GRIMETHORPE

Barnsley Libraries

P.S.442

Return Date		
10/12		
05. DEC 13		

By the same author

The Comfort Zone

THE SMILING AFFAIR

JEREMY SHELDON

BARNSLEY LIBRARY SERVICE	
10011116	
Bertrams	21.01.06
	£12.99

Jonathan Cape
London

Published by Jonathan Cape 2005

2 4 6 8 10 9 7 5 3 1

Copyright © Jeremy Sheldon 2005

Jeremy Sheldon has asserted his right under the Copyright, Designs and Patents Act 1988 to be identified as the author of this work

This book is sold subject to the condition that it shall not, by way of trade or otherwise, be lent, resold, hired out, or otherwise circulated without the publisher's prior consent in any form of binding or cover other than that in which it is published and without a similar condition including this condition being imposed on the subsequent purchaser

First published in Great Britain in 2005 by Jonathan Cape
Random House, 20 Vauxhall Bridge Road,
London SW1V 2SA

Random House Australia (Pty) Limited
20 Alfred Street, Milsons Point, Sydney, New South Wales 2061, Australia

Random House New Zealand Limited
18 Poland Road, Glenfield, Auckland 10, New Zealand

Random House South Africa (Pty) Limited
Endulini, 5A Jubilee Road, Parktown 2193, South Africa

The Random House Group Limited Reg. No. 954009
www.randomhouse.co.uk

A CIP catalogue record for this book
is available from the British Library

ISBN 0-2240-6281-6

Papers used by Random House are natural, recyclable products made from wood grown in sustainable forests; the manufacturing processes conform to the environmental regulations of the country of origin

Printed and bound in Great Britain by
Mackays of Chatham plc, Chatham, Kent

Permissions

'Foolin' Myself'. Words and music by Jack Lawrence and Peter Tinturin. Campbell Connelly & Company Limited.

'I Must Have That Man'. Words by Dorothy Fields and music by Jimmy McHugh © 1924, EMI Mills Music Inc/Cotton Club Publishing, USA. Reproduced by permission of Lawrence Wright Music Co. Ltd/EMI Music Publishing Ltd, London WC2H 0QY

'You Go To My Head'. Words by Haven Gillespie and music by J Fred Coots © 1938, Remick Music Corp, USA. Reproduced by permission of B Feldman & Co Ltd, London WC2H 0QY

'This Year's Kisses' by Irving Berlin © 1937 (renewed) Irving Berlin Music Corp. USA. Warner/Chappell Music Ltd, London W6 8BS. Reproduced by permission of International Music Publications Ltd. All Rights Reserved.

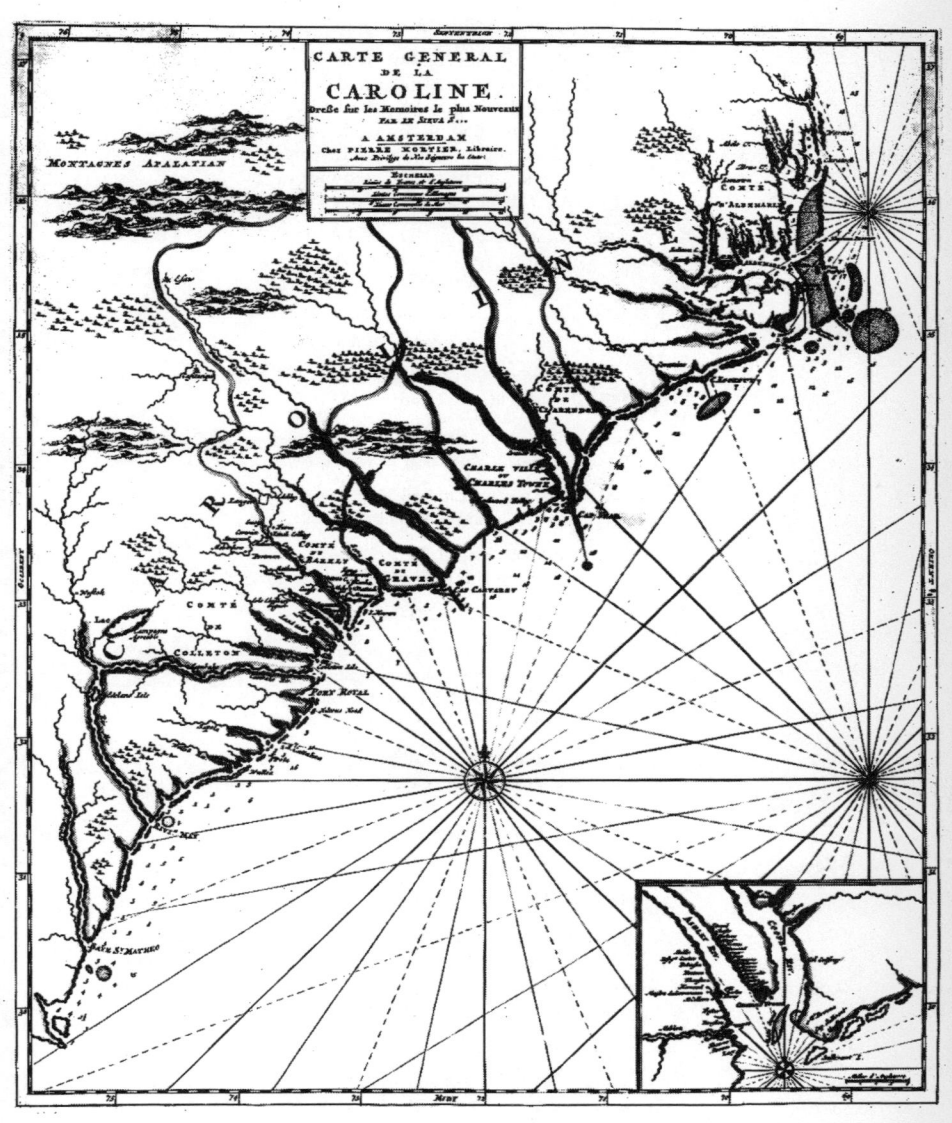

'Human life is but a series of footnotes to a vast obscure unfinished masterpiece.'

Pale Fire, Vladimir Nabokov

I set it down that one may smile, and smile, and be a villain . . .

Hamlet, William Shakespeare

THE SMILING AFFAIR

1

San Francisco. Jay often looked back on it as a city of Fs: a city of fault-lines and 49ers, Fisherman's Wharf and Fillmore, a city of farraginous skin-tones and people never certain whether he was saying 'Fulton' or 'Folsom' (although this rarely seemed to affect their overall conclusion that his English accent was 'fabulous'); a fool's paradise whose lethargic pleasures included dodging the bright yellow trams on the F-line and buying flawless focaccia at Liguria on the corner of Washington Square and getting high in Golden Gate Park before flopping out in the middle of Fish Roundabout; a city of hills and bridges continually fading in and out of view in the fogs that rolled in from the Pacific, even on bright days, drifting as far as Stanyan by late afternoon and blotting out the sun over Sunset and Richmond. It all started there last April.

'As my pop used to tell me: "*You can paint racin' stripes on a pig . . . but it's still only a pig*".'

This from Mike Penny as they all sat in Jay's office, his single unit above the Espresso Express on the corner of Kearny and Sacramento. Jay himself slouched behind his desk, shuffling through the morning mail like a Scrabble player with a rack of bad tiles. Marlowe, his Scots terrier, dozed in the corner of the room, the light from his small TV flickering over his damp nose. Christoph and Mike lounged in the easy chairs by the open window with their feet up on the ledge, the two of them loudly disagreeing with anything the other said.

'Heck,' Mike continued in his flat Nebraskan drawl, tossing Christoph's *Need For Speed* magazine back at him with open contempt and pulling out a cheroot, 'your bread ain't done if you seriously believe a communist's capable of buildin' a high-quality sports car.'

Recently Jay had watched them both sit there for hours, arguing about anything from the inferiority of American beer, capitalism and the nationality of the inventor of the ballpoint pen to the issue of whether Jean-Luc Picard had been a better captain of the *Enterprise* than James Kirk. Most contentious of all was the subject of *Casablanca* and whether Ilsa should have stayed with Rick Blaine rather than Victor Laszlo, not least because it always triggered a variety of disputes about the political reality (or 'moral' reality as Christoph was fond of saying) of the Second World War, disputes that usually sent Jay scuttling downstairs for a round of half-and-half lattes and a smoothie for Marlowe. Now Mike and Christoph were arguing about the competence of the Czech auto industry and, more precisely, whether the latest incarnation of the Zvuk V12 could outrun a Comanche Arrow, Christoph continuing to tell Mike that the Czech Republic hadn't been a communist state for over a decade but that it was typical of an American to be unaware of political change occurring further away than the nearest tub of chicken wings.

'Buddy,' Mike scoffed (everybody is Mike's 'buddy'), 'admire your pride in your homeland and all. But it takes years of dedication and perseverance to perfect the art of designin' and constructin' a GT-class vehicle. And, with all due respect, it's your Czech automotive *heritage* that I was referrin' to as communist . . . prohibits me from takin' your li'l runnerbout too seriously'.

'Forgive me,' Christoph replied, 'if I don't take an American assessment of another culture's heritage too seriously. Nor anything they have to say about cars. There isn't even any such thing as an *American* industry, not now it's all been bought up by the Japanese . . .'

And so it would continue until Christoph drove home to

the house he and Jay shared on Quintara and Mike responded to the call of his own bleating stomach acids. Did Jay mind that the two of them had started to treat his office like some kind of social club or group therapy centre? It wasn't as if he had any work to do and given that Christoph at that point in time covered their entire rent with the proceeds from selling weed and writing jingles for MuzakCorp down the Peninsula, Jay had little urge to do anything else but extend him a *mi casa es su casa* run of the place.

As for Mike? Jay stared across at him with a fascination that had recently started to border on obsession. Jay knew little about him except that he'd grown up on a cattle farm 'a hundred klicks west of Omaha', that he'd worked in Detroit as a private eye for ten years and that he too had become a paranormal investigator after a recent move to California, one who the previous December, by way of a freak combination of harmless coincidence and available office space, had taken up the next unit down the corridor. Jay watched Mike as he lounged in a late-morning sunbeam, Cuban heels up on the ledge, cheroot burning away in his right hand, its heavy smoke drifting carelessly out of the window. Mike would sit there whether Christoph was around to banter with or not, reclining like a victorious prizefighter in a pair of Oscar Goldman sunglasses and an Oscar Goldman suit while he read his magazines and told Jay stories about Nebraska and old cases and scarfed down Toaster Tartz ('you just heat 'em and eat 'em'). Around noon he'd pull himself up on to his feet, saunter down to his Madison in the street below and cruise the ten blocks to his regular table at House of Prime Rib where he would linger until late afternoon. Mike rarely bothered to come back to his office until the following morning, Jay noticed, usually appearing at Jay's door with a coffee in each hand and rarely without yet another story of a ducked payment. But Mike never grumbled and never complained: whenever he got stung by a client, and this happened at least as regularly as once a fortnight just as it did with Jay, he seemed simply to *absorb* it. '*If you climb into the saddle, be ready for the ride,*' he would say stoically (and somewhat unhelpfully, Jay felt) whenever Jay happened to engage him on the subject. How the hell did Mike survive? Did he have a private income? A cannily structured investment portfolio? Was there a rich Mrs Penny waiting at home over in the Western Addition? Jay didn't know.

Christoph and Mike continued to argue while Jay stared at the pile of bills in front of him. There were the standard bills for utilities but also the CT for the office and the arrears on the new Geiger counter which Jay had been forced to pay for in instalments. Amongst these, he found a second rent demand for January and a first rent demand for February. There was a also a third rent demand for January and, yes, there it was: a first rent demand for April, right there behind a reminder that February's rent was still outstanding and that March's hadn't been paid either. Besides these, Jay found a bill for the Apache's new exhaust (this particularly irked him given that it still sounded like a cheap lawnmower being driven across a bed of nails every time he started it up). And there was always the coffee tab from downstairs, always three figures and only ever settled after it had mitotically sired an identical double.

Jay dropped it all on his desk and sat back in his chair. *What was it Tommy Cheung had said in those first tentative days of Jay's apprenticeship as a p.i.?* He glanced at the old man's photo up on the wall. *You wanna be rich? You wanna drive around the city in a brand new fuel-injection Kaiser, drink champagne and fool around with all the pretty girl?*

At the time, they'd been driving back to the city from Merced in Tommy's black Buccaneer Supreme as the first light of the breaking day turned the speeding freeway from blue to grey beneath their spinning wheels. 'Go be a stockbroker or banker,' Tommy had advised him. 'Go be a rock star or a football player. *No such thing as a rich paranormal investigator.*'

The two of them had spent the night before monitoring a property on a side street off East Olive where a woman with hair like stale tobacco and a voice like an ashtray had claimed she was being haunted.

'Miss Shirleen Sherlay, yeah that's me,' she'd rasped through the screen door when they first arrived, two toddlers hanging off her arms as if they were handcuffed to her.

'My name is Tommy Cheung. We spoke on the phone. This is my assistant, Jay Richards.'

Ushering them into her cramped kitchenette, Shirleen had taken the cigarette out of her mouth and told Jay and Tommy that she 'had a poltergeist' as if she were confessing to suffering from some kind of incurable disease.

'What leads you to believe this, Miss Sherlay?' Tommy had asked.

'I've recently been hearin' strange noises at night,' she'd replied, '*ghostly* breathin' sounds and *ghostly* footsteps.'

Mia, Shirleen's third and eldest child, a pierced and pimpled teen in hotpants and a t-shirt with JAILBAIT emblazoned across the front, added that there was an old Indian burial ground rumoured to lie beneath the street. 'It's been rilly freakin' me out,' she confessed from the lurid sofa as she painted another toenail and listened to the cartoons on the TV.

Tommy had proceeded by making a big deal of telling Shirleen that he was going to conduct a scan of the electromagnetic field surrounding the property. If there was a poltergeist or some other paranormal phenomenon in the house, he told her, it would show up on the instruments out in the car, all the time playing the Wise-and-Avuncular-Karate-Mentor that Jay soon learned was his standard MO when it came to dealing with clients. When it came to setting up the equipment that night, however, all Tommy did was deploy a couple of motion detectors, one in the alleyway that ran down the side of the house and the other at the back gate. 'Remember,' he advised Jay when they were alone later on, 'a mystery almost always have something simple at its centre.' He smirked, then added, 'This one, I think, have something more simple than most.'

Sure enough, just after four-thirty the next morning, while Tommy and Jay were slumped down in the Buccaneer on the other side of the street ('all us Chinese oldies drive them,' he once told Jay, 'make us think we're successful Americans'), the remote unit linked to both motion detectors had vibrated as a shadow shuffled through the bushes outside Shirleen's living-room window. On Tommy's signal, they crept out of the car and across the street before fixing the dark figure with the hand-held spots. Lights went on in the house. Shirleen appeared downstairs in her robe, Mia at an upstairs window.

'Your poltergeist is called "Kyle",' Tommy had said simply, glancing at the name badge on the blue pump-attendant's shirt. But it had quickly and dramatically transpired that Shirleen already knew the man, a pale little thug in his early thirties with widow's peaks that reached for the back of his neck and teeth like nubs of melting candy. On the days that Kyle worked the day shift at the Gas 'n' Go on G Street, Shirleen would usually spend the night with him, leaving the two toddlers with Mia and the TV. What Shirleen hadn't realized was that on the nights Kyle worked the night shift, he'd pass by Mia's bedroom on his way home.

Pretty soon Shirleen's front yard had thronged with the sound of circulating accusations and revealed betrayals, lights appearing in the nearby windows and disturbed neighbours not needing a second invitation to make their own grievances heard. While fingers pointed and voices yelled and doors slammed and slammed again, Tommy had retrieved the two motion detectors and signalled a deft retreat back to the Buccaneer.

'Aren't you going to bill her?' Jay asked as they pulled away down the street.

'Bill? Ha! You can send her one first thing in the morning if you want, first job of the day,' Tommy replied. And it was then, as they sped back to San Francisco along 99, under a dirty dawn sky the colour of the sole of an old bowling shoe, that Tommy and Jay had indulged in the first of many discussions about money and the paranormal, Tommy lighting a continuous trail of Delta Menthols tail-to-tip and jerking a hip-flask of fifteen-year-old Glen Achall to his lips every few miles or so.

'No such thing as a rich paranormal investigator,' Tommy told him. 'Sometimes you get lucky and get honourable customer. But usually it's very hard to get paid. Partly to do with the nature of the job itself. Paranormal investigation is difficult, not like being a pool-boy. You can't simply turn up and find the blocked filter and say to the client "Look, *there's* your problem!" and everybody go home happy.'

Tommy had paused, coughed and wiped his mouth on the sleeve of his sports jacket before taking another sip of scotch.

'Also, you got problems with the type of client you're usually dealing with. Most likely you're working for frightened people. Sometimes they're stupid. Sometimes they're educated which can make things worse. But one thing is true for all of them: they've all seen or heard something they can't explain, eerie voices, a strange figure downstairs or maybe some picture fly off a shelf in the middle of the night . . . by the time they come to you, they've tried every logical solution they can think of to explain what's happened to them but nothing's worked and they're scared *shitless*.'

Tommy had chuckled, smoke appearing in front of his wrinkled face.

'At that point, they so scared they'd sell their grandmother to have it all explained away. It's different afterwards, of course. If it's a hoax, or if you show the client there's some ordinary explanation, then the customer quickly get all defensive, as if you'd told them they'd been stupid or hysterical. And even if you manage to show them something anomalous is occurring, what they gonna do? Seventy per cent of the time the client has to coexist with the phenomenon anyway, or move away which isn't usually possible, and they end up blaming it all on you. And, of course, you got all the crazies . . .'

Jay swivelled gently on his chair and looked around the office: the dust and the cracked plaster, the dead insects piled up inside the grimy up-lighters, the torn furniture that had been sealed and re-sealed with duct tape and the battered filing cabinet that hardly opened any more, not even when he gave it a smack on its alleged 'sweet spot'. *No such thing as a rich paranormal investigator?* Jay would have settled for being an investigator who broke even, an investigator who sustained manageable losses. Unfortunately, like Mike Penny, Jay was making nothing. Zilch. Nada. Zip.

As usual, this kind of thinking soon had him indulging in his recurrent mid-morning debate about whether he should quit the world of the potentially paranormal. But, as always, this train of thought soon came to a gentle rest against the buffers of certain irresolvable realities. Even if he decided to give up the whole business, what else could he do? It was a problem that he was qualified for nothing else, he conceded that, but he was also sure that the fact that he couldn't even *think* of something else to do was a more serious and fundamental problem. Also, though Tommy had exacted no guarantees from Jay when he'd first taken him on, and exacted no promises about the business from him during those final days before he died, the office had been the old man's and Jay felt as responsible towards it as he did towards Marlowe.

And it hadn't always been this bleak. Sure, he'd worked with Tommy for six months before the old man had become too ill to continue and they'd suffered together the steady stream of time-wasters and defaulters who'd knocked on their door or called them. But after the four month break that followed (four months that saw the old man fade away in San Francisco General, four months of daily visits to the mortal claustrophobia of Ward 86 that ended with a tearful but resolute flight to Scotland where Jay hurled Tommy's urn into the windblown murk of Rhidorroch Sound as requested in the old man's will), Jay had been pleasantly surprised that his first few solo forays into the world of paranormal investigation met with relative success. Yes, there had been the geriatric hoaxers and lonely widows and desperate divorcees looking for someone to talk to. But there'd also been a few notable if minor successes. There'd been The Case of the Chinese Bride (jumpy EMF readings at the client's home had prompted Jay to suggest that the memory of the daughter of one of Tommy's old poker gang, an old Sunset patriarch called Wally Chu, hadn't been appropriately mourned by her husband's family after the two newlyweds died in a car crash); there'd been The Marsh Road Bridge Murder (a few miles outside of Milpitas, a trail of cold spots and EMF analysis had led Jay to find a skeleton in an abandoned reservoir pump house, the wrists and ankles bound with rotting rope, forensics eventually identifying the victim as a woman who'd gone missing in the summer of 1978); there'd been The Hillsdale High Hanging where he'd found his instruments peaking under the branches of a tree where a former pupil had hung himself in '94 (there'd been little for Jay to do except call in a local clergyman and leave him to it while the school principal tried to come to terms with the whole thing as best as he could).

Jay had been paid on each of these occasions even though his findings might have been best described as *circumstantial*. He'd never been able to show the client any tangible evidence of the paranormal except for the readings on his machines and their apparent correlation with the client's own experience. Yet on each occasion he'd received the agreed fee. Were these the 'honourable customers' that Tommy had talked about? Jay guessed that they had to be. And that hadn't been the end of it either. There'd been a few other minor successes besides these, cases like The Legend of the Lady in the Lake, The San Pablo Playhouse Poltergeist and The Incident at Occidental Cemetery.

And of course there was his role in The Lockwood Murder Mystery. Perhaps six months after Tommy's death, Marlowe and Jay were finishing a takeout from Jose's 1001 Bocadillos while Lester Young breathed his way through 'Ghost of a Chance' in the background when the office intercom buzzed.

'Who is it?' Jay had asked.

'Mr Patrick Norton,' a voice replied in the most regal Queen's English that Jay had heard for a while outside the four walls of a TV screen. 'I'm looking for the business premises of Mr Tommy Kwong Ming Cheung.'

Jay had canned his sandwich wrapper, lit some incense and turned down the music before letting the guy in, a tall man in his sixties wearing a black jacket, striped grey trousers and a dark overcoat.

'Can I take your hat and coat?' he offered.

The man shook his head and said that his business wouldn't take long and Jay gestured towards the client's chair before sitting down in his own, guessing that the man was an undertaker, his second that week.

'Sorry, could you give me your name again?' he asked, flipping open a notebook.

'Norton. Mr Patrick Norton,' the man replied slowly, removing his hat and staring at Jay as if he was continuing with some internal and ongoing assessment. Nothing new there, Jay thought. Clients were always suspicious to begin with.

'So,' he tried, wanting to break the silence, 'it seems we're both English . . . whatever *that* means.'

'Indeed,' Norton replied. 'Is Mr Cheung available to see me?'

'I'm afraid he died a while back. I'm now here in his place.'

'I'm sorry to hear about Mr Cheung. My condolences.'

'Thank you.'
'And you are?'
'Richards. Jay Richards.'
More silence.

Then Norton reached inside his coat and withdrew a patent leather billfold from which he extracted a neatly trimmed cutting. He placed it on the desk and his gloved fingers slid it towards Jay. It was Tommy's old advert, the one the old man had been running in the *Guardian* and other publications for years.

SPOOKED?

**Hear things go bump in the night?
Seen something you can't explain?**

Call TOMMY KWONG MING CHEUNG

'MYSTERY IS MY BUSINESS'

— Paranormal Investigator for hire —
— Professional and discreet service —
— Reasonable rates —

**600 Sacramento Street — #2
San Francisco, CA 94111**

CALL: 415-SPOOKED

'Mr Richards, perhaps you'd tell me what kind of "mystery" it is that you deal with exactly?'

Jay cleared his throat. 'Well Mr Norton,' he started, 'I'm

usually hired by private individuals to investigate supposed paranormal events . . .'

'Paranormal events?'

'Anomalous phenomena. In layman's terms: *suspected* hauntings, situations where evidence seems to indicate the existence of what the general public refer to as a "ghost" or "poltergeist" or "spirit". I'll tell you now, Mr Norton, because hopefully it'll reduce the possibility of later recrimination: I'm almost always the last resort for my clients, a person they've come to because they've exhausted all other possibilities. Also, the way I work has little to do with the supernatural or the mystical and a lot more to do with exposing and identifying logical explanations to the problems my clients come to me with.'

Jay sat back in his chair. Norton seemed satisfied with this answer, at least for the time being, as if it passed some kind of test predetermined by him or whoever employed him.

'As I've said, my name is Patrick Norton,' he started eventually, his palms spread on his striped knees, 'the butler to a General Lockwood of Stinson Beach, Marin Country. I am here representing the General who has found himself embroiled in a delicate and difficult matter and is most keen to talk to someone with your . . . *skills*. To this end, would you consent to being the General's guest for dinner this evening, or perhaps another evening this week? You have my assurance that you will be generously compensated for your time and any expenses incurred.'

2

As Jay walked out of the door that November evening and climbed into his battered car, the clouds had surged ominously overhead and by the time he was guiding the Apache across Golden Gate, he found himself snailing his way through a frenetic downpour that only got worse on the other side of the bay. By the time he arrived at the Lockwood mansion itself, the building positioned on a headland overlooking the black havoc of the ocean, fist-sized spats of rain pounded the windshield like suicidal locusts.

Norton was waiting for him at the front door with an umbrella.

'Mr Norton,' Jay extended a hand.

'*Norton* will be fine, sir.'

The butler hustled Jay into the panelled hall where he took his anorak before leading him down a long corridor to a dining room that was all Ms, Marine Corps memorabilia hanging from all four walls, including regimental awards for marksmanship, monochrome photos of groups of young men in battle fatigues and others of men in ceremonial dress and of Lockwood himself receiving various decorations. Along with these were a regimental flag with the Corps' eagle, globe and anchor and a marine scimitar hanging on the wall next to it. General Lockwood, already sitting at the head of the table, gestured that Jay should sit to his left but then continued to stare down at his cutlery while Norton ladled thick chowder into bowls the size of crash helmets. The General didn't say anything so Jay didn't say anything and instead catalogued a few details about his prospective client. Lockwood was in his seventies, still broad and powerfully built despite his age. His lead-grey hair was still buzz-cut in a military style he'd probably maintained since he was an eighteen-year-old cadet at Parris Island and he had hands that looked like fists even when they weren't clenched.

'I fought hand-to-hand on Guam and Iwo Jima,' he said as if they were already in the middle of a conversation. A clock ticked away in the background and punctuated the muffled sounds from the kitchen beyond.

'I didn't know that,' Jay replied quietly. General Lockwood's voice may have had the torque and bulk of a Mack truck but nothing could camouflage the confusion in his sandstone eyes.

'You're British, like Norton . . . and also a young man, late twenties if I'm not mistaken.'

'My father was English. My mother was Chinese-American. I'm twenty-nine.'

'I wonder if you even know what happened on Iwo?'

Jay looked back at the General. He'd seen *The Sands of Iwo Jima* starring John Wayne but didn't think it worth mentioning.

'When I say that we fought hand-to-hand,' the General continued, 'I don't mean that we overran their lines and I stuck my bayonet into a few cowering Japanese infantrymen along the way.' He turned his eyes away from Jay and back to his bowl as if the croutons floating there were a model of the island itself. 'It should have been a cakewalk, a formality,' he continued, scattering black grains of pepper over his soup. 'We'd bombed the island for almost six months and expected to outnumber a dispirited and degraded enemy by at least four-to-one. Of course, in retrospect, we know that this wasn't true. They'd dug sixteen miles of tunnels into nearby Mount Suribachi – "Mount *Sonofabitchi*" we used to call it – and more than twenty thousand Japanese soldiers had survived the bombardment and had their guns trained on the beach.'

Lockwood stopped and asked Jay to pour wine for the both of them before he picked up his spoon.

'It was a massacre. We came ashore in our landing craft at high tide and as we clambered on to the beach it seemed as if High Command's plan had worked. The whole place was as silent as a church for a single, beautiful moment ... then they opened fire.' Jay watched as Lockwood dipped his spoon towards his soup but then hesitated before replacing it beside his bowl. 'Some companies suffered over ninety per cent casualties in the first hour,' he continued. 'We tried to dig foxholes in the sand while the Japanese brought down barrage after barrage right on top of our heads. We might as well have tried to hide under paper plates.' The General moved forward in his chair. 'Even after we got off the beach, there was still the mountain itself to assault, five hundred and fifty-four feet high, one hundred and forty millimetre guns raining down treebursts on us while we got cut up to pieces by twenty-millimetres to our left and seventy-fives from higher up the slope.'

The General stopped to sip some wine and noticed Jay hadn't yet touched his soup. 'You're not going to eat yours?' he asked.

'I have a certain kind of sito-myxophobia.'

'Which means what?'

'Which means that I eat sandwiches and little else,' Jay replied, hoping they weren't going to get sidetracked. 'Why don't we forget about me for now and carry on with your story?'

The General looked at Jay suspiciously before shrugging his shoulders and continuing.

'We lost over seven thousand marines in a month. Sometimes we thought we'd pushed back their front line only to find them coming out of their tunnels behind us. One night, during the second week of the assault, I remember lying down on the floor of a Japanese position we'd taken the day before. I knew I only had a few hours but I just couldn't fall asleep and I lay there looking up at the stars while artillery boomed away in the distance. It was then that I heard voices. I couldn't believe it at first, thought my head was playing games with me. But the voices were getting louder, Japanese voices echoing out from under the ground and getting closer all the time . . . and then they were in the room.'

The General picked up his knife and reached for the butter and the dish of bread rolls.

'What I'm trying to tell you is that I've seen a lot of death in my life. I've been up close to it. I'm not someone who scares easily — or if I am, I know how to deal with it.'

'I've no doubt about that, General,' Jay replied.

'So if I now tell you that something has happened in this house that has scared me to the core of my body, you will understand that I am being neither frivolous nor weak.'

'Of course, General.'

According to Lockwood, he'd started to suffer an alternating series of cold flushes and mild fevers a couple of weeks before, as well as periods of disorientation and insomnia that he attributed to the onset of flu.

'One night, it was particularly bad,' he told Jay. 'I went to bed and lay there for a few hours, unable to fall asleep. The room was either too hot or too cold and I even considered disturbing Norton to ask him to call my physician. I must have dozed off eventually because I distinctly remember the sensation of waking up again and lying there for a few moments while I stared up at the moonlight flickering across the ceiling. And then I remembered that Norton had closed the shutters as he did every night, as he has done every night for the last fifteen years . . . where was the light coming from?'

Jay listened as General Lockwood told him that he'd lain there paralysed for a few moments, his blood pumping, an idea forming in his mind that he might stop breathing at any moment. 'I thought I might be dreaming,' he told Jay. 'I didn't know what to think. I thought that *this* was finally what it was like to die. Eventually, I summoned up the courage to look down to the end of my bed and it was then that I saw her, floating a foot or so above the floor.'

'Who?' Jay asked.

'My granddaughter.'

Did Jay know who the General's granddaughter was? He didn't. Hadn't he read any newspapers or watched the news recently? Jay somewhat sheepishly told the General that he didn't *do* current affairs.

'She died a month ago.'

'How?'

'She fell from the thirtieth floor of the Gibson Hotel.'

'What was her name?'

'Dana. Dana Amanda Lockwood.'

As the General filled him in, Jay realized that he'd glimpsed of reports of the incident on a few news items as he'd cycled through the channels in transit from one cartoon or sitcom or movie to another and seen headlines for the story on the front of newspapers at downtown magazine stalls. Now Lockwood revealed in detail how Dana, the daughter of his son, Lloyd (himself a decorated soldier who'd served two tours as a young marine in Vietnam), had gone off the rails sometime during her teens.

'Perhaps you know the kind?' the General asked Jay. 'Pampered girls who fall in with the wrong crowd and are too young, too vain and too wilful to know that some of the steps they are taking might be irreversible. I suppose it was partly her father's fault for spoiling her. But this feels like a rather feeble conclusion, like remembering that my son was once a sensible and decent man, a son that I was proud of, but that he became an idiot ever since he made his money.'

While Norton cleared the soup bowls and Jay turned the main course into a series of sandwiches as best he could (like many of Jay's uninitiated dining companions, Lockwood's tolerance of this quickly changed from semi-curious incredulity to grudging acceptance), the old soldier related how Lloyd had gone into banking after his military career and bruised, duked and hard-balled his way to success.

'I don't for one minute believe that my son is a gifted financier,' he elaborated, 'but he has always been a bully and I imagine that skills in this area might be all that one ultimately requires to make a success of oneself. Anyway, I digress.'

Lockwood continued to sketch out a picture of Dana's life to Jay as they sat there in the dining room, telling Jay that he might be old but he wasn't naïve. He knew Dana's life was one 'spent in the bleary thrall of cocaine and fast cars and ambitious young men who knew a good opportunity when they saw one'. And now Dana was dead, having toppled over the balcony of a penthouse suite at the Gibson and fallen the thirty storeys between her room and the ground.

'When they found her, she had high levels of both cocaine and alcohol in her blood.'

'Who rented the hotel room?' Jay asked. 'Was anyone in the room with her at the time she . . .'

'According to the police, she was on her own. According to the hotel, Dana paid for the room in cash though whether the money was hers in the first place is a different matter entirely. My son finally had the presence of mind to cut off Dana's access to the family money last year. According to various sources, including San Francisco detectives, it's likely that Dana was replacing her lost income through prostitution. It's also believed that she'd begun associating with known pornographers.'

There'd been an inquest, the coroner's office eventually passing a verdict of death by misadventure rather than suicide. After that, the Lockwoods had gathered to consign the whole pitiable episode to the past, the clan convening in Walpole, West Virginia to see Dana buried in the ancient family plot. 'Unfortunately,' the General said as he pulled the cord that summoned Norton, 'it may be that the past won't let go of me.'

Was it a dream? Was it a fantasy? Was it a delusion or an extreme instance of sleep paralysis or something similar? Jay didn't know and the General didn't know either. After they'd moved to a drawing room, he told Jay about something that happened when he was temporarily stationed at a military base in the Philippines. One of a crew of soldiers assigned the task of delivering the camp's mail to the other men, Lockwood had spent half a day looking for a Captain Jones Cartwright.

'I remember that it took the whole morning to deliver this huge sack of letters and parcels,' he said as he clipped and lit a cigar. 'It was a boring job and we all hated doing it. But the size of the pile steadily dwindled throughout the day until all I had left was this single letter for Captain Cartwright. Well, I looked for him everywhere. It was franked for special delivery which meant that it had to be delivered personally and I first reported to his quarters only to find that he wasn't there. Another soldier told me that he'd seen the Captain at the medical shack an hour before only for an orderly there to tell me that he hadn't seen Cartwright all day but that if he was on the base, he'd probably be in the mess. He wasn't in there either but a few men were still at the tables so I asked them if they'd seen Cartwright and a few said they had and a few said they hadn't. And then an engineer, this New Yorker called Tony Vizio, he told me that he'd just passed the Captain outside the Command Tent. Vizio had been on his way out, the Captain had been on his way in. "When was this?" I asked him. "Only a few minutes earlier," he replied.

'Lord knows, I ran all the way. I was sick of this goddamned letter and wanted rid of it as soon as I could. Finally I got there and told the guard that I had a special-D for Captain Cartwright but he just stared back at me like I was crazy. I held the letter out as proof and told him that I could take it in or he could,

I didn't care just as long as the Captain got his mail and signed for it. Then this Lieutenant Colonel appeared and asked us what was going on and I told him that I had a special for Captain Cartwright and that I'd been told that he was in the Command Tent. "Soldier," the lieutenant colonel told me solemnly, "somebody's been playing tricks on you. Captain Cartwright isn't here." I replied that I didn't know about any tricks and that I was just trying to do my duty. But he was strangely insistent. "No, son," he said, "you're misunderstanding me." Apparently Captain Cartwright had been killed in action forty-eight hours before on a reconnaissance patrol in the Angara Heights.'

In the drawing room the General told Jay that until recently, the details of this incident defined the way he thought of ghosts. 'Forget the hoaxes,' he said, dipping his head for a small, efficient sip of Armagnac, 'and the superstitious fantasies – they can be written off without a second thought. But perhaps there are instances when events align themselves in a certain way, during times of great distress or emotional upheaval, and these delusions take on an extra kind of force . . .'

He broke off suddenly. He'd been talking more or less non-stop for a couple of hours and Jay wondered if he'd exhausted himself in spite of being formidably sturdy for a man his age. But then it became clear that General had probably reached a different kind of limit: the limit of understanding what it was that had appeared at the end of his bed a week or so before and had returned on two occasions since.

That night, they sat in the General's bedroom in a pair of large leather armchairs that Jay lugged in from a spare bedroom. Around them, Jay's equipment stood poised and primed: a video camera perched on a tripod scrutinized the spot at the foot of the bed where the apparition had so far appeared; a selection of sensors placed throughout the room burbled around the baseline zeroes that Jay had recalibrated them to earlier on, these including the usual EMF detectors and Geiger counter but also a thermal scanner and a hydro-thermometer to monitor ambient humidity. Besides these, he'd set up a couple of microphones linked to two digital audio recorders and placed his small compass on the arm of his chair. Neither Jay nor the General said a word after they'd sat themselves down. And if Jay had gradually acclimatized to the static of apprehension that had built up in his spine ever since he'd stepped out of the rain and into the mansion the same way that his ears had learned to filter out the faint sporadic clicks of the Geiger counter in the corner of the General's bedroom, then as time passed this process seemed to reverse itself. The clock on the mantelpiece chimed midnight. The rain continued to fall. The clock on the mantelpiece chimed one . . . and then two, and then three, Jay's Adam's apple like a rock in his throat as his eyes darted from the end of the General's bed to the shivering blue point of the compass and back again. Every thirty minutes or so, Jay and the General passed the flask of coffee back and forth. Other than that, the General sat completely still with his fingers loosely interlinked in his lap, eyes down on his hands, and Jay sat there trying to keep his breathing deep and regular while every passing hour saw the tension intensify behind his eyeballs and in his knuckles and in the soles of his feet. In order to counter this feeling, Jay tried to go back over the General's earlier account of the apparition in his mind. But there were few facts for him to chew over. There were the details of Dana Lockwood's life and the details of her death. There was the apparition that the General had seen – or *believed* he'd seen – and claimed resembled his dead granddaughter. But there was no reason yet to connect these things together. The hands on the clock continued to run their strange relay race across the roman numerals of its squinting white face while Jay battled to stay awake but also battled to stop his mind from wandering, which would surely be the most efficient way of letting himself fall asleep. If he wasn't careful, he'd drift off. One moment, he'd be sitting there imagining Dana Lockwood's last moments, imagining General Lockwood storming the beaches of the Pacific, his eyes aimlessly sweeping around the room, his gaze moving over the swirling grain of the panelled walls, the nap of the brown leather on which he sat, another image coming to him of Dana falling through the sky towards the waiting ground. The next moment, it would be six in the morning and he'd be coming round as Norton leaned down to shake him awake and . . . the hand on the compass stirred as did the hairs on the back of Jay's hand beside it, a wave of adrenalin breaking between his legs and crashing up his back towards the thin outer rims of his ears. And there it was, an apparition crystallized in the air in front of them, at first nothing more than a vaporous blur that poured light over their faces while the Geiger counter roared like a buzz-saw and the compass needle by Jay's arm blurred on its axis and the sensors flashed like disco lights. Jay looked across at the General who stared back at the figure but didn't move, not even when it seemed to extend a pallid limb towards him, and then a hand, its fingers outstretched.

By noon the following day, the General had thrown enough political weight around City Hall to succeed in having the case reopened. Within a week investigating detectives discovered that a bent police pathologist called John Merdesley had been paid to cover up the fact that Dana had been poisoned before being pushed over the hotel balcony, most likely with cocaine spiked with chloroacetophenone and a dimethyl sulphoxide catalysing agent. Soon after that, it was discovered that Lloyd Lockwood had been laundering money for former army colleagues who'd been smuggling pure heroin into California from Cambodia ever since the end of the Vietnam war but that Lloyd had recently got cold feet and tried to back out of the arrangement only for the smugglers to throw Dana over the balcony of the Gibson as a warning. Lloyd Lockwood was promptly arrested, sentenced and subsequently incarcerated as were several of his accomplices.

In the meantime, the news was full of details of the case, journalists hungry for the kind of story that usually appeared on the screens of the world's multiplexes.

And so the case made Jay a star of a kind for a short and un-expected moment. He was already used to contributing occasional articles about his work to various zines and 'grass-roots' publications, titles like *Visitors From Beyond* and *Celestia* and the *Journal of Anomalous Phenomena* that one tended to find in headshops along Haight, on the shelves next to the UFO magazines and the stoner pamphlets. But in the wake of the discovery of the truth behind Dana Lockwood's death, Jay also found himself paddling for the first time in the shallow back-waters of the mainstream media. He saw a picture of himself attached to a news report about Dana's murder on the second page of the *San Francisco Examiner* with a small article on one of the inside pages dedicated solely to his role in uncovering the murder; he appeared on the third page of *The Chronicle* and even made it across country on to the inside pages of the *New York Post*. And he seemed to be on the radio endlessly, talking about himself and promoting the business, and managed to appear on both *Bay Today*, Baxter Swerdsferger's current affairs show on KCBR, and Derwent Benton's *Breaking News*. In addition to this, he was commissioned to write a syndi-cated weekly column about the strange and wonderful world of the paranormal, a piece that appeared in newspapers as widespread as Redding and Otis to the north and Lost Hills to the south, and was even invited to appear on a few local TV talkshows. These were banal, of course, the level of the debate pitched somewhere between 'Do Angels Exist?' and 'Pet Aromatherapy' after the hosts had managed to get over his accent and the fools in the audience had stopped tittering. But the money had been good, there was no doubting that, and all Jay had needed to do was tell the story of that night at the General's house. His mode on these occasions was always High

Gothic, his Englishness often maximized to *Masterpiece Theatre* levels of exaggeration. '*I first received a visit from General Lockwood's batman late last November,*' he would start. '*Would I consent to being the General's guest for dinner that evening or perhaps another evening that week? Full of curiosity, the paranormal investigator's religion, I duly drove north through the gathering gloom . . .*' And so on. Nothing too technical. Nothing too far from the paranormal-by-numbers methodology of Hollywood and the networks.

And for once Jay felt like a success, felt that he'd done something that might have made Tommy Cheung proud of him. All the publicity had resulted in a sharp rise in the number of cases he took on and soon Jay was out on assignment fourteen hours a day with as many as eight investigations on the go at any one time while the messages banked up on his answerphone back at the office, messages containing reports of alleged poltergeists and disembodied voices and phantom figures. None of these cases resulted in anything as dramatic as the events that had taken place at the Lockwood mansion and most ended with Jay arriving at the standard explanations for the allegedly paranormal phenomena. But a gratifying if small percentage of the cases still pointed to the manifestation of something out of the ordinary and his clients seemed happy enough to pay him the agreed fee, even when he found nothing or found that the 'supernatural tremors' were caused by vibrations from the rails of the nearby Muni or that a glowing figure in a hallway was simply a stray moonbeam or that the disembodied voices were in fact *embodied* voices, those usually of the client's children and sometimes – as in the case of The Mystery of the Trapped Mynah – their pets. Jay even got to the point where he thought about hiring his own apprentice or taking on a partner or maybe just a receptionist. *Was he just a fad?* he asked himself. *Perhaps the only way to capitalize on this recent success was to take on more staff and expand the parameters of his operations?* Or was hiring extra personnel the quickest way to drain what resources he'd managed to accumulate (as well as the fifty-thousand dollars of reward money that the General had given him)?

In the end Jay hired no one. And, as expected, business soon flattened out before flatlining altogether. He was still invited to various functions to offer his views on paranormal investigation but the quality of his audience seemed to diminish by the booking: an Alternative Realities Institute fund-raiser, the *Ghostbusters* Fan Forum, the California Affiliation of Sherlock Holmes Readers' annual get-together, the tenth Bay Area Paranormathon, the Scooby Doo Club's Christmas Ball (where Jay told ghost stories to the kids and a stoned elf doled out the candy). He was even invited to speak at the Stanford University parapsychology department's New Year's Eve dinner but suspected that this was only because listening to an in-the-field paranormal investigator was the faculty's equivalent of hiring a clown when they'd all sniggered like prurient schoolkids throughout the entirety of his presentation.

And now where was he? Jay looked around his office. Marlowe snoozed in front of his TV. Mike Penny and Christoph sat by the window arguing about *Breathless* and *A Bout de Souffle*. The money was spent, the phone dead as always. And if it rung? It would be some lost soul on the other end of the line requiring Jay to play a role somewhere between Visiting Mental Health Nurse and Dial-a-Schmuck. It would be a frail widow who claimed, with no small degree of vulnerable apprehension, that her husband was trying to reach her from 'the other side' but who would be equally as bilious when Jay demonstrated that the 'ghostly knocking sounds' were simply the neighbours' cats playing on the roof. It would be a clock that struck thirteen (ninety-nine times out of a hundred, these were simple cases of weak springs, ailing gear-meshing and faulty rack hooks as every experienced paranormal investigator knew). It would be a widower with a wild and improbable story or a solitary drunk or some other category of lonesome desperado who called only because Jay had put his number in the paper and because they needed company, needed someone, anyone, to come in from *out there* and break the ritual of their lonely and repetitive lives.

3

'Jay, forgot to mention it, buddy,' Mike called from his seat, 'some of your mail's been gettin' delivered to my office by mistake.'

He got up and left the room, coming back a minute later with a stack of envelopes which he dumped on Jay's desk. Jay filtered through them, ignoring anything that looked like a demand for money until he came across a small parcel. A little bigger than a pack of cigarettes, it was wrapped in brown paper and had his name and address written on the side in navy blue ink. Jay didn't recognize the handwriting but a throb of anticipation beat away in his gut when he saw the postmark stamped on the package's top corner.

Wilmington, NC

Jay tore away the paper and opened the box, its contents spilling out on to his doodle-strewn blotter: the delicate silver chain, the hazelnut-sized diamond set in a silver disc.

'You alright, Jay?' Christoph asked.

'You look like you've been hit by a lightnin' bolt,' Mike observed.

'It's nothing,' Jay replied, 'just something from an old acquaintance. It's a bit of a surprise, that's all.' He searched for a note or letter but couldn't find one. Then he picked up the necklace itself and stared at it.

Helena Smiling.

Why had she sent it to him? Jay pictured her for a second (it was as easy as blinking, even after all these years, simply a matter of choice), the diamond lying there on her tan skin like a teardrop stolen from the cheek of some cosmic being, remembered the kamikaze Ks of her kinetic kisses and the pressure of her fingertips on the back of his head and the faint gravity of her breasts crushed against his chest.

'From where I'm sittin', that looks like a mighty fine piece of jewellery to be sendin' through the mail, buddy,' Mike said. 'This acquaintance of yours, she wouldn't happen to be an old flame by any chance?'

'Kind of,' Jay replied, hearing his voice flutter like a panicked bird as it cleared his throat. 'She lives in North Carolina. I haven't seen or heard from her in almost five years, not since that summer Christoph and I worked on Ibiza . . .'

Christoph and Mike stared across the office at him with level expressions.

'Say no more, buddy, say no more. Sounds as if it's all something you left *way* back in the past and you still want it left there.' Mike pushed his sunglasses back up his nose. 'You ever want to talk to someone about it, you know my door is always open.'

Jay considered telling Mike that he seemed to spend more time in Jay's office than in his own but Mike chose that moment to look at his watch and stand up.

'You off to lunch?' Jay asked.

'Yes, buddy,' the Nebraskan replied, smoothing down his suit. 'It's chow time and there's twelve ounces of prime rib with my name all over it. Either of you guys want to tag along?'

Jay shook his head.

'Maybe tomorrow, Mike.'

'Sure thing, buddy.'

And Christoph was out of his seat too, heading home to work on a jingle. And then they were gone. Jay sat there for a few more minutes, staring at the diamond, letting the chain slip in and out of his fingers. Why had she sent it? He thought back to those afternoons years before, her body whorled up in the white sheet with his, his fingers reaching for the diamond and holding it up to the light, Helena telling him about the day her mother had given it to her (and given an identical necklace to her twin sister Zelda) just before she'd died. They'd been children, seven years old, and the necklaces were impossibly precious to both of them.

Why had she sent it after all this time?

For a few years now Jay had been congratulating himself on feeling better about Helena Smiling. There'd been a time when her memory had been a detailed and extended torture for him, when the merest thought of her had elicited deep plunging sensations in his chest, sparked long bouts of unrelenting insomnia or forced him to stop what he was doing (whatever it was) and ride out a moment of emotional vacuum. Eventually he'd managed to come up with a version of events that he could live with. Jay Richards and Helena Smiling? The same old tale of Boy meets Girl, Boy gets Girl, but Girl ends up going back to her Rich Robust Fiancé. The Boy in this case was Jay, five years earlier (young, naïve and stupid?), bumming around Ibiza and running errands for Pepé the Waterman. The Girl was Helena Smiling. As for the other guy? Well, he'd been Jean-Marc, heir to a French pharmaceutical empire whose products lined the shelves of every bathroom cabinet in the country.

Yes, Jay thought as he rolled a joint and then whistled a few bars of 'Something To Remember You By' at Marlowe to signal that it was time for lunch: these days, Helena meant nothing. If his heart had jumped at the thought of her (and Jay had to admit that it *had* jumped when he'd first seen the parcel, the handwriting, the Wilmington postmark), then it was like an old biology experiment he'd seen at school. His teacher, in order to demonstrate the relationship between electricity and the animal nervous system, had once wired up a pair of frog's legs to an electrical current. '*Observe what happens when I connect the power,*' he'd warned the class before flicking a switch. The frog's legs had twitched and spasmed, kicking out at the teacher's command . . . well, this was how Jay defined any feelings that surfaced these days on the subject of Helena Smiling: they were nothing more than the meaningless side effect of neural electricity. They meant nothing. They meant nothing. They meant nothing. He took one more look at the necklace. Then he put it back in its box and slid the box into the back of the desk drawer which he locked before walking out of the office.

Down on the sidewalk a few moments later, with Marlowe trotting beside him and the joint smoking discreetly away in his cupped hand, Jay felt a little better. Occasionally, perhaps a couple of times a year, usually during the long spell of indecisive weather that the Bay Area passed off as winter, he'd feel a sharp hunger for London in his stomach, a longing that also registered as a tingle in the nose and across the backs of his hands, a desire to stand on its cold rainwashed streets as the dove-grey afternoon light started to turn and schoolkids hurtled back and forth over its slick pavements. But not that day. The sky was still clear, a warm breeze floated in off the bay and the streets of San Francisco were all Rs: a gang of chain-smoking Chinese boys stood around admiring the racing alloys on an ultramarine Rapier outside Old St Mary's; a giant advert for Regret perfume high up over the diggers and dumper-trucks renovating Union Square presented a model's face in extreme close-up in an attempt to persuade people that it was 'A Beautiful Thing' (across the square, their competitors offered the public a half-naked redhead ravaging a male contemporary in a grimy alleyway, presumably in order to get him to hand over the vial of Redemption that he seemed intent on denying her); a woman in a red dress roared away from the lights on the corner of Post and Mason in a Rhapsody Royale with white rims and the sun burned the sky a raw shade of blue above them all. In San Francisco, there were probably more theories on the nature of God than anywhere else in the world. *He* was a man. *She* was a woman. *It* was a marmot or a turnip or simply an idea. But on a perfect Californian day, Jay could only think that if God existed, then whatever form he, she or it took, the being would have blue eyes and that the universe sat nestled in one of the being's brilliant irises.

After fifteen minutes of casual strolling, Marlowe and Jay had crossed over Geary and stepped into Ernie's Elvis Diner where Big Ernie served a themed selection that included Blue Hawaiian Pizza and Love Me Tender Beef Fajitas but where Jay ordered his usual, a Heartbreak Hotel Hamburger with nothing on the side. Sitting there amongst the old gas-station pumps and antique pinball machines and authentically rusted dairy signs, the King crooning away in the background, Jay sipped juice and told himself that the best thing he could do would be to get rid of the necklace as quickly as he could, to toss it into the bay and forget about it. He should be quite good at that, he considered, especially if the pronouncements of some of his recent dates were anything to go by. During his first year in San Francisco, these brief connections tended to see Jay temporarily sharing airspace with the kind of women who drank and smoked anything he put in front of them, pale raven-haired waifs who favoured the heavy application of dark eyeliner and interrogated him about his job with a feral intensity in the guttering light of black candles while he lay there in the double whammy of stoned post-coital torpor. During Jay's second year in the city, however, he seemed to find himself transiently coupled with a more maternal type of woman, the kind of woman who filled his weekends with trips to the houses of other couples where yet more couples congregated and used each others' first names a lot, or else obliged him to collaborate on group picnic trips to Sonoma or Carmel where he got the feeling that he *wasn't* meant to talk about what he did. If Jay was a little mystified by this undeniable reformulation in the texture of his romantic life (if that's what one could call it) then at least he could now extract a small degree of consolation from it: both groups of women were consistent in proclaiming him 'terminally distracted' and 'emotionally disengaged'. If it were all true, Jay mused (also remembering other perennial accusations, 'emotional cowardice' and 'reality evasion' to name just two), then surely forgetting about the necklace would be child's play?

In the end, Jay didn't so much forget about the necklace (or Helena) as find himself gradually and increasingly preoccupied with other concerns. A few weeks later he managed to earn gas money after getting to the bottom of The Mystery of the Monterey Mental Asylum, nearby residents claiming that spirits of former inmates haunted the abandoned building at night but Jay only finding a bunch of kids smoking dope and drinking Red Dog. And there was The Case of the Headless Hardware Store Cashier where he was called to investigate the supposed ghost of a former employee at the Daly City branch of FixIt, an employee who'd been decapitated in a car accident on his way to work and whose spirit the store manager believed was still turning up for his shift. This time Jay found nothing, was paid nothing for his time, and it seemed clear that the whole thing was just a ruse to get the store more publicity. And it was the same when Jay investigated an alleged haunting at The Bastille Bar and Grill down in Bakersfield (the owner claimed that the ghosts of men who were incarcerated in the building when it was formerly a prison roamed the parking lot at night). And it was the same when Jay was called to Cinemaniacs Videos in Carlton where employees claimed to have seen the translucent figure of a man who'd held up the store a couple of years previously and ultimately taken his own life when police officers had surrounded the building. To begin with, Jay couldn't get Helena's necklace out of his mind. It sat there in the back of his desk drawer (he didn't open it for weeks at a time) but also in the background of his thoughts, like tape hiss, a faint murmur that accompanied everything: it was there when he was sitting in the office with Mike Penny and Marlowe; it was there when he sat around with Christoph at home, smoking whatever weed Christoph hadn't already sold to the city's red-eyed youth or when the two of them were out mixing records at Rabbit City; it was there when Jay investigated a supposedly haunted telescope at the vista-point on the north side of Golden Gate and when he took his instruments into the Ghost Train ride at the Thrillville FunDome and when he staked out a barber's in North Beach where Mickey 'Mugsy' Malloy had been shot while receiving his weekly trim. And there were more cases and more disappointments. Jay investigated an alleged haunting at the preserved mission down 101 in San Juan Bautista where two women had fallen from the historic bell tower on two separate occasions in the last twelve months. As he expected, Jay discovered nothing anomalous and it was the same when he investigated an alleged poltergeist at a luxury housing complex up in Petaluma and revealed that the books and ornaments weren't flying off the shelves and ending up smashed on the floor of the clients' home because of paranormal activity but because the family's teenage daughter hated her new stepmom. And Jay was busy dodging Flora Arfenstein, his elderly landlady, and ignoring her rent reminders. And there was the time he killed taking Marlowe for long walks, usually along Ocean Beach but sometimes out along the pier in the Marina or around the sculpted grounds of the Palace of Fine Arts and the Legion of Honor Museum. Soon, the necklace was nothing more than an idea and no more real to him than his memories of Helena (after a while, he'd stopped using the desk drawer and simply left it closed) and how long had Jay been dealing with those?

Months passed. Then one day during the last week of August, a stack of mail arrived at the office, the standard assortment of trash and demands except for a single cream envelope addressed to Jay in lilac ink near the bottom of the pile. As soon as he saw it, Jay put his joint down in the ashtray (and thought of Helena's necklace sitting in its box for the first time in days) and turned it over and over in his hands, examining it carefully while he rubbed his fingers across the powdery grain of the paper. Like the parcel he'd received before, it looked strange, old-fashioned and almost other worldly amongst all the other word-processed correspondence. Was the looping purple handwriting the same as that on the wrapping paper he'd stuffed into his desk back in April? After a frantic search through his pockets for the key, Jay yanked open the drawer and pulled out the scraps of brown manila. The handwriting was the same. *Had Helena written to him?* Jay then saw that there weren't any stamps on the envelope which meant that it had been delivered by hand. *She'd come to the office . . .* he took out the key to the Apache from his pocket and used it to slice open the envelope. Inside was a single folded sheet of cream paper.

The Buchanan Hotel
San Francisco
24th August

Dear Jay,

 I can't imagine what you must be thinking, receiving a letter from me out of the blue like this. All I can say for now is that I've come to San Francisco to contact you in person and ask for your help with an urgent matter.

 As anxious as I am to go into more detail, I think it's best that I explain it all to you face to face. I will be waiting for you in the bar on the roof-terrace of my hotel at 7pm this evening.

 Please meet me there. It may be that you do not wish to take up my invitation. That is your prerogative, I will be waiting nonetheless.

 Yours,
 Zelda Smiling

Zelda. Helena's identical twin. Where had she got his address from? Jay read the note again, picturing her somewhere in the city, somewhere, anywhere, perhaps at that very moment walking back to her hotel having made her delivery. Why did she want to see him? Whatever the reason Zelda had for writing to him, she hadn't stated that it concerned Helena but Jay couldn't stop himself from wondering if Helena wanted to contact him and had sent Zelda as a go-between and . . . Jay realized how stupid he sounded, felt a flood of shame at his own foolishness and told himself that turning up at the Buchanan at seven o'clock could only make things worse. He thought back to that September evening five years earlier, the last time he'd met Zelda (the only time he'd previously met Zelda): Helena had gone, she'd told him, no message, no goodbye. Helena had disappeared out of his life and why did he still pretend, even for a second, that any of it held significance, that it had been anything more than a brief and meaningless affair, a small footnote in Helena's larger agenda, the whole thing nothing more serious than the opening scenes to *Grease*: 'summer dreams ripped at the seams' (wasn't that how the line went?).

And yes, the sleepless nights had persisted for a while. And yes, after that last evening Jay had left Ibiza and circled the planet gripped by something that seemed, at least at some level, like paranoia. He'd hallucinated her repeatedly in the crowds ahead of him as he penetrated the shifting heat of tropical streets with their whirling neon and argon, the strangely familiar clamour of oriental voices all around him, the kiosks at the side of the road selling grilled insects and bowls of steaming noodles. He'd imagined her in the windows of restaurants and in the flickering worlds of airport departure lounges and on the platforms of heaving railway stations. Once, when Jay was working as a valet at the Peninsula in Kowloon for a few months, he'd prepared himself to see her screen-goddess heels stepping out on to the forecourt every time a cab or limousine pulled up (would she even recognize him?), and it was only when he'd finally made it to San Francisco that the whole issue of Helena had started to fade, the past put gradually where it belonged, entered into the ledger book of Life one figure at a time, in a column labelled 'Experience', a lesson endured if, indeed, little had been learned.

And now Zelda was there, in the city, in San Francisco.

It didn't matter, Jay concluded, looking up and nodding to Mike Penny who strode into the office at that moment with a couple of cappuccinos from downstairs. Whatever it was Zelda Smiling wanted to talk to him about, it didn't matter and Jay didn't care. It wasn't his business.

4

Jay arrived at the Buchanan a little after seven and stared at the hotel entrance from outside the tropical bird shop across the street while he finished a joint and wondered over and over if he should go inside. By the time he was treading the roach into the sidewalk he still couldn't make up his mind and retreated to a nearby bar where he sipped at a Venus Flytrap until he'd convinced himself that he had nothing to lose. *Ten minutes*, he told himself, *he would listen to what she had to say, that was all he was committing himself to* . . . a few moments later he was negotiating the revolving doors of the hotel and the lobby beyond them, wondering if Zelda would still be waiting. Thirty-three floors up, the roof terrace of the Buchanan was all Zs, executive looking zaibatsu convened at various tables discussing zillion dollar deals in hushed voices while waiters in zinc-white jackets zipped methodically between them with trays of drinks, but it only took a second for Jay's eyes to zero in on Zelda, sitting in zazen stillness at a table on the far side of the terrace. He froze when he saw her, felt a twisting beneath his ribs and a sensation in his dry mouth that seemed far too large for such a small space. Then he approached, tractor-beam slow, and she didn't see him until he was a few feet away.

'Zelda.'

She stood up.

'You made it. I'd just convinced myself that you weren't going to come.'

Another internal contortion. She was Helena's replica . . . but he'd known that already (and what else should he have expected?). Jay managed to compose himself enough to wonder whether he should kiss her on her cheek or offer her his hand to shake. In the end he did neither and left the two of them standing there awkwardly for a few moments.

'Shall we sit down?'

They took their seats, once again facing each other, the bay shining away to Zelda's left as Jay stared at her face and tried to catalogue the differences between it and his memory of her sister's. There were hardly any to consider if she didn't move. Like Helena, Zelda's hair was the same searing chrome yellow as sun-bright dahlias, her eyes the same dusty delphinium blue. And there were the same arching eyebrows and forehead above them, the same thin nose. Was it his imagination or the product of faulty recollection or was Zelda's face slightly fuller than his memory of Helena's? He couldn't tell, watching as a smile struggled to arrange itself on her face. And then she spoke and the exact resemblance was lost, Jay adjusting to the extra quartertone of depth in Zelda's voice and the strange rhythm of her painfully familiar features.

'Thank you for coming. It's been a long time.'

'Yes, it has.'

'I haven't ordered a drink yet. What would you like?'

'Whatever you're having.'

Zelda ordered two glasses of Zinfandel from a passing waiter and asked them to be charged to her room and then turned back to Jay.

'You're obviously wondering how I got hold of your address and why I'm here.'

'How did you find me?'

'I got your number and address from George Lockwood . . .'

'You know General Lockwood?'

'No,' she replied. 'How I came to contact him will become clear once you've heard what it is I've come to San Francisco to tell you. Perhaps I should get straight to the point? In my note, I wrote that something serious has happened . . .'

Zelda stopped for a moment and Jay noticed how tired she

looked, the dark clouds around her eyes, the pale skin of her face. Perhaps it was all the result of jet-lag or some other kind of fatigue but suddenly Jay found himself imagining the worst.

'I'm not sure where to start,' she said.

'Is Helena . . . *dead?*'

Jay was surprised at his own insistence.

'Jay, she's missing.'

'Since when?' he asked but had to wait for his answer while the waiter placed their drinks in front of them.

'Helena went missing a couple of weeks ago,' Zelda continued eventually. 'Let me tell you what's happened in full. If I tell you the whole story, you'll see that it all might have a perfectly reasonable explanation.' She scanned Jay's eyes for a second. 'You probably don't know this but Helena broke off her engagement with Jean-Marc a few months after they returned home for our father's funeral. A short time later, she met and married an Englishman, a man called Toby Charteris.'

As it happened, Jay *did* know this. He'd already seen an article about Toby and Helena's marriage in the society column of a discarded English newspaper while he'd sipped a beer in a bar on the Quai de Mekong in Vientiane. He'd raised the bottle and toasted them before draining it and tracking back into the city in search of opium or some other kind of easily won oblivion though he didn't bother to share any of this with Zelda.

'After they were married, they moved into Willoughby, my parents' house,' she continued. 'They seemed happy for a short while. Then . . .' Zelda stopped. For some reason that Jay couldn't work out, she seemed hesitant to continue.

'What happened?' he asked gently.

'Jay, I don't know how well you think you know my sister but she's never been the most stable person, certainly not when it comes to responsibility nor when it comes to other people's feelings. As for Toby . . .' Again, she hesitated for a second, as if she were choosing her words with extra care. 'I think he's a deeply unlikeable man: selfish, vain and stupid. Perhaps it's no surprise they turned their marriage into a disaster.'

'How?'

'Jay, in four years of marriage, I'd say that the two of them must have had at least three times that number of affairs. I've got a whole shoe-box of Helena's letters telling me that she's run out of patience. But she's never left him, or at least she's never left him for longer than a few days.'

'What about Toby?'

'Toby's a lot simpler about the whole business. He just sleeps around with local women, anything in a skirt as I understand it. Why they stick together is anyone's guess. I thought, like a lot of people, that things might change after Helena gave birth to Jacob . . .'

'Helena's had a child?'

'Yes,' said Zelda. She told Jay, almost reluctantly, he thought, that Helena had given birth to a boy the previous January.

'He's called Jacob.'

'But nothing's changed?'

'It doesn't look like it. Helena's more recent letters have suggested that Toby's been making more of an effort since she became pregnant. But she's never been convinced that it was anything more than an act. And now . . .'

'And now?'

'And now it seems as if Helena's run off with a local man.'

'When?'

'Almost two weeks ago.'

Zelda told Jay that Helena and Toby had been married on the fifteenth of August and that each year since they'd invited close friends to stay at Willoughby to celebrate the occasion.

'This year the anniversary fell on a Saturday and they also invited a few hundred people to a party on the day itself. I think it was Toby's idea, another of his pathetic attempts to show that he's some kind of reformed father and husband. The whole thing certainly sounds like one of his ideas: ostentatious, expensive and requiring minimum emotional investment.'

'What happened?'

'Well, I wasn't at the party . . .'

'Why not?'

'I decided not to make the trip,' Zelda replied clinically. 'I've been working in Kosovo with the UN for the last two years and it's a long way to travel, especially as I've been unwell recently. And I don't like going home all that much . . . anyway, it was the night of the anniversary party that Helena and this guy went missing.'

'What's his name?'

'His name's Wallace Kelly. He lives nearby at Thackeray.'

'What's Thackeray?'

'Another old plantation house a mile or so from Willoughby.'

'And where are Helena and this Wallace guy now?'

'No one knows. They haven't contacted anyone yet, not even me.'

Jay asked Zelda if the police had been notified and she nodded.

'Of course. Toby contacted them straight away but I don't think they're taking the matter too seriously. It's widely known that Helena and Wallace were having an affair. Apparently, or at least according to the people I've spoken to in the area since I returned home, the two of them as good as flaunted their relationship.'

'Have the police taken any kind of action?'

'They've asked for a complete list of the guests that attended the party that night and they've asked all the guests actually staying at the house to remain there until they've completed an initial investigation though they expect to allow them to go home any day now.'

'You say you weren't at the party,' Jay asked. 'How did you hear about all of this?'

'Toby sent news to me in Kosovo a few days after Helena disappeared and I flew home as soon as I could arrange it. I have to say, it's the last thing I need right now. I'm still recovering from a bout of viral pneumonia I contracted in the spring and if I were my patient, I'd tell myself to rest up in bed for a couple of months. But I'm worried about Jacob and I'm not convinced that a drunk like Toby is the best person to be responsible for a small baby under any circumstances, let alone these . . .'

'Zelda?'

Zelda stopped. 'What is it?'

Jay leaned forward in his chair. 'Zelda, I haven't seen Helena for five years.' He took a breath, a sip of wine. 'And now I've listened to everything you've told me, that Helena's missing and that she's run off with this Wallace guy. How does any of this concern me?'

'There's more to tell you.'

'So tell me.'

Zelda shifted in her seat and Jay wondered if she'd recently given up smoking. Her restlessness seemed to need the action of lighting a cigarette in order to resolve itself.

'Jay,' she said finally. 'Your work, it must be a strange business?'

'My work?'

'Your work. Hunting . . . for ghosts.'

'How do you know about my work?'

'One morning a while back, I was reading the *Daily Planet* during a coffee break when I saw an article about the Lockwood murder case. I have to say that at the time I was surprised to see the *Planet* dealing with what seemed like a tabloid story. And I was even more surprised to see your name and picture there.'

Zelda stopped while the same waiter who'd brought their

drinks returned to light the gas heater behind Jay's shoulder.

'So you remembered me?'

'Don't be too flattered,' Zelda replied, allowing herself a brief smile. 'I can't even remember if I mentioned it to Helena the next time I wrote her.' She stopped to push a strand of hair away from her forehead and then turned back to face him. 'What's it like being a famous ghostbuster?'

'I prefer to call myself a *paranormal investigator*,' Jay replied with a smile. 'And you should know that reports of my celebrity have been greatly exaggerated. Most of my work is exceptionally routine and has a lot more to do with exposing obvious reasons why strange things are happening rather than proving the existence or non-existence of anything supernatural.'

Zelda stared back at him. 'You think *I* believe in ghosts, Jay?' She laughed. 'I'm a doctor. Do you know how many people I've watched die over the last four years? One thing I'm convinced of is that once you're dead, *you're dead*. There's nothing spooky about it, though in my particular experience it's inevitably sad, brutal, and almost always unnecessary.'

'So what's happened,' Jay asked. 'You've not come all the way to San Francisco to tell me about Helena's latest fling. I presume something's happened at Willoughby?'

Zelda looked at him for a moment but didn't speak.

'What's wrong?' he asked.

'Does everyone feel like this when they come to you?'

'Feel like what?'

She stared out across the water towards Treasure Island and the lights on the Bay Bridge for a moment.

'Ridiculous.'

'A lot of people find it hard. But I'm more suspicious of clients who *don't* find it difficult, to be honest. Why don't you just tell me what you know?'

'It all happened the week before I arrived back so I'm really reporting to you what others have told me.'

'That's okay for now.'

'The first thing that happened occurred last Tuesday. To put it in context, two of our father's aunts live at Willoughby. Clemmy and Lobelia are their names and they're both in their nineties, both very ill and very frail. They have to spend all day in bed and need all their meals and medication brought to their room.'

'Why do they live at Willoughby?' Jay asked.

'They've both got nowhere else to go so Toby and Helena are obliged to have them at the house. Anyway, last Tuesday night, everyone was in bed when they heard Clemmy and Lobelia crying out. When Toby and the others rushed to their room, the women claimed that they'd seen our mother "floating" across their floor.'

'This Clemmy and Lobelia, they hardly sound like the most trustworthy witnesses,' Jay suggested.

'I agree,' Zelda replied. 'But the next night, the housekeeper was walking home across the estate when . . . well, she's not exactly sure what happened to her.'

'What's this housekeeper's name?'

'Sara. Sara Taft.'

'*Mrs Taft*?' Jay asked. 'Your nanny from when you were both children?' Zelda nodded and Jay remembered that he'd often heard Helena talk about her. 'How did Mrs Taft describe her experience?'

'Sara said that she was making her way back to her house through the garden after shutting up Willoughby for the night and that she thought she heard a noise behind her. She went to take a look . . .'

'Could she describe what she saw later?'

Zelda shook her head.

'Apparently Toby was the first to reach her. He was still

reading in his study when he heard her scream and rushed down to find her collapsed on the ground. When she came round she insisted that she hadn't seen anything, that she'd overreacted.'

Jay asked Zelda if anything else had happened at Willoughby and she nodded. She'd arrived at the house the previous Friday morning around midday to find Toby, Sara and the guests sitting in one of the drawing rooms.

'To be honest, it looked ridiculous, like a scene out of an old film where some fat detective tells everyone the butler did it. I asked what was going on but no one said anything. Then Toby took me out into the entrance hall. Jay, there are twenty-two paintings in that hall, some of them as tall as you . . .'

'What happened to them?'

'They'd all moved in the middle of the night.'

'What do you mean by "moved"?'

'I mean that each of the paintings was hanging in a different position in the hall when everyone came down to breakfast last Friday morning. I grew up in that house and I don't think I saw anyone move those paintings, not even once.'

Jay said that one of the guests could have moved them and Zelda quickly agreed.

'But they all deny it,' she continued. 'Toby was furious and demanded that someone own up but so far no one's admitted it was them.'

'Let me get this last bit of the story straight,' Jay said. 'You're telling me that twenty-two paintings moved in the middle of the night.'

'That's right,' Zelda replied.

Jay swilled back some wine. The two of them stared at each other while the nacreous evening sky stretched out towards the horizon above them.

'Will you come to Willoughby and . . . and *do* whatever it is that you do?'

'You say you don't believe in ghosts yet you're hiring me to investigate a possible haunting?'

'Jay, you're not the only one who's sceptical. The sooner you can prove that there's something logical behind all of this, the better it is for all of us: me, Toby and the guests in the house. At the moment, everyone is going crazy and they're driving Clemmy and Lobelia mad while all the time there's a baby in the house without its mother.'

'Why me?' Jay asked. 'I'm not the only paranormal investigator around.'

'No, you're not. I rang a few numbers I found in the paper – a couple of guys in Charleston and a woman in Raleigh. The woman wanted to read my palm. One of the guys in Charleston wanted to hold a séance while the other wanted me to undress. Then I remembered the article I'd read about you in the *Daily Planet*. I couldn't remember your name at first so I called Helena's friend Bessie. Do you remember her from Ibiza?'

Jay said that he vaguely remembered her (Helena's oldest friend, staying at the villa with her and Jean-Marc and the others?).

'She remembered *your* name anyway and I looked you up on the internet and found a few reports about the Lockwood case. You can pretty much work the rest out for yourself.'

Zelda stopped and held Jay's gaze for a few seconds.

'I can imagine that you might not want to have anything to do with my sister. And I certainly can't make you take up my offer of a job. If you decide that you don't want it, I'll be forced to look for someone else. But I'd like you at least to give it serious consideration.'

Two envelopes appeared on the table.

'Listen,' she continued, 'it feels strange enough having this conversation in the first place. And forgive me for being direct but it feels pretty strange hiring someone like you. But you seem to have been successful in the past ... and at least you're not a complete stranger.'

'Perhaps a stranger is what you need,' Jay replied but realized that he was starting to sound petulant. He glanced down at the envelopes. Zelda looked down at them too.

'Here is a ticket for a flight tomorrow morning – it'll get you to Wilmington International which is about a half-hour's drive from Willoughby. And here is a small advance to cover your initial expenses.'

'What if I don't want the job?'

'Do whatever you want with the money. If you decide to come, I promise you'll be paid for your time.'

'Whose money is this?' Jay asked, keeping his hands where they were for a moment. 'Toby's?'

'It's mine,' she replied firmly. 'I'm responsible for you, not Toby. He's convinced that one of the men staying in the house is behind what's been happening.'

Her voice dropped into a low, fervent cadence that had her reminding Jay of Helena more than at any other point so far in their conversation.

'Jay, please decide to help me. I'm flying back in a few hours. If you decide to follow me, call ahead to Willoughby and leave a message. I've written down the phone number for you.'

She got up and Jay also rose from his seat.

'I have to go. See you again, I hope. Goodbye.'

'Goodbye.'

Jay watched her weave through the tables and twilight towards the elevators where she took one last look back over her shoulder and flashed him a troubled smile. And then she was gone. He sat down and looked at the table in front of him. The two envelopes sat on the pressed linen, one with a plane ticket, the other loaded with dollar bills. C-notes. There were thirty-five of them, not the usual dirty dishcloths people were always palming off on him and pretending it was money, but the real deal: taut, clean notes as smooth as freshly razored skin.

5

As Jay drove back home, the city seemed to be all Gs: a Giants game on the radio as he trawled down Geary past the Gibson Building where gravity had pulled Dana Lockwood to her death and on through the swerving g-forces of the bend at the bottom of the hill where the glare of headlamps gathered in the fog. He stopped off for sandwich materials and a pack of Spirits at Golden Gate Groceries on 18th and then substituted the baseball with a Count Basie disc (the Prez in perhaps his best post-army form as he burned and churned his way through 'Sent For You Yesterday' in front of a mesmerized Newport '57 crowd) before proceeding home through the park to Quintara Avenue. For once the house was quiet. Most evenings, it resembled the designated smoking cubicle of some humid oriental airport, waves of people arriving and leaving, a short overlapping passage of time in between that saw the arrival and departure of others, Christoph's customers ranging from the pierced students in the inevitable skatepunk clobber and retro colours to the corporate technology drones and Financial District hustlers in soft cashmere vests and rimless eyewear looking to unwind after a hard day at their screens. But that night Marlowe snoozed in his basket while Christoph sat alone in his ALL DJS ARE WHORES t-shirt, smoking a joint in front of his computer screen while the latest micropiece he was composing trickled out through the speakers.

'You been out on a case?' he grunted, eyes on the rolling cursor.

'Kind of.'

Jay didn't say any more about it and instead made himself and Marlowe a sandwich before he and Christoph climbed into the Apache around ten o'clock and drove across to the Mission where they played their usual four hours at Rabbit City to the usual graveyard shift crowd. It was a relief for Jay that he and Christoph rarely talked about anything other than records during these weekly excursions (these days Jay spared Christoph the ugly details of paranormal investigation and there was little he didn't already know about the ten second soundbites Christoph composed or the pot he sold). And it was a relief to stand there and stare down at the spinning simplicity of labels of the records and their spiralling text, the systematic passage of the beats in the headphones synchronizing and falling in line while his hand manipulated the pitch control and the reflection of his face stared back at him from the wavering surface of the vinyl. But Jay ultimately couldn't stop himself imagining Zelda flying through the night. And he couldn't stop himself from thinking about Helena, imagining the possibility (or was it a ridiculous fantasy?) of seeing her again outside the old house that so far he'd only seen in photographs. There he was, he told himself, yet again at the unavoidable core of the matter. How much space-time had he already travelled trying to get away from Helena and her memory? And how much dream-time had he already wasted watching himself do his best to retrace his steps?

Jay also considered another detail of Zelda's account of recent events. Helena had disappeared with the neighbour. What was his name? Wallace Kelly. Imagining them together offered Jay another strong and painful flash of her, memories of drifting to sleep in her arms, memories of *that* afternoon they went swimming off Cala Carbo, memories of the energy that he'd felt in his taut fingertips whenever the three of them – him, Helena and Jean-Marc – had been in the same room together, the cut of Helena's fingernails sometimes still fresh in his skin, the sensation of their clashing mouths still there in his gums and his lips and his tongue. Why would Jay even consider getting involved?

At two-thirty Jay and Christoph packed up their records while the bar staff cleared the dirty glasses and the dead drinks.

'So,' Christoph asked, 'what's up? You've hardly said a word all night.'

'I'm deciding whether I'm going to go to North Carolina on a case,' Jay replied after a while. 'I'm not sure how long it'll take.'

'You sound unsure about it. Why?'

There seemed to be nothing else to do but tell him the whole story or tell him nothing at all. They spluttered through the sleeping city in the Apache and reached home just after three, Jay telling Christoph the story of Helena, Jean-Marc and himself as they passed the bong back and forth in the den. 'What do you think?' he asked when he'd got to the end. As expected, Christoph remained entirely practical about the whole matter.

'Is she going to pay you, this Zelda?'

Jay nodded. 'And she's already given me a retainer up-front.' He pulled out the envelope of cash she'd given him and handed it to Christoph.

'She must want you to solve this one pretty badly,' he replied handing it back. 'You should go. You're a paranormal investigator and she's a paying client. Christ knows you spend enough time running around for people who never pay you.'

Typical Christoph. It wasn't so much a case of him liking to be pragmatic about money, more that money gave him yet another opportunity to be pragmatic. Jay counted out five of the notes and gave them to him for Marlowe's sandwiches and any other expenses the mutt might incur. Then he packed some clothes, some mini-discs and his equipment and lined it all up by the front door. By then, it was almost six, time left for one last walk along Ocean Beach. Jay drove over to Café Judah where he chatted to Don and the girls while he helped them open the place up, and then bought a triple-shot, a juice box and a ham 'n' cheese tostada which he took outside on to the sand. Out to sea, the grizzled Pacific toiled through its heavy negotiations under a mackerel sky. Inland, the roads stretched away towards the Peaks where the massed girders of the Sutro radio tower broke through the gloom and continued with their daily impersonation of an invading mothership. Once he'd finished his share of the sandwich, Marlowe sniffed his way through the driftwood towards the water to get a closer look at the seabirds digging in the wet sand for worms while Jay sat down and watched the waves fall over themselves. Then he dropped the dog back with a Christoph and said goodbye to the two of them before getting in his cab. Twenty minutes later, he was outside the Penny residence on Broderick, a three-storey Victorian with a jacaranda in full bloom beside the front steps. Mike eventually appeared after two tries on the doorbell, dressed in a long dragon-print kimono and a pair of Chinese slippers, a cup of coffee in his right hand.

'Jay, buddy, this is an unexpected pleasure. What can I do for you?' he asked.

'Sorry to disturb you so early. There's something I need to talk to you about.'

'You best be comin' in off the street then.'

Jay signalled to his driver that he'd be five minutes and then followed Mike through the hallway into a kitchen where a Chinese woman stood at the stove manipulating various frying pans. 'This is my wife, Mei Han. You want some chow, buddy? We got eggs, muffins, hash browns, pancakes, waffles, bagels, bacon steaks, pork chops. Mei Han can put any and all of it between a coupla slices of bread if you like.'

Jay declined, saying that he'd already eaten and wondering at the same time if Mike ate like this every day before consuming his morning ration of Toasty Tartz.

'So, what's the story, buddy?'

'I have to go to North Carolina on a case and I don't know how long I'm going to be. I could be back next week or I could be back next month, you know how it is.'

'North Carolina, you say? Is this all on account of that romantic attachment you alluded to a few months back?'

'Something to do with it, yes.'

'And you want me to keep an eye on your office while you're gone?'

'Actually, I was thinking of something a little more drastic than that . . .'

Mike hooted. 'Drastic, you say? Shoot.'

'I was wondering if you'd like to become partners. I've got enough money up-front for this case to get things straight with Mrs Arfenstein. As for the future, it seems to me that you and I don't need two offices between us. You could give up your office and move in with me. We could cut costs, share our work load, help each other generate business. And I only say that we should share *my* office because it used to be Tommy's and I'm sentimentally attached to it.'

Mike took a piece of toast from his plate, bit into it and thought for a moment.

'What do you think, honey?' he called over to his wife who was stirring something on the stove. She replied in Cantonese and whatever it is she said, it seemed to satisfy him. 'Hell,' Mike said, 'let's do it. We'll be like "Spade 'n' Archer". We'll paint our names on the windows and everythin'.'

Jay decided not to remind Mike that Miles Archer died in the first act and instead counted out two thousand dollars and handed them to him along with spare keys to the office. After that, Mike led him back to the front door.

'I'll call once I get a sense of what's going on at the other end,' Jay said when they were standing on the porch. Mike thumbed through the wad of hundred dollar bills and said he'd take care of Flora Arfenstein.

'Hell, *this* and some good ol' Nebraskan charm should do the trick.'

Mike leant on the door jamb and Jay noticed a tattoo on his usually suited forearm for the first time, an eagle in a plunging dive with its wingtips on fire and its talons murderously extended.

'A li'l souvenir from my time with the hundred and first,' Mike said, seeing Jay stare at it.

'I didn't know you'd been in the army.'

'Well, I guess there's a whole lot you don't know,' he replied affably, 'and vice versa. Guess we'll have a lot to yack about when we're stakin' out graveyards after you get back.'

'I guess so.' They shook hands. 'Like I say, I'll call in the next few days.'

'You know where I am.'

After they'd pulled away from the Penny residence, Jay asked his cab driver to stop by the office where he dug out the box containing Helena's necklace and settled his coffee account downstairs before continuing on to the airport, the freeway outside the capsule of the car all Is, a billboard above the skyway with the slogan 'Into the Future?' mystically tagged across its glossy face in giant iguana-green letters, a bus bearing the latest advertisement for Infinity along its side, indium clouds above the bay and a blonde woman in an indigo Intrepid with Illinois plates who drew abreast with the cab for a second and beamed an impish smile at him before flashing her indicators and sweeping imperiously across the freeway for the off-ramp. *Why had Helena sent her necklace to him*? Jay still didn't know and no amount of staring at the diamond as the car sped down 101 seemed to help him arrive at an answer or hush the infrasonic voice throbbing away somewhere inside his head that told him to turn around and head for home.

I'm smoking the first joint of the day in my bedroom at the French former ambassador to Cuba's mansion and listening to the whirring grind of the *grillos* out on the hillside when my mobile rings. It's Pepé.

'*Hey*,' he growls down the line (Pepé always refuses to anglicize his pronunciation of my name), '*Hey*, I need you to come over and pick up a delivery.'

It's almost eleven by the time I get myself over to Portinax and the tables in the Restaurante S'Illot have started to fill up with Spanish families, parents drinking coffee and eating sandwiches, dripping children wandering back and forth with ice cream and chocolate. Pepé's waiting for me as he always is, at a small table in the storeroom out back with a bottle of water, a café solo and a Ducados burning away in an ashtray next to a pile of receipts and he tells me that he wants me to drive five cases of wine over to Ibiza Town. After that, he wants me to collect a pile of tablecloths from the cleaners and drive them over to his hotel in San Rafael. After that he wants me to pick up some water from his warehouse by the airport and deliver it to a series of villas he's listed on the back of an old business card.

'And *Hey*,' he says as I'm turning to leave, 'after that, I need you to take a look at the generator over at Can Jazmín.'

'What's the matter with it?' I ask. Pepé tells me that he doesn't know.

'There's a new crowd of rich French kids staying there, arrived this morning. They just telephoned to tell me they haven't got any power.'

●

What am I, Jay Siu Fu Richards, doing on Ibiza? And how come I'm living in the mansion that belongs to the French former ambassador to Cuba (or, to be more precise, the mansion that *formerly* belonged to the French former ambassador to Cuba)?

•

I'd been living in Amsterdam prior to my arrival on the island. I'd left London on the promise of a DJing gig that never materialized and ended up working in a coffee shop where I weighed out bags of weed and hash for stoned tourists and lived in a flat in a street off Overtoom with a posse of indistinguishable New Zealanders. Two years passed, my life looking exactly the same at the end of it as it had when I'd arrived, and it was around then, just as I wondering where else I could go and what else I could do, that I got a call from Christoph, a Hungarian-Czech guy I'd become friends with in London after we'd run adjacent stalls in Kensington Market for a while. What did he want? He'd rung to tell me that he was on Ibiza.

'What are you doing *there*?' I'd asked.

'I've been working in this strip club the past six months.'

'Doing *what*?' It was hard to see anyone paying Christoph for a lap dance in the back room. And at five foot three, he was hardly bouncer material.

'DJing. Sort of.'

'What do you mean by "sort of"?'

It turned out that Christoph was in charge of the music in the club, 'not a position without responsibility,' he told me given that the girls timed their private dances to the length of each track.

'Okay, so it's not as if I'm dropping two hours of house in front of a packed dancefloor at Pacha every weekend,' he said, 'but the job has its obvious perks. And a paid gig is a paid gig.'

'I guess.'

'Thing is,' he continued, 'I'm going back to Prague to work

for this technology company. I'm off in a week's time and my boss wants me to find someone to take over from me. I thought of you.'

•

Christoph's boss turned out to be Pepé, of course, and I duly presented myself to him in the backroom at the Restaurante S'Illot when I arrived only to discover that he'd already found someone else to fill Christoph's headphones, an Iraqi guy called Ziad who was friendly with one of Pepé's tribe of sons.

'I'm sorry you've come over here for no reason,' he said, stubbing out a Ducados in the ashtray next to the pile of receipts on the small table. 'If it is useful to you, I need to hire a driver. One of my drivers, I just caught him stealing from me so . . .'

•

Pepé never finished the sentence and I soon came to see this as symbolic of the man himself. On the face of things, he came across as the good-humoured paterfamilias of an old and respected Ibicenco family, a landowner and businessman, a community figure. And most of the time, he was little more threatening than the vacationing Santa Claus he so much resembled with his white hair and gut the size of a beachball. But it was also clear, right from the start, that to believe that he was simply a genial restaurant owner was probably a dangerous mistake.

•

I soon found out that my assumption that Pepé came from an old landowning family was entirely wrong. But pretty much everything else I subsequently discovered about him was founded in hearsay and island gossip rather than in anything Pepé told me himself. According to Pedro, who tended the bar at one of Pepé's restaurants up in the old town, during his teens Pepé had supported his impoverished mother and sisters by delivering water all over the island from the back of his horse-drawn cart (this was why one still heard people on Ibiza refer to him occasionally as *Don Agua*, though never in his presence nor in the presence of any of his family). Then, in the early sixties, he'd apparently left the island for the mainland to work as a carpenter for production companies building film sets for westerns on the dusty plains of Almeria. According to Pedro, Pepé even did some acting, usually as an extra, but also getting the chance to play a couple of bandits with a few lines of dialogue that were later dubbed. 'He never talks about it,' Pedro told me, but if I ever got the chance to see *Gunfight At Black Sand Ridge*, I'd see Pepé in all his cinematic glory.

•

Pedro was less sure of what happened next to Pepé in real life, or less willing to talk about it anyway. But Marga, one of the women who serviced Pepé's luxury apartments in Talamanca, seemed to know the next chapter of the story. 'My mother,' she told me, 'she was a childhood friend of Pepé's.'

•

According to Marga (or her mother anyway), Pepé's own mother had died just as the shooting of *Six Bullets Before Sundown* had come to an end and Pepé had duly returned to the island to perform the customary rituals, though not before he'd become friendly with the film's leading actor, Montgomery Swain. Importantly, this all took place at a time when Ibiza was a hippy haven and also a paradise retreat for the English aristocracy and American jet set wallowing in Camelot-era glamour, a romantic and little visited island in the middle of the blue Mediterranean where the rich and famous idled away their summers. And it seems as if Swain wanted to be part of the scene. His previous film, *The Ballad of Prairie Gates*, had met with considerable success and *Six Bullets* seemed destined for the same, and it was on the strength of these accomplishments that the actor came back to Ibiza with Pepé and bought a large plot west of San Mateo on which he planned to build a luxurious villa.

•

Now, perhaps Swain had initially intended to oversee the construction of the house himself, perhaps not. Whatever the case, he'd been forced to leave the island for Los Angeles almost as soon as he'd signed for the land, suddenly required to audition for the leading role in megalomaniac director Gianni Passero's forthcoming epic, *A Hundred Days Under The Sun*.

•

What happened next? It seems as if Swain was still intent on building a summer palace in the dust and dirt of the San Mateo hillside and to this end had an architect design the house before hiring a team of Spanish builders to start work. Pepé was hired to supervise the project and to administrate the massive sum Swain had put up in advance to cover the costs of construction.

'It was his plan to check on the progress of the work by way of a series of photographs that he asked Pepé to send him every few months or so,' Marga told me, taking a second to look over her shoulder, 'which Pepé did without fail. Except that Pepé, seeing an opportunity that would be unlikely to come his way again, swindled the American for everything he had.'

•

According to the story, Pepé gathered together a couple of cronies from his days as a set construction worker and only built a façade of a mansion on the hillside. Every month, he would send the actor carefully taken photographs, images that suggested that the building of the mansion was progressing without too many setbacks (though he would rarely forget to include a request for extra money to cover some unforeseen expense). And every month Swain would send back more money to add to the thousands of dollars he'd already invested in the house. It seems evident that Swain was guilty of an ill-conceived faith in the goodness of human nature, or Pepé's anyway, but also of titanic arrogance. But to be fair to him, he must have been inevitably distracted by the now legendary problems that attended the filming of the ultimately doomed *Hundred Days*

('A Hundred Years Under The Sun?' ran one famous headline at the time, commenting on the interminable delays prolonging principal photography) and Passero's hubris-accelerated charge towards creative meltdown. By the time Swain eventually set foot on Ibiza again two years after his previous visit (broke and with his career in pieces), all he found was a windswept skeleton rising out of the dirt that was less inhabitable than a lot at Universal Studios.

•

Inevitably, the enraged actor scoured the island for Pepé. But Pepé was nowhere to be found and in the end Swain returned to California and the Santa Monica motel room where they eventually found his body, or at least what remained of it, though the circumstances of his suicide have usually been reported differently.

•

Pepé, of course, reappeared on the island a few years later as the proprietor of several businesses and the owner of several properties.

•

The rest is, as they say, history. And Pepé doesn't just own holiday villas and apartments nor just a string of bars and restaurants all over Ibiza from Portinax to Cala Vadella. He owns The Blue Rose, the island's only strip club. He owns chip shops in San Antonio and Playa d'en Bossa. He owns car rental businesses that have offices at the airport and in Ibiza Town and Santa Eularia. He owns launderettes and boutiques that sell cheap jewellery and postcards and t-shirts with 'I ♥ IBIZA' on them. He owns chemists and commercial properties and sells ferry tickets and even bread from a number of bakeries around the island.

•

And Pepé also smuggles cocaine on to the island, a hundred kilos at a time. It comes over from Colombia and Uruguay before being brought to Ibiza in Pepé's Gibraltar-registered yacht where it is stashed until it's taken to Barcelona for distribution. Needless to say, Pepé takes a large cut. Needless to say, it all makes Pepé very rich.

•

And Pepé is still *Don Agua* in the sense that he is still has the monopoly on Ibiza's water delivery, if not in name then certainly in reality.

•

As for the other question: how come I'm living in an eight bedroom mansion (complete with swimming pool, tennis court and roof terrace) that formerly belonged to the French former ambassador to Cuba? Again, it all comes down to rumoured events that occurred before I arrived on the island.

•

According to various sources (including Elena and Elvira who work at the Restaurante S'Illot and Rico who manages Pepé's car rental office at the airport), Alejandro, one of Pepe's sons, was caught piloting a yacht loaded with cocaine into the harbour in the mid-eighties and promptly arrested. The details of what happened next aren't known but Alejandro was released from custody the following day and a week later the French former ambassador to Cuba moved from his comfortable (if modest) villa just outside of Santa Gertrudis into the mansion on the hillside near Cap Blanc where he lived until only a few weeks ago. The reason for his departure? No one knows or is prepared to say. From the uncomfortable silences that meet my enquiries since I moved in (I passed two of Pepé's sons on the drive as they loaded up the last of a pile of boxes of the former ambassador's belongings into the back of a truck), I don't think anyone even knows where the erstwhile emissary is. All they know, or are prepared to say, is that a couple of weeks ago, he ordered the felling of a fir tree on the edge of his land and that when Pepé found out, the old man went *loco*.

•

It takes half an hour to get to Ibiza Town and I ride the whole way with the windshield down, the wind breaking across my face as the landscape flies past, groves of olive trees corralled by low stone walls, cedars and squat palms skirted with sprays of ferns and bullrushes, pink swathes of bougainvillea flashing by, the occasional field of maize. By the time I get to the outskirts of the town itself, Saturday traffic clogs the roads and by the time I've parked the Scout and shunted the wine into the bar, the midday sun has turned my t-shirt into a damp rag. Afterwards, I take a seat outside and drink a Coke while I watch the people crossing Plaça des Parc, the locals, the groups of boys in bright board-shorts and surfing t-shirts and sunglasses, the tanned girls in bikini tops and sarongs. After that, I score a *tolla* of charas from a guy I know in the lanes at the foot of the old town and smoke a polite joint with him before stepping back out into the hustle of the scalded street and its line of indistinguishable stalls selling postcards and cigarette lighters and cheap jewellery.

•

On the corner there's an argument taking place. A cop stands between two people, a patch of sweat the shape of South America soaked through the back of his light blue shirt, a brown leather bag in one of his hands. On one side of him, a shop owner screams in Spanish, gesticulating wildly with his stubby hands.

'*Te digo la verdad, ella me la ha robado. Yo soy la única persona en la isla que vende este tipo de bolsas.*'

On the other side of the cop *you* lean back against the wall, waiting patiently for the shop owner to finish ranting, your amber skin dark and glossy against the whitewash. Looking around, I can see that I'm not the only one who's stopped to watch and not the only one who's noticed you. The men in the small crowd that has gathered in the street (the waiters from the nearby café, the stall holders, a huddle of tourists, a couple of other delivery boys) can't take their eyes off you, can't help but gawp at the deep neckline of your loose cheesecloth shirt and the diamond necklace hanging there between your breasts, can't stop themselves from staring at the pink discs of your nipples visible behind the gauzy material or your golden hair or your brown legs that stretch away towards a pair of cream leather sandals. In the meantime, the cop seems to be trying to calm the shop owner down.

!*Por favor, cálmese señor!*

He repeats this several times but this only seems to infuriate the shop owner more.

¡*Ella me ha robado la bolsa! ¿Qué más quieres saber?*

The cop now turns his back on you and faces the man squarely and you're content simply to stand there and watch.

'*Vale. Se lo estoy diciendo por última vez: tranquilícese.*'

Whatever it is the cop says to the shop owner, it seems to work because he falls silent for a moment and takes several deep breaths. The cop also takes a moment to collect himself and then turns back to you. Looking at him more closely, I can see that he's a rookie in his early twenties and that he doesn't stand a chance.

'How much English do you speak?' you ask slowly, in an American voice with a low, Southern twist to it, a voice that seems assured yet somehow diffident at the same time, as if your mouth itself was reluctant to surrender its electric potential.

'A little,' the cop answers, shifting his weight slightly. 'What is your name?'

'Smiling. Helena Smiling.' You pronounce 'He*l*ena' with the stress on the middle syllable, all the time giving the cop a full blast of your blue eyes, your lips parting to reveal the pink slip of your tongue and the white light of your teeth.

'Do you have identification?' he asks. You nod and dip your hand into the back pocket of your shorts and pull out your passport, his eyes following your hand the whole way. You give it to him and he opens it, his eyes looking up from your photo and lingering on your face.

You smile. It's all you need to do.

'This man, do you understand what he is saying?' the cop asks as he hands back the passport (I watch as your brown fingertips brush against his for a second, the white arches of your nails bright against his tanned skin).

'I think so,' you say, tucking the blue book into your back pocket and then bending one long leg at the knee so that the bottom of your right sandal comes to rest against the wall behind you, the muscles in your thigh and calf tensing (a nice touch), your eyes returning to the cop's.

'He says that you stole the bag from his shop?' The young cop now takes off his hat and runs a hand through his black hair before replacing it.

'And I'm saying that I bought the bag earlier today, in Santa Eularia.'

'Receipt?'

'No,' you say simply.

Then it's all over. The shop owner tries another outburst but the cop waves him back to his shop while I watch you stroll off towards the harbour. Before I can stop myself, I'm following you, transfixed by the pale tan lines around the soles of your feet and the delicate skin on the backs of your knees, and I watch as you throw the bag into a bin along with the parking ticket that's been slapped against the windshield of your Silentium 4x4. Before you start the engine, presumably headed for the ring-road and wherever it is you're staying on the island, you take your necklace from around your throat and hang it from the rearview, the diamond dangling there above dash. Then you take a last look in the mirror (did you spot me watching you? I can't tell), light a cigarette and thrust your way into the traffic.

•

I finally get back to the mansion around four-thirty. I've collected the tablecloths from the cleaners and driven them over to San Rafael and delivered Pepé's water to the eight addresses he's given me and decide that I've got time to stop by the mansion for a joint. Can Jazmín is only on the other side of the bay from me and can wait another five minutes.

•

Up on my roof terrace, I imagine the scene at the villa, a crowd of haughty French brats sitting around complaining that I haven't shown up earlier. *Why not see what they're like in advance?*

•

I spark the joint, take a few drags and then aim the telescope I've set up at the opposite hillside. I'd found the thing while snooping around on my first night in the mansion, wrapped up in a drawstring bag in the garage between an empty petrol can and a pair of warped tennis rackets. Rarely short of high-minded intentions, I'd originally thought I might use it to learn the constellations though so far I've fallen asleep after not getting much further than Ursa Minor and Cepheus.

•

I soon have Can Jazmín in focus: the shutters and windows on the upper floors of the villa have all been opened; the long table on the veranda by the kitchen has the remnants of a meal scattered across it; the loungers by the swimming pool are strewn with towels and books and bottles of suncream. But there's nobody in the water or anywhere else as far as I can make out. Panning left and right, I finally manage to bring the lens to bear on a couple at the far end of the pool. A man stands at the foot of a lounger, talking to a woman who's lying down on it though I can't see what she looks like because the man's body obscures her from sight. I tweak the focus and eventually see that the man isn't talking but shouting. I watch as he takes a drag on the cigarette he's smoking before flicking it into the pool behind him and driving an accusatory finger towards the face of the woman he's screaming at.

•

She gets up off the lounger, pushes the man out of the way and starts to walk off towards the steps that lead up to the veranda and the house itself.

•

It's the girl from earlier on, still in her pale shirt and shorts.

•

It's you.

•

I watch as the man comes after you, grabs you by the wrist and pulls you back before you make it to the step. You push him away and shout something into his face. Whatever it is he says next, you don't like it because you slap him, right hand to left cheek, and at that point it looks like its only a matter of time before he slaps you back.

•

He doesn't. His arm flies up, palm flattened for contact, and I'm sure that the next thing I'm going to see is you crumpling to the ground. But the man pulls up short, his hand trembling in the air by your left ear while you stare back at him. Neither of you move for a few seconds. Then you turn on your right heel and slowly walk up the steps and into the house leaving him standing there.

•

Ten minutes later, I'm rumbling up the jagged camino to Can Jazmín and bringing my Scout to a halt in the driveway.

'Hello?'

I look around the swimming pool but all the loungers are empty as is the veranda and kitchen and reception room. Nothing but cool shadows and more luggage lying around waiting to be unpacked. I call out again.

'Hello?'

Another few seconds of silence. Then the man I saw through the telescope appears at the top of the stairs leading up to the first floor.

"*'Allo?*" he calls down to me. One of the 'rich French kids' that Pepé mentioned. (So how do you fit in?)

'*Bonsoir,*' I say, 'Pepé's sent me to take a look at the generator.'

He comes down the stairs, pulling the drawstring of his beach shorts tight without a trace of self-consciousness. I expect him to ask me why I haven't shown up earlier and complain that the house has been without power all day and that he's paying good money for the place and so on and so forth. But he simply holds out a hand and introduces himself.

'Jean-Marc,' he says, his cheekbones and teeth assembling themselves into a confident grin.

'I'm Jay. I work for Pepé.'

He shakes my hand. It's warm and slightly slick (his face and bare chest are smeared with a light film of sweat) and I imagine how his fingers had been all over you moments earlier.

6

Jay slept for almost the entire flight to Wilmington. After he boarded, he found his row near the back of the plane, stowed his carry-on in the overhead locker and then strapped himself into the narrow box of his seat between a woman who wept as she stared listlessly at the first of a series of lesbian vampire comics she'd piled on to her lap and a skatepunk with the letters L, O, V and E tattooed across the knuckles of his left hand and the letters H, U, R and T tattooed across the knuckles of his right. Jay did his best to snooze during takeoff, semi-conscious at best after his sleepless night, only dimly aware of the flight attendants demonstrating how to put on the life-vests and pointing out the location of the emergency exits. After that, he heard the soaring pitch of the engines and felt the explosion of thrust in his eyeballs and then the insulated sensation of being airborne. Sometime later he heard the sonic *boing* of the seatbelt lights followed by the impatient clacking of a hundred seatbelts being unclipped and he reclined his own seat and pulled his anorak up over his head to block out the light. For a moment, he lay there with his eyes shut, a flash of Helena's face streaking through the northern skies of his imagination as he listened to the sound of his own breathing. Then nothing. When he came round five or so hours later, he stretched like a periscope breaking the water to see the attendants serving lunch while the grid of people in the seats around him slouched dozily in front of their TV screens, slowly drinking in the entertainment along with the booze and food. Next to him, Cruella snored while his other neighbour clocked in for another hour of *Pac Man Millennium*, pierced eyebrows knotted in concentration over the screen of the hand-held unit between his busy fingers. And there were the bookish types frowning over their thick thrillers and there were the retired couples in their terrycloth and leisurewear and the women practising yoga in the aisles and the students making out sleepily in the shadows and the vague impatience of the line of weary passengers camped out by the toilets. Jay yawned, dying for a joint. More than that, he was starving, but when the stewardess eventually presented him with his sandwich, it looked like the *fossil* of a prehistoric sandwich, one recently excavated from some muddy pit and then wrapped in protective plastic. Jay stared at it for a while, gauging his hunger against his reluctance even to look at the thing (it looked like moonrock, like rare elephant dung, like forensic evidence). Then he unwrapped it and took a tentative bite that confirmed it tasted of dead fish and pushed it away before digging out his headphones and dozing in his seat to the sounds of Lester Young and Billie Holiday floating through 'Foolin' Myself' on a magic carpet of pure tone . . . *I tell myself I'm through with love and I'll have nothing more to do with love* . . . there couldn't be more than an hour's flying time till Wilmington . . . *I stay away, but every day I'm just foolin' myself* . . . there was nothing else he could do but lie there with his eyes shut and wait for the wheels to hit the ground.

An hour later, Jay was standing in the terminal at Wilmington International, with his cell phone pressed against his ear. There was a long series of ringing tones before a woman's voice came on the line.

'Willoughby. How can I help you?' she asked, her politeness flattening the list and lurch of her Carolinan accent but not suppressing it entirely.

'Good afternoon,' he said, 'my name is Jay Richards. I've just flown into Wilmington from San Francisco at the invitation of Zelda Smiling. She's expecting me.'

'I'm Sara Taft, the housekeeper here,' the woman replied. 'Miss Smiling isn't available to speak to you right this moment but she has notified me of your arrival. What can I do for you, Mr Richards?'

'Zelda told me that the house is a short drive from the airport. Would it be convenient for me to arrive in half an hour or so?'

Mrs Taft grunted that it would be fine and Jay asked for directions to give the cab driver only to be told that any driver would know the way if he asked simply to be taken to Willoughby.

'If he doesn't know how to get here,' she told Jay loftily, 'tell him to take the River Road south-east towards Southport and make the turning for Sunny Point Naval Base. The first left after you cross Sixty Bridge will bring you to the house.'

Jay thanked her and hung up before wheeling his trolley of luggage out of the comfort zone of the terminal and into the dry afternoon heat. At the cab stand, he hailed the first driver in the line of waiting cars, a bald man in his fifties with hairy upper arms that poked out of a t-shirt with the words 'Tony's Surf 'n' Turf Trattoria' streaked across the front and an image below of a cartoon fish smiling up at the viewer as it toasted away on a sizzling grill. 'Where to?' he asked as he loaded Jay's bags and flight cases into the trunk with practised reluctance.

'Willoughby,' Jay replied. 'Do you know the way?'

The driver nodded and climbed into his seat with a gentle sigh while Jay slotted himself into the back and settled himself on the scorched leather as the cab trawled across the ocean of roasting tarmac and out on to the freeway.

'You from England?' the driver asked.

'Kind of,' Jay replied.

'I never been there.'

And that was it in terms of conversation which was fine with Jay who was more than happy to say nothing and stare out at the landscape of Bs beyond the smeared glass, the billboards at the side of the road advertising B&B motels and all-you-can-eat BBQ buffets and stores selling bait and boating equipment, the bridge that carried them away from the airport and over what Jay assumed was the Cape Fear River towards road signs for Belville and Big Neck, for Brunswick Station, Bell Swamp and Boiling Spring Lakes. Other signs told Jay that he could take the next exit for the *USS North Carolina* Memorial (the battleship itself suddenly visible through a gap in the trees before the road bent round to the right and it disappeared from view again), that he was now entering Brunswick County, a babble of short news items on the local radio station the driver had tuned into relating stories about places and incidents that felt familiar and unfamiliar at the same time as they turned off the main freeway and dropped down into a low forested valley. The trees at the side of the road intermittently gave way to a view of the farmland that stretched away to the car's right, pale yellow scrub in the bright distance, the occasional cluster of houses flashing past as well as the white box-like churches and signs for Black Bear Hollow and Big Buck Trail. But mostly the road was banked by tall pines that rose up on each side, damp sunlight filtering through their thin black trunks and sending shadows slithering all over the windshield. Eventually the driver made a left, the car crossing a narrow creek and a sign bearing the words 'Sixty Bridge' visible momentarily as sunspots bombed across Jay's vision and the light changed and pulsed. Then the driver made another left on to a long drive that cut between ranks of chunky oaks, the car passing under the canopy of their thick branches before breaking clear into the sunlight again and Willoughby suddenly appeared like a massive white elephant crouched amongst lush vegetation. The driver eventually brought the car to a stop and lined up Jay's bags on the brick pathway that ran up towards the front of the colossal house between two small lawns as immaculate as putting greens, the windows staring down as Jay paid the driver what was on the meter and gave him a five dollar tip before he disappeared back up the drive, a screen of dust hanging in the air behind his rumbling wheels. Turning back to the house, Jay wiped his hands on the front of his t-shirt and took it all in. He'd expected either Zelda or Mrs Taft to be standing at the front door by now but no one had appeared under the massive portico nor at any of the windows (there were twelve of them across the width of the ground floor of the house, he noted, the central block of the building standing three storeys high with a wing extending out to the building's right and an old stable block or coachhouse extending away to the building's left). Jay walked up to the doorway, found a round white button marked PRESS on the wall and leaned on it, the aura surrounding the house seeming even more impenetrable as the mid-afternoon sun bounced off the pale silent gravel. He'd expected to hear some gong or ancient bell system chime away on the other side of the door but heard nothing. Was the button defunct? He waited on the doorstep for a few more moments before there was the sound of footsteps and the door finally swung inwards and Jay found himself staring at a woman in her late forties.

'Good afternoon,' she said in a voice that was as compact as her square face. It was the same woman he'd talked to on the phone earlier.

'You must be Mrs Taft,' he said. 'I'm Jay Richards.'

'Miss Smiling's guest, come inside. I'd ask Alfred to come and help you with your things but he's somewhere in the gardens at the moment so you'll have to do it yourself.'

Jay said it didn't matter, presuming that Alfred was a butler or groundsman, and he stepped inside with the first of his bags only to be struck immediately by a breathless sensation. As his eyes struggled to adjust to yet another sudden change in light, a constriction took hold of his throat and the roots of his hair murmured their first cries of alarm.

'Are you all right, Mr Richards?' Mrs Taft asked him.

'Yes, I'm fine,' he replied though his heart still felt as if its rhythm had yet to step back into sequence. Had he sensed something there in the hallway? Jay reminded himself that it was probably nothing more than adrenalin and remembered that Tommy had continually warned against these kinds of melodramatics, perennially dispensing appropriate advice while they ate dim sum at Harbor Village or when they were out on the freeway in the hearse-like Buccaneer or as they sat in the office discussing old cases. 'Superstition is the enemy of successful paranormal investigation,' the old man would tell him. 'Let the client flounder in panic and fear.' So far, both under Tommy's tutelage and as a solo operator, Jay had managed to go about most of his work in a state of analytical detachment. Even in Milpitas, as they'd all stood there outside the rusted door of the pump house, the farm manager poised with the glinting crowbar, the cops flanking him with their flashlights and the machines going crazy in Jay's hands while the reservoir turned quicksilver in the deepening twilight behind them, he'd managed to stay calm and professional. It made no difference that a minute later they'd busted the door open and found the slumped skeleton on the concrete floor, the frayed twists of fluorescent climbing rope hanging off the pale bones suggesting all kinds of degradation. Jay had refused to let himself entertain any moral sense of the supernatural nor make any clear connection between a feeling that he might define as *foreboding* and the potential manifestation of the paranormal, circumstantial or otherwise. Even at the Lockwood mansion where Jay's body had quietly tingled with apprehension the moment he'd stepped inside out of the rain, he'd succeeded in not letting his unease cause him to presume a single detail about the case. But as Jay stood there in the hallway at Willoughby, the feeling intensified second by second, sparking nerve endings deep in the meat of his back and neck that felt as if they'd been in cold storage for a lifetime.

'Are you sure you're okay?' Mrs Taft asked again.

'Yes, absolutely,' he replied.

'Then I'll leave you to bring the rest of your bags in while I go and see where Lord Charteris and Miss Smiling are. I'll be back in five minutes.'

She walked off down a side corridor and he carried in the rest of his things and dumped them on the dark floorboards at the foot of one of two symmetrical flights of stairs that led upwards to a half-landing that in turn gave access to the floor above by way of another set of steps, all the time trying to swallow down the bitter taste of unrest in his mouth so that it could be digested into nothing. *Twenty-two paintings moved in the middle of the night* . . . Jay stared up at the cream walls. There they all were (he counted them) except that the dark lines where the dust had gathered over the years clearly showed that their positions had been switched. Perhaps he should take a reading? Jay was about to unlock one of his flight-cases and pull out his EMF detector when Mrs Taft reappeared.

'Miss Smiling is still resting in her room. Lord Charteris is upstairs in the nursery but he should be down in a minute or so. You can wait in the library if you like.' She opened a door to one side of the main hall and led him inside. 'Would you like a drink?' she asked.

Jay said he could wait until he'd spoken with Toby and she nodded before closing the door behind her and leaving him to sit down in one of a pair of leather wing-backed armchairs. Looking around, Jay took in the walls lined with shelves of leather-bound books that looked as if they hadn't been read for decades, an antique globe in a wooden cradle in the opposite corner of the room, an old pool table in another corner sitting parallel to a long window seat. There was a low table next to where he sat with a pile of newspapers on top of it and he reached over and picked up the first only to see Helena's face staring back at him when he unfolded it.

SOCIETY WOMAN STILL MISSING AFTER 10 DAYS

Underneath the headline was a monochrome photo of Helena. It looked as if it had been copied and cropped from a professional portrait shot but only crudely reprinted on the cheap paper. Helena wore a strapless gown, its exact colour impossible to make out amongst the smudged pixels. But the material seemed at least as pale as the skin of her throat and chest against which hung the thin chain of her necklace. And there it was, that expression in her eyes that had haunted him through so many sleepless nights, a raw lickerish thirst that also revealed itself in the pout of her lips and the diagonals of her cheekbones that even now had Jay's insides turning flic-flacs. There was a short article below the picture.

> Brunswick County Sheriff's Department refused to comment today on the continued disappearance of society woman, Lady Helena Charteris (29), except to confirm that they are following 'standard investigative procedures for incidents of this type'.
> Lady Charteris, heiress to the Smiling shipping fortune and wife of English entrepreneur, the Honourable Toby Charteris (34), has been missing from Willoughby, her family's home for over two centuries, since the night of Saturday 15th August with her family having heard no word from her since.
> A spokesman for the Sheriff's Department also refused to speculate as to whether Lady Charteris' disappearance is connected with the recent disappearance of neighboring man, Wallace Kelly (32). Mr Kelly, owner of the historic Kelly Plantation, was also reported to sheriffs as missing

on the night of August 15th by his wife, Madeleine, but so far neither she nor Lord Charteris has offered further information.

It felt strange to see Helena referred to as 'Lady Charteris' but Jay had little time to think about it or read more of the article for the door to the library opened at that moment and a man walked in. Jay got to his feet and they both stared at each other before the man offered his hand for Jay to shake.

'Sorry to keep you waiting. I was just attending to my son. I'm Toby Charteris.'

'Jay Richards.'

So this was Toby. This was the man Helena had married.

Toby glanced at the paper in Jay's hand, then took it from him, screwed it up into a ball and tossed it into the unlit fireplace before walking up to a drinks tray.

'Want a drink?' he asked. Jay said that he did, knowing he would leave it untouched by the side of his chair, and Toby poured them each a tumbler of scotch before sitting down in the armchair opposite.

'You've been reading about what's happened.'

'Yes.'

'Bastards.'

For a moment, Jay thought he was referring to Helena and Wallace but it became clear he was talking about the staff at the newspaper. 'Quite why my wife's latest infidelity should be the concern of every idiot in the county is beyond me. It's not like they bothered to splash details of any of her other deceptions across the front of the paper.'

Jay didn't say anything. He'd only seen a single photograph of Toby (the picture he'd seen in Laos years before of Toby and Helena on their wedding day), an image seemingly branded on to his occipital lobe even though he'd attempted to void it from his mind immediately by spending the next four days with his lips clamped around an opium pipe. Now, he took a good look at the man in person. In the picture Toby had appeared handsome, in possession of the kind of face and physique that women might have fawned over. Now it looked as if someone had attached him to an air pump and gently inflated him. His face seemed to have swollen up around his eye sockets and mouth, his leonine nose sitting squat in the middle of his face between a pair of cheeks that looked as if they'd been simmered in champagne, the thinning hair as brittle as rice paper as it sprouted out of his scalp.

'So, how do you know my wife and her sister?' he asked, content to slug back his drink while he waited for his answer.

'I met them both several years ago,' Jay replied vaguely, 'on Ibiza. We became friendly but haven't been in touch regularly since then.'

Jay wondered if Toby would probe further. He didn't.

'She must have really despised me,' the man continued suddenly. 'The fifteenth of August was our wedding anniversary.' He stopped to light a cigarette, the match failing to spark immediately, his hand striking it against the box with increasing agitation until the flame fizzed into existence.

'Zelda told me that you were holding a party on the day Helena disappeared,' Jay said.

'Yes,' Toby replied. 'We had several hundred people here at the house.'

Jay pictured him standing right there in the library on the night in question, his wing collar splayed and his bow tie flung amongst the whisky bottles as he absorbed the news of Helena's disappearance while crowds of guests continued dancing and drinking in the blue garden beyond.

'By midnight, no one had seen Helena for hours. I called the police but received little help from them. Helena has made a habit of this sort of thing throughout our marriage and they've become pretty tired of it.'

'She's disappeared before?'

'Several times. My wife is rather good at losing herself to various little whims,' he said as he drained his glass, the signet ring on the little finger of his left hand catching a ray of light. 'Anyway, Madeleine Kelly rang me early the next morning to say that Wallace hadn't come home either and it became pretty clear what had happened.' Toby got out of his seat to refill his glass. 'I have to say that I'm surprised,' he continued while he drowned the ice cubes with liquor.

'By what?'

'Helena's pulled stunts like this more than a few times before, but never with anyone quite like Wallace Kelly. Usually it's been some flash hustler who offers her a few moments of pretty distraction. Take last summer, for instance. She had a fling with a local doctor, a real slick piece of work who seems to have been through half the women in the county. The two of them even ran off to Cabo San Lucas for a weekend. He learned, like all the others, that it never means much, and never lasts long.'

Toby sat down again. 'And there were others before that,' he continued.

'Did you call the police each time she disappeared?' Jay asked, shifting in his seat.

'Not always. Sometimes it was obvious where she was . . . or, at least, *who* she was with. What was I going to do then? Ring the police to inform them that my wife was cheating on me? Other times, it was less clear what was going on, less clear that Helena wasn't in danger, and it was on those occasions that I informed the police of her disappearance. My wife has been prone to bouts of mental instability throughout her life — depression, nightmares, sleepwalking, episodes of extreme and groundless anxiety, episodes of inexplicable amnesia and so on. I woke up one morning last March to find a pair of cops from Myrtle Beach at the front door and their squad car parked out on the drive with Helena in the back. They'd found her on Cherry Grove Pier at five in the morning in her nightdress. She'd got out of bed, left the house and driven for over an hour yet she couldn't remember a thing. I've asked myself if her latest disappearance could be the symptom of some form of postnatal depression. But she refuses to talk to anyone about it. And of course she drinks too much and still uses cocaine.'

Toby stared down at his hands.

'I thought that she might have changed once Jacob was born. But it looks like I was wrong.' He raised his head and looked at Jay. 'And now that's the end of it. She won't get the chance to humiliate me again.'

Toby knocked his drink back with one jerk of his neck and put the glass down on the pile of newspapers between them.

'Shall we talk about why I'm here?' Jay asked.

Toby nodded. 'I'm presuming that Zelda's already told you something about what's been happening when the two of you met in San Francisco.'

Jay nodded and then picked his words carefully. 'She told me that her great-aunts *believe* that they saw a ghost. She also told me about the incident involving Mrs Taft and about the pictures in the hall.'

'What do you make of it all?'

'I haven't made anything of it, not yet at least . . .'

'Well, I'll tell you what I think . . .'

At that moment there was a knock at the door.

'Yes?' snapped Toby.

The door opened and Mrs Taft appeared. 'There's a phone call for you. It's Sheriff Bryar.'

'Thank you, Sara,' he said. 'I'll take it in my study. If you could tell him I'll be right there.'

Mrs Taft disappeared and Toby settled back in his seat.

'We'll talk more about this later on. But it's pretty obvious that someone here is very bored and being very childish, most likely John or Will or both of them. And I'll be frank with you, Jay: I'm not happy about *you* being here, not happy at all. In fact, I'd go as far as saying that it's laughable. If Zelda thinks that I can't see what she's trying to do then she's a fool, but I won't give her the satisfaction of refusing her this concession. So I'll simply warn you now: this is *my* house and I decide what happens here. You'll report to me. When you find out which of my guests is fooling around, you'll come and tell me. And if I change my mind about you, you'll be out of here within the hour. Is that understood?'

7

After Toby had gone to take his call, Jay walked out of the library and stood by his bags at the foot of one of the staircases. The unease he'd felt earlier seemed to have subsided (either that or he'd simply got used to the feeling) and he took another look around the hallway, eyes passing over the cream walls, the paintings, the large grandfather clock on the far side of the room, the chandelier hanging above him, the bunch of white roses wilting in the heat in a vase on a side table next to a line of polished straight-backed chairs that looked as if they'd never been used. Mrs Taft was nowhere to be seen and he still had no idea which room he was sleeping in. Should he go look for her?

Jay realized that he didn't feel like penetrating the interior of the house quite yet and instead walked back through the door into the warm light with its birdcall and insect hum. It was clear, he told himself out on the gravel, that the Englishman was bitter about Helena's latest affair. That was far from being a surprise (and something Jay could identify with only too easily) as was Toby's certainty that nothing paranormal was going on in the house. But something about their conversation still circled around Jay's mind. What was it Toby had said? He'd said that he considered Jay's presence at Willoughby 'laughable' but that he'd agreed to it as 'a concession to Zelda'. *If Zelda thinks that I can't see what she's trying to do then she's a fool, but I won't give her the satisfaction of refusing her this concession,* he'd said, as if he suspected Zelda of hiring Jay in a deliberate attempt to provoke him into . . . *into what?* Toby had also stated that Helena's latest act of infidelity would be the last one that he would endure and Jay presumed that he was preparing to instigate divorce proceedings whenever Helena finally resurfaced.

How was this connected with Zelda beyond the fact that she was Helena's twin sister?

Jay walked around the left hand side of the house, round the coach house and along an alley of cypresses before ducking through a brick archway into the first of a series of walled gardens between the house and the nearby woods. There was a paved quad framed with crimson roses and Persian lilacs and Chinese honeysuckle, another filled with jasmine bushes and redwood violets and another with a small circular pool crowded with fat goldfish and lilies. After that, Jay negotiated a box maze in whose centre he found a pair of bronze nymphs grappling in the shadow of twin sycamores and a circular suntrap complete with four wooden benches and dense beds of lavender. Looking around, he imagined Helena and Zelda playing here as children while Sara Taft looked on.

'Jay?'

Jay turned to see a woman coming through the archway on the far side of the suntrap, a small basket in her right hand. She stopped in front of him and put the basket down.

'Bessie,' she said, extending a hand.

Jay shook it, remembering her more clearly now that she was standing in front of him. Her hair was still the colour of milky tea (although it was cut shorter than it had been years before) and her cheeks still reminded Jay of a hamster's. Besides that, Jay could remember little about her except that she was a lawyer and that she'd joined Helena and Jean-Marc and the others staying at the villa halfway through the summer, accompanied by her husband about whom Jay could remember nothing except that his name was Stevenson and that he was also a lawyer.

'Bessie, I remember you. Bessie Stevenson.'

'It's *Stevlingson* actually, or it was. Ed and I divorced a couple of years back so now I'm back to being Bessie Flowers. But I'm amazed you remember him. Or me for that matter.'

They took a seat on the nearest bench.

'How was your flight?' she asked.

'Good, though it's left me a little hungry. I thought about asking Mrs Taft if there was anything to eat but she doesn't seem to be in a very approachable mood.'

Bessie laughed. 'We used to call her "Sourpuss" when we were little girls.'

'Who?' Jay asked. 'You, Helena and Zelda?'

'Oh no, not Zelda. Zelda would never say anything derogatory about Sara. She's much closer to her than Helena. It was the same when we were children.'

'How long has she worked here?'

'I don't know exactly, but it's been decades. I think John and Esme hired her and Alfred when they were teenagers. They took her on as the maid and him as a gardener. Eventually Sara became the cook, and then the housekeeper and eventually Helena and Zelda's nanny when John and Esme separated.'

'What about Alfred?'

'Alfred's always just been the gardener.'

'And he looks after all of this on his own?'

'A bunch of guys come in and help him out every so often, maybe once a month. Their daughter Lara also helps out around the house.'

'I guess Helena isn't the kind to do the housework.'

'No, she isn't.'

Bessie reached down and pulled the basket up on to her lap. 'Anyway, you said you're hungry? We've all been having a picnic by the lake.' Her hands came to rest on the wicker handle of her basket. 'The others are still there. We could go and join them.'

Jay shook his head saying that he was still too tired from his flight to meet people. So they stayed there in the suntrap instead, talking while Jay inserted slices of ham and salad between pieces of bread that had started to dry out but were still soft enough to eat. Bessie pulled out a bottle of wine that was still half full and poured two glasses. Jay asked her if she was still a lawyer and she shook her head.

'I quit a couple of years ago. I found out I was infertile,' she said bluntly, 'so I decided I needed a change of lifestyle. I gave up my job, gave up being a New Yorker – which was sad because it was kind of fun for a while – and came back here. I thought I might as well enjoy my life if I didn't have any children to save for.'

'Where do you live now?'

'In Southport with my mother. She's getting old now so it's a relief to be close by.'

'And near Helena?'

'That's a little more complicated.'

'You see a lot of her?'

'Yes. I'm around a lot, especially now that I'm looking after Jacob while Helena's gone.' Bessie took a sip of wine. 'From what I remember, you don't seem to have changed much. How long have you been living in San Francisco?'

'A couple of years. After I left Ibiza at the end of the summer . . . *that* summer . . . I drifted around for a while and ended up in San Francisco. Been there ever since.'

'Being here must be pretty strange for you. Christ, it's been pretty strange round here for all of us.'

'Who's staying at the house?'

'Let's see: there's Will Hooper, an old friend of Helena's who's an artist and who lives in New York. Then there are the couples, Tony and Nina Shipman who've come down from Boston, and Jim and Molly Remick from Louisville – Molly is a distant cousin of Helena and Zelda. And there's John Fulton, one of Toby's friends from England, and Meliza, his current date. She's nineteen, Italian and a model. John's been showing her off in front of the guys who're trying their hardest not to stare at her breasts *all* the time. Meliza, of course, says very little, but it all sounds like pornography in that accent of hers.'

'When did they all get here?'

'Most of them got here the third week of July except for Johnny and Meliza who flew in from London a week later.'

Jay asked Bessie how long everyone had originally intended to stay at Willoughby and she replied that most of the guests had planned to leave after the party.

'Now they've all been asked to stay by the police and everyone's pretty bored of the whole thing. Johnny seems happy enough to spend the rest of the summer here draining Toby's wine cellar one bottle at a time. But the others are starting to get desperate. Jim Remick has to have at least one rant to his lawyer each day before he calms down while Molly is getting more and more anxious about her children who are due back from their grandparents' house in Maine in a couple of days. In the meantime, Tony's mistress back in Boston has started ringing the house which causes its own set of problems while Meliza needs everything explained to her twice.'

'How's Toby holding up?' Jay asked.

'I think he's pretty devastated.'

'He told me that Helena's run off before and that the police hardly take him seriously now.'

Bessie nodded. 'Yes, Helena's run off before, more than a few times. The police say it's part of their normal procedure to ask everyone here to stick around but they've never done anything like this before. It's almost as if they're doing it just to spite Toby. He and Sheriff Bryar have never been on the best terms.'

She picked up a piece of bread from inside the basket and began picking at it with her fingers.

'I don't know what kind of friends you have, Jay, in San Francisco or anywhere else. But it's been pretty hard watching my oldest friend continually screw up her life these last few years. Recently there's been Oliver Floramor. But there've been many others, and now it's Wallace Kelly's turn.'

Jay searched her voice for any oblique reference to his own affair with Helena but there didn't seem to be one. 'Toby mentioned that Helena ran off with a local doctor?' he asked.

'That was Oliver Floramor.'

'And how did it end, their affair?'

'The two of them hid away in some villa in Cabo San Lucas for a week or so. Then Helena suddenly arrived back at Willoughby. I asked her what had happened and she simply said that she'd got bored of him.'

'What about this Floramor character?'

'He limped back home a few days later and kept his head down for a while. I think he's the sort of man who takes pleasure in humiliating the husbands of the women he sleeps with. But with Helena, he was the one who ended up looking used.' A butterfly weaved in through the swollen heads of lavender and distracted them for a second, moving from purple cluster to purple cluster in an ecstasy of pollen and heat. 'Helena's always been the same, ever since we were teenagers,' Bessie continued. 'The summer she turned fifteen, she was going to parties at beach houses up the coast with recruits from Camp LeJeune and breaking a different heart every weekend. A couple of soldiers even got to fighting over her. And it just got worse and worse as time went on.'

'Worse?'

'Jay, we were just little girls. But there she was, dating soldiers, dating married guys who fell over themselves to be with her, anyone who came near enough and showed her any kind of interest. Needless to say, there were lots of willing victims.'

'She sounds very different from Zelda,' Jay said.

Bessie looked up at him. 'That's true. Zelda was a very serious and introspective teenager. So was I, if I'm honest. I don't think we were the kind of girls who found adolescence very easy, more like a punishment in fact. And you can imagine what it was like being friends with someone like Helena. At parties, you'd have to sit and watch while crowds of boys ignored you and drooled over her, boys always asking you out only so they could meet her and so on.'

'Zelda suggested to me in San Francisco that Toby's been just as bad as Helena.'

'In the early days, certainly. But he seems to have kept his pants on ever since Helena got pregnant, at least as far as I know.'

'So why have they stayed together?'

'Who knows? They were happy together at the beginning, but it was short-lived. After that, they started carrying on as if they were trying to punish each other for something. It was a mystery at first. But after it happened a few times, it just seemed as if it was part of their lives. I tried to talk to Helena about it a few years back . . .'

'What did you say?'

'I told her to think about divorcing Toby. I didn't like saying it, you understand, but what the two of them were doing to each other was terrible.'

'What was Helena's response?'

'She said she'd think about it but nothing changed. I suppose there's nothing anyone else can do if two people are prepared to treat each other like that and put up with it, I should know that more than anyone, and who knows what happens between two people in the privacy of their own bedroom or anywhere else for that matter? Maybe they need the reconciliation or the anger or the sex that follows? It'll be the same when she's finished with Wallace.'

'You think that it won't last, this fling with this Wallace Kelly guy?'

Bessie nodded.

'She'll be back in a few days time. She and Toby will scream at each other. Then there'll be these grand romantic gestures before it happens all over again.'

Bessie stopped and Jay refilled their glasses and they sipped at them, watching the upper branches of the trees all over the garden start to glow pink in the first of the twilight.

'This will sound a little idealistic, I guess,' he said, 'but you'd have thought that two people with so much might have found it a little easier to be happy. This place . . . it's paradise.'

'Yes, Willoughby is beautiful,' Bessie replied. 'As for money? Well maybe that's been the problem. They've been running out of it for years and it's made things between them worse, especially because neither of them is very practical. Helena's really only ever had the house – she's never had a lot of cash, not since her father died – and Toby's spent all his money, either on fast living, usually with someone other than his wife, or else on luckless investments.'

Jay asked Bessie if Toby's family in England had a lot of money and she nodded but also told him that Toby was the youngest of three brothers. Because the family was Catholic, the eldest son had got the family house when their parents died and the majority of the money.

'So Toby *didn't* get much money after his parents died?'

'Oh no, Toby got plenty. As I understand it, he inherited several properties in London that his family owned. But that was it when it came to assets and he's sold most of them I think, not least to underwrite his rather misguided business sense. He's tried it all, restaurants, internet companies, organic food – ultimately, it's all failed. And his latest venture's been no different.'

'What is it?'

'A few years ago, the County Development Commission awarded a contract to a consortium of investors to build a new marina complex over at Windy Point, one with a hotel and a mall and restaurants and a new building for the yacht club and so on.'

'Where's Windy Point?'

'Along the coast from Southport towards the state line. The whole area's been developed. Anyway, Toby became one of the major shareholders, saying that it was a sure thing. But it's been a disaster. The building work was meant to be finished by May last year in time for the tourist season. But the place was only half-built and they missed a whole summer's revenue.'

'Is the building work finished now?' Jay asked. Bessie nodded.

'Just about. And business seems to be picking up slowly. But Helena's told me that Toby and the others investors are still barely managing to meet the interest payments on their original loans. There's no doubt that the project will eventually break even in the long run but they may not be able to afford to wait that long. As you can imagine, it's made everything between Helena and Toby worse, especially since they had a child.'

Jay sat there for a minute absorbing everything Bessie had told him.

'I'm surprised about one thing,' he said eventually. 'Given the number of affairs Helena's had, I'm surprised that Toby didn't contest Jacob's paternity. How could he be sure that the child is his?'

'That was another terrible episode. Toby *did* contest Jacob's paternity and demanded that Oliver Floramor take a blood test. Floramor tried to refuse but Toby threatened to report him to the Medical Board. Again, it all did very little to make things around here any better for Helena and Toby.'

They sat in silence for a moment, the two of them looking up at the sky as a flock of starlings rose into the air and swung back and forth across the falling sun.

'And now there's this other problem,' Bessie said eventually.

'You mean the paintings?'

She nodded. 'And everything else.'

'What do you make of it?' he asked her. 'Who do you think's behind it all? Toby's convinced it's one or two of the guys staying here.'

'I don't know. I've been going back and forth between Willoughby and my mother's house so much that I'm probably not the best person to ask. What I do know is that the atmosphere in the house stinks at the moment. Toby sits brooding and drinking in his study for most of the day. Sara is more grouchy than usual while everyone else is bored out of their minds. I love Zelda dearly but her arrival won't improve things.'

'Why?'

'Her and Toby hate each other. Neither of them has ever said it to me in person, but Helena told me that they've both admitted it to her. At least she's done her best to stay out of his way.'

'How is she?' Jay asked.

'She's been exhausted ever since she got here.'

'Which is her room?'

'It's on the top floor. But Helena's been sleeping in there for a while now so Zelda's taken the spare room above the old coach house.'

'Miss Flowers?'

Sara Taft appeared at the other side of the lavender garden. 'Miss Flowers?' she called out.

'Yes, Sara?'

'Could you help me for a few minutes? I need to take tea up to Misses Clemmy and Lobelia.'

'I'll be right there, Sara.'

Jay followed Bessie through the garden to the house and the massive kitchen where Mrs Taft had arranged two trays, an identical place setting on each: a cup and saucer, a silver spoon, a mound of sugar lumps in a silver bowl, a minute set of silver tongs, a saucer of tablets and capsules. Mrs Taft herself was standing by the sink warming two identical china teapots. 'We're putting you in the Green Room, Mr Richards,' she said briskly, putting down one teapot and picking up the other and swilling a cupful of boiling water around the inside of it. 'That's next to Misses Clemmy and Lobelia. Follow us up and see where it is.'

'You're witnessing one of the Willoughby rituals,' Bessie said with a smile. 'Tea for the great-aunts.'

Mrs Taft snorted. 'Miss Flowers is dressing things up with prettier words than she needs to as usual. If you'd be kind enough to take Aunt Clemmy's tray for me, Miss Flowers, I'll take Aunt Lobelia's. We'll take the main stairs so that Mr Richards can collect his bags and follow behind.'

Jay couldn't see a difference between the two trays, not even in the spectrum of the colour-coded tablets that had been counted out on to each, but Mrs Taft authoritatively picked up one and Bessie picked up the other and Jay followed, carrying as many of his bags as he could as they all filed up the main stairs. On the floor above, Jay followed the two women through the corridors of the house, through shadowy passageways lined with dressers and bookshelves and old photos of the house and the surrounding landscape and old maps of North Carolina in gold frames, doorways offering glimpses of bedrooms and bathrooms. They passed by a stairwell and down another corridor before Mrs Taft came to a halt, Bessie and Jay stopping behind her.

'That's your room there, Mr Richards,' Mrs Taft said, nodding towards an open doorway, 'Misses Clemmy and Lobelia are through here.'

The two women proceeded into the room adjacent to Jay's and he stood at the doorway watching them administer the contents of their trays to two skeletal women with skin like worn polythene. Neither spoke, both staring at the middle of the room with blank expressions while Bessie and Mrs Taft moved around them, fiddling with cushions and blinds and bedcovers. 'Would you like me to turn on your radio?' Mrs Taft asked, addressing neither of them in particular and turning on an old transistor on a dresser anyway when neither of them answered, a light ragtime seeping out of the speaker. Then she and Bessie watched as each woman lifted the first of their tablets up to their quivering mouths and washed it down with a sip of pale tea. The whole thing took a minute, all sixty slow seconds of it, and there were at least ten or more to get through. Jay watched for a while, then looked in on his room. It was green all right, not a bright Lincoln green nor a deep fir green but the colour of peas that had been over boiled and then left overnight to cool. There was a damp smell and everything looked as if it had been only carelessly dusted. Jay dumped his bags on his bed and walked over to the window that had been opened, presumably by Mrs Taft and presumably only recently. It looked out over the front of the house, the drive veering away between the heavy trees, some of the ornamental gardens visible to its right. Then he ferried the rest of his luggage up to his room, kicked off his sneakers and lay down on the bed. He was exhausted. He needed a joint or something else to take his mind off the hollow feeling in his stomach that was more than just hunger and more than just sleeplessness. Lying there, staring up at the ceiling, he pictured Toby and Helena arguing with each other in the library, on the stairs, in the garden. However hard he tried to think about something else, his mind eventually returned to images of them fighting. Why had they stayed together? After a while, he found himself imagining Helena in some shadowy interior, the Mexican sun blazing down outside on the empty swimming pool and throwing shafts of light through the closed blinds and across her glistening skin while Oliver Floramor ground her hips into the mattress (and he didn't know what the doctor looked like but it didn't matter – in Jay's mind, the man was just heaving shoulder blades and buttocks, Helena's hands clasped around him and pulling him closer) . . . Jay forced himself upright, rubbed his eyes, held on to the sensation of his knuckles against his eyeballs. Trying to get his thoughts to move in a rational direction again, he asked himself why Toby hadn't divorced Helena if accounts of her serial infidelity were true (and who was *Jay* to dismiss them as false)? Was it her money? Toby had his own didn't he? No, Bessie had told him that Toby's money was running out – but then she'd suggested that the Smiling fortune was also dwindling. If Helena had been rich, then perhaps that would be a reason to stay with her. But neither of them had any money.

Jay lay back down again and closed his eyes, wondering where in the world she was, wondering what she was thinking and what she was feeling. How many times had he tortured himself with this question? (As many times as he'd sat up waiting for lights to appear amongst the shadows, waiting for the disembodied voices to manifest themselves out of the dark silence, waiting for something to happen, anything.) Perhaps Helena *hadn't* run off with Wallace Kelly and she was on her own, crushed by the kind of hysteria that Toby had earlier described, Wallace's own disappearance merely a coincidence? For a moment, he imagined her on Cherry Grove Pier (again the same problem as with Oliver Floramor: he didn't know what it looked like but imagined her staring out to sea nonetheless, a haunted look in her eyes while the waves crashed around her). What was it Toby had said in the library: *he learned, like all the others, that it never means much, and never lasts long* . . . well, Jay knew all about that, as much as anyone. But if that was the case? Jay imagined the moment, just before sleep came, of the taxi pulling up outside in the darkness and Helena stepping out and he wondered what she would say when she found him waiting for her.

8

When Jay woke up, it had just gone seven which meant it was still mid-afternoon in California. He lay there for a while, imagining Christoph taking Marlowe for a walk along Ocean Beach, then hauled himself out of bed and into the adjoining bathroom where a junkyard of antique plumbing failed to flush the journey from San Francisco out of his system. Then he pulled on some jeans and a clean t-shirt and wondered what to do next. Should he look for Zelda? And what about the other guests? He wondered if he should wait downstairs, either in the library or in some drawing room where the others would presumably congregate, and simply meet people as they appeared. Entering the corridor outside his room, he also noticed that the door to the great-aunts' room was still open.

'Helena, is that you?'

He peered in.

'Helena?'

The two old women sat there, both of them propped up in bed and staring into space, their glassy pupils like four shiny black olives as the last of the evening sun fell through the windows on to the rug on the floor.

'Helena, is that you?'

They didn't seem to notice him or seem to be in any kind of distress and Jay decided not to answer, instead walking on past linen cupboards and bathrooms until he found himself in the long central corridor. Bessie was coming up the main stairs.

'Hi there,' she said cheerily. 'You unpacked? Need anything?'

'I'm fine. The great-aunts were calling out for Helena just now but it didn't seem urgent.'

'I wouldn't take much notice of them if I were you. They stopped making sense years ago.'

Jay said that he wanted to take an initial tour of the house and asked Bessie if she could show him round. She nodded and they moved through Willoughby together, Jay making a mental note of where he might place his equipment later on. The middle floor of the house, what he still called the 'first floor' in his English way, seemed to contain most of the bedrooms. There were his and the great-aunts' rooms in the north-west corner of the house but also four others. Along the main central corridor sat two guest bedrooms that were currently being used by the Remicks and the Shipmans, and also Toby's room in the south-eastern corner, all of them overlooking the main gardens. After these, the corridor bent round past Toby's study and led to a bedroom in the south-western corner of the house that was being used by Will Hooper and a staircase that led up to the top floor. At the head of this were two matching rooms that had been Zelda's and Helena's when they were little girls. Helena's old room now belonged to Jacob while Zelda's old room had been taken over by Helena as Bessie had told him earlier on. They looked in on these, Jay feeling his insides stir when he saw Helena's things scattered around her borrowed room, make-up and hairbrushes on a dresser, clothes folded in piles or hanging up on a hook behind the door. Thankfully they didn't linger, continuing through the top floor, Bessie pointing out a room that had formerly been Helena and Zelda's nursery and the bedroom that was being used by Johnny Fulton and Meliza as well as several attic rooms that were being used for storage. Bessie opened the doors to some of these to reveal piles of boxes and crates stacked up against one another, dead furniture and more paintings shrouded with dust sheets that had Jay thinking of the others three floors below in the hallway. And it was to the ground floor that they descended next, taking a stairwell on the north side of the house down past the first floor to the end of the main ground-floor corridor. The bottom of the stairwell sat directly by a side door that led outside. Next to this was the door to the kitchen through which Jay could see Sara Taft stirring a selection of pots on top of the huge gas-fired range. Further along the corridor there was a door that opened on to a set of stairs that led down to the cellars as well as the dining room and a drawing room. Next to this, on the south side of the house, lay another drawing room that gave way both to the library (on the south-western corner of the house under Will Hooper's bedroom if Jay wasn't mistaken) and to the cavernous ballroom that extended from the second drawing room out into Willoughby's gardens. Besides these, there were two other rooms just off the hallway, a small den (where some old sofas and a cheap coffee-table were aimed at a large television) and a small office (with a computer and a fax machine on a desk and shelves full of box files on the walls). And there was the hallway itself, dominated by the twin staircases that swept up towards the half-landing that also doubled as an archway through which one could walk back through to the main corridor below. It was underneath this arch that a woman appeared and Bessie introduced her to Jay.

'Molly, this is Jay Richards. He's here to sort out the . . . the . . .'

'The ghost?' Molly asked. Jay offered his hand and she shook it a little gingerly, almost as if he was the ghost himself, before telling them that everyone was waiting out on the loggia. 'The police are here,' she elaborated. 'They want to speak to everyone and let them know what's going on.'

Out on the terrace, what Jay presumed was the full complement of house guests sat around a massive wooden table. There were six others as well as Bessie and Molly but Jay had little time to take in much about them besides their generalized air of boredom before Toby appeared, coming through the French doors that led back into the dining room, a drink in his right hand, a cigarette in his left, two uniformed men following him.

'Good evening everyone,' he said, looking round after the murmur had fizzled out. 'Where's Zelda?'

'I looked in on her,' replied one of the women Jay hadn't met yet. 'She didn't answer when I knocked and the curtains are drawn so she must be asleep. I didn't wake her.'

'Then we'll begin without her.' Toby turned to address the group as a whole. 'I don't need to introduce most of you to Sheriff Bryar nor Deputy Benson,' he started, Jay wondering how much effort it took for him to sound polite, 'just as I don't need to introduce them to most of you.' Bryar and Benson merely stood there eyeballing everyone, Jay in particular. 'Anyway,' Toby continued, 'it seems fair to let you know what's been going on, especially as you've all been asked to extend your stay here at Willoughby longer than might have been ideal. Sheriff Bryar here is ready to summarize it for you. Sheriff Bryar?'

Bryar coughed, walked a step forward and removed his hat with a freckled hand. Without it, he was perhaps a couple of inches under six foot, in his late forties with a face like stirred oatmeal and green veins visible on the side of his head through the copper stubble.

'Good evenin' ladies and gentlemen,' he began. 'Firstly, I'd like to thank you all for bein' so patient with me these last few days. I know that your extended stay here at Willoughby has been a matter of some inconvenience and your understandin' has been greatly appreciated.'

Bryar paused for a moment – for no apparent reason that Jay could determine except that he was used to being listened to – and spent a moment picking something off the rim of his hat.

'Secondly, I'd like to bring you all up to speed with our investigations into the whereabouts of Lady Charteris. Thus far, nobody we've questioned has seen or spoken to Lady Charteris since twenty-one hundred hours on the night of August fifteenth. As you all know, we've also been conductin' another routine Missing Persons Investigation into the whereabouts of Mr Wallace Kelly who hasn't been seen since approximately the same time on the same night. As a matter of routine, we're investigatin' these events independently of each other but also not rulin' out the possibility that they're connected with one another.' Another pause. More hat inspection. 'Mr Kelly's car's also missin',' he continued finally, 'and details have been sent to all relevant law enforcement agencies. Strictly speakin', I shouldn't be tellin' you all this, but it seems a like fair concession considerin' your extended cooperation: thus far, we've ascertained that Lady Charteris' passport can't be found on the premises and that a number of items of clothing and luggage are also missin'. We've also discovered that similar items are missin' at the Kelly residence, including Mr Kelly's passport, and we are continuin' to investigate these facts to discover whether there is a connection.'

He stopped again and there was another moment's silence. Jay took a look at Toby who stood there next to the cops trying his best not to look angry or humiliated. He wasn't doing a very good job of it, staring down at his feet, his cheeks flushed as he killed his cigarette with one last pull and dropped it into the dregs of his drink.

'Any questions?' the sheriff asked.

Molly Remick spoke up. 'Can we go home yet?' she asked simply.

'I'm afraid not, Mrs Remick,' Bryar replied. 'We're askin' that you all remain here at Willoughby for a few more days . . .'

'This is ridiculous!' spluttered the man sitting next to her, presumably her husband. 'This has got to be against the law, detaining innocent people against their will. We've all done everything we can to assist you, Sheriff, but enough is enough.'

The Sheriff stared back at him wearily. 'Mr Remick, sir,'

he said, 'I'll be straight with you: I *don't* have reasonable grounds to detain you here any further. An' if you want to make this a legal matter, why, that's your right, sir. What I will say is that should I or my fellow officers require you to answer any more questions in the next few days, what seems certain is that it's easier for you to remain here rather than return to . . .'

He paused and looked at his deputy who consulted his notebook. 'Louisville, Sheriff.'

'. . . rather than return to Louisville only to have to travel all the way back down here again so that we might speak to you.'

Jim Remick sank back in his seat, muttering that it was 'all ridiculous'.

'I would say to you all that our investigations should only take a few more days and that by then we should've been able to rule out any untoward explanations as to what's happened. After that, there shouldn't be anythin' else that requires your assistance.' Bryar paused again. 'Does any of you have anythin' more you want to ask?' he asked. No one said anything. It hadn't been a question and everyone sitting around the loggia knew it.

'No? Then I thank you all again for your continued cooperation and bid you all a good evenin'.'

And that was it. Sara Taft appeared at the French doors and announced that dinner was ready and everyone filed slowly inside. Jay followed them but then stopped when he heard Sheriff Bryar call after him.

'And you are?'

Jay turned and faced him.

'Your name, sir? We haven't been introduced.'

'My name? Richards. Jay Richards.'

Deputy Benson scribbled it down in his notebook with a pen that looked ridiculous in his huge farm boy hands.

'Address?' Bryar asked. Jay gave it: Quintara Avenue, San Francisco. More scribbling.

'Jay is a friend of my sister-in-law,' Toby added. 'He arrived today at her invitation.'

Bryar focused his grey eyes on Jay's. 'And how long are you planning to stay Mr Richards?'

'I'm not sure yet,' Jay replied.

Bryar didn't respond but simply leered at him for a few seconds before telling Toby that he would contact him soon and that he and the deputy could show themselves out. After that, Toby led Jay into the dining room where everyone else had taken their seats. There were three spare places, one at the head of the table for Toby and two more at the other end, presumably left for him and Zelda. Toby gestured towards one of the empty chairs.

'Jay, why don't you sit at the other end of the table?'

Jay did as he was told and as the women passed bread and bowls of soup around and the men opened bottles of wine and he exchanged murmured introductions with everyone, he had a chance to take his first undistracted look at them all. Toby sat at the head of the table and to his immediate left sat Meliza Milo in a white cotton top with half-length sleeves. Her black hair was cut short and exposed the boyish shape of her head and her scrubbed childish features (the negligible nose, the small arch of her brown forehead, the wide cheekbones that curved down to the edges of her thin, wide lips). When she was asked to pass something by one of the others or when Johnny filled her glass, she responded with a smile that revealed the exacting symmetry of her flawless teeth. But when she thought no one was looking, Jay could see the boredom in her lowered eyes, in the tangle of her folded arms, in the slump of her shoulders. She'd probably been whisked away to North Carolina with promises of a luxurious week in a beautiful old plantation mansion but never expected to be detained there by the police. And the same went for most of the others, of course. If Johnny Fulton sitting next to Meliza seemed unaffected by his enforced stay at Willoughby, gulping at his wine happily and starting on his soup as soon as it was placed in front of him, then everyone else around the table seemed weary of each other and the same old conversations that had worn as thin as one of Meliza's forearms. Next to Johnny sat Molly Remick who stared joylessly down at her plate and next to her sat Tony Shipman who stared at his cutlery with a dead-end smile under his broad nose. To Jay's right sat Tony's wife, Nina, a bottle-blonde who looked like a stouter proposition than Molly, the kind of woman who worked in PR and whom Jay could imagine priding herself on her ability to 'hang with the boys', the kind of woman who showed her molars when she laughed and continually told people about her 'hunger for life'. Like Johnny, she seemed to be enduring the boredom with a greater sense of equanimity than some of the other guests, though also like Johnny she wasn't shy about guzzling back the wine as soon as it was opened and Jay noticed that she kept her pack of cigarettes in easy reach.

As for Jim Remick who sat to Jay's left, he stared across the table at his diminutive wife with a look that seemed to contain both concern and annoyance. And next to him was Will Hooper. If Jim and Tony seemed to resemble each other with their sandy hair and their polo shirts and khaki slacks, and if Toby and Johnny seemed to resemble each other, both of them blond, both of them English (though Toby seemed to have aged faster than his childhood friend), then Will Hooper seemed different to all four of them. He sat there in a black linen shirt and black jeans, still smoking even though Bessie who was sitting to his left had started eating. Most of the people around the table looked bored by two weeks of each other's company but Will looked as if he'd *arrived* bored, looked as if he was *always* bored. How had Bessie described him? 'An old artist friend of Helena's.' Jay wondered if he'd slept with Helena.

'Bessie tells us you've flown in from San Francisco,' Nina Shipman asked eventually.

'That's right.'

'Beautiful city, San Francisco,' said Tony Shipman authoritatively, 'not in the same league as Boston or New York, but a beautiful city nonetheless.'

'I like it,' Jay replied casually.

'How long have you lived there?' Nina asked.

'A couple of years. I used to live in London,' he told her, wondering for a moment whether Tony Shipman thought that London was in the same league as Boston and New York. 'Then I travelled for a few years before ending up in California. I was born there so it kind of feels like home.'

'And do your parents live there or in England?' she asked.

'My parents are dead,' Jay replied. Bessie and Mrs Taft appeared at that moment with plates of grilled chicken and dishes of vegetables, a break which conveniently allowed Nina to let the subject drop and left Jay staring down at the meat that was put in front of him. As usual, anything that wasn't served between two pieces of bread tended to look gelatinous to him, formless, a sludge smeared on to his plate. Perhaps he could turn it all into some kind of sandwich? Before he could reach for the bread, Toby clinked a spoon against his glass at the other end of the table.

'Everyone,' he started, 'why don't I take this opportunity to formally introduce you all to Jay who'll be staying here for a few days.' There was a murmur and then silence again. 'As you all know,' Toby continued, 'a few strange things have been happening here at the house recently . . .'

'I thought we might talk about this after dinner,' Jay interrupted as politely as he could.

'Now's as good a time as any,' replied Toby. 'Everyone's here except for Zelda, but she already seems to know all about you.' He looked around the table. 'Jay's being here is Zelda's idea. It seems as if she has the same taste for the . . . *exotic* . . . as my wife.'

Toby paused and no one said anything. The women looked

down at their plates while the men looked at Jay with impassive faces.

'Anyway, as I was saying, a few strange things have been happening here around the house and Zelda has taken it upon herself to hire Jay. How is it that you describe yourself, Jay?'

Jay looked around the table to see nine pairs of eyes staring back at him.

'I guess you could call me a paranormal investigator.'

Will Hooper immediately sniggered while Meliza tapped Johnny Fulton on the shoulder and whispered something in his ear.

'What's a *paranoid investigator*?' asked Nina Shipman.

'Jay, I'm thinking it might be best if you explained your working methods to everyone,' Toby leered from the far end of the table, lifting a forkful of chicken to his mouth and washing it down with a glass of wine.

'Well, it's simple really,' Jay replied, clearing his throat and deciding to take a direct approach. 'If people think they've seen something they think is supernatural, what you might crudely call a "ghost" or "poltergeist", they hire me and I come and investigate it.'

'And do you think a ghost *is* responsible for what's been happening?' Molly Remick blurted out.

'Will you stop being so stupid Molly,' muttered her husband. 'Ghosts have got nothing to do with it. It's just Will and John screwing around.' He turned towards them both. 'You two clowns should own up. It's bad enough being kept here by the police without you making everything worse.'

'It's got nothing to do with me,' said Will.

'Me neither,' said John, stroking Meliza's hair. 'I've got better things to do than hump art around Toby's gaff in the middle of the night.'

Jay spoke up. 'To be honest,' he said, 'and to answer Molly's original question: no, at this point I don't think a ghost is responsible for what's been happening. Something I should say about my work is that I'm used to scepticism. *I'm* always highly sceptical myself, in fact, not least because nine out of every ten so-called mysteries I become involved with end up being explained away by something mundane. My work is more about revealing rational explanations for events that my clients misinterpret as paranormal than proving or disproving the existence of what people ordinarily call "ghosts".'

'Can you give us an example?' asked Nina.

'I can give you a hundred examples,' Jay replied. 'You wouldn't believe the number of times I've been called to investigate a disembodied voice and find that it's simply floated in through a ventilation duct from another apartment. Other recurring explanations behind so-called ghostly noises are structural subsidence in old buildings, the echoes of railway lines through the ground and plastic lightshades.'

'Why plastic lightshades?' she asked.

'There's a certain material used in the construction of the kind of cheap lightshade popular amongst many of my clients, if not most homes throughout North America. When it cools down, the plastic contracts and makes a crinkling sound,' Jay replied. 'Of course, some people are prone to superstition and jump to the wrong conclusion, especially in the middle of the night. That's where I come in. And of course there are all the hoaxers and all the attention seekers, but they're fairly easy to rumble.'

'What about the other ten per cent?' challenged Tony Shipman. 'You say that nine out of ten of the cases you deal with are ultimately resolved by logical explanation. Are you seriously suggesting that one in ten incidents involves something supernatural?'

At the other end of the table, Jay could see Toby sitting there with a cigarette burning away in his hand, observing him through a cloud of smoke.

'No, not exactly. I think that what I'm saying is that a small percentage of my investigations force me to concede that I'm only part of the way towards discovering a truth that I might never fully understand rather than uncovering a truth that I previously didn't know about.'

'Now *I* don't understand,' Jim Remick said. 'Either ghosts exist or they don't.'

'I don't think it's that simple.'

'How so?'

Jay didn't answer.

'Let's put this another way,' Remick continued. 'Do *you* believe in ghosts?' Jay still didn't answer.

'Zelda mentioned to me that you'd helped the police in San Francisco with a murder investigation,' Bessie added from the other end of the table. 'Is that true?'

Jay nodded, thankful for her intervention. 'Yes, that's true. I was involved with the investigation into the murder of a young woman called Dana Lockwood, a Californian heiress.'

'I read something about that,' Nina Shipman said.

'What happened?' asked Molly Remick.

Jay once again proceeded to tell the story of The Lockwood Murder Mystery, this time leaving out any dramatic embellishments that he might have indulged in if he'd been with a different audience at a different time in a different place. *Just the facts*, he warned himself. But given that he'd already detected an underlying confusion amongst them all as to exactly what *had* been going on at Willoughby the last few days, perhaps the facts of the Lockwood case would be all it took to settle everyone down and give him a chance to start a systematic investigation. After a few minutes, Jay got to the end of his story. Jim Remick spoke immediately.

'So, you're claiming that in this instance, a ghost *did* appear to this General . . . this General Lockwood. That's ridiculous.'

'Honey,' whined his wife, 'the police in San Francisco believed him.'

'I don't care about the police in San Francisco,' he snapped back.

'I *didn't* claim that a ghost appeared to General Lockwood,' Jay said, trying to calm them both down.

'Yes you did. You told us that the ghost of his granddaughter appeared to the General and revealed to him that she'd been murdered.'

'Jim, I think you misunderstood what I said. Yes, the true nature of Dana Lockwood's death wasn't initially obvious. And yes, this was later revealed and yes, *something* happened in the General's bedroom in between. But you haven't heard me make any explicit connection between what happened that night at the Lockwood mansion and what happened to Dana Lockwood, nor have I ever made such a connection. Nor have the San Francisco police. If it helps you better understand how I approach what I do, I'll happily say that I *don't* know what happened that night in the General's bedroom except that my instruments recorded anomalous readings and that the General and I witnessed something that defied conventional explanation and that afterwards, once the General had been in contact with the SFPD and Dana's killers had been brought to justice, these strange events stopped occurring. One could read all sorts of things into this, and into this last fact especially. But whether such interpretations are founded in superstition or reality is something one could hardly be confident about. You'll have noticed that you never hear me use the word *ghost* except with some kind of qualification.'

'What about the video camera you said that you'd set up?' Tony Shipman asked. 'Did it record pictures of the phenomenon that you claim to have witnessed? I imagine television stations all over the world would be very interested in paying a large sum of money for live footage of a ghost, though of course you refrain from using such a word.'

'The camera cut out on that occasion,' Jay replied, remembering the black rectangle of static he'd scrupulously examined the following morning while Norton had supplied him with an endless series of cups of coffee.

'How convenient,' Shipman replied.

'It often happens, or else the camera seems only to capture a mass of light with no distinct shape or form.'

'Again, very convenient,' Jim Remick butted in.

'Do you mind if we finish with the philosophical debate?' Toby yawned.

'How are you going to go about investigating what's been happening *here*?' asked Molly.

'Can you tell us more about your equipment?' Bessie asked.

'Well, once I've heard from you all what's been happening here at Willoughby, I'll proceed exactly as I did that night in the Lockwood mansion. I'll set up cameras, microphones and motion detectors in the areas of the house where people claim to have experienced something out of the ordinary as well as take readings with EMF detectors, thermometers and a Geiger counter. If something paranormal moved the pictures and it returns to the hallway at any point over the next few nights, they should all pick it up.' Jay glanced across quickly at both Will and Johnny but the two of them seemed the most bored out of everyone. 'I'll take this opportunity to clarify that I won't be trying to infringe upon anyone's privacy and that I don't expect to position my equipment anywhere except in the common parts of the house. But before that, I'll need to know exactly what you all believe has been happening here.' He turned to face Toby. 'What do you think?'

Toby didn't answer for a moment. 'Okay,' he said finally, 'I suppose the sooner we get this started, the sooner we get it finished. But we should all move to the drawing room. I'll ask Sara to bring in some coffee and also fetch Alfred and Lara. If we're all going to sit here and discuss this, they should probably be here too.'

As they all moved silently through into the adjacent drawing room, the garden appearing briefly beyond the windows in swirls of grey, silver and purple before Bessie drew the curtains, Jay wondered if interviewing the whole group together was likely to get him anywhere. As Tommy had once put it, it was like *Twelve Angry Men*. 'You ever see that old Henry Fawnda movie?' the old man asked him. 'Take a rare kind of individual not to just say the same as everybody else.' But then Jay realized that he didn't feel the need to know what the guests thought individually. Looking schematically at what Zelda had told him in San Francisco, there had been three allegedly paranormal events. For now, Jay could all but forget about the first of these, could dismiss the great-aunts' experience as a product of their senility. As for the second of these, Sara Taft's experience out on the drive, usually it would have been better for Jay to have taken her to one side and interviewed her separately. But then she'd already denied that she'd seen anything, and what Jay really wanted to hear about was what the guests at Willoughby thought had happened on the night the paintings had switched positions. Several independent witnesses with no apparent motive to collude had witnessed the same anomalous event and one look at the pictures up on the walls of the hall when he'd first arrived had immediately suggested that it was unlikely (though not impossible) that human agency could have moved them in the middle of the night without disturbing those who slept nearby.

Soon everyone was arranged around the room, Mrs Taft pouring coffee as her husband walked in on his own and took a position at the back of the group near the door. She poured him a cup too and he accepted it from her without saying anything and without expression.

'Somebody should tell you,' Bessie whispered in Jay's ear as she handed him his cup, 'Alfred's mute.'

'Thanks for letting me know,' he whispered back, staring at the man over her shoulder. He was a giant, perhaps six and a half feet tall with the same square face as his wife and the same fluid blue irises that were only a little darker than the surrounding whites of his eyes.

'So,' Jay started, 'are we still waiting for your daughter, Mrs Taft?'

'Lara's working in Wilmington tonight,' she replied.

'Okay.' Jay looked at Toby. 'Shall we start?'

Toby nodded and Jay turned to face the group as a whole.

'What was the first strange thing that anyone witnessed?'

'It was the night Clemmy and Lobelia woke us all up,' said Molly Remick. 'Last Tuesday night. Three nights after Helena . . .' She stopped mid-sentence. 'Three nights after the *party*.'

'What happened?' Jay asked.

'Either Clemmy or Lobelia had a nightmare and woke up screaming,' said Toby. 'Obviously, whichever one of them it was, she woke the other and soon they both had us all out of our beds.'

'Bessie, you helped me calm them down until Sara arrived,' said Nina Shipman. 'What was it they were saying?'

Bessie looked around the table.

'They said they saw Esmerelda Smiling walking around their room.'

'They *both* said that?' Jay asked.

Bessie nodded. 'They both said the same thing . . .'

'This is ridiculous,' scoffed Jim Remick. 'With all due respect, I refuse to sit here and discuss the nightmares of two senile old women. If that sounds harsh, I'm sorry, but it's hardly unreasonable.'

'Be nice, Jimmy!' wailed his wife.

'Why don't we calm down for a second,' Jay said, trying to keep everyone focused. 'Jim's reservations are understandable given the circumstances . . .'

'I don't need you to tell me if anything I think is "understandable".'

Jay saw Toby smirk out of the corner of his eye but ignored it. 'What happened next?' he asked, trying to move things on. Everyone looked at Sara Taft who kept her eyes on him, as if Jay were the one who was being asked a question and she the one who was asking it.

'Sara, Toby found you out on the drive in a great deal of distress,' Bessie said.

'What time was this, Toby?' Jay asked.

'About midnight,' he replied. 'I was in my study when I heard Sara cry out.'

Jay looked at Mrs Taft. 'Mrs Taft, what happened?' he asked gently.

She didn't say anything but everyone continued to look at her. 'I had a dizzy spell, that's all,' she replied eventually.

The tension in the room seemed to deflate.

'Then what happened?' Jay asked. 'I'm presuming the paintings moving in the middle of the night was the next suspicious event?'

Everyone started talking at once and he had to wait for them all to fall silent before he could work through the details one at a time. Eventually they were all listening again and he asked them which night it had been that the paintings had moved.

'It was last Thursday night,' answered Nina Shipman. 'It was the night before Zelda arrived. Or very early that morning.'

'Who was the first person to see that they'd moved?' Jay asked. No one answered so he asked the question again.

'Who was the first person to see that they'd moved?'

'I was.'

This from Mrs Taft. 'Can you describe what happened as you experienced it?' he asked her.

She nodded. 'Friday morning, I came across to the main house at six-thirty like I usually do.'

'Which door did you use to come into the house?' Jay asked.

'The side door, same as always.'

'What happened next?'

'Well, I did everything I usually do. I put the water on to boil, I put out breakfast for everyone, and then I started opening up the shutters on the ground floor. First the dining room, then the drawing rooms and then those in the hall. I was just about to go upstairs when . . .'

She broke off.

'What happened?' Jay asked.

'Someone had moved all the pictures in the night. It was too dark to see anything at first. But I turned round from opening the shutters to the window by the side of the front door and I couldn't believe my eyes. Those pictures haven't been moved since their frames were cleaned when John Smiling was alive.'

'Who saw them next?' Jay asked.

'I did,' Nina said. 'I came down the back stairs around eight o'clock and found Sara sitting in the kitchen with a cup of coffee in front of her. She hadn't touched it. I said good morning to her but she didn't reply. I asked her if she was okay but she still didn't say anything, just got up out of her seat and led me down the main corridor to the hall. When we got there, she stared up at the walls. All the pictures were hanging in different places.'

Jay looked around the room. No one, not even Tony Shipman or Jim Remick disputed that. Toby sucked away on the cigarette that now seemed to live in his face and silently observed the discussion.

'It was then that Molly came down the main stairs,' Nina added.

It transpired that Molly Remick, already spooked by previous events, had fainted when she'd looked up at the walls and that Nina and Mrs Taft had revived her right there on the half-landing as the rest of the guests slowly filed down for breakfast.

'This is getting out of hand,' Jim Remick said. 'John and Will, will you just own up for Christ's sake so we can all get some peace. You've scared Molly and Sara and the Aunts . . .'

'For the last time, I haven't scared *anyone*,' Johnny replied, a combative edge creeping into his voice.

'Me neither,' Will added and suddenly everyone was talking again. Jay managed to calm them down, Toby all the time saying nothing and watching his every move. 'Has anyone else witnessed anything strange that they haven't yet shared?' he asked. No one spoke. 'Don't be embarrassed,' he encouraged. 'Even if it sounds stupid, it's best to get it out in the open so we can dismiss it and no one has to waste any time worrying about it.'

Everyone remained silent.

'I have to say,' Bessie started after a moment, 'Will and John were so drunk on Thursday night that I have difficulty believing that they could walk let alone move over twenty paintings in the dark without waking anyone.'

'Can we go and look at the paintings themselves?' Jay asked, looking directly at Toby who eventually got to his feet.

'Follow me.'

Toby led them all along the main downstairs corridor and through the archway into the hallway where everyone stood in a crowd staring up at the walls like tourists in a cathedral. Jay counted the pictures again: twenty-two in total, most of them dark and sombre portraits of various Smiling patriarchs though there were also a few landscapes, a few paintings of the house and a few pictures of various Smiling women from the past as well. One of these, the second in a line of four hanging above the left of the two staircases portrayed a young woman who reminded Jay of Helena and Zelda. She had the same long and delicate neck, the same luminous blue eyes, the same direct gaze that had Jay thinking of Helena years earlier as she'd moved towards him on the rain-washed night they'd first kissed. Was it their mother? No, it couldn't be. The painting was much too old.

'Who's that,' he asked Bessie who was standing directly behind him.

'Her name was Katherine Smiling,' Bessie answered. 'She lived here in the nineteenth century.'

'I see . . .'

'Why don't you zap the wall with one of your gadgets?' Jim Remick interrupted from somewhere further behind them. 'See if there's any trace of the ghostly hands that did this?'

'I *will* take some electromagnetic field readings once you've all gone to bed,' Jay replied as evenly as he could. 'But I can't do it with all of you standing here. It's impossible to adjust the equipment to compensate for background levels with so many people around and so many lights on.'

Turning back towards the paintings before Jim Remick could answer, Jay guessed that some were as wide as six feet, a few of the landscapes even wider.

'What do we do now?' Toby asked.

'Will? Johnny? Could you help me?'

The two men stared at each other, knowing what was coming next. 'This is stupid,' Will muttered.

'Please, indulge me, for just a moment.' Jay led them halfway up the right-hand staircase and came to a stop by the largest frame on the wall, a huge oil painting of the back of the house. It looked as if it weighed over a hundred pounds.

'Can you both try and take the picture down off the wall?' Jay asked. 'As long as Toby's okay with this.'

Will and Johnny looked down the stairs at Toby who nodded back at them. Then they stood below the painting and reached up towards it. Will, who was as tall as Jay, a decidedly average five-ten, could barely get a suitable grip on the bottom corner of the frame that was nearest to him. Nonetheless, he and

Johnny stretched and grunted until they'd shunted the picture up off its supporting hooks. Even then Will was on tiptoe, his footing precarious on the carpeted steps, and everyone watched as the two of them made a few abortive attempts to lower the picture to the ground without damaging it. The frame made a scraping sound as it slid down the cream wall and left two dark marks against the plaster.

Watching them struggle seemed to stun everyone: no one spoke.

'What time is it?' Bessie suddenly asked, breaking the silence.

'Just after ten-thirty,' Tony Shipman replied quietly.

'The clock,' his wife pointed, 'it's stopped.'

Everyone stared at the large grandfather clock at the side of the hallway by the door to the library. Its hands were frozen at twenty-eight minutes after four. Sara Taft went pale, Jay noticed, also hearing Molly Remick's breathing accelerate as she reached a hand out towards her husband's shoulder.

'Does anyone remember the last time they looked at it?' Jay asked.

'I took a look at it this afternoon,' Sara Taft admitted, 'as I was coming to the door to let you in. I thought it was telling the right time.'

'Does anyone else remember looking at the clock at some point during the last few days?'

No one said anything.

'It could have just stopped,' Jim Remick muttered.

'That clock hasn't stopped since I came to work here,' Sara Taft mumbled.

'Like the paintings . . .' Molly cried out.

'My watch has been playing up the last few days,' Bessie offered.

Then the whole group started talking all at once until Toby's voice rose above them all.

'Okay, that's enough,' he called out above the noise. 'This has turned into floorshow.' Somewhere, a bell started ringing as if to emphasize his point.

'That must be Clemmy and Lobelia,' said Bessie. 'I'll go and see what they want, and check on Jacob.'

'Maybe they've seen another ghost,' Will Hooper said, lighting a cigarette. 'This whole thing is a freakin' farce.'

'I agree,' said Toby before turning to Jay. 'I need to speak to you in the library.'

9

'I am *this* close to throwing you out.'

Toby launched a finger towards Jay's chest, stopping a few centimetres short. It lingered there in the air for a few moments, pointing at Jay's heart before it moved to pull a lighter out of Toby's trouser pocket and light the cigarette his other hand had placed in his mouth. Before he could speak again, there was a knock at the library door.

'Who is it?' Toby snapped. The door opened to reveal Zelda.

'It's me.'

She walked across the room to the window seat where she turned to face them both.

'What happened?'

'I will not be humiliated in my own house,' Toby replied.

'I was merely trying to establish what's happened,' Jay cut in. 'Toby says he's certain that Will and Johnny are responsible for moving the paintings. But when I asked them to lift just one of the paintings off the wall a few moments ago, they only managed to do so with extreme difficulty. To believe that they, or anyone else, could have moved them *all* without making a noise is unreasonable, not least because they would have had to have done it in the dark and after having had a lot to drink.'

Toby didn't have an immediate reply to that. 'He was trying to make me look like a fool,' he said eventually, but with less conviction.

'The pictures *moved* in the middle of the night, Toby,' Zelda insisted. She walked over to a shelf on the far side of the room and picked up a small photograph in a frame which she handed to Toby. He put it down without looking at it. It was a picture of him and Helena in the hall on their wedding day and Jay was glad to be standing far enough away not to be able to see it in any detail.

'There they are,' Zelda continued, her voice not breaking rhythm once, nor rising in volume. Jay imagined that it was a voice she used when she was working amongst the dead and the dying. 'All the pictures,' she said, 'in their original places.'

The glowing tip of Toby's cigarette flared and subsided.

'What are you trying to prove Zelda?'

'Whether something moved the pictures in the middle of the night. At the moment, you seem as if you're still unsure as to whether they moved in the first place . . .'

'Of course they moved, I'm not denying that!' he snapped back. 'Just don't ask me to believe in ghosts, that's all. You were pretty sure yourself a couple of days ago that it was Johnny and Will who were behind all of this. "They're a couple of bored little boys," you said, "they're . . ."'

'It sounds like things just got a little bit more complicated out there in the hallway. I'm as hard-headed a rationalist as you are, Toby, but Jay's just doing what I've hired him to do . . .'

'That's exactly my point, Zelda. This is *your* idea. But this is still *my* house . . .'

'Yours and *Helena's*.'

This seemed to stop Toby for a second. Jay watched them, standing there in the low light and imagined Toby and Helena standing in the same spot arguing with each other. And there it was again, the issue of Willoughby and to whom it belonged.

Toby turned to Jay. 'I will not have you humiliating me in my house, do you understand?' he growled. Before Jay could say anything, he turned back to Zelda. 'And before you bring up Helena again, can I remind you that your sister obviously had a questionable commitment to Willoughby before she abandoned her child and ran off with Wallace Kelly?'

'You can,' Zelda replied. There was the merest hint of a

challenge in her voice, enough to start Jay thinking that Toby might strike her at any moment — he was furious, and drunk.

'What do you want me to do?' Jay asked, clearing his throat. 'Do you want me to go? Do you want me to stay but do nothing? Or do you want me to stay and do what you've hired me to do? If you want me to leave, I'll leave.' He purposefully didn't address his comments to either one of them in particular.

'Jay is my guest, Toby,' Zelda said firmly.

Toby didn't reply, stepping over to the drinks tray by the globe and pouring a scotch. After he'd swallowed it down, he turned to Jay and asked him what it was he proposed to do next, swaying a little on his feet.

'Can we all sit down?' Jay asked. Toby nodded and Jay sat in an armchair opposite him, the same two chairs they'd sat in that afternoon when he'd first arrived, while Zelda sat down on the window seat.

'I'm going to go about this the same way I go about every incident of this type,' he started, deciding to keep it brief. For the moment, he just wanted Toby to remain neutral. 'My first objective is to see if Will and John or anyone else is responsible for what's been going on here, however unlikely it now seems. As you've said already, your friends have been bored for days, stuck here for longer than they planned. That two or more of them have been playing up is still an explanation that we can't rule out.' Toby stared back at him, some thought that Jay couldn't read flickering in his eyes, while Zelda watched the two of them from across the room. 'So I'll continue to proceed from the premise that at least *someone* here is responsible for moving the pictures however difficult it might have been. I'm going to set up cameras in the hall and also motion detectors around the house at strategic locations, probably in the main corridors on each floor . . .'

'You're going to spy on my guests?' Toby interrupted.

'I think that's a little simplistic . . .'

'And you're going to insult me, call me stupid?' Toby interrupted.

'. . . if someone *is* creeping around at night,' Jay pressed on, 'then at least you'll know about it. And then you'll be rid of me too. Also, I'll be up most of the night looking out for anything strange. If anything potentially paranormal happens, my equipment should pick that up too.'

Toby still looked sceptical. 'I don't like the idea of *you* creeping around my house at night,' he said eventually.

'All I'm looking for is the simplest explanation, *the investigative path of least resistance*,' Jay told Toby, borrowing one of Tommy's favourite maxims. 'Like I say, once we find out that John or Will or one of the others is messing about in the middle of the night, I get on the next plane back to San Francisco. What you do after that is your business. You'll never see me again.'

Jay wondered if Zelda would add her point of view but she remained silent.

'Okay,' Toby said finally, 'but you will report to *me*. This is my house and I don't want you sneaking about in it without letting me know exactly what's going on.'

Jay nodded. 'There's one last thing, Toby.'

'What is it?'

'Do you have any plans for Willoughby? I'd like to look at them if possible, and also any architectural notes concerning the plumbing, the house's foundations and the rock formation beneath it. As I told everyone in the dining room earlier on, structural subsidence in buildings, especially old buildings, often causes noises that are misinterpreted as hauntings. The same goes for plumbing. Perhaps it was something of this kind that startled Clemmy and Lobelia.'

'I haven't a clue about any of that kind of thing,' Toby replied.

'Our father loaned a lot of historical documents to do with

the house to the City Library in Wilmington,' Zelda added. 'You could call them in the morning.'

Jay nodded.

'Well, if that's all, I'm going up to my study,' Toby said. 'I'll see you both tomorrow.'

Once Toby had slammed the door behind him, Zelda stood up and bounced a ball around the pool-table. It twanged off three cushions before colliding with a pack of three or four others. 'So, you came after all.'

'I guess I just couldn't pass up the opportunity of seeing where you and Helena grew up,' he replied. 'She told me all about this place that summer, showed me a few photos. They hardly did it justice.'

'Helena loves it here,' Zelda replied briskly, but then stopped. 'Don't take this the wrong way,' she said, 'but I've always remembered that day you and I met on Ibiza. I don't have any reason to remember you especially. It's not like you were Helena's first fling, nor her last.' Jay felt himself contract inside momentarily. 'But I've always been able to remember that entire day with complete clarity. Every second of it, including you right at the end, this strange figure drifting around that villa . . .'

'I'm not surprised you remember the whole day in such detail,' Jay interrupted, deciding to change the subject, 'given what had just happened and how far you'd had to travel.'

Jay imagined that journey for a moment, Zelda getting on a plane for Europe, the initial shock of her father's death still there in the clotted wells of her tear ducts, still there in the tundra of her tongue, in the burning beds of her fingernails, in the slow thump of her heartbeat as she sat stuck in her seat with nowhere to go for ten hours. He remembered what it had been like when he himself had flown to Scotland with Tommy's ashes, boarding the plane for Heathrow and changing there for Inverness (in the terminal in London, it had been mercifully dark outside allowing him the chance to forget that he was standing on English soil, to pretend that the lights and the solid impact of the black sky beyond the plate glass belonged to somewhere else, to pretend that it was nowhere or at least nowhere in particular). Jay remembered the inertial ritual of the journey allowing him not to say anything to anyone for three days except *please* and *thank you* and to ask the grim cabbie outside Glasgow airport to take him south to Rhidorroch Sound. Once they'd agreed a price — a hundred pounds each way — Jay had dozed in the back while the driver had drilled his beige Chieftain through the scarred hills and gaining light. He'd waited by the car, smoking a roll-up and watching from a distance with his collar up against the wind while Jay did what Tommy had asked in his will and then driven Jay back to Glasgow without question or comment. From there, another eighteen hours to America, Jay sleeping all the way with a mini-disk on loop in his headphones, the stewardess shaking him awake just as the Prez fell into 'I Guess I'll Hang My Tears Out To Dry' and 101 appeared in the plane window, the San Bruno hills in the distance rolling towards the sea.

And Jay imagined one more journey, another journey back to America, Jean-Marc flying back to North Carolina with Helena in his arms.

'And now I'm flying all over the place again,' Zelda said, interrupting Jay's thoughts.

'How are you feeling?' he asked her. She still looked weak, the skin on her face scalp-pale.

'A little better now,' she replied.

'When did you recover from your pneumonia?'

'Only a couple of months ago.'

Zelda paused, the library around them all Hs for a moment: the hypnotic presence of the picture of Helena and Toby on their wedding day standing on the shelf across the herringbone floor where Toby had put it down earlier; the pictures of her parents and of Zelda on the walls amongst the antique prints of horses and the house. Even the halation of the library's low light at the edges of Zelda's hair had Jay thinking of her sister.

'Can I ask you something?' he asked hesitantly.

'Go ahead.'

'Toby keeps reminding you that this is *his* house, as if you could dispute that in some way. So I suppose what I'm asking is this: even though your father died unexpectedly, he was a wealthy man and would have drawn up a will even though he was relatively young and in good health. Why did he leave Willoughby to Helena and not to you?'

'He didn't.'

'What do you mean?'

'The house was left to both of us. I legally gave my half to Helena soon after he died.'

'Why did you do that?'

'I'm not like my sister. I don't feel that close an attachment to Willoughby or to the Smiling family name. Naturally this place is bound up with many of my memories, some good, some bad – but I weighed it all up and decided to give her my half.'

Jay asked Zelda if she'd bought another property. She shook her head.

'But that means you don't have a home.'

'I have a home here. Even if it belongs to Helena.'

'Helena *and* Toby.'

'It doesn't really belong to Toby, and never could. The inheritance of the house is controlled by a set of legal conditions.'

'Such as?'

'For a start, the house and the estate have always been kept in the Smiling name, ever since the early 1700s. Our ancestors took certain steps to make sure of this.'

'What happened when a generation failed to produce a male heir?' Jay asked.

'Bizarrely, it's only ever happened twice. The first time they forced the poor thing to marry a paternal cousin. Her name was Katherine Smiling. Her painting's in the hallway next door.'

'And you and your sister are the second time.'

'Yes,' Zelda replied. 'Fortunately, no one's forced either of us to marry anyone and now that I've given my half to Helena, it'll all be passed on to Jacob . . .'

'Which means the house *will* finally be owned by a Charteris rather than a Smiling?'

'Yes it does,' Zelda replied, staring across at Jay from the other side of the pool table. 'To be honest, it's exactly all this kind of bullshit that motivated me to give Helena my half in the first place.'

The two of them fell silent. 'Perhaps it's time I went to bed,' Zelda said, gathering her wrap around her shoulders. Jay said he would walk her to her room and they stepped through the hallway and along the corridor past the dining room and the kitchen until they'd come through the side door and were standing in the narrow passageway between the coach house and the house itself. Out on the front drive, fireflies moved in the darkness in a frantic imitation of the stars that loitered above their heads in a sky that was the colour of an over-ripe plum.

'So, what's this Wallace Kelly guy like? He lives nearby, right?'

'He owns the old plantation on the other side of River Road. Most of it is rented out but he still has a few acres and the house itself of course.'

'Toby said something to me about him,' Jay said. 'What was it: Helena's run off with men before, but "never with anyone quite like Wallace Kelly"?'

'Well, I'm not sure what Toby means by that exactly. I haven't seen Wallace for years. If he's anything like he was when he was younger, then he's a quiet and romantic kind of guy. He was the only child of elderly parents so I guess that's to be expected.'

'Does he have any other relations nearby?'

Zelda shook her head.

'And the two of you knew Wallace Kelly when you were younger?'

'Of course. Our families have lived side-by-side for centuries. Our father used to play golf with Gideon Kelly every other weekend. *Their* fathers were friends.'

'And were Wallace and Helena attracted to each other when they were kids?'

Zelda laughed and Jay asked her what was funny.

'I suppose there's no reason why you should know this . . . I lost my virginity to Wallace on the night of our sixteenth birthday. We weren't in love or anything, or, at least, I wasn't in love with him and what he felt for me probably didn't amount to much more than a crush. Helena was too busy dating the entire football team to notice a guy like Wallace.'

'And did the two of you continue to have a relationship?'

'No,' Zelda replied. 'Wallace was probably too attached to his own solitude to let a girlfriend into his life. He was always out in the swamps and forests on his own, reading books, painting pictures . . .'

'Was he any good?'

'At which?'

'Either?'

'I don't think his actual paintings were anything special. But he was, and probably still is, a tremendously sensitive guy, always talking about poets and writers and making trips to New York and Europe every summer to visit museums and galleries.' Zelda raised a hand to the door-knob of the coach-house. 'Not that I *wanted* a relationship with him, you understand,' she added suddenly. 'I'm just telling you the way he was.'

'And probably still is,' Jay replied. They were silent again, Zelda's face in the moonlight a perfect replica of her sister's. Jay wanted to asked her another question but also didn't want her to speak or move.

'Zelda?' he said eventually.

'What is it?'

'Your great-aunts reported that they saw the ghost of your mother. How do you feel about that?'

'Nothing,' Zelda replied.

'Nothing?'

'I'm guessing that Helena and you talked about our parents. I don't know exactly what she said to you but as far as I'm concerned, whatever my feelings are about my mother, her life or her death, they're complicated and something I've had to live with since we were seven years old. As much as I love Clemmy and Lobelia, any claim of theirs to have seen our mother's ghost hardly scratches the surface. It would be ridiculous for me to take it seriously. Does that answer your question?'

'Yes,' he replied. 'But I have another.'

'What?'

'This house is old, at least a couple of centuries old, which means a lot must have happened here. Did you ever hear any ghost stories about the place when you were growing up?'

'I thought you said you never used the word *ghosts*?'

In the darkness, Jay saw the corners of Zelda's lips bend into a thin smile.

'You know what I mean.'

'Yes, I know what you mean,' she said. 'And yes, there are a few old legends about the place. Apparently our grandfather used to frighten our father with a couple of gloomy stories about old relatives whose spirits were meant to haunt the house, and also one about an old Cape Fear pirate who used to be seen marching around the grounds at night. But I don't think our father took these very seriously. Certainly, he never mentioned seeing anything and nor has anyone else, not since we were born. I think the stories were designed to scare and entertain and were nothing more serious than that.' They both stood there for a moment longer. 'Are you really staying up all night?' she asked.

Jay nodded. 'Most of it anyway. That's what you're paying

me to do. Tomorrow morning, I'll show you pictures of Will Hooper wandering around the house with a sheet over his head and that'll be that.'

'With a cigarette sticking out of his mouth,' she laughed softly. 'Good night, Jay.'

10

Once Zelda had closed the door behind her, Jay turned and walked out on to the front drive and stared up at the house. It glowed in the moonlight, pale aquamarine against the impenetrable mass of croaking trees that loomed up into the night beside and behind it. The light in Clemmy and Lobelia's bedroom window on the north-east corner was already out as were all the lights on the floor above. But the light in Jay's room was still on and so was the light in Will Hooper's room at the other end of the first floor.

As he made a circuit of the outside of the house, rounding the ballroom protruding from its southern face, Jay could also see that the light in Toby's study still burned away. And on the side of the house looking out over the loggia and main body of the gardens towards the Cape Fear estuary, he waited while the lights in the upstairs bathrooms and bedrooms flashed on and off in a strange sequence of chess moves before they all were extinguished. Then he ducked back through the passage between the coach house and the kitchen to check that Zelda's light was out (it was) before walking back into the house through the side door by the kitchen. All the rooms downstairs were empty until he came to the small sitting room adjoining the downstairs office where Will Hooper was slumped with a beer in front of the muted baying of a basketball game on the TV.

'Everyone's gone to bed,' he said without looking up from the screen. 'Sara said she didn't know if you needed a key but she's left you one for the side door anyway. She put it on the kitchen table.'

Jay picked up the key on the way back to his room where

he collected the cases that contained his equipment and brought them back down to the hall. There he laid them out on the floor and flipped the lids open, the gilt letters T.K.M.C. still not quite worn away from the black leather, and made a list of what he'd brought with him while he tried to formulate an opening strategy in his head.

Powerpad	Ion Detector
Compass	Hydrothermometer
Notebook	Thermal Scanner
Flashlight	3 Motion Detectors
Handheld EMF Scanner	Remote Unit
(w/earpiece)	2 Digital Videocameras
Geiger Counter	

Where to put it all? After thinking for a few moments, Jay decided to set up most of the stationary equipment in the hall itself and placed his powerpad on the low table next to the vase of white roses and the ion detector, hydrothermometer, thermal scanner and Geiger counter underneath one of the shuttered windows to the side of the front door. He also placed one of the cameras there so that the frame in the viewfinder encompassed both the staircases and the half-landing they led up to and almost all of the hallway itself including the archway leading through to the main ground-floor passage and the entrance to the side passage leading north past the downstairs office and den. Jay then synced this camera to a motion detector that he duct-taped to the upper frame of the front door and did the same thing with a camera on the main corridor on the first floor. He put this one at the north end of the corridor so that it had a clear view of all the bedroom doors: the Remicks,' the Shipmans' and Toby's at the far end. If anyone left their room and came down the corridor, they'd trigger it (as well as the remote unit in his pocket) and his powerpad would record and timecode the data. The same went for the hall. And an added advantage to this system was that Jay could move between the floors of the house without setting off the sensors by using the stairwell at the north end of the house.

Jay put his last remaining motion detector in the main corridor on the top floor near the door to Johnny and Meliza's room, again setting it to send an alarm signal to both his powerpad and his remote unit if it registered any activity. Then he returned to the hall. Checking the den, he saw that Will Hooper had gone upstairs at some point in the last half hour, a half-empty bottle of beer left on the table, strata of cigarette smoke moving in the lamplight, the static still live on the TV screen at the side of the room. Jay turned off the lights and shut the door and then followed the corridor round to the side door and stepped outside into the night where he made one last circuit of the house to clear his head and see who was still up. The lights on the first floor were all out except for the bedside lamp in his room. Toby's lights were out as were the lights in all the other bedrooms overlooking the loggia. Someone, presumably Johnny or Meliza or Bessie (who was staying in the old nanny's room), turned on a light in a bathroom on the top floor and then turned it off again a few moments later. And that was it. Jay checked his watch, Tommy's old Shitronic digital that he'd picked up in Chinatown for $4.99 (the old man had sworn that it was the only 'spook-proof' watch he'd come across in twenty years), and saw that it was half past midnight. Everyone was in bed.

He walked back into the house, locked the door behind him and started up the software on his powerpad before taking a chair from the kitchen and placing it in the middle of the main corridor on the ground floor. He would cover this area himself with his hand-held EMF detector, 'the magic wand' as Tommy used to call it, and keep an eye at the same time on the hallway on the other side of the archway.

After that, there was nothing else to do but get used to the waiting. Jay fitted the wand's earpiece into his left ear and flicked the power switch, a turmoil of signals beaming in from every direction, electricity cables, telephone lines, background static in the carpet and on the walls and curtains. He turned the base calibration on the unit down a couple of clicks, fifty milliguass and then another fifty, before fine-tuning the last couple of integers, the squawk of the background signal fading into a single neutral hum that sat poised above a milky black silence: it would take something wielding a hundred times the standard EMF of a normal person to disturb the signal unless he was stupid enough to point the thing at his computer or the microwave in the kitchen.

In the hallway, Jay took a reading of both the clock and the paintings on the wall, got nothing back for his time and then sat himself back down in his seat and stared down the corridor towards the kitchen, occasionally glancing over his left shoulder towards the hall where he could hear the Geiger counter clicking quietly away.

What were the chances of something happening that night?

Jay remembered asking Tommy this exact same question the very first night he'd accompanied the old man on a case. They were in an old house on Clay where the newlyweds renovating the place swore that they'd seen the translucent image of a ten-year-old girl dancing in the top bedroom on a couple of occasions since buying the property.

What were the chances of something happening that night?

'Does the fish ever know when the fisherman's net is about to fall?' Tommy had replied. 'We're dealing with something we know very little about. Better to forget all about mathematical probability for now and just wait to see what happens.'

'But we could wait here all night and not see anything?' Jay had insisted.

Tommy's wrinkled face had simply stared back at him.

'But we could sit here for *weeks* and not see anything?' Jay had continued.

Tommy had tossed the tub of caffeine pills at him. 'I doubt it. I don't think this nice couple want two untidy guys like us in their new home for any longer than they have to.'

Sitting there in the corridor at Willoughby with the earpiece droning away in his left ear and the faint clicking of the Geiger counter in the hall echoing in his right, Jay tried to summarize what he knew about the case so far. There'd been three incidents that might have been connected with the paranormal, perhaps four. First: the great-aunts' alleged sighting of the ghost of Helena and Zelda's mother. Second: Sara Taft's experience out on the drive. Third: the paintings in the hall. Fourth: the clock that had stopped at some point during the last few days.

Jay immediately dismissed the first and last of these from his thoughts. The great-aunts were hardly the most reliable witnesses, as he and Zelda had agreed in San Francisco (and as everyone else was quick to point out when the subject was raised earlier on), and what they claimed they'd seen couldn't be used as the basis for an investigation. As for the clock? It could have stopped for any number of reasons and at any point. Moving on to the incident involving Sara Taft, it was hard to know what to do. Any kind of investigative angle bound up in the woman's personal testimony was likely to lead him into all kinds of investigative dead ends. For a start, the event was now six days old and Sara's account of it would almost certainly be corrupted by her own feelings of embarrassment, feelings that would have steadily grown in the interim until she'd convinced herself that it had all been a construction of her imagination, even if she had actually seen something. That Toby was her employer and that he was openly sceptical of the idea of something paranormal moving through the house and its grounds at night would have only added to her sense that she'd been frightened by shadows. That Toby and the other guests were also unsettled by recent events concerning Helena and Wallace Kelly's disappearance would also have added to the pressure on Sara Taft to believe that she'd encountered nothing more uncanny than her own heightened nerves.

That left the paintings. It had been plain to everyone in the hall earlier on that it was highly unlikely, if not impossible, that they'd been moved on the night in question by any kind of human agency, individual or collaborative. The Remicks' bedroom was nearest to the short staircase that led down to the half-landing and the hall beyond, its door not more than twenty feet away from the nearest of the paintings that had switched positions. Could one or more of the other guests have pulled the whole thing off without waking the Remicks? Perhaps the Remicks had moved them all? It wasn't likely. Molly Remick had fainted on seeing the paintings the following morning in clear sight of two witnesses and nothing about her suggested that she had either faked this or that she had any reason to conspire with her husband, her only possible co-conspirator, in an attempt to spook everyone. Jay also ruled out the Shipmans for similar reasons. What about Will Hooper and Johnny Fulton? As Johnny had said at the dinner table, he had better things to be doing with his nights. And if he had been involved, he would have either had to have let Meliza in on the plan or he would have had to have sneaked *out* and then back *in* to their room without waking her. Also, if he and Will Hooper had drunk as much as everyone else suggested they had the previous Thursday night, then surely it was a safe bet that it would have been difficult for them to have pulled off such a stunt without waking up the guests sleeping on the first floor at the very least.

But if none of the guests were responsible, then who or what was? Jay realized that he was reaching the end of what he knew and the beginning of the next phase of the investigation: the waiting, the watching and the wondering. He could sit there, looping through supposition after supposition trying to guess what had happened and never make any real progress. As Tommy had put it that first night up on Nob Hill: *best to wait and see if anything happened.*

Jay stretched and checked his watch again. It was coming up to one o'clock and time for his first tour of the house. Deciding to start from the top and work his way down, he took the stairwell all the way up to second floor where he made a slow circuit of the rooms and corridors. He looked into the attic rooms and scanned them with both the flashlight and the wand but found nothing but flat black signal. After that, Jay moved along the corridor to the door of the old nanny's room where Bessie was sleeping and saw that she'd left it slightly ajar, probably to allow a breeze to move through it. He peered through the crack between the door and the frame and could just about make out her sleeping figure in the darkness, her body and legs bunched up in a ball under the sheet, her face thrust into the skin of her elbow joint, the speaker unit for the baby's intercom perched on the spare pillow beside her head. Directly across the corridor was Jacob's room and Jay also peered in there, twisting the handle of the doorknob as far as it would go before gently pushing it open and sticking his head through the gap. More hot dry air, moonlight at the edges of the room's curtains giving Jay enough light to see without turning on his flashlight. He made a quick sweep of the room with the EMF wand and got a low burble in his left ear that most probably originated from Jacob's intercom unit. Then he switched the wand off for a moment and looked around. Bessie had told him that the room had been Helena's when she was a girl and there were still photos of her on the walls if little other evidence of her youthful occupation: a picture of her and Zelda in the hallway downstairs (five or six years old, he guessed), their hair bobbed short around their necks, a spangled Christmas tree behind them with a cityscape of parcels and boxes at its base;

a picture of an adolescent Helena in t-shirt and sweatpants receiving a trophy from some hoary headmistress at the side of a high school pool while a muscled swim coach stood by clapping, his lips pulled back into what looked like a proprietorial smile; a shot of the two girls blowing out the candles on a birthday cake the size of a golf cart while a blurred sea of adoring childish faces looked on; a picture of the two girls in what looked like Central Park; a picture of Helena at her junior prom, golden hair left to hang around her neck, glacial make-up (no adolescent garish splashes of rouge and lip gloss for Helena), one hand round a white bouquet, the other round a grinning young lad who looked at least three years younger than her though he was probably the same age. A few inches away there was a photo of Helena at her senior prom. Eighteen, perfect, beautiful and in total control of her considerable powers. Even her earlobes seem to radiate a staunchless and overpowering lust that suggested the smug quarterback at her side didn't stand a chance.

Jay moved across the room, treading silently across the carpet until he came to Jacob's cot. The baby lay there on the mattress, his translucent eyelids and thin amphibian lips shining in the moonlight, and as Jay looked down he couldn't stop himself from wondering what would *their* child have looked like, his and Helena's (what mix of her pale perfection and his own mongrel genes would have surfaced in their child's face?). For a moment it was all too easy to believe that Jacob was *his* son as he watched the rise and fall of the child's tiny torso and imagined the delicate clutch of his small fingers around his own. Jay reached down and touched the baby's foot, the toes like small peas, Jacob's skin like liquid in his fingers (Helena's child, he told himself, half *her*), before he tucked it back under the blanket's edge and moved on to the next room along the corridor. As Bessie had told him, the room had been Zelda's when she was a girl but had been used by Helena after she'd stopped sleeping in the same room as Toby earlier on in the year. Jay entered, his nose tingling as if it might catch some latent scent of her, and switched on the flashlight. Again, there was scant evidence of Zelda's childhood, but also an absence of any pictures on the wall except a watercolour of Willoughby that showed the east side of the house viewed from the Italian garden that lay beyond the loggia. A pile of clothes, presumably Helena's, were folded in piles on top of an armchair, a robe thrown across its back and a few personal effects scattered across the surface of a dresser next to it, and Jay passed the beam of his flash over each of these in turn: a pile of small change, tubs of creams and lotions and other cosmetics, some hairbrushes, a tangle of silver bracelets, an old watch, pairs of earrings, a box of tissues in a silver case.

Helena. Where was she?

She could be anywhere, he realized, and imagined her standing on a hotel balcony, looking out over a city horizon throbbing with light and traffic noise while Wallace slept in the room behind her. It could be New York, Paris, Milan, Barcelona, perhaps even London, he told himself, anywhere. There was the other possibility, that she was alone, Wallace's disappearance just a coincidence, but it seemed unlikely. Moving to the far side of the room, Jay came across a pair of photographs on the dresser propped up against the base of a small lamp. He picked them up and saw that the first was of Jacob lying in his cot in his blue romper suit, bright eyes looking up at the camera lens. The second showed Helena staring down at the child as she cradled him in her arms, also taken in the room next door, fingers stroking the child's forehead. Had she really abandoned Jacob? *Could* she have abandoned Jacob? It was hard to imagine but not impossible, not impossible for Helena, he realized, not for Helena Smiling who seemed to have made skipping out on people her lifetime's specialty.

Jay put the photos back where he'd found them and moved

out into the corridor where he checked that the passage outside Johnny and Meliza's room was empty before making his way to the top of the stairwell at the other end, taking the long way round to avoid triggering the motion-detector he'd positioned by the door to their room. On the floor below, there was less to do. All the rooms had people sleeping in them except the study adjoining Toby's bedroom and Jay simply looked in on his own room and that belonging to the great-aunts before peering down the main corridor from behind his camera and the motion detector and then descending to the ground floor. No paranormal phenomena. No ghouls, no ghosts. Not even a flicker of disturbance in the signal coursing into his left ear.

He switched the wand off. It was all useless, he told himself, but then also remembered Tommy's regular pronouncement, especially in those early days, that he was continually guilty of impatience. They'd be sitting there in the ruined mission, in the box of the dilapidated theatre left to crumble and rot, in the knave of the old church, in the car at the edge of the fogbound cemetery, the two of them staring at the lifeless read-outs hour after hour and it would always be Jay who'd be first to crack. The old man would try to calm him down, usually giving him some menial task to perform like cleaning out the coffee flask or driving to the local All-Nite to refill it and buy him more Deltas. 'That's why you smoke all that dope,' Tommy would say in his slow voice. 'You want the truth to come all at once, in a rush. If so, maybe this is the wrong job for you. No hard feelings if you want out. Not everybody is cut out for the life of a p.i.' The old man was at least partly right, Jay told himself, moving towards the door to the stairs that led down to the cellars and turning the wand back on. The humming flared slightly as he approached it, a tiny explosion of midrange static burning away in his left ear like a sunspot flaring on the surface of the gigantic black star. A junction box, Jay thought to himself, or some other accumulation of domestic circuitry. He flicked on his flash and guided the outstretched finger of light down into the cooler air of the basement. He could smell dust and moist cardboard and could hear the faint snoring of Willoughby's boilers, more electrical wiring figuring in his left ear like a lone wasp as he picked his way slowly down the steps. The sound of the boilers grew louder as Jay reached the bottom of the stairs and turned a corner, the door of the first cellar appearing to his left in the narrow shaft of white light. He brandished the EMF wand out in front of him and then twisted open the handle and let the door swing open. The footprint of the flashlight moved over trunks and boxes. Old furniture lay piled against the far wall, unneeded chairs stacked seat-to-seat and tables stacked top-to-top so that the upper partner's legs curled up into the air like those of a dead cockroach. There was also an old sofa piled high with cartons of discoloured linen (bedclothes? curtains? old table-cloths? Jay couldn't tell) and an old sewing machine that threw a shadow like a set of gallows on the side wall when he angled the beam at the upper corners of the cellar roof.

Jay let the door swing shut and scanned the next door on his right, a toilet that looked as if it had been the cutting edge of plumbing technology around the time Clemmy and Lobelia might have shared their first chaste kisses with handsome young troopers off to fight the Kaiser in the killing fields of Flanders and never used since. As for anomalous EMF readings? Nothing. The next room on Jay's left contained Willoughby's wine cellar (again, nothing) while the next door on his right housed the boiler room. As he scanned the room from the doorway there was the expected surge of murky bass noises in his ear like a section of tenor saxophones tuning up. The signal was loud and fluctuating but seemed cyclical enough to suggest that there was nothing out of the ordinary lurking amongst the hot moist shadows. Then Jay took one last look around the corner of the basement passage and found a door that led out to a short stairwell that looked as if it brought one up to ground level outside between the coach house and the kitchen. The door was locked and the wand picked up nothing and Jay turned and climbed the stairs. Back in the main corridor on the ground floor, he took a reading (nothing), and then another in the kitchen (nothing but the subdued peripheral vibrato of the appliances) and then more after that in the dining room, drawing rooms, ballroom, library and hallway (again, nothing). After that, he made a note of the time – it had gone one-thirty – and resolved to make another circuit of the house in an hour before walking back to the main corridor. There, Jay settled himself back on his seat and decided to review again the facts of the case so far. Yet going through it all seemed to throw up nothing new. All he had to go on were the paintings in the hallway. He sat there, staring down the corridor and soon found himself working through the events of the evening instead. Sometimes thinking about the *personalities* involved with a case rather than the *facts* gave one a fresh angle. But he'd already been through all this too. The only people who seemed convinced that there was something paranormal at work in the house were the two old bats in the room upstairs and nervous little Molly Remick. Even the sensation that Jay had felt when he'd first stepped into Willoughby's hall seemed to have disappeared and not returned. Yet something still tugged at the sleeves of his curiosity, a feeling that he'd missed something vitally important gossiping away with itself somewhere in the background of his mind while the earpiece crackled and fizzed in his ear.

Sunday is officially my day off (though it rarely seems to stop Pepé from ringing me and asking me to run some kind of errand for him) and I get up late and make myself a coffee before I pad around the mansion's gloomy corridors wondering what to do with myself.

•

The mansion itself fascinates me. It sometimes feels like a ghost town, except that a ghost town would probably have more in it, the possessions of the absent settlers lying around wherever it was they'd last been used or had last stood when catastrophe or *force majeure* had driven or removed their owners from their homes. The mansion is different in that it's almost completely empty. There's the small array of kitchen utensils (*one* plate, *one* knife, *one* fork and so on) and the coffee machine that Alita, Pepé's wife, lent me when I first moved in, but not much else. The cupboards and drawers in all the bedrooms are bare. The bathrooms are scrubbed clean and show little evidence of human occupation, not even a ring of dirt around the baths or around the vaulting golden dolphins whose job it is to spit water into them. The shelves in the reception rooms are empty though the occasional faint ring of dust hazily implies the footprint of the object that once stood on the spot in question just as the rectangles of dirt on the mansion's walls imply the presence of pictures and photographs at some point in the recent past. Even the beds in the seven other bedrooms are stripped down to their mattresses.

•

Can Jazmín, in comparison, buzzes with activity. From my vantage point up in the sunshine of the roof terrace, I spend a while surveying the villa on the other side of the bay.

•

The night before, you'd appeared at the top of the stairs and stared down at us, a towel wrapped loosely around you. 'Jean-Marc, who is it?' Again, your voice with its magnetic farrago of intensity and vulnerability. Jean-Marc introduced us but his mouth might as well have belonged to a fish in a tank. I was far too embroiled in the mauled disorder of your golden hair spilling around your flushed neck and shoulders to hear what he was saying, a helpless and hopeless wretch trying to keep his balance while the world ground round on its axis beneath his feet, a delirious jester bracing himself for the shockwave when you inevitably blinked and a million blue butterflies took off all at once in the summer skies of your eyes. Once I'd managed to restore electricity to the villa, you'd told Jean-Marc you were going to take a bath and disappeared again while he pulled a pair of beers out of the fridge and told me that the other guests had scurried off soon after they arrived to spend the day on Beniras beach where they could swim, shower and eat in the beachfront restaurant (I listened to him absent-mindedly, all the time picturing you upstairs as you undressed and slid into the water).

•

Now the other guests at the villa lounge around the side of the pool, the girls reading paperbacks and magazines or else just lying there in the sunshine while the boys smoke joints, drink beer and toss a football around in the water. I can make out twelve guests but neither you nor Jean-Marc are amongst them which suggests that there might be more of them inside or else in Portinax or San Joan (where are you and Jean-Marc, I wonder: in Portinax or San Joan? Or are you upstairs behind one of the shuttered windows?).

•

Over the next few days, I get a closer look at the latest inhabitants of Can Jazmín, dropping by the villa intermittently to deliver more water, to skim insects out of the pool, to check on the generator, any excuse to drive over and get a closer look at everyone, to get a closer look at Jean-Marc, to get a closer look at you. I learn that there are eighteen guests in total including you and Jean-Marc, and most of them soon adjust to my sporadic presence at the villa. Conversely, I steadily become familiar with most of them. Because I can't speak French, I can never be entirely sure of my conclusions but I gradually glean more and more about the network of their relationships from their intonation, their body language and the matrix of their questions, answers and silence as I steer the net though the glittering water and trim back the jasmine outside the kitchen. There's a short lad called Laurent, a stocky little joker whose easy familiarity with Jean-Marc suggests he's known him since childhood. There's Alain who also appears to be another childhood friend of Jean-Marc's, another sybaritic six-footer around whom the girls continually cluster like adoring moths even though none of them seem to be sleeping with him. As for the girls themselves, they're a fairly colourless bunch, silent and skinny and immaculately dressed, with remote sounding names like Jenay and Raissa and Céleste, the cadence of their voices (when they deign to open their mouths to speak) always flawlessly composed. When they need me to do something, to change a light-bulb or oil a whining shutter, they never ask me directly but get one of the boys to do it.

•

And, of course, there's Jean-Marc at the centre of everything. That he's rich and confident and handsome (if one can consider his thick yellow slop of hair, his blue eyes and fleshy face as *handsome*) is as self-evident as the five thousand dollar watch on his left wrist and the uncompromising timbre of command in his voice that is as decisive in asking for things as it is in giving them. Though everyone else at Can Jazmín seems to be rich too, or at least the product of a wealthy background, none of them seem to be as wealthy as him.

•

I'd first thought that the group's expedition to Ibiza had been a joint venture. But I soon learn that Jean-Marc has paid for Can Jazmín for the whole summer by himself and that the others are there as his guests. And this isn't the limit of his extravagance either. A few days after I first show up at the villa, Jean-Marc takes me to one side and counts out a wad of cash into my palm before asking me if I can hire him six jet-skis for the following day. I thumb through the money: about two and a half thousand pesetas.

'Most places, they hire them one hour at a time, I know,' he says authoritatively, 'but if you know someone who can offer a better price for the whole day . . .'

I say that I'll see what I can come up with and he tells me to make sure that I take a hundred pesetas for my time.

•

The more I get to know him, the more I'm staggered that someone my age might possess so much money. That such people exist isn't, of course, a surprise. But to see such a large wedge of pelf tangibly extracted from Jean-Marc's jeans as if it's spare change causes me to hesitate for a second before taking it, while his trust in me to handle his cash only makes his life seem even more remote from mine (though curiously it makes it seem *less* remote as well). After all, my sketchy existence – on Ibiza but also in Amsterdam before that and in London before that – still feels like the life of a teenager working a summer job. *Where did all his money come from?* I want to ask, though I know that this isn't so much a mystery as simply remarkable.

•

And Jean-Marc's at it again a day later, pressing another seven hundred pesetas into my palm and asking me to buy him as many cases of champagne as I can and to take another tip for myself, as much as I think is reasonable.

'I don't mind spending the money,' he confides as we stand in the sunshine in Can Jazmín's driveway. 'But I hate getting swindled just because I'm a visitor. I imagine you know someone who can do a deal.'

•

And what about *you*?

•

A few days earlier, I'd watched you almost get yourself arrested for shoplifting and the memory of the contemptuous flick with which you tossed the leather satchel into the bin comes back to me again and again as does the memory of the silky backs of your knees and thighs as you'd strolled calmly away from the smitten cop. Yet it quickly becomes clear that you, or your boyfriend anyway, can afford to buy a towering mountain of cheap handbags.

•

As for seeing more of you, it doesn't seem to happen during my first few visits to the villa. You're never there and you evade all of my rooftop vigils. And not only do I want to see you: I also want to see you and Jean-Marc *together*. What are the two of you like together? Do you seem to be in love with him? Do you have long and soulful conversations in the moonlight? Does he neglect you? Unfortunately, you're never there in the splash of light in the telescope's eyepiece and my guiding image remains the exchange I witnessed that first evening.

•

And what I really want, of course, is to find myself in the villa alone with you.

•

On your fifth day at the villa, I spend the morning driving around the island making a series of deliveries and then return to the mansion where I trudge up to the roof terrace, spark a joint and take my seat behind the telescope. Across the bay, the residents of the villa are scrambling their squadron of hire cars, presumably heading off to the beach, or lunch, or both. Three of the girls climb into a white Egret, three more into an amber Topaz. Alain tools down the camino in a cherry-red open-topped Alpha with another girl in the passenger seat and everyone else follows him in a series of 4x4s, a coral-green Switchback, a mean-looking Nullabor and a lumbering black Kodiak. *Why haven't you gone with them?* I lean back in my chair, take a drag on the joint and run a hand through my hair, a hot blast of sunlight hitting my forehead. Then I hunker back down behind the eyepiece. Your Silentium sits in the driveway on its own while the dust around it falls slowly back down to the ground. *Am I sure that I saw Jean-Marc climb into one of the cars? And am I sure that you hadn't been in any of them?*

I count back through the departing guests: three . . . three . . . two . . . four . . . two . . . three. That made seventeen including Jean-Marc who I was sure I'd seen behind the wheel of the Kodiak as it hurtled around the bend and down the hill through the trees. You hadn't been one of them.

●

Moments later, I'm sliding my jeep alongside yours and pitching across the drive with a couple of the twenty-litre cylinders of diesel from the huddle of spares Pepé keeps stored in the garage at the mansion.

'Is anyone home?'

I put down the containers and knock on the door to the main hall after I've opened it (it's unlocked, further confirmation that I'm on the right track). No answer. Then I pad into the main reception room and its inevitable disarray of handbags, sunglasses, beach towels and bottles of suncream. Crushed packets of cigarettes, lumps of hash and piles of rolling papers lie scattered over the coffee table along with piles of coins, rolled notes and CD cases with coke smudged across them. But the room is as empty as the kitchen and the veranda beyond it. You don't seem to be anywhere downstairs and I realize that I don't have an excuse to go upstairs and look for you.

'Hello?'

I turn around to see that you're lying on a wicker sofa in the corner and start slightly as if you've seen me doing something I shouldn't.

'It's Jay isn't it?'

•

You're lying back in the shadows with a book, a novel, *Fragments of Paradise*, a pale sarong swaddled around you, the diamond at the end of your necklace lying in the valve of your tanned throat.

'Yes, that's right,' I say.

'Helena,' you say, even though you've told me before.

'I've . . . come to top up the generator,' I say. 'I saw the jeep outside and thought I'd better warn whoever was in here that the power's going to be off for a couple of minutes.'

'The power's already off,' you say.

'Pardon me?'

'It's already off. I just turned it off. I wanted total silence for a few hours and the humming of the fridge was killing me.'

•

I don't know what to say to that. But then your eyes are already back on the page you're reading and an answer doesn't seem to be necessary so I go up to the roof and fill up the generator's fuel tank. *What are you trying to do here*, I ask myself, *what on earth do you think is going to happen?* As I screw up the cap to the tank, I shudder for a moment at the thought of the telescope across the bay, at how many hours I've spent up on the roof (I glance across at the mansion: it's a pale block, barely distinguishable from the other buildings sitting amongst the tumbling hillside vegetation.

Up there on my roof terrace, I'm probably nothing more than an indistinguishable light speck). *Get down there*, I tell myself as I trudge back to the ground floor, *say goodbye and leave before you make a fool of yourself.*

•

Back in the kitchen, I poke my head through the doorway to the veranda.

'I'm just going to wash my hands and then I'll be out of your way.'

'Okay,' you nod, licking a slender fingertip and turning a page as I slope over to the sink and twist the tap.

'Do you want a beer?'

'Pardon?'

'Do you want a beer?'

You're in the kitchen now, opening the door of the fridge and pulling out a couple of cans of Dos Equis. You've left the sarong out on the veranda and are standing there in a white bikini (I'm was standing metres away but feel the hairs on my forearms tremble), the diamond hanging from your necklace lying just above your breasts.

'I think they're cold enough,' you say, handing one to me before I've had a chance to dry my hands, an infinitesimal contact between your fingertips and mine. 'Let's see.'

You hoist yourself up on the counter-top and cross your legs, the bottom half of your bikini stretching across the tattoo of a Chinese dragon in green and red and black that arches over the jutting parabola of your left hip bone and down between your thighs. I open my beer and gulp a mouthful of froth.

'Where are all the others?'

'Three of the girls have got a lunch date in Talamanca with some American guys they met at some bar a couple of nights back. Everyone else has gone fishing. Jean-Marc hired a boat so I guess they won't be back till this evening.'

'Why didn't you go with them?'

'I felt like a day off.' You sip your beer, a glob of condensation dripping off the end of the tilted can and on to the upper surface of your left thigh (a fingertip lazily swipes at the drip). 'It's gets a bit tough being the only girl around here who's not French.'

'So how did you guys meet?'

'Me and Jean-Marc?'

I nod.

'We met at a party last Christmas.'

'Where?' I ask, imagining some exclusive reception.

'At this resort on Langkawi,' you reply.

'Where's that?'

'Western Malaysia, maybe eighty or so miles north of Penang. Jean-Marc was there with a girlfriend, some Austrian countess called Etti his father set him up with. He fell out with her halfway through the trip and sent her home.'

'And who were you there with?' I ask, taking another sip of froth and not bothering to ask what it was that Etti and Jean-Marc had argued about.

'How do you know I wasn't there on my own?' you ask.

'I don't.'

'I *was* there on my own.'

You slide forwards off the counter and land on your bare feet. 'I travelled around Asia last year and ended up hooking up with this exiled Cuban poet. I stayed at his house for a while on the coast near Da Nang in Vietnam. When I got tired of that, I left and ended up in Langkawi.'

You walk across the room, then twist and drop on to a sofa.

'And where do you live now,' I ask, 'with Jean-Marc?'

You bite your lip.

'I guess I don't really live *anywhere* at the moment. I mainly grew up in North Carolina though we used to spend some time in New York. My family has a house on the Cape Fear River and has lived there for centuries so I guess that's the place I'd call home. But I've been travelling pretty much straight for three years now, first through South America, then Africa and then Asia last year. I only go back home every once in a while. I've been staying with Jean-Marc in Paris for the last few months but I don't really like it there. It's like that old song from the sixties says: Europe's *too old, too cold, and too settled in its ways.*

We're talking across the distance of several metres. It seems stupid for me to stay in the kitchen so I walk over and sit down on the sofa leaving maybe half a metre between us.

'What about you? You look part Asian.'

'I'm half Chinese,' I tell you. 'I was born in San Francisco but my parents moved to England soon after. I lived there until a couple of years ago. I moved to Amsterdam, stayed there for a while, and now I'm here.'

Then neither of us says anything. Somewhere outside, a dog barks, a scooter putts its way up the hill, the sound of the engine getting louder and then Doppler-shifting away into the distance. A distant door slams. Insects fry in the undergrowth.

'You want to listen to some music?' you ask eventually.

'Why not?'

'I'll go and turn the power back on.'

You get up, your hips drifting past my face as you walk out of the room. A minute later, the villa fridge starts to hum with life and you reappear with a small bag which you put on the floor and open up, pulling out CDs and make-up and spare bikinis. A couple of photographs fall out from between the pages of a notebook tied together with pieces of string and when you notice them lying face down on the rug beside your knees, you slide one back out of sight and hand the other to me.

'That's Willoughby, my father's house in North Carolina,' you say, reaching across and putting on some old jazz. 'You know Billie Holiday and Lester Young?'

'I know Billie Holiday,' I reply, wondering about the photograph you'd tucked away and wondering why you've just described Willoughby as your *father's* house.

'My mom's favourite music. "Lady Day and The Prez" she used to call them. Apparently they both had terrible lives.'

So there *was* a mother somewhere or there had been at some point in the past. The sound of a piano materialized in the room's hot air, followed by the soft, fleshy undertone of a saxophone. You say that you're going to roll a joint and I take a look at the photo you've put in my hand, a picture of a you outside a sprawling white house. You're squinting into bright sunlight, eyes narrowed, your mouth tensed in a flat line across your face.

'How old were you when this was taken, sixteen?' I ask.

'Seventeen,' you say, kneeling beside me and looking over my shoulder at the picture, your shoulder grazing mine (do you hear the breath stop in my throat?).

'But I only *took* that one.' You point at the girl outside the house. 'That's not me. It's my sister, Zelda.'

'You're twins?' I ask idiotically.

'What do you think?'

•

I don't know how long it is that we sit there in the prismatic light of the villa, smoking joints and drinking warm beer with the music pulsing away in the background. I listen to you tell me about Zelda ('desperately serious,' you say, 'training to be a doctor back home') while my eyes suck up every last detail about you, the tortoiseshell comb in your golden hair, the smoothness of your gathered knees, the glistening film of fine hairs on your forearms.

•

For identical twins, you tell me, you and Zelda are very different. You were born ten minutes apart: Zelda first, you second. But immediately after that, your lives operated for several years as mirrors for each other, a repetitive cycle of matching clothes and hairstyles, of parallel meals and parallel bedtimes and presents given in pairs, comments always addressed to the both of you, rarely to each of you individually.

'I guess all parents think of their children as miracles,' you say (I wonder what my parents thought of me, for that brief and unreachable time), 'just think of all the generations of family resemblances our parents have seen in our faces and gestures. It must be like seeing ghosts. And when it comes to twins, it must seem like the same miracle *squared*.'

It was only later on, you tell me, that you and Zelda gradually developed separate personalities.

'We didn't go around finishing each other's sentences,' you say, 'we didn't go around playing tricks on our parents or on boys or teachers, pretending to be one another or anything like that. And we had separate friends and separate interests.'

•

You're sitting centimetres away from me, the photograph of Zelda and Willoughby the only thing between us, a faint and humid flush spread out across your cheeks, your mouth glistening with beer. The skin at the small of your back seems to be made up of a magical substance as are the cobalt pools of your eyes and when you push a strand of hair away from your face, the sensation of what it would be like to crush you back against the cushions feels like it's been lurking dormant in my synapses since birth.

'Of course, there *is* the telepathy,' you add.

'Telepathy?' I stare at you.

'Telepathy,' you repeat, leaning closer (there are strips of silver rainclouds in your blue irises). 'You've heard of *twin's intuition?*' you breathe. I nod slowly. 'Well, sometimes Zelda and I know what the other is thinking.'

'Seriously?'

Your lips press together in a line, like Zelda's mouth in the photograph, like the wings of a hovering seabird. Then they move and the seabird disappears to reveal the glinting tips of your teeth. 'No, of course not,' you laugh. Our faces are centimetres from each other and I can feel the percussion of your breath on my skin. A song finishes and another one starts, some piano and then the words drifting towards us through greywhite nebulae of hash smoke . . . *don't want my mammy, I don't need a friend* . . . I must have listened to Billie Holiday a hundred times like everyone else on the planet . . . *my heart is broken, it won't ever mend* . . . but this time feels like the first . . . *I ain't much caring just where it will end, I must have that man* . . . I could place a hand on each side of your face and kiss you. What would you do then? Your mouth is apparently forming words. You seem to be telling me that this was your mother's favourite song and that you remember you and your sister watching your parents dancing to it when you were little girls . . . *I need that person much worse 'n just bad, I'm half alive and it's drivin' me mad* . . . *I must have that man* . . . they used to have lavish parties at the house in the photograph every summer, hundreds of people converging on Willoughby's gardens, a live orchestra playing till daylight, tables of cocktails on the terrace, fireworks in the garden. I just sit there, barely making sense of what you're saying as I imagine rubbing my lips against the nape of your neck and placing a hot dry hand on your naked stomach (a mystified expression would dapple your face, your eyelids would flutter shut, your hips searching out my hand). I'm vaguely conscious of the sun lowering itself into the sea beyond the garden as my arm finds itself draped across the back of the sofa towards the supple skin of your bare shoulders. Again, a song finishes and another starts. You gaze out through the window, start to sing along in a low whisper and the profile of your lips blanks out everything else in the universe for a slow and beautiful second . . . *like a summer with a thousand Julys, you intoxicate my soul with your eyes* . . . you turn back to face me (fine, nothing else exists for now except you) . . . *and I'm certain that this heart of mine, hasn't a ghost of a chance in this crazy romance* . . . and there's a moment that you know that I know that you've let me touch your hair (it hovers there, sunlight light on the back of my hand) . . . *you go to my head* . . . surely there's nothing left for us except the voluptuous abyss of a kiss?

11

When Jay came round on the floor of the corridor, daylight hazing in through the side door by the kitchen, the image was there in his mind already, as if it had quietly sneaked in during the night, taken a seat next to him and patiently waited for him to notice it hanging around: the argument in the library between Zelda and Toby. *Can I remind you*, Toby had said the night before, *that your sister obviously had a questionable commitment to Willoughby before she abandoned her child and ran off with Wallace Kelly?* Toby had used the pluperfect: 'your sister *had* a questionable commitment . . .'

Why?

Jay pulled himself up on to his feet, planted himself back on the chair and considered how Bessie and Toby had each independently characterized all of Helena's previous affairs as transient: Toby had been insistent about this and had seemed just as certain in the library yesterday afternoon that Helena's latest affair would be similarly brief. Was there any secret reason for the Englishman to believe that Helena's fling with Wallace Kelly was going to be any less fleeting? In the library the night before, he'd talked about Helena as if she was now an irrevocable part of the past, that she wasn't coming back, that she wasn't coming back to Willoughby.

Jay told himself to dismiss the idea as soon as he'd had it (that Helena was *dead*, that Toby had killed her). He was being ridiculous. More than that, he was being ridiculously jealous. But the thought still remained in his head: some kind of paranormal force had moved the paintings. Though nothing out of the ordinary had occurred the night before, Jay was still sure of it . . . *how else could the twenty-two paintings have switched places in the middle of the night?* The rest of the theory fell into place with the precision and velocity of a freeway pile-up: there could be no haunting without a death ... the potentially paranormal events occurring at Willoughby had occurred in the days directly following Helena's disappearance ... Toby was running out of money ... he'd killed Helena to gain control of the Smiling fortune. Nothing about their marriage suggested that there was any love left in the relationship and weren't the highest percentage of homicides carried out by spouses?

Jay also reminded himself that there wasn't a Smiling fortune any longer if Bessie's account of things was to be trusted, just the sprawling house that would one day be passed on to Jacob. As for Toby's emphatic insistence that Helena belonged to the past (this bound up in the way he'd talked about her), his grammar hardly identified him as a murderer and Jay was almost certainly reading far too much into it. Perhaps Toby really believed that Helena might stay with Wallace and leave him for good this time? Also, Helena had run off with Wallace Kelly as she had with many other men previously (including Jay himself), but this time she'd cuckolded Toby in front of two hundred assembled guests and done it while their child slept in a room upstairs, all reason enough for Toby to feel more bitter than ever before and to accept that she was lost to him.

Jay now remembered that Toby had even admitted as much to him in the library yesterday. The man seemed to have had enough, seemed ready to dissolve the marriage. *But what about the paintings?* Jay realized he was going round in circles and told himself that he was tired and homesick for San Francisco and locked into some kind of process of perverse wish fulfilment that had him imagining that Toby and Helena's marriage had ended in the ultimate failure.

It was then that the light flickered in the corridor and a figure appeared at the side door. It was Mrs Taft. She caught sight of Jay as she stepped inside and paused before speaking.

'Good morning, Mr Richards,' she called out down the corridor.

'Good morning,' Jay replied.

'I'd like to open up the downstairs rooms if that's all right.'

Jay asked her to give him five minutes and she walked into the kitchen while he went out into the hall and scanned the screen of his powerpad. Thankfully nothing seemed to have happened while he'd slept and there were only three entries in the log.

00:38:52	Camera 01
01:32:23	Camera 01
06:44:22	Camera 01

Jay checked the three files, three clips of him bank-robbing his way around the hall, the first showing him priming and checking his equipment the night before, the second showing him checking the hallway at the end of his first and only tour of the house, the third showing him walking up to the table and deactivating the software seconds earlier. No footage from the camera on the first floor and no signals recorded from the motion detector on the top floor, not even after he'd fallen asleep. Jay stared up at the walls, half expecting the pictures to be back in their correct places. But they were still where they'd hung the night before.

Mrs Taft appeared in the hall.

'Are you done here, Mr Richards?'

Jay could see the question, the *other* question, poised on her lips, a question that she couldn't quite bring herself to voice out loud. *Had anything happened*? And he felt that her opinion of him was victim of a similar indecision. She thought of him as a meddling outsider, some kind of conman from California who earned a living from claiming that ghosts existed. Of course, in Mrs Taft's universe, ghosts didn't exist – but how could she then explain what had been going on in the house?

'It must have been a real shock,' he said, as gently as he could, 'for you more than any of the others, to see that all the paintings in the hall had moved.' He wondered if she'd take the bait and open up, perhaps say something about what she'd witnessed out on the drive. But she didn't answer.

'Well, nothing extraordinary happened last night,' he continued, seeing that this also did little to soothe her unease. She told him that she'd laid out some breakfast on the table in the kitchen and then proceeded towards the first of the shutters while Jay went through to the kitchen where he inhaled a jam sandwich and a cup of coffee. Mrs Taft re-entered the kitchen just as he was draining a second cup and he asked her to mention to the guests that they shouldn't touch the equipment before going upstairs to his room where he slept in his clothes. A couple of hours later, the ceiling reappeared in front of his eyes. Jay stared at it for a while and then negotiated the shower on automatic pilot, all the time telling himself that his earlier suspicions were ludicrous. After he'd dressed, he came out of his room to find Mrs Taft in the great-aunts' room next door. The two old maids looked as is if they hadn't moved since Jay had looked in on them the previous evening.

'Can I help you, Mr Richards?' Mrs Taft asked as she poured a cup of tea.

'I was just wondering if you'd seen Zelda this morning.'

'I think Miss Smiling is still asleep. She hasn't come in for breakfast so far.'

'What about Toby?'

He was in his study, she told him, or maybe in the nursery. Jay tried the study first, knocking on the door with two short taps of his knuckles.

'Who is it?'

'It's me, Jay.'

'Come in.'

Jay breathed in . . . *this was the man he suspected of murdering Helena* . . . if it had all seemed like an intellectual exercise earlier on, then as Jay reached for the doorknob he was struck by the reality of what he was proposing, that Toby had killed her, that she was dead, that she didn't exist. He noticed his hands trembling.

On the other side of the door, Toby sat in a leather chair by his desk, CNN muted on a small TV on one of the bookshelves that covered the entire right side of the room. A cigarette smoked away between his bristled lips and Jay was surprised that a tumbler of scotch wasn't sitting on his blotter next to his copy of *American Venture*, even though it was just after ten.

He swivelled to face Jay. 'Anything to report?' he asked briskly.

Jay shook his head. 'Nothing.'

Toby exhaled as if to say he'd thought as much, his bloodshot eyes seeming to settle on Jay's because they couldn't be bothered to look anywhere else. 'What did you do?' he asked.

'As you might have seen already this morning,' Jay replied, 'I've set up various pieces of equipment around the house. Most of it is in the hallway because that's where the paintings are. But I've also placed devices on the main corridor on the first floor and on the corridor above. None of it registered anything potentially paranormal last night.'

He watched as Toby absorbed this information, the idea in his mind that Toby had killed Helena seeming more and more ridiculous. The man didn't look guilty, he just looked bitter and angry.

'So what do you propose to do next?' Toby asked.

'All I can do is monitor the house again tonight and see what happens.'

Toby's eyes narrowed but he didn't say anything. Jay guessed he'd said all he had to say on the subject the night before and wasn't about to repeat himself. 'Today, I'm going to travel into Wilmington and have a look at the plans of the house as I mentioned yesterday. To be honest, I don't think they'll tell me anything tremendously useful. But I haven't got much else to do and I might as well be as thorough as I can.'

Toby blew smoke out of his nostrils and looked at Jay with an expression in his eyes that suggested that he didn't care how thorough Jay was.

'Is there a car I can borrow to get to Wilmington?'

Toby replied that Sara might be able to spare hers and Jay went to look for her, eventually finding her in the nursery watching Jacob stare listlessly at the toys on his plastic mat. Might Jay be able to borrow her car? No (she might need it, she told him), but Lara was due to leave for another shift at the restaurant where she worked in a few minutes. Perhaps she could give him a lift? Mrs Taft called home to arrange things from a phone downstairs while Jay watched over the baby, hoping that it wouldn't move or do anything that required him to engage with it. In the end, Jacob simply lay there and stared back at him until Mrs Taft returned and told Jay that he could wait for Lara outside the front of the house. A few moments later Jay loitered under the portico until an old blue Gazelle came clanking down the short drive that led to the Taft's cottage.

'You Jay?' the girl behind the wheel asked after she'd leaned across and opened the passenger door.

Jay nodded.

'Hi, I'm Lara.'

She pulled away down Willoughby's drive, the Gazelle's suspension almost as bad as Jay's car back home. And by the time they'd got to the end of the drive, everything else about the Gazelle seemed as bad as the Apache, if not worse: the torn upholstery, the broken air-con, the tangled seat belt that strapped Jay back in his seat like a deer caught in a net, the passenger window that only wound down a couple of inches, the clutter of candy-wrappers and empty soda-cans on the floor. But it was also similar to the Apache in that there was the unmistakable odour of marijuana in the car behind the stale cigarette smoke and the smell of the brittle foam of its shabby seats. As for Lara herself, it seemed to Jay that she resembled her mother more than her father. She didn't seem particularly tall, though it was hard to tell while she was seated and driving. And she had her mother's muddy hair, pulled back behind her ears to reveal a cheap jangle of earrings hanging from her earlobes, and her mother's heavy forehead and eye sockets.

'So, *you're* the ghosthunter?' she said eventually, looking sideways at him as they pulled out on to the main road. Jay could hear the mixture of suspicion and fascination in her voice that ended up sounding gently sarcastic. Typical smart teenager.

'Yup, that's right,' he replied, allowing his mouth to form a smile. 'Your mother told you about me?'

Lara nodded.

'I don't think she trusts me.'

'She's just been scared is all,' Lara replied.

'And what about you?' Jay asked. 'I've spoken to everyone else but I haven't yet asked you if you've seen anything strange happen around the house or the gardens.'

'Well, nothin' except all the pictures in the hallway movin' around. Isn't that fucked up enough?'

'You think something paranormal moved them?'

'I dunno anythin' about anythin' paranormal. But they sure didn't move by themselves. And I don't think anybody could've moved them all without wakin' everybody up. What do you think? You're the expert.'

'I think pretty much the same as you at this point. The difficult part is proving it. What about your mother's experience out on the drive?'

'I just figure she had a turn. She was tired from the night before. And this whole business goin' on recently with Helena runnin' off again.'

Lara pulled out a pack of Naylor Lights and took one out before offering them to Jay. He extracted one, really wanting a joint, and lit it after she'd lit hers.

'That's all I know,' she continued, blowing smoke against the windshield.

'Me too. So far.'

They drove for a few minutes without speaking, travelling back along the route Jay's cab had taken the day before, back over Sixty Bridge and on through the trees that tilted in close over the tarmac. Jay asked Lara where she worked.

'Place called "Nicole's".'

'What's that?'

'It's a restaurant in the city. I wait tables there.'

'Is it a good place to work?'

'S'okay. The owner, guy called Dan, he can be a bit of an asshole. But it's only a job. And it's not forever.'

Jay asked her how long she'd been working there and she told him: a couple of years. She was saving up to go travelling.

'I want to go to Europe and see shit, y'know? Thought I might even go to England. What's *that* like?'

Jay laughed.

'What's so funny?'

'Nothing. I couldn't think of anywhere more boring. It's like that old song says: England's just too old, too cold and just too settled in its ways.'

Lara looked across at him with a blank expression.

'Say *what*?'

'Never mind.'

Jay looked out the window as the car moved through the landscape. Soon they hit the main freeway and were flying across the Cape Fear River a few minutes later, the *USS North Carolina* lying in the water to their left, Wilmington spreading itself out in front of them on the far bank in neat orderly lines.

'Where do you want me to let you out?' Lara asked. Jay had been planning to ask her if she knew any car rental offices in the city but then felt his stomach gurgle. He was starving. He probably hadn't eaten more than a couple of mouthfuls since leaving San Francisco.

'Do you know anywhere where I can get a decent sandwich?'

'A sandwich?'

'Yes, a sandwich.'

Lara thought for a second, tapping her ringed fingers against the steering wheel as they came to a stop at an intersection on the other side of the river. 'I could take you to Chandler's Wharf. It's like this new development with a whole load of cafés and restaurants, should be able to find somethin' there.'

Jay said it sounded good to him and Lara cut across a lane of honking cars to make a left. A minute or so later, she pulled over.

'This is it. Hope you get somethin' to eat.'

Jay thanked her for the ride and unbuckled his belt.

'See ya back at the house,' she called out through the passenger window, her hand reaching for the handbrake.

'Lara, wait, before you go . . .'

The girl looked at him.

'What?'

Jay opened the door again – no use trying to talk to her through the inch of air between the top of the window and the door frame – and tried to sound as casual as he could.

'Lara, this is a difficult thing to ask. But do you know where I can score? I figured you might know someone.'

Lara stared at him.

'You talkin' about weed?'

'Yes.'

'And you're being straight with me, no bullshit? My mom would kill me if she found out.'

Jay held up his hand. 'I don't want you to get into any trouble. I just want to get high. If you can put me in touch with someone you know, that would be great. If not, well, that's the way it is.'

Lara looked at him to see if he was being honest. Then her shoulders dropped. She trusted him.

'I'll talk to my friend Eric,' she said. 'He might be able to sort something out. I'll let you know.'

Jay nodded and they exchanged numbers before he watched her drive away and then started his search for food. Ten minutes later, he was sitting on a bench staring out across the river with a pastrami-on-rye, mustard spread across one piece of bread, mayo across the other, red onion, pickle, lettuce and slivers of steak tomato folded into the layers of meat. It wasn't anything special, not by the standards of his regular sandwich establishments back home. It wasn't a bacon 'n' Brie on seven-grain with salad and cranberry mayo from DeLucchi's in North Beach. It wasn't even a hot asparagus, ham and melted Swiss from Café Baroni in Menlo Park or a chicken cutlet caprese from Molinari's or a club supreme from the San Francisco Sub-Machine on Haight. But it was food, food orthogonal enough for him to eat, and he was hungry. Jay sat there, chewing away for ten minutes. After that, he flagged down the next cab that passed and climbed in.

'Where to?' the driver asked.

'I need to rent a car. Do you know a rental firm based near here?'

'Your best bet would be the airport,' the driver replied.

At Wilmington International, jetliners rumbled through the sky while the rep who herded Jay around the lot insisted on telling him that every model they passed 'was an extremely good deal'. Jay eventually found a gleaming black Apache that made his own look like something that had been left at the bottom of a river for a couple of years and duly handed over a wad of Zelda's money for a week's rental. Then he was back on the open road, the leathery interior of the polished car all

Ls as he headed towards the city. He slid a disc into the player, a rampant piano introduction from Johnny 'The L' Lewis heralding the arrival of the one and only Lester Willis Young ('President of the Tenor Sax' or 'The Vamps' depending on whose story you believed) who scorched his way through 'Lester Swings', ride cymbals clattering in the background courtesy of Jo Jones, Gene Ramey's bassline lamping away underneath it all. Jay's next stop was Wilmington City Library, the map in the glove-box telling him that it was over on the east side of the city.

12

Spectacled staff at the reception desk told Jay that 'Local History and Culture' could be found on the second floor. Up he went, the other library users drifting around him like ornamental fish in a tank, and he eventually found the department he was looking for on the far side of the building from the elevators. There was a wooden counter with a pile of ledgers on it, a clipboard that looked like some kind of petition next to an assortment of leaflets and a name plate that read 'Ms Pandora A Wyatt'.

'Can I help you?' a middle-aged woman asked, peering up at him from a computer at least a couple of feet beyond the other side of the counter.

'Yes,' replied Jay. 'Are you Ms Wyatt?'

The woman nodded.

'My name is Jay Richards. I'm currently engaged in a project for Toby Charteris and Zelda Smiling over at Willoughby. Lord Charteris said you might be able to let me have a look at the old diagrams of the house that John Smiling loaned to the library.'

'Which diagrams are you referring to specifically, Mr Richards?' the woman replied, still not bothering to move from her seat. The clipped way she spoke left a space in between each word, tiny but discrete gaps during which Jay could almost hear the whirr of the air conditioner above her computer and the cooling fan of the computer itself.

'I'm not sure yet,' he called out, hoping they weren't going to have to continue yodelling at each other. 'What have you got?'

'You won't be able to look at *all* of them,' she replied briskly, remaining in her chair. 'The documents are very old and are *painstakingly* stored by the library so as to preserve them. This isn't a dentist's surgery where we just hand out them out like magazines.'

Jay took a deep breath and tried to keep a grip on his manners.

'Has the library archived them on microfiche?' he asked, even though several other responses jostled at the back of his throat.

'Yes.' Ms Pandora A Wyatt still didn't move. 'Do you have some kind of documentation on you?' she challenged.

'No,' Jay replied. He pulled out the envelope which had previously contained the money Zelda had paid him and on which she'd written the number for the house. 'You could call Willoughby and talk to Lord Charteris or Miss Smiling if you like, or, failing that, even Sara Taft who's the housekeeper there. They'll be able to verify who I am if that's what you require.' He struggled to keep his voice even and just about managed it. 'I have the number here if you've mislaid it.'

'No one here at the library is in the habit of mislaying things,' she replied, putting up no kind of similar struggle of her own and placing her emphases with as much painstaking care as she seemed sure the library lavished on its historical documents. Then she got out of her chair with a reluctance that Jay could almost smell, straightened her blouse and skirt, and told him to wait where he was while she disappeared into a back office. A moment later she reappeared with a tray of small brown files.

'All information pertaining to historic architecture is catalogued alphabetically by county,' she informed him, 'with the name of each property logged alphabetically after that. You'll find a viewer just beyond the aisle over there.'

Ms Wyatt pointed over to a set of terminals just visible through a corridor of book spines and Jay thanked her as graciously as he could before taking his seat at the first terminal of three. He turned on the machine and filtered through the tray while it warmed up: Beaufort County, Bertie County, Bladen County . . . *Brunswick County*. He pulled the file, took out the envelopes inside and started looking through them, fingering his way through the indexed labels that had things like 'Bald Head Lighthouse' and 'Brunswick County Courthouse' and 'Fort Anderson' and 'Walker-Pyke House' written on them. Amongst them, he found an envelope labelled 'Thackeray' and finally one marked 'Willoughby' right at the end. Jay opened this last one and extracted the first of several slim sheets of celluloid from its paper wrapper and placed it in the viewer.

A blurred map was the first thing to appear on the screen, Jay focused the image until he could see it.

Carte General de la Caroline

There was a legend underneath the title in French that was more or less unintelligible to Jay except for the words '*Chez PIERRE MORTIER (Libraire)*' and a date: 1696. Printed in black ink underneath this was a map of the state as it had appeared to cartographers back then. Nothing much there for Jay except a pretty picture. He twiddled the dials and scanned through more of the records. Much of it turned out to be text, lists and legal documents and contracts and certificates that may or may not have been land licences or title deeds of some kind, many of them in French. But there were also pictures, schematics of the house when it was first built (a comparatively modest set of two-storey accommodations completed in 1730 as far as Jay could make out), maps of the surrounding land as it had evolved throughout the eighteenth century and illustrations of the various facilities vital to the running of a vast plantation: a saw mill, a clay pit, a brick works, wharves on the banks of the river, stables, a blacksmith's workshop, slave quarters some distance from the main house and a cemetery even further away, probably reserved for the slaves once they'd toiled their way into early graves. There were also pictures of old Smiling (or 'von Smiling' as it was sometimes written) patriarchs, some of whom Jay thought he recognized from the pictures in the hallway at Willoughby though he couldn't be sure, admitting to himself that one smug and pudgy-faced autocrat in a wig looked pretty much like another. Scrolling on through the archives, it looked as if the von Smiling estate had originally stretched much further south towards the Cape than it did now and was made up of land that now belonged to the naval base. And as he scrolled on further, Jay finally found diagrams of Willoughby as it now existed. The date of the completion of the rebuilding of the house, as far as he could make out, had been 1826. And there it was, a floor-by-floor layout that tallied with the mental picture he'd constructed the evening before.

For a moment, Jay wondered if he should ask Pandora Wyatt if he could see the originals and perhaps even if she could make him some copies. But the diagrams didn't tell him anything he didn't already know and there didn't seem to be any other plans on file relating to plumbing or the laying of the house's foundations or underground water sources or any other information that might have been useful, however tangentially. Jay considered this for a moment and also realized that even if there had been, these probably wouldn't have taken him much further in terms of his investigation than where he was already. Perhaps there might have been something useful to discover if he was taking the great-aunts' testimony seriously. They could have been disturbed by a noise that was simply a product of the house shifting on its foundations or old and ailing pipes and interpreted this in the confusion of waking as something uncanny. But nothing in the diagrams could explain why the paintings had moved, nothing at all.

Jay scrolled on a bit further, almost for the sake of it, a whim, and it was then that he came across a map of the eastern section of Brunswick County, '1855' in a box in the top right hand corner with the von Smiling plantation delineated by a thick black line that surrounded an area of faint grey shading. It showed the house, represented by a small black rectangle, sitting at the northern tip of the shaded area and also two large bodies of water that sat within the plantation's boundaries. The largest of these was labelled 'Willoughby Pond', a long thin stretch of water that was approximately half the size of the entire Willoughby plantation and sat directly to the northwest of Willoughby between the house and the River Road, its eastern end narrowing at a point where Jay guessed the Sixty Bridge sat before flowing onwards towards the Lower Cape Fear River in a thin wavering line that was labelled 'Willoughby Creek'. The second body of water sat a little to the south of this and was much smaller even though it was curiously labelled 'Willoughby *Lake*', a small circular opening in the surrounding forest directly to the north of where the house's ornamental gardens now stood and not more than a quarter of a mile from the house itself.

Also shown on the map was Thackeray, the Kelly house, another black rectangle that sat just on the other side of Willoughby Pond and River Road from the von Smiling land. It couldn't have been more than a mile from Willoughby. As for the Kelly Plantation itself, it was delineated by a series of light cross-hatchings that stretched west from the house and described an area that was at least half as big again as its neighbour's property. Jay whistled softly to himself. If the Smilings were (or, at least, *had* been) rich then what did that make the Kelly? Did Wallace Kelly still own it all? Yes, he did. Zelda had told Jay that Wallace only rented out his land to various farming concerns.

Jay snapped off the terminal's backlight and rubbed his eyes. Somehow he felt as if he was making progress even if he couldn't actually define what this progress was. Perhaps it was just knowing more about Willoughby: its history, its surrounding landscape and its proximity to the Kelly land. It all seemed to mean *something*, though what this was exactly, he couldn't tell. One thing was clear: the microfiche archives were a highly frustrating way of going about finding more information. There were simply too many blurry old documents concerned with insignificant details. Jay got up and returned the box of files to the counter where Pandora Wyatt muttered barely audible thanks before taking them back into the far office. When she reappeared she seemed surprised to see Jay still standing there.

'Is there anything else I can help you with?' she asked.

'Yes. Could you point me in the direction of the library's card index? I need to look up a few things.'

'You won't be able to take any books out,' she replied smartly. 'This is a reference department except in the rarest of circumstances.'

Jay almost snapped but caught himself just in time. 'I won't be taking them much further than the nearest reading table.'

'The department's index can be found over on the far wall,' she said in a thin voice. 'An electronic index of the library's complete catalogue can be found on the first floor.'

Ten minutes later, Jay was pulling a series of hardbacks he'd listed on a piece of scrap paper from the bookshelves, aware of Ms Wyatt staring across at him occasionally. *A History of North Carolina's Coastal Plain* by D R Pell. *Great Plantation Houses of the Carolinas* by Lucas Crocombe. *The Economic History of the Lower Cape Fear River, 1710–1945* by Professor Patrick Gary. A dry bunch of titles by anyone's standards, Jay thought to himself as he carried them to a reading table (though perhaps not by the standards of the Wicked Witch of the Reference Section). But they allowed him nonetheless to collate a coherent history of Willoughby and the Smiling family. In 1714, after massacring the majority of the local Tuscarora Indians in a final ambush that ended a three-year war with the natives, a Swiss playboy (this was the exact term used by Pell) called Herbert von Smiling parcelled off just over twenty-two thousand acres of swampland on the banks of the Cape Fear River which he then drained at colossal financial expense and at the cost of hundreds of slaves' lives, both indigenous slaves and 'new' slaves brought over in ships from West Africa. In spite of this (or, to put it more accurately, *because* of this), the land soon started yielding vast rice harvests that brought von Smiling a substantial annual profit. Then, in 1724, the huge plantation was split in two, an eight thousand acre plot to the east retained by von Smiling himself while a larger twelve thousand acre plot further inland was sold to a man named Francis Kelley, a distant cousin ('by marriage' one of the writers specified) who also wanted to build an empire in the New World. Exactly why the land was partitioned seemed to be an issue on which the three historians couldn't agree. One rumour in the Gary book suggested that the land was lost to Kelley in a card game that took place one notorious August night at Willoughby. But the historian was careful to reiterate the anecdotal provenance of this explanation and also suggested, like the others, that it seemed more probable that the land was divided as part of a larger set of transactions that included the sale and exchange of vast plots both in Ireland and in Africa. Whatever the reason for the partitioning of the estate, both Kelley and von Smiling constructed their voluminous mansions throughout the remainder of the 1720s, the original Willoughby completed at the end of the decade, Thackeray a year later, and both families continued to prosper in parallel, their wealth and prestige accumulating side-by-side. According to Professor Gary, the Willoughby plantation produced over half a million pounds of rice each year during this period and turned a remarkable profit, so much so that Herbert von Smiling's great-great-grandson, James Morrison Smiling (they'd evidently dropped the 'von' somewhere along the way, just as the Kellys had dropped the second 'e'), rebuilt the house in the early 1820s, extending the footprint of the building in both directions, adding an extra floor, the ballroom extension, the coach house and spending an unprecedented sum designing and constructing the house's new ornamental gardens.

Yet if this was all proof of the inexorable rise of the Smilings then potential catastrophe lay just around the corner in the form of the American Civil War. Jay discovered that North Carolina had initially held back when it came to choosing between Confederate grey and Union blue. Eventually the state threw its lot in with the South three months after the start of the conflict, a disastrous decision for some forty thousand North Carolinan men who subsequently marched off to die on behalf of the losing side. Nonetheless, and according to all three writers, James Morrison Smiling continued to try and keep the Smilings out of the war. In the early months of 1861, the Union imposed a naval blockade on Confederate ports that stretched along the three thousand miles of coastline between Virginia and Texas in an attempt to put a stranglehold on the South's access to and distribution of vital supplies. But the geography of Cape Fear with its outlying multitude of barrier islands meant that ships could still move in and out of Wilmington, if not without considerable risk. And though Smiling added members of his fleet of transport ships to this number of 'blockade-runners' during the early years of the war, it seemed as if this contribution dwindled as the war progressed. By early 1864, according to Pell, no Smiling-owned vessels had broken the Unionist's *cordon de guerre* for a year. A few of Smiling's ships were ordered to remain docked off the Willoughby plantation's wharves but most were ordered to remain on the other side of the Atlantic where they continued to earn an income plying comparatively less dangerous trade routes between Europe and Africa or the Orient. If this caused inevitable resentment amongst his peers, then so did what followed. Eventually, in early January of 1865, the last year of the war, the Unionist fleet breached the South's defences at Fort Fisher at the mouth of the Cape Fear estuary and swarmed up the river towards Wilmington. Immediately, and in a move that struck Jay as particularly and ironically Swiss, an ageing James Morrison Smiling and the then head of the Kelly family, Jerome Kelly, were tipped off by contacts in Union high command and quickly offered up their mansions as field hospitals for wounded Unionist troops, the workings of this convenient agreement oiled by high-ranking diplomatic contacts in France and England. The deal seemed to achieve its intended objective for both families' houses and holdings were spared the destruction that was visited on almost every other major plantation for miles around. And the benefits of this were not just confined to the immediate post-war period. While the rest of North Carolina's economy took decades to recover, the Kellys and Smilings were able to make their privileged position count. Both estates were the first to establish themselves as major producers in the region's new economy as it switched from the production of rice to the astronomically profitable production of tobacco, and the money flowed in, continuing to swell both families' coffers faster than ever before for almost a hundred years until the outbreak of the Second World War. According to the books, it was at this point that a John Herbert Smiling (Helena and Zelda's grandfather?) sold most of his estate to the government so that it could be used as a naval terminal, what was now the Sunny Point base, and used the proceeds of this to start a new career in finance, moving the family to New York though Willoughby was kept as a second home. As for the Kellys? It appeared that Wallace's father Gideon also grew tired of agricultural life and took the decision to subdivide the Kelly plantation into a number of smaller holdings.

Jay sat back in his seat, his eyeballs like eggs that had been broken and left to fry on a dirty sidewalk. What was it someone had once written? *Follow a fortune to its source and you'll uncover a crime.* It seemed as if both the Smiling and Kelly ancestry was comprised of criminals and carpetbaggers of the worst kind, genocidal maniacs, shameless turncoats and cynical cowards. But there was also a more immediate and useful set of conclusions to draw from what he'd learned: Willoughby was steeped neck-high in bloodshed and betrayal. Jay considered the cemetery of dead slaves that lay just to the south of the estate but also imagined the rooms and corridors of the old house crammed with wounded and dying soldiers, the screams of those undergoing amputation, the groaning of those ravaged by gunshot and gangrene, the whimpers of those who couldn't be saved and whose lives must have inevitably trickled away second by tortuous second. It certainly added a new dimension to Jay's suspicions that any paranormal activity in the house was potentially a result of Helena's murder (though he still shuddered at the idea, his spine flushing with cold fear at the thought of her dead). If there was a ghost it could be the product of any of the violent and bloody events that the house had witnessed during the first two turbulent centuries of its existence.

And Jay wasn't the only one who seemed to think as much. In the chapter on Willoughby in the Crocombe book, the writer had included a section dedicated to two alleged hauntings that had been associated with the house through the years. Were these the stories Zelda had mentioned the night before? There was the pirate she'd referred to, Jay discovering that he'd been called Jan Hendricks, a Dutch outlaw who'd achieved notoriety up the coast in the 1740s, robbing and sinking cumbersome freight ships coming in and out of New Bern as they negotiated the treacherous waters of Pamlico Sound. When the city fathers of New Bern had dispatched ships to capture the Dutchman, he'd played cat-and-mouse with his pursuers in the rough waters off the Outer Islands or else hidden in the alligator-infested swamps inland. More than once,

Crocombe suggested, Hendricks had evaded capture by skilfully leading ships on to the rocks off Cape Hatteras and Roanoke Island before escaping by way of his superior seamanship. The historian also singled out a notorious incident in 1744 when a platoon of soldiers pursued Hendricks up the Alligator River and were never seen again. And this wasn't the only reason for Hendricks' notoriety. According to Crocombe, it was the region's worst-kept secret at the time that the pirate also conducted an affair with Caroline von Smiling, the wife of Herbert von Smiling's eldest son, William. It was rumoured that Hendricks and Caroline had been lovers in their youth before Caroline's magistrate father had married his daughter off as part of a business arrangement, though Crocombe was careful to concede that this was unsubstantiated. Whatever the truth, it seemed as if Hendricks and Caroline pursued a clandestine relationship throughout the marriage, this inevitably enraging Caroline's husband. Things came to a climax when William von Smiling locked his wife in Willoughby's attic sometime in November 1744. What he hoped to achieve by this in the long run wasn't clear but it prompted a daring raid on the house five months later. While William von Smiling and his father were away on business, Hendricks and his pirates sailed up the Cape Fear estuary, docked at the plantation wharves at Willoughby and came ashore under cover of darkness, storming the house and killing anyone who stood their ground, though they spared Marie and Anne von Smiling, Herbert's wife and daughter respectively. Caroline herself was sprung from her incarceration and spirited away, William and his father inevitably outraged at such a violation when news reached them. A large reward was put up and a small fleet hired to search the waterways for the pirate and the stolen girl though neither could be found. Then, after four months had passed, a former member of Hendricks' crew, a man named Jack Mullins, was arrested and sentenced to be hanged for stealing in Edenton. In an attempt to escape death, Mullins had blabbed, revealing that Hendricks was hiding up in the Blackwater swamps just across the border with Virginia and four boats of soldiers were duly sent there to investigate. Mullins' information had proved correct (though it didn't save him from the gallows) and more than two hundred marines surrounded Hendricks' camp and took the man prisoner.

What followed? Caroline von Smiling was brought back to Willoughby and locked back up in her attic prison where it seemed she languished for the rest of her life, never allowed out unless accompanied by four armed guards. As for the pirate? *According to local legend,* Crocombe wrote, *Hendricks was executed in the grounds of Willoughby House a couple of days after his capture, beheaded with his own cutlass on August 18th, 1745 while Caroline von Smiling was forced to look on from a window on the upper floor. Since then, some of Willoughby's inhabitants have reported seeing the ghost of the pirate in the grounds at night while others have claimed to have heard light footsteps echoing around the top floors of the house, both at night and during the day, these footsteps sometimes accompanied by the sounds of a sobbing woman.*

Jay read the last couple of paragraphs again. Hendricks had been executed on the eighteenth of August, the same day that Clemmy and Lobelia had woken the other guests in the middle of the night. Underneath these paragraphs was an old illustration of Hendricks in all his roguish tricorne pomp, his ill-fated cutlass in one hand, a pistol in the other. Had the old women been woken by Caroline von Smiling's ghost reliving her lover's last moments?

Underneath Hendricks was another picture, one that Jay recognized, a reproduction of the painting of Katherine Smiling that hung in the hallway at Willoughby, the only female heir to be produced by the Smiling family for as long as anyone could remember, until Helena and Zelda came along. Crocombe himself made a reference to this fact, describing it as a 'genetic idiosyncrasy' before going on to offer a short account of her story. Like Caroline's, it was a tale of an arranged marriage and absent love, if also one that was far less glamorous than that of her tragic forebear. Jay, of course, already knew the beginning of the story but now found himself reading the details of its conclusion. Desperate to keep the house in the family name, Katherine Smiling had been married off to a spare paternal first cousin, a Johann Smiling brought over from Europe in 1881. Crocombe reported that the man had been a brute, 'a drunkard renowned for whipping slaves and horses until they died' and not above dishing out similar treatment to his wife. Eventually she was found floating in Willoughby Lake after two years of unhappy marriage, some rumours at the time suggesting that she was drowned by her husband who wished to marry one of his mistresses although her death was officially registered as a suicide. According to Crocombe, subsequent inhabitants of Willoughby have occasionally claimed to have seen a female figure drifting through the corridors of the house and attributed it to this sequence of events while others have reported seeing a figure at the edge of Willoughby Lake at twilight.

Enough was enough. Jay's head felt like a laboratory maze into which someone had let loose a score of febrile black rats and he decided he'd done as much homework as he could bear. He returned the books to their shelves before walking out of the library and climbing back behind the wheel of the Apache, thirsty, tired and desperately wanting to smoke a joint. But at least the hours in the library had been worth it. He had a better sense of the house and the Smiling family and their connection with both the history of the area and, more crucially, with the Kelly family. Jay recalled what Zelda had told him the night before about losing her virginity to Wallace Kelly. And now Helena had run off with Wallace herself. There was no getting away from it, he told himself, it seemed as if the descendants of Francis Kelley and Herbert von Smiling still couldn't get enough of each other, even after almost three hundred years of living in each other's pockets. And it had been absurd to believe that Toby had killed Helena. Like any semi-sentient student of cop shows, Jay knew that suspicions of this kind needed to identify a killer's *motive, means* and *opportunity* and that so far he was falling at the first of these three hurdles. Earlier on, Jay had connected any idea that Toby had killed Helena with his financial problems, including his latest investment project. Jay had placed this fact at the root of any kind of suspicion that Toby had killed Helena to gain control of the Smiling fortune . . . *which didn't really exist . . . why couldn't Jay simply accept that Helena had run away with yet another lover?* She'd had affairs with Oliver Floramor and other men before the womanizing doctor, himself included. So why was Jay resisting the idea that she hadn't changed?

He pulled out his cell phone and dialled home, realizing that he was sick of talking to himself and hoping to speak to Christoph but only getting the answerphone and Christoph's recorded message, Marlowe barking in the background. *Please leave a message after the short musical interlude* . . . one of Christoph's jingles sounded out down the line and Jay hung up before checking the time. It was still before one in the afternoon in California and he might just catch Mike Penny before he left the office for his lunch. Seconds later, digital bleeps cooed in Jay's ear.

'Penny 'n' Richards Paranormal Investigations . . .'

For a second Jay thought he'd got the answering machine but then realized that it was Mike himself on the line.

'. . . *Mike Penny speakin'. How can I be of service?*'

'Mike, it's Jay. How are you? Nice phone manner.'

'Well buddy,' Mike replied, 'It's like my pop told me back

home in Omaha: you can't expect to fly with eagles if you sound like a turkey, you know what I'm sayin'?'

'I think so.'

'So how're you doin' down there in rebel country, partner? How's the case? You breakin' hearts or havin' yours broke?'

'I'm making progress.'

'Sounds promisin'. What's the state of play?'

'As far as I can make out, there could be a poltergeist in the property in question, though there's little corroborating data beyond the primary evidence: there are twenty-two paintings hanging in the hallway of the property. They all switched places a few nights back and so far no one has claimed responsibility.'

'What y'gettin' in terms of your EMF and GC readin's?'

'Zip.'

'What about your historical data?'

'I've just come out of the library here. The house has a history of alleged paranormal activity so there's something there to work on. I guess I'm still collecting information and doing the groundwork.'

'Ain't got no investigation without the proper groundwork. S'all in the preparation.'

'I agree. What about your end? Anything interesting happening?'

'Not much,' the Nebraskan replied. 'Gotta go check up on a convent school up in San Rafael this afternoon. Apparently a pupil drowned herself in the pool there a few months back and now all the girls is refusin' to take a swim in it. Been claimin' they feel someone or *somethin'* tuggin' at their legs durin' their physical education classes. Had the Mother Superior on the line at her wits' end this mornin' so I'm gonna go up there and take a look right after I had my chow.'

'Well, good luck with it. Try not to break too many hearts yourself, Mike.'

'Fat slob like me? Some chance. And by the way, I had words

with Mrs Arfenstein. She's stoked at you and me partnerin' up. Told me "it makes her heart warm", her exact words, and wanted me to pass that on the next time we spoke.'

'Well that's a blessing of a kind, I suppose. I guess the good old Nebraskan charm worked?'

'I guess it did. That and the hard cash. If you need anythin', just give us a call. And good luck with your poltergeist. I hope you get lucky.'

'I'll speak to you again soon, Mike.'

Mike hung up and Jay put his phone down on the passenger seat. What next? Perhaps another coffee and another sandwich and then he could call Lara Taft to see if she'd spoken to her friend? Jay reached into the glove-box and pulled out the courtesy map. Where was Windy Point? He checked the index and found that it was twenty miles or so along the coast from Southport. It wouldn't take much more than half an hour to get there. Why not take a look at the place, get something to eat and see what it was that Toby had got himself involved with? It wasn't as if he had anything else to do . . . Jay folded up the map and replaced it, then started up the engine as Lester and the gang plundered their way through 'Easy Does It' at high volume. He could be in Windy Point before they reached 'It All Depends On You'.

13

Wandering around the seafront, Jay sipped a coffee through the teated lid of a paper cup while he dodged gangs of rowdy children waving ice creams around like sparklers. Besides the children, there were couples in bright clothes and fishermen on collapsible stools and hawkers offering tickets for fishing trips and boat rides to look at shipwrecks and cheap deals for cheap restaurants. On the face of it, Windy Point looked to Jay like any other quayside tourist trap attempting to extract as much money as it could from its visitors while the sun shone and seabirds hung in the air above the bunting that crisscrossed the promenade and snapped and fluttered in the ocean breeze. There were shops selling fridge magnets and key chains and t-shirts and sweatshirts and sweaters and sweatpants and mugs and glasses, anything that could display the words 'Windy Point' and the accompanying logo, an image of three fish in silhouette jumping over a lighthouse and leaving a rainbow in their wake. And there were shops selling bumper stickers and plastic pirate hats and models of old sailing ships and stalls selling cotton candy and doughnuts and cameras and film and batteries and lucky pennies and personalized necklaces and personalized nameplates ('Aaron', 'Abe', 'Ada' and so on) and decorative plaques and more t-shirts and more mugs. Amongst these were more shops selling bait and fishing gear. And there were shacks selling plastic tubs of seafood and restaurants with names like *The Captain's Table* and *The Feasting Fisherman* whose terraces spilled out on to the sidewalk, families mulching away at the perimeters of checked tablecloths, guzzling fried food and desserts the size of small dogs.

Jay hadn't seen what the town had been like a few years

before so maybe it was all progress of a kind. What was certain was that the whole place looked as if it was far from failing. Wandering further along the promenade, he found the marina itself, sailboats and fishing launches crowding the water and elbowing each other gently for space along the low wooden jetties. The bars and restaurants around the edge of the quad of black water clinked and clattered with the sound of people sipping pale liquids of various kinds. And on the far side of the marina sat a three-storey building gazing out over it all. Constructed from steel, smoked glass and concrete, the top floor looked like the bridge of a battleship, a crested flag flapping on a pole in the air above it, the floor below a series of huge windows through which Jay could see diners wielding glinting cutlery and crystal. Money was being spent up there, he thought to himself, as it was on the floor below, a mall through which he wandered, observing the shops selling 'formalwear' and 'weekendwear' and leather goods and golf clubs and cut crystal and oil paintings of the coastline. Out behind the mall and up a short slope, there was a parking lot full of elegant cars, grids of Jupiters, Centurions and Empresses protected by security staff who patrolled the area with an air of paramilitary superiority, gleaming Banshee Coupes, snub-nosed Bullits and Tempesti convertibles sending heatwaves up into the air. There was another incline on the other side of the lot at the top of which stood a collection of white buildings beyond a thin line of trees. Jay presumed it was the new hotel complex and he followed the signposts until he'd found a pink path that wound its way up through the toy landscape of bushes and plants and brought him out opposite the building's canopied entrance. Uniformed staff bustled around with carts of luggage. The sound of splashing water echoed out from somewhere unseen and Jay wandered past a set of doors leading to a reception lobby and through an archway into a cloistered patio where palm trees stood in each corner and waiters moved around a collection of tables with plates of food. Through another archway Jay found a swimming pool and more palm trees and he took a seat at a white metal table in the shade. A couple of hotel guests swam lengths in the water but most lay around looking at the pictures in magazines or reading detective novels or just staring up at the sky. After a while a waitress presented herself and Jay asked for a '*mineral* water', having given up asking for just 'water' in America long before (no one understood him unless he made the word rhyme with *harder*, something that he wasn't prepared to do).

It was then that he thought he saw her.

Helena?

'I've got Alaska Chill, Appalachian Spring, Black Mountain, Cold Mountain, Clear Mountain . . .'

A blonde flame disappearing through the archway on the other side of the pool.

'. . . Hidden Spring, Loon County, Mountain Forest, Oasis, Pagosa, Seven Creeks, Stone Clear and Zephyr Hills . . .

Perhaps it was Zelda?

'. . . we've also got a couple of foreign waters, San Pellegrino and *Badoyt* . . .

Jay gave the waitress a five and asked for a bottle of Loon County, saying he'd be back for it in a moment and getting to his feet. Had he seen Zelda (or Helena?), moving through the glare on the other side of the water. Replaying what he'd seen in his mind was useless – he'd picture what he *wanted* to see – but so was staring at the archway waiting to see if she reappeared.

Jay walked towards it, vaguely aware of the blue water to his left and a lifeguard perched somewhere above him, and stepped through the horseshoe of creeping ivy to find a path on the other side that wound round a corner and up a hill. Jay followed it, all the way up to the top, Zelda nowhere in sight (had it really been her? Surely it couldn't have been *Helena*?), not even one level up where Jay discovered a club house and terrace where tartan-clad sexagenarians pointed putters and Bloody Marys out towards the sea with olive oil hands. Jay walked along the seaward balustrade. Golf carts whirred back and forth beyond a line of pines to his right. Bright figures in primary colours moved across a kaleidoscope of a hundred different shades of green. Jay couldn't see Zelda anywhere, just the sun-toasted tourists and the waiters bringing out their drinks and a couple of suits at a table. One of them was blond, in his mid-twenties, white linen shirt without a tie (perhaps it was *him* that Jay had glimpsed across the pool earlier on?). The other man was older, some way into his forties, listening to the younger guy map something out in exact detail. Before Jay could hear what they were saying, the older man noticed him and stared at him for a second and Jay realized that he might have been able to lurk in the background unnoticed down by the pool, able to pass off his t-shirt and jeans as pool-side attire but that up here amongst the check and hounds-tooth of the golfers' creased pants and their crisp hundred-dollar polo shirts, he might as well have been wearing a clown costume. As if to confirm it, the older of the two men got up from the nearby table and approached him.

'Excuse me?' he called out. Before Jay could answer, the man was standing beside him.

'You look as if you've come out in the wrong place,' he continued. 'Perhaps I can ask one of my staff to show you the way back out?'

He stared at Jay, waiting for an answer though they both knew he didn't care if Jay gave him one or not and that Jay would end up in the same place whether he gave one or not. Jay answered him anyway.

'I'm just looking for my uncle but I must have taken a wrong turn.'

'Perhaps one of my staff can take you back to reception.'

'No, I'm okay,' Jay replied. 'I'll just go back the way I came. That should bring me out by the pool, right?'

'Correct. Let me get one of my staff to assist you anyway.' The man signalled to a nearby waiter who hurried over.

'Yes, Mr McKelvy?'

'Please will you show this person the way back to the hotel entrance,' McKelvy answered. He took one more look at Jay and then added, 'If he needs to put a call through to his uncle's room, will you escort him to the reception desk and take him to the Head of Security who will be more than happy to make that call for him personally.'

The waiter, six-foot six tall and built like a tight-end, nodded and gazed down at Jay. 'This way please,' he gestured with one of his paddle-sized paws.

14

As far as Jay could make out, Thackeray seemed bigger than Willoughby. It was as tall as the Smiling house but also half as long again, a gleaming white castle standing amongst obedient sun-blazed trees. Jay walked across the gravel towards it through the rippling light and climbed the nine steps up to the front door that was shielded from the afternoon glare by a portico supported by eight white columns. At the front door itself, Jay pressed a button with the symbol of a bell on it next to a digital keypad screwed into the woodwork and waited. After a minute, a maid appeared at the door, drying her hands on the checked blue tongue of the apron wrapped around her waist.

'Good afternoon?'

'Hi,' Jay replied. 'I was looking to speak to Madeleine Kelly.'

'Is Mrs Kelly expecting you?'

Jay said that she wasn't.

'I'm a guest staying at Willoughby. If she had five minutes to talk to me, I'd very much appreciate it.'

The woman disappeared back into the house, shutting the door behind her. It opened again a few moments later to reveal a tall woman in her early thirties. She was wearing a loose linen shirt, black cargo pants and black sandals. Her long black hair was tied behind her shoulders and a cigarette smoked away in her left hand which had come to rest on the frame of the door. There was a pair of rings on the third finger, a wedding band and bright cluster of diamonds.

'Can I help you?' she asked.

'Mrs Kelly?'

'Yes,' she replied. 'Madeleine.'

For a second, Jay thought that she seemed too beautiful to

be married to someone like Wallace Kelly but then immediately told himself he was being foolish. What did *he* know about Wallace Kelly? Only that the man was languishing at that exact moment in some remote paradise with Helena. And of course there was always the small matter of the Kelly fortune to consider. Perhaps Jay had expected an abandoned wife, pale, tearstained and humiliated, not this assured looking woman who lifted her cigarette to her mouth with slim brown fingers and gazed calmly back at him.

'You are?'

'My name is Jay Richards.'

'What can I do for you, Jay Richards?'

She stared at him, flecks of bronze and mocha in her dark irises amongst spirals of cinnamon and butterscotch. As for her accent? A trace of French? Spanish? Italian? Somewhere Mediterranean anyway, Jay thought to himself, maybe even Israel or somewhere else in the Middle East.

'I'm a guest at Willoughby, a friend of Zelda Smiling,' he said. 'Perhaps, if I could come in and spend a few moments explaining why I'm here?'

Madeleine Kelly stared at him for a moment longer before leading him through the house into the back garden, Jay following her through a cavernous hallway that reminded him of the entrance to a museum and then a drawing room that seemed like a museum itself. He had time to take in the paintings on the walls as they passed through into the garden. No dim mahogany symbols of gloomy colonial decadence here, he thought to himself, comparing them to the images on the walls of Willoughby's walls and corridors. There was a voodoo priestess above the fireplace, eight feet tall and splashed on to the canvas in brash primaries and streaks of bone-white light. On the far wall hung a mosaic of a Chinese dragon in funereal black and bloody crimson that immediately had Jay thinking of Helena's tattoo (and grudgingly accepting that Wallace inevitably made the same connection every time he looked at it also). Further along, a Mexican farmboy in a large corn-yellow sombrero and sea-blue smock sat smiling up at the viewer from a milking stool while pedestals around the room variously displayed Maori war masks and Native American ceramics rendered in cobalt and sandstone, a ten-inch sculpture of Kali rearing up to deliver a *coup de grâce* on some unsuspecting universe, a pair of long-limbed lovers carved from a single piece of pale jade.

'That's an impressive collection,' Jay said as they passed through a set of open doors and took their seats at a wooden table in the garden. A lawn stretched away to a line of trees and what Jay presumed was originally the Thackeray plantation beyond them, a harlequin patchwork of greens and yellows rolling towards the horizon. Behind them, Thackeray's white brickwork rose up towards the flawless sky.

'My husband is interested in ethnic art,' Madeleine replied simply. 'Most of his collection is loaned out to various places.' She lit a cigarette with a silver lighter and put it back down next to a glass of water. 'Can I get Liza to bring you a drink?'

Jay shook his head. 'No thank you. This won't take long.'

'So,' she said, exhaling before she spoke, 'you're a guest at Willoughby, a friend of Zelda Smiling's.'

'Yes,' replied.

'Are you her boyfriend?'

Jay shook his head. 'Just a friend.'

'Okay. How can I help you?'

'I'm not sure how much you know about what's been happening at the house . . .'

'Typical English. Always ready to make things sound so complicated. Are you referring to the fact that Helena Charteris has run off with my husband?'

Her voice was calm. She almost sounded as if she was describing two strangers.

'Well, not exactly.'

Madeleine didn't say anything and waited for him to continue.

'Some strange events of another kind have taken place at Willoughby over the last week. I'm not sure how well you know Toby and Helena's housekeeper, Sara Taft, but she believes she saw a ghost in the garden. Also, the guests have been waking up to find that objects around the house have moved in the night with no apparent explanation.'

Madeleine took another drag on her cigarette. 'I find this hard to believe,' she said.

'Everyone does,' Jay replied.

'Tell me more about these objects that have moved around the house.'

'Last Thursday night, the paintings hanging in the hallway at Willoughby switched places during the night. Everyone at house swears it wasn't them.'

'And you think this has "no apparent explanation"? I think a house full of trapped people would be explanation enough. I can't believe that the police have insisted that they all remain there when it seems more than clear what's happened.'

Madeleine paused for a second, then stubbed out her cigarette. Jay tried to picture her at Willoughby on the night of the party as the transmission of the news that Wallace and Helena had both disappeared became visible in a series of whispered conversations and sideways glances that filtered through the crowds of guests around her. She didn't seem like the kind of woman that men discarded and Jay imagined her driving away from Willoughby at the earliest opportunity, a cigarette between her teeth, the house behind her like a giant paper lantern.

'Tell me Jay,' Madeleine continued, 'what's *your* connection with these strange events?'

'I investigate them,' Jay replied.

'What do you mean by that?'

'Someone experiences something they can't explain and they think it's the product of something paranormal. If they hire me, I come along and find an explanation, usually a rational one.'

'That must be a very lucrative line of work, being paid to chase shadows.' Madeleine replied. 'So what brings you to Thackeray?'

'I guess I wanted to check with you that nothing strange has been happening *here*,' he replied.

'Jay,' Madeleine replied crisply, 'my husband has run off with another woman. The only mystery is that he's stupid enough to believe that his little fling will last. Of course, Wallace has a hopeless romantic streak in him and likes the idea of being helplessly in love – *she* played him like an eager puppy.'

Madeleine leaned forward and looked Jay full in the face.

'I knew the *exact* moment their affair started,' she said. 'It was earlier this year, at the beginning of April. There was a small party at Willoughby to celebrate Helena's birthday, maybe twenty local people invited to dinner at the house. It was clear from the beginning that Helena and Toby were in the middle of a fight. No one could mention it, of course, and it made everyone very uncomfortable. You could see that everyone wanted to leave as early as they could without looking impolite.'

Madeleine took out another cigarette from a pack on the table and lit it. 'Eventually it was time for Wallace and me to leave. We wanted to say goodbye to Toby or Helena but couldn't find them. I said that we should just leave but Wallace wanted to do the right thing, of course, and eventually we found them in Toby's study. Helena was screaming at Toby that he'd been flirting with one of the waitresses all night, that girl who works at the house, and screaming that she was going to leave him. And we were standing there just beyond the doorway having to listen to it all and not knowing if we should leave them to it. And then Toby started shouting back at her and something got knocked over. Wallace walked in at that point. I don't know if Toby was about to hit Helena but Wallace walking in like that stopped him dead whatever he was about to do.'

'Did they exchange words?' Jay asked.

'Nothing really. Wallace told Toby that he was drunk and that he should calm down. Toby stormed out, past me and back downstairs to the library where the other guests were finishing their coffee.'

Madeleine took another sip of water.

'It was pathetic really. Wallace was doe-eyed for days afterwards, like some kind of smitten teenager who's just had their first kiss. And then it started. We'll see how romantic he's feeling when he turns up here in a few weeks after she's grown tired of him.'

'So you think Wallace will come back?'

'No, I think that Helena Charteris will get bored of him and the two of them will come crawling home, one after the other, the same as last year after she went running off to Mexico with that sleazy doctor.'

Jay didn't say anything, not about Oliver Floramor nor Toby nor Helena. Nor did he suggest that Thackeray itself was as good a reason to come home as any.

'All things considered, it makes for a fairly tasteless story,' she continued. 'As I've said, this isn't the first time Helena's done something like this. She's the type of woman that thrives on a rather flimsy kind of adoration. Wallace wasn't the only one round here Helena had losing their minds over her. There were others.'

'Like the doctor you were telling me about?'

'Yes, like him, and men like Buck and Dan Harrington.'

'Two brothers?'

'No, a father and his son. Two local businessmen. Helena *knew* Dan Harrington was after her. And what did she do? She started playing up to his father.'

Madeleine stopped and drained her glass. 'We seem to have been diverted. I'm not sure how much any of this helps you with your assignment. Do you have any more questions?' she asked.

'I don't think so.' Jay got to his feet. 'Thank you very much for your time.'

Madeleine Kelly got up and led Jay back through the house to the drive on the other side. Under the portico, Jay asked her to call him at Willoughby if anything strange occurred at Thackeray. She remained sceptical.

'I don't expect that to be necessary,' she replied. 'Goodbye.'

Back at Willoughby, Jay parked the Apache at the far end of the coach house and entered the house through the side door. No one was in the kitchen, nor in the library nor any of the other rooms on the ground floor. He eventually found Nina Shipman and Bessie Flowers sitting by the pool which, along with the tennis court, lay between the house and the Tafts' cottage, both surrounded by tall yew hedges.

'Hi there,' Jay called out as he walked up to them. Nina raised a wine glass.

'Sara tells us you didn't see anything last night,' Bessie said.

'That's right,' he replied. 'And my equipment failed to pick up anything out of the ordinary.'

He didn't want to talk about the investigation so he tried to change the subject. 'How are you all? Have the police said you can go home yet?'

'Bored,' Nina replied.

'And no word from Sheriff Bryar today,' Bessie added. 'So they're all stuck here. What have you been doing?'

Jay considered whether he wanted to tell them that he'd called on Madeleine Kelly. Was there any reason to be secretive? He didn't think so.

'I went to Wilmington this morning to look at plans of the house. After that, I visited Madeleine Kelly.'

'Why did you do that?' Bessie asked.

'To see if anything strange has happened at Thackeray.'
'And has it?' Nina asked.
'No.'
'Nothing?'
'Nothing at all, which is what I expected. I guess I was just trying to be thorough.'

'And what did you make of *her*?' Bessie asked.

'She's certainly not what I expected,' Jay replied, trying to remove the emphasis from his voice. 'What's her background? Where's she from? I can't place her accent.'

Bessie said that as far as she knew, Madeleine's father was American and her mother French. 'No one really knows very much about her,' she added.

There was an open bottle of wine lying nearby and Jay noticed that the women's glasses were empty. 'She seems very . . . *confident*,' he said, reaching for the bottle.

'She's certainly a fast operator,' replied Bessie. 'She arrived in the area about a year and a half ago and was married to Wallace Kelly not much more than six months later.'

'Did they get married at Thackeray? What are her family like?'

'I don't know,' Bessie replied. 'They got married in the Caribbean. *That* had a lot of people round here raising their eyebrows, I can tell you.'

'What does she do?'

'Nothing. She worked for a while as the PA to Frank McKelvy . . .'

'Frank McKelvy?' The man who'd confronted Jay at Windy Point.

'Yes, one of Toby's business partners,' Bessie replied. 'I think she worked in Wilmington before that. And now she's married to Wallace.'

'Wallace must have been one of the most eligible bachelors in the county.'

'Try one of the most eligible bachelors in the state, and one with no relations.' Nina couldn't stop herself from laughing at that particular detail and spilled some of her wine in the process. 'But I'm not so sure anyone should be surprised,' Bessie continued. 'Now you've met her, I'm sure you don't need me to tell you that she's more than capable of persuading most men to do anything she wants.'

'Helena introduced me to her at the party,' added Nina Shipman, dabbing at her blouse with a tissue. 'I've seen women square-up before, but nothing like *that*. At one point I thought they were going to go at it right there.'

'So Madeleine and Wallace were invited to Helena and Toby's wedding anniversary party even though Toby knew that they were having an affair?'

Bessie nodded.

'I can't understand why he insisted on inviting them. He knew what was going on between Helena and Wallace. Everybody did.'

'Maybe he couldn't face up to the truth?' Jay suggested, knowing that it was possible but not the only possibility.

'Either that,' Bessie replied, 'or he couldn't face admitting the truth in front of everyone else.'

'And look what happened,' Nina added, 'they humiliated him.'

Jay asked what happened on the day Wallace and Helena disappeared, filling up both Nina and Bessie's glasses. According to the women, the celebrations had started early in the afternoon, a couple of hundred guests meeting at the yacht club in Windy Point for lunch. After that, everyone was free to do what they wanted for a few hours before meeting back at Willoughby at seven: more drinks in the ballroom, a band, dancing, food for those who wanted it in a marquee erected over the veranda.

'When did Toby realize that Helena had gone?' Jay asked.

Bessie said that Toby had been due to give a speech at nine.

'He delayed it for ten minutes while I went to look for Helena. I couldn't find her anywhere. Sara was looking as well but she couldn't find her either. Then Madeleine Kelly took me to one side and told me that she'd been searching for Wallace but he was missing too.'

'Poor Toby,' Nina sighed. 'He had to get up there in front of everybody and thank them all for coming, aware the whole time that they all knew what had happened. I felt sorry for him — he's not perfect but no one deserves to be shown up like *that* in front of so many people.'

Jay asked who else attended the party. Had any of Toby's family from England come over? Apparently not. 'Zelda was invited but said that she was too busy to make the trip. Mainly it was just a lot of rich local people.'

Nina got up off her lounger, saying she was getting too hot and was going inside to change into her swimming costume. Jay waited until she was out of earshot before he spoke again. He'd been looking for a natural point in the conversation to ask Bessie about Buck and Dan Harrington but there hadn't been one and he had little choice except to force the issue.

'Bessie, who's Buck Harrington?'

'He's a local man. Why?'

'Madeleine Kelly mentioned that he was interested in Helena,' Jay replied as neutrally as he could. Bessie didn't respond immediately and he wondered if he'd made her suspicious.

'I guess I can't criticize her for spreading gossip,' she said cautiously. Jay noticed that she was slurring slightly (how long had they been sitting out there drinking wine in the sun? Two, three hours?).

'So it's true?'

'Yes. I suppose.'

'Who is he?'

'He lives a few miles away in Parton, and remains something of a mysterious figure. Apparently he grew up there but went off to Chicago sometime in the seventies.'

'What do you mean by "mysterious"?'

'Well, a lot of people say that he made his money in "organized crime". I don't know what that means in this case exactly, and I don't think I want to find out. What I do know is that he came back about four years ago, bought a large plot of land off old Gideon Kelly just before he died and built a stud ranch there. Whatever he did before, all he seems to do now is rear horses and play golf. His son's a different matter of course. He's a thug, plain and simple. Twenty-six years old and he thinks he's Al Capone.'

Jay presumed it was Dan Harrington that Bessie was talking about, the son who Madeleine Kelly claimed had also been attracted to Helena, but didn't interrupt her. According to Bessie, when Buck Harrington returned to Brunswick County, he'd invested his money in various tourist businesses. He bought a hotel in Wilmington and a few restaurants and bars dotted around the surrounding area.

'Sara's daughter, Lara – she works in one of their places,' Bessie told him and Jay now remembered that Lara had described her boss as 'a bit of an asshole'. 'Anyway,' Bessie continued, 'I get the impression that Buck Harrington came here wanting a quiet life. Whatever he did in Chicago, I think he's just another quiet middle-aged guy looking for his money to earn him a simple return while he gets on with his golf.'

'So what makes Dan Harrington a thug?'

As Bessie went on to describe it, Dan had been given a mandate to manage a section of his father's businesses when they moved to the area. And whether his father was looking for a quieter life or not, Dan had operated a policy of aggressive expansion that seemed to skirt the bounds of criminality.

'He seems to have acquired an alarming array of businesses

and commercial properties in a very short space of time,' Bessie told Jay, 'bars, video game arcades, restaurants, nightclubs. None of the rumours can be proved but there is something very suspicious about the way he operates. His father's reputation doesn't help, of course. And nor does the crew of thugs he cruises around with.'

'Does he live with his father on the ranch?'

'I think he used to split his time between the ranch and the suite he keeps at the Harrington.'

Bessie stopped for a moment and looked across at the surface of the pool.

'He even made a move on Helena,' she said, her voice lowered.

'But I thought that it was Buck Harrington that was interested in her?' he asked giving no indication that this was what he'd been wanting to talk about the whole time.

'That's my point. When Buck found out, he beat Dan up.'

'How do you know that?'

'My friend who works at Wilmington General – she didn't see it herself but the story amongst the staff there is that Buck Harrington stumbled into the emergency ward with his son one night last summer. Dan needed six stitches across his left eye. Buck needed a few across the knuckles of his right hand. You do the math.'

'They sound like a lovely family. So how are things between the two of them now?'

'Who knows? I don't think they see each other much.'

'And Buck Harrington continued to approach Helena?'

'Well, yes . . .'

'You sound uncertain?'

'Well, there can't be any doubt that Buck was interested in her. But you make it sound like he cornered her in a bar or asked her to meet him in motel rooms. It wasn't like that.'

Bessie told Jay that Buck had first invited Helena to his home sometime in the spring. That time, it had been to offer Buck advice on some redecoration he was having done at the ranch.

'Helena told me he made some big pretence of inviting her to the ranch claiming he wanted a woman's opinion or something lame like that. But after that he kept on inviting her to meet with him, perhaps as much as once or twice a week, sometimes for lunch, sometimes for tea.'

Jay asked Bessie if Buck Harrington had ever made a pass at Helena. Apparently he hadn't. Had these meetings been kept secret from Toby? They had, and from Wallace too. Jay asked Bessie if Helena had ever told her what her own feelings were towards Buck and she replied that Helena had always maintained that she believed Buck was just being 'neighbourly'. Was that plausible? Jay asked Bessie what she thought: would Helena have kept the meetings secret if they were innocent? The woman shrugged.

'I'm not sure that I can say I've had a real sense of any of Helena's motivations for several years. I might have thought I did. But I now realize that I haven't had the faintest idea. It wasn't as if Helena wasn't aware of his reputation.'

'What reputation?'

'For having a thing about younger women. Just last year he was running around with this teenager, one of Lara's co-workers.'

'What was her name?'

'Delman, I think. Roxanne Delman. I'm sure that she's not the first. I guess his infatuation with Helena shows that she's not his last.'

'So you think Buck's interest in Helena wasn't innocent?'

Bessie gave Jay a what-do-you-think stare back.

'I think he's obsessed with her, just like all the rest. He crashed the anniversary party even though he wasn't invited, making a big show of having brought gifts for Toby and Helena as if that made any difference. And all he did was look out of place, stomping around the garden with his bodyguard. It seemed a little pathetic to me. Who knows what would have happened under any other circumstances? That night I think Toby was so preoccupied with looking for Helena and Wallace that he was only too happy to welcome Buck in just to get it over with.'

The preparation of Clemmy and Lobelia's tea and medication brought the conversation to a sudden halt, Bessie suddenly noticing the time and rushing off to the kitchen so as not to keep 'Sourpuss' waiting. Jay also stood up, considering going upstairs to his room to sleep for a few hours but deciding instead to take a walk down to the lake he'd seen on the map at the library. He stepped along a short path that took him into the maze of gardens he'd walked through the previous afternoon, and came across Will Hooper sleeping in the suntrap that he and Bessie had sat in the day before, a book crushed open on his trembling chest, an open bottle of wine by his splayed fingers, a half-smoked joint lying next to it on the tartan picnic rug. What was he reading? Jay tilted his head. *The Money Takers*. 'The most exhilarating financial thriller for years . . .' read the blurb under the title. Jay bent down and picked up the joint (Will wouldn't miss it. He'd wake up in an hour or so with a headache, sunburned, disorientated . . .) and continued on through the garden until he eventually found an opening in the treeline. There Jay fumbled around in his pockets for a lighter but only found an old book of matches from Rabbit City. He used one to spark the joint, took a long drag and then continued along the path winding ahead of him through the pines, the air in the wood all Ss, birdsong straying through the saphenous black stems of the trees, the air sticky with the spongy scent of pinesap, slanting sunlight, slanting shadows, the smell of the hissing grass, the white noise of the insects sizzling around his shoes and ears, the sapid marijuana smoke that Jay breathed out in front of him. He reached the lake after ten minutes of slow ambling and came to a stop by its edge. The water spread out in front of him, a couple of mauve clouds slipping across its surface, the branches all around him stirring with a sound like a thousand ride cymbals being gently brushed all at once. There was a boathouse about fifty metres to his right and a domed cupola to his left. Jay walked over to the boathouse first, looking inside and finding a couple of rowing boats hanging on the walls and a third beached on a small wooden platform sloping down into the water. As for the cupola, it sat on five thick pillars and offered protection to a round stone platform on which stood a long iron table and eight small drifts of leaves shored up against the legs of the metal chairs surrounding it.

Jay swivelled one of these chairs around to face the lake and sat down on it, wishing he had another joint to help him think. He'd started the day trying to convince himself that Toby had killed Helena. *The paranormal events had started directly after Helena and Wallace's disappearance . . . there was Toby's slip of speech in the library the night before . . .* it felt more speculative than ever before to Jay given what he'd learned about Helena over the course of the last two days and her turbulent passage through the lives of most of the men she came into contact with, the Harringtons, Oliver Floramor and the others. And what about Madeleine? Jay questioned his own reservations about her (and he still had them). Just because she hadn't been what he'd expected didn't mean she was anything other than an abandoned wife, if only temporarily. Examining what he knew about her so far, Jay wondered if he was suspicious of Madeleine simply because she was beautiful (and again, more beautiful than he'd *expected*), a feeling that was an analog of the jealousy that Nina and Bessie had displayed earlier when gossiping about her. And it didn't matter which way one looked at it, Madeleine wasn't the only beautiful woman to have married an astronomically rich man. They were doing it all the time.

It was then that Jay remembered something Bessie had told

him by the pool: Madeleine had worked for Frank McKelvy, Toby's business partner and the man who'd ordered Jay's smooth ejection from the hotel on Windy Point. Was there anything suspicious about this set of interpersonal connections? There didn't seem to be, not on the face of it, not in a community the size of Brunswick County.

Gazing out across the lake, Jay also reviewed what he'd learned about the entwined histories of Willoughby and Thackeray and the generations that had lived at both. If there was something haunting Willoughby, it could have been the product of any of the terrible events he'd read about earlier in the day. Was it only a coincidence that Jan Hendricks had been executed on the same day that the great-aunts claimed to have been woken by an apparition? Sitting there, Jay wished he'd had his EMF wand with him. What if the figure of Katherine Smiling appeared at the water's edge as it was rumoured she had in the past? He wondered how the woman had died. Her death had been registered as a suicide. Had she filled her pockets with stones and then rowed herself into the middle of the lake before throwing herself over the side? And if her husband had killed her (which the book had suggested as a possibility)? Perhaps he'd forced her into a boat and rowed out into the middle of the water before tossing her in? Wouldn't she have put up a struggle? Not if she hadn't suspected that she was about to die. Johann Smiling could have asked her to accompany him in the boat and then surprised her – most likely she wouldn't have been able to swim and Johann would have known that in advance. Or perhaps she'd accompanied him on a walk along the water's edge and he'd suddenly overpowered her and thrust her down into the silt until she'd stopped struggling?

Jay shuddered, for a moment picturing the woman under the water, her husband's hands round her neck, his thumbs crushed against her windpipe. She would have struggled, but not for long. Perhaps, given the historians' account of her husband and her other options, she hadn't really wanted to go on living?

And what about Helena? Was she really another murdered Willoughby wife? Why couldn't he accept that she'd run off with Wallace? It was ridiculous to believe that she was dead, or that he'd seen her (or Zelda for that matter) at Windy Point or anywhere else. Was he really going to start with all *that* again? No, it was ridiculous to believe that Helena was anywhere except by Wallace's side. They were on a beach in some far flung time zone, somewhere idyllic of course, somewhere they could sleep outside, the surf caressing the sand metres away, Helena's head bent into the crook of his neck and his arms closed protectively around hers while the jealous stars and green-eyed moon spun through slow trajectories around their still and perfect world.

15

Jay drove across the Cape Fear River for the third time that day, the oblong of sky in the Apache's rearview banded with purple and orange striations of distant light from beyond the horizon, the sky ahead of him dark and cloudless. It would still be bright and warm in San Francisco he realized for a moment, perfect weather for sitting up in Delores Park and gazing at the San Francisco skyline while Marlowe quietly dispatched his ice cream or for taking a walk along JFK with a joint before ambling over to Café Deluxe for a couple of beers, perfect for scouting out strange books in Bound Together or Sunset Books or City Lights or the glut of second-hand stores on 9th, perfect for taking in a triple-bill at The Red or for sitting in Vesuvio with a Bloody Mary or thumbing through the records in Amoeba or a late-afternoon sandwich at Andiamo.

After ten minutes Jay found Nicole's Bar and Grill a couple of blocks off Wilmington's main drag and parked across the street. It stood on a corner of a block that also housed another bar directly to its left, an Irish pub called McKittrick's and a restaurant called Ranoshoff's next to that. Nicole's was bigger and more modern than both of its neighbours, Jay noted, and a lot more successful. Waiting inside the Apache, he watched as a procession of blazered men and their burnished dates walked up to the quadrant of red carpet where two hundred and fifty pounds of doorman processed them before allowing them to pass under the halogen-lit logo. Why hadn't he checked if there was a dress code when he'd spoken to Lara on the phone? Jay got out the car and zipped up his jacket to hide his crumpled t-shirt and approached as confidently as he could, the doorman inevitably manoeuvering to block him with a mere shuffle of his tiny leather shoes.

'Can I help you?'

The man's face was like a screwed-up rag and the peppercorns of his eyes glanced down at Jay's sneakers over a broken hump of a nose, the clipboard nothing more than a playing card in his hairy left fist (the other hand pointed a fat finger at Jay's throat).

'I was looking to come in for a drink,' Jay replied.

As expected, the doorman went through the pointless ritual of asking him if he had a reservation and then telling him that he couldn't come in without one while a group of people accumulated behind him, shiny cufflinks glittering away at the end of the men's shirtsleeves, the women with matching purses and shoes.

'I'm here to meet a member of staff,' Jay tried.

'You still can't come in here dressed like that. Now will you stand to one side so I can let these people through?'

There was no point in arguing. Jay sloped back across the street and parked in the lot behind the restaurant where he put on 'Shoe Shine Boy' and let Count Basie, Carl Smith and The Prez fight it out amongst themselves while he called up the operator on his cell and got the number for Nicole's. Eventually a young male voice came on the line that seemed as if it only just remembered to be polite as the telephone completed its journey from its cradle to his mouth.

'Nicole's Bar and Grill. This is Steve. How may I help you?'

'Hi. Could I speak to Lara Taft please?'

'This line is for reservations and enquiries only, not for personal calls. If you need to speak to her, you'll have to call her during non-work hours. Is there anything else I can help you with?'

Jay said there wasn't, let the guy put the phone down on him and gazed across the parking lot. He could see the back entrance to the restaurant from where he was sitting, a small light high up over the flyscreen-door flickering in the steam from a nearby vent as it dispersed over a large garbage dumpster. What could he do next? He had her cell number and could leave a message but there was no guarantee as to when she'd get it. After a few minutes, Jay saw a couple of girls come out of the back of the restaurant and take a seat on a railing where they lit a pair of cigarettes. Neither of them looked like Lara but he still got out of the car and walked over to them.

'Hi,' he called out when he was ten metres away.

'Hi,' they replied warily, their shoulders tensing as he approached. The girl sitting nearest to him was dressed in a waitress's standard black and white, her friend in a dirty chef's coat and check trousers.

'Do any of you know Lara Taft?'

'Sure,' the waitress replied while her friend smirked behind her. She had a nametag pinned to her white blouse with the name 'Roxanne' printed on it. 'She's inside. What do you want?'

'Can you pass on a message for me?' Jay asked, studying her. Roxanne was tall, as tall as Zelda (or Helena for that matter), chestnut hair falling flawlessly straight to her shoulders, her blouse unbuttoned to show exactly two quarter-cups of black lace against her young skin, a silver sea-horse hung there to draw male eyes to the crease above. In San Francisco or another large city, she might not have stood out. But here in Wilmington she seemed to him like the kind of girl who was well aware of her disproportionate advantages.

Was she Roxanne *Delman*? Perhaps.

'I'm meant to be meeting Lara in her break,' Jay told her. 'The guy on the door wouldn't let me in. Can you tell her I'm waiting for her in my car . . . over *there* . . . my name's Jay.' He walked back to the Apache, ignoring the girls' smug conspiratorial glances at each other, climbed inside and sat there listening to the music and watching Roxanne and the other girl smoke before they flicked the butts out on to the concrete, straightened down their clothes and went back inside. How long would he have to wait?

Jay had been eating a sandwich in the kitchen at Willoughby, Sara Taft busy at the range on the far side of the kitchen preparing dinner, when her daughter had called him. 'I've got that *thing* you asked for,' she told him, the clang of pots and pans in the background at her end of the line as well as his. Jay had agreed to meet her at the restaurant then finished his sandwich and gone upstairs to his room to get some money and his jacket. Back on the ground floor moments later, he'd walked out on to the loggia and looked out towards the Italian garden between the two groves of cherry trees. The houseguests stood around in the twilight laughing at something Will had said, even Zelda who sat on a bench a little distance away with Bessie who joggled Jacob around in her arms. While the others had continued to banter and Bessie cooed at the child, Zelda seemed to drift off into her own world, staring up through the branches of the cherry trees at the sky over the river that beat away somewhere in the distance. She'd had her hair tied up and the skin on the back of her neck glowed white in the failing light.

'How are you Jay?' she asked once she had joined him on the loggia. 'I'm sorry I haven't seen you today to discuss how things went last night. Toby's told me that nothing happened.'

'That's right. Today, I spent a fair amount of time in the City Library researching the history of the house. A few of the books there mentioned the pirate in the ghost story you said your grandfather used to tell your father. He was called Jan Hendricks and was executed by one of your ancestors here at Willoughby on the eighteenth of August, 1745.'

'The eighteenth of August? But that's the night Clemmy and Lobelia . . .'

'Exactly. One of the books I looked at suggested that Hendricks had an affair with Caroline von Smiling, the wife of William von Smiling whose father built Willoughby. Apparently Hendricks abducted her at some point in 1744 but was captured the following year.'

'What happened to him?' Zelda asked.

'William von Smiling had him beheaded.'

'Here?'

Jay nodded. 'Apparently Caroline von Smiling was forced to watch from an upper floor of the house. Given that the house was only two storeys high in those days, it's not impossible that she watched the event from your great-aunts' bedroom. I know that so far I've been fairly dismissive of what Clemmy and Lobelia claimed to have witnessed. But we may have to start taking what they've said a little more seriously.'

'You think they were woken by the ghost of this Caroline von Smiling?'

Jay shrugged. 'I can't say at this point. It's a possibility, one of many. There's also a rumour, for instance, connected to Katherine Smiling, the woman whose painting hangs in the hallway. Apparently she committed suicide . . .'

'Suicide?'

'Yes,' continued Jay, deciding to keep it simple. 'She drowned herself in Willoughby Lake. Since then, previous occupants of Willoughby have intermittently claimed to have seen an apparition there and associated it with her death. Again, it's impossible to tell if any of this is connected with what's been happening at the house over the last few days. It's useful to have this secondary data to hand. But until something else happens, we shouldn't really start assuming too much.'

He stopped for a moment and examined Zelda's face, trying to work out her feelings about what he'd told her. She didn't seem the type of person to believe in old ghost stories let alone new ones, not hard-headed Zelda who'd chosen some of the world's most unforgiving landscapes for her place of work with bullish zeal, not Zelda who'd surrendered her share of the family estate to prove a point to *herself*. Yet even she hadn't been able to stop herself being startled by the fact that the date of Hendricks' execution coincided with the aunts' claim to have seen the figure of a woman in the room.

'How about you?' he asked. 'What have you been doing today?'

Zelda said that she hadn't been feeling well and had spent a lot of the day in bed.

'So you didn't visit Windy Point today?'

'No. Why?'

'I drove over there this afternoon. I thought I saw you,' he replied.

'I haven't left Willoughby all day.'

'I must have been seeing things.'

'Bessie mentioned that you'd called on Madeleine Kelly.'

'Yes,' Jay replied. 'I wanted to see if anything out of the ordinary had happened at Thackeray. Should I have consulted you first?'

Zelda looked back at him. 'I guess not,' she said after a pause. 'What did she say?'

'She told me that ghosts don't exist and accused me of being a fake.'

'I guess you get that a lot?'

Jay nodded.

'I've not met her yet,' Zelda said. 'What's she like? People say that she's beautiful.'

'She is,' Jay agreed, 'but also pretty tough. I guess you've heard that as well.'

Zelda nodded.

'She's convinced that Wallace and Helena will come back in a few days,' Jay continued, 'like everyone else.'

'Like everyone else.'

Jay looked at Zelda and wondered how she'd react if Helena did appear on the front drive. It could be that very night, he realized, or any of the nights to come, Helena on the doorstep (pale and tan simultaneously) bracing herself for impact with Toby and his rage while the driver assembled her luggage and lights appeared at Willoughby's windows one by one like distant stars at dusk, Wallace either abandoned at the lover's paradise they'd been holed up in for the past twelve days or else on his own way back to Thackeray to face Madeleine. They'd been gone twelve days: was that a long time by Helena's standards?

'You look like you're about to go somewhere.' Zelda said, interrupting Jay's thoughts for a moment.

'I have to drive to the city,' he replied. 'I'll be back in an hour or so to start on tonight's investigation. Will you tell Toby I'll be back later if he asks where I am?'

Jay had waited for her to ask him what he was doing in Wilmington but she hadn't enquired. In the parking lot behind Nicole's Bar and Grill, the Prez and Lady Day slipped through 'All of Me', Nat King Cole's fingers pirouetting across the piano in the background. Lara appeared nearly thirty minutes after Roxanne and her sidekick had gone back inside, standing in the twitching pool of light by the dumpster and gazing out across the lot until Jay flashed his headlamps and she spotted him.

'You rented yourself a stick shift Apache,' she said as she climbed into the passenger seat. 'That's pretty cool. How you doin'?'

'I'm good. How are you?'

'I'm okay. Double shift always takes it outta me.'

She pulled a small ziploc bag out of a pocket and handed it over. One look through the plastic at the dry olive-drab clumps was enough to tell Jay that it was schwag and nothing like the moist spongy buds that Christoph sold back home. Jay didn't even have to open the bag. Still, schwag was better than nothing.

'How long have you got?' he asked Lara. She said she had a half-hour and Jay asked if he could borrow some Zig-Zags.

'Hey, I'm sorry you had to wait,' Lara said, passing them across. 'I should have told you they run a door policy here.'

They sat in silence while Jay rolled a joint which he then offered to her. She looked at it before taking it. 'I shouldn't,' she said but still put the end between her lips.

'This Dan, your boss . . . that's Dan *Harrington*, right?'

Lara nodded.

'I've heard his name mentioned.'

'Oh yeah? Where?' she asked.

'I heard some of the guests at the house talking about him this afternoon. Bessie Flowers mentioned him . . . and his father.'

'That figures. Those guys just sit around drinkin' and bitchin' all day. What did she say?'

'She told me Buck Harrington and his son are gangsters and that no one round here likes them much. I couldn't really tell if she was being melodramatic.'

Lara handed the joint back. 'She kinda is and she kinda isn't. People say that Buck used to be some kind of mafia big shot in Chicago back in the eighties. Who really knows? Some of it's probably true. What does it matter anyways?'

'What about Dan?'

Lara didn't answer for a second. Jay watched her stare out through the windshield, her front teeth grating down against her lower lip.

'People say that Dan's up to all kinds of shit. Some of it's probably true, same as his father. But none of it's got anything to do with me.'

'That's not what I heard.'

'Whaddya mean by that?'

Jay took a deep breath. He'd prepared this routine earlier on, before he'd left the house.

'I heard that you and Buck hooked up?'

'Who the fuck told you that?' Lara twisted in her seat and

glared at him. Jay didn't reply. He wanted her to get more angry — a second ago, she'd been ready to clam up and he had no choice.

'I asked you who the fuck told you that?'

'I don't know what you're getting so angry about. I didn't say I believed it . . .'

'I don't give a fuck what you believe. And I know it was that Flowers bitch who told you that shit about me an' Buck Harrington.' She reached for the door handle. 'It ain't fuckin' true. And you owe me thirty bucks for the weed.'

'Lara, look, I'm sorry . . .'

'Who the fuck do you think you are? I don't even fuckin' know you and you come out with this shit.'

Jay didn't say anything for a moment. If he pushed Lara too far, she'd get out of the car and stomp across the parking lot back into the restaurant, screw the money, she'd get it later on. And if not? He counted to five slowly.

'Bessie Flowers and I were talking about Buck and Dan Harrington,' he said quietly. 'She told me that Buck was interested in Helena. I said that Helena was young enough to be his daughter and she told me that wouldn't stop him, that Buck had a thing for younger women. She said he was shameless about it, dating the girls who worked in his and Dan's restaurants. For a moment, I wondered if she meant you. She also told me that Toby came on to you and him and Helena had a fight about it . . .'

'You fuckin' asshole . . .'

'I'm sorry . . .'

'. . . and that's just kinda what I'd expect from her. If I were you, Jay, I wouldn't take too much notice of what comes out of that woman's mouth. I don't mean to be a bitch but she's kinda twisted because of her personal problems. First, *yeah*, Toby came on to me, for like all of five seconds. All I did was ignore it. He was drunk like he pretty much always is. And it was *my friend*, Roxanne, who had a thing with Buck, not me, not that it's any of your fuckin' business.'

'Roxanne?'

'The girl you talked to earlier, the girl who told me you were waitin' out here for me. Bessie Flowers' just jealous.' Jay passed the joint towards her one more time and she took it. 'You wanna know another thing?'

'What?' he asked.

'Bessie Flowers likes to make a big deal about how she's such a good friend to Helena. But it's pretty fuckin' clear to everyone else that she's jealous of her too. Helena's rich and lives in a big fuckin' house. Helena had a fuckin' kid this year. Helena's got every guy for miles around turnin' tricks for her. Bessie's got jack shit.'

Jay let Lara finish what she was saying and didn't reply straight away, as if he was conceding a point. He counted to five again, slower this time: *one, two, three, four, five*.

'Bessie told me that Buck was interested in Helena but so was Dan and that they've both fallen out over her. It seemed a bit far-fetched to me – maybe she was just being spiteful?'

'No, it's kinda true.'

'Is it?'

Lara nodded. 'Buck beat the shit out of Dan when he found out.'

'How do you know?'

'It was last February. Dan took Helena to lunch up the coast. A couple of days later Dan came into work with his face all bandaged up. No one at the bar dared say anythin' and I asked my mom later if she knew all about it. She wouldn't tell me at first, but I went on at her and she eventually told me that Buck had done it.'

'How does *she* know?'

'Mom's been livin' in the area since she was born. She knows everythin' that's going on.'

Jay asked what things were like between Buck and Dan now and Lara repeated what Bessie Flowers had told him by the pool that afternoon, that Dan used to spend his time between the ranch in Parton and a suite he kept at the hotel he and his father owned in Wilmington.

'They bought it five years ago and renamed it the *Harrington*. How does that suck for a name?' She went on to tell him that her friends who worked at the Harrington told her that Dan hadn't been back to the ranch since the previous summer.

'This Dan character doesn't sound like he's the kind of guy to take a beating,' Jay said, 'even from his own father. If I was Buck, I'd be watching my back.'

'Yeah, well Dan better watch his back an' all.'

'What do you mean?'

Lara paused for a second.

'What?' Jay asked.

'Sometimes they switch the staff round and we get sent to work at the hotel or at Solaris, the club Dan owns down at the wharf. Anyways, back last April I was workin' a late shift here at Nicole's and had an early shift at the Harrington the next day so I arranged to stay over at my friend Alicia's over in Wrightsville Beach. I was drivin' over there around three in the morning when I saw this red Firefly pullin' out of this motel on to 76. It looked like Dan's and when I took a closer look, I could see Dan sittin' behind the wheel. Helena was sittin' next to him. I'm sure you can figure the rest out for yourself.'

'Are you certain it was Dan and Helena?'

'I only took a quick look. But yeah, I'm sure.'

They sat there for a few moments.

'Did you tell anyone else? Roxanne? Your mother?'

Lara shook her head. 'To be honest Jay, I think what's been going on at the house recently is pretty sick and I just try to stay out of it. I guess that's why I got kinda angry earlier when you said that Bessie Flowers thought that there was something goin' on between me and Buck Harrington. I'm just not part of any of that kinda thing. And I hate people spreadin' shit about me . . .'

At that point there was a sudden banging on Lara's window, a shape looming into the glass.

Open the fuckin' door!

'Who is it?' Jay asked, reaching for the ignition.

'Fuck . . . it's Dan.'

'Open the fuckin' door!'

Lara's door wasn't locked and it was yanked open to reveal a stubbled face leaning down out of the parking lot's indigo sky, a scarred eye socket . . . *the man Jay had seen earlier on at the marina hotel had been Dan Harrington . . .*

'What the fuck are you doing out here?' the man bawled at Lara.

'Dan . . . I . . .'

'Who's this?' he asked, nodding towards Jay.

'Dan . . .'

Dan had been with Frank McKelvy at Windy Point . . .

'You gettin' high again on my time?'

'I was takin' a break . . .'

Did he recognize Jay? Jay wasn't sure . . .

'Takin' a fuckin' break? Get the fuck out of the car and get the *fuck* back inside. I don't fuckin' pay you to sit out here gettin' high.'

Lara didn't move for second and Dan grabbed her arm and started pulling her out of the Apache.

'Hey, there's no need . . .' Jay started.

'*You* don't say a fuckin' word to me!'

By now Lara was out of the car. Dan ordered her back inside again and watched her walk slowly across the lot before bending back down inside the frame of the passenger door.

Jay tried to open his mouth again. 'There's no need . . .'

'I told you to shut the fuck up. You're takin' drugs on my

property. If you're not out of here in twenty seconds I'll call the cops and have your ass hauled down to the station. If I ever see you round here again, I'll have you bust in half. You wanna tell me there's anythin' else I don't need to fuckin' do?'

Jay stared at Dan. Dan stared back. If he recognized Jay from earlier, he didn't show it.

'Get the fuck out of here!'

Dan slammed the door and gave it a kick as Jay started the engine and pulled away, not stopping until he found a gas station near the river where he finally pulled over and got out of the car, his heart rate still high, his breathing shallow. There was a toe-shaped dent in the Apache's passenger door that ended his chances of getting his deposit back. And there was the sudden glut of new information about Dan Harrington. As Jay pulled himself together, he considered what Lara had told him, that Dan had gone ahead and had an affair with Helena despite Buck's warning. And now Helena and Wallace had disappeared. Was there a connection? Jay remembered what Bessie had told him: that Buck (and his surly henchman) had gate-crashed the anniversary party at Willoughby. Was Dan connected with Helena and Wallace's disappearance? Did Buck Harrington know something about it, perhaps even crash the party to stop Dan from . . . Jay walked a few paces to the wharf's edge and looked out towards Cape Fear's lost horizon. Again, the idea that there was a ghost in the house, that it was Helena's, that she was dead.

Jay walked back to the gas station forecourt and into the strip-lit cubicle where he bought a pack of Spirits and pack of E-Zs and returned to the car where he rolled another joint. He reminded himself that he'd seen Dan Harrington earlier at the marina with Frank McKelvy. McKelvy was Toby's business partner and Dan had also had an affair with Toby's wife: was there anything important to glean from *this*? And what if one factored in the information that Madeleine Kelly had once worked for McKelvy, if only for a short time, and that her and Toby's spouses had now disappeared simultaneously?

One could read almost anything into it, Jay realized, sparking the joint and starting the Apache's engine. One could read almost anything into it when there was perhaps nothing there at all. As he crossed the river he put the music back on to calm him down, the capsule of the car was all Ws, the whirring contact of the Apache's wheels with the tarmac beneath it, white letters on the road signs flaring in the passing glare of the headlamps as Jay turned on to River Road, the swollen white moon ducking and diving amongst the speeding black wracks high up in the sky, the white glare of a pair of headlamps in the rearview some fifty metres behind him. Five minutes later, with The Prez bouncing his way through 'Taxi War Dance', Jay noticed that they were still there in his mirror, two blurred points of light that swung in and out of view as he negotiated each successive bend in the road. Was he being followed? Were they even the *same* headlamps? He turned off the music and kept an eye on the lights as he sailed past the small towns at the side of the road, the red beacon at the summit of a radio tower he hadn't noticed before visible in the dark sky above the forests to his left. The lights continued to stay with him. Was it his imagination or was the car getting closer? Whoever it was behind him had closed the gap to less than thirty metres and seemed to be getting nearer and nearer. A right turn that was marked 'Funston Road' came into view and Jay watched to see if the beams of the headlamps would swing away into the murk and disappear leaving him to get on with feeling stupid and paranoid. No, they stayed on the main road, perhaps gaining another ten metres on him. Jay tried to work out what kind of car it was but couldn't, the glare blotting out what moved behind them. Whatever it was, its chassis was set high up off the ground which suggested that it was some kind of pick-up or 4x4, a Raider maybe, or a Scout or a Kalahari. In the end, it didn't matter what it was: was it tailing him? Jay toed the Apache forward and tried to draw away but the car behind did the same, matching him in terms of speed and acceleration. Who was it? Maybe it was someone trying to overtake and the best thing he could do was slow down and let them pass? For a moment, Jay considered the possibility that it was Dan Harrington or one of his cronies but then told himself that he was being alarmist. *Was* he being alarmist? The car closed the gap further. Twenty metres. Then fifteen. Then ten. Then five. Jay tapped the brakes to flash a warning at the driver with his rear-lights and the headlamps behind retreated for a moment before coming in close again, two bright beams angled right into his eyes as the road straightened out. Then Jay saw the amber wink of an indicator . . . *it was just some idiot who wanted to overtake but had been too timid to make a move until now* . . . the lights moved sideways and in a few seconds he'd see some middle-aged couple in a Searcher glide past on their way back from the city or maybe a gang of teenagers drunk after a night out in mom's Cruiser.

Then everything behind him went black. The lights on the car behind snapped off and Jay was left blinking in the sudden darkness, trying to concentrate on the lights of his own car ahead of him, hands moving the wheel for a moment with a blind trust that he wasn't about to skid off the road, the shadow of the darkened car behind lost in the blind spot between his mirrors before it loomed up just behind his left shoulder and he felt its clanging impact and the altered velocities that attended it in the core of his stomach and the wheel spun out of control in his hands.

16

And then the whole world turned white.

'*W'thef'ck?*'

It took Jay a moment to synchronize the necessary elements of reality: the single thump of the initial contact, the sound of the Apache's wheels careering across the verge, the rumbling vibration of the tarmac giving way to the strangely silent mud and the torsion of the steering wheel going glassy in his hands. His feet trampled down on the pedals and he felt the ratchet vibration of the useless handbrake in his right palm, then the first impact of the fender with something at the side of the road (accompanied by the thought that it was a tree and that *that* would be *it*) and a hissing sound that preceded the taught fuzz of the plastic airbag that now pressed against his lips and nose.

'*W'thef'ck?*'

Jay took a first tentative breath, expecting a flash-fire of pain in his ribs and frantic bulletins coming in from the rest of his body with reports of similar disasters. But he seemed to be okay except for a soreness in his neck and a stunned, blunt sensation on the back of his head. He took another breath and then located his fingers (they were at the end of his hand where he'd left them) before pulling at the door handle and falling sideways on to the grass. At some point, he remembered that the car might catch fire and slithered away to a patch of grass where he lay panting at the star-haunted sky. Minutes later, Jay and the Apache were still in the same positions, neither of them in flames, both of them lying in the mud and ejecting steam out into the air where it joined the whooping of the bullfrogs and the sound of the insects ticking away like a million clocks counting out the pieces of the night. Slowly he picked himself up and walked up to the car and saw that it hadn't struck a tree but a fencepost that had half-buckled under the force of the collision. The front right corner of the Apache was crumpled but there seemed to be little more damage than that.

In the distance, coming from the direction he'd originally been heading (and the direction in which his assailant had disappeared) came the glow of headlamps bouncing off the trees at the next bend in the road, a car then appearing, moving at a cautious pace. Was it the same car as before, returning to check if he was dead, maimed or merely dazed (and what if he was discovered merely dazed and not maimed or dead, what then)? It didn't look like it and Jay hobbled to the side of the road and held up a hand. The approaching car slowed down further, a sleek looking Mamba that eventually came to a standstill a couple of feet away.

The window lowered.

'Are you all right?' the voice asked before a light came on inside and Madeleine Kelly appeared in the frame of the driver's window.

'Jay? Are you okay?'

She climbed out of the car and came over towards him, dressed in a pair of jeans and a plain white t-shirt, black hair tied back with the same black ribbon Jay had seen earlier in the day.

'Madeleine, I . . .'

'Don't try and talk. Are you sure you haven't broken anything?'

'I'm fine . . . I think.'

'If you can stand then you can't be too badly hurt,' she said. 'Lean on my car and let me check.'

Madeleine guided Jay over to the Mamba and he leaned back on it, thankful for the support, while she pushed aside the flaps of his jacket, placed her hands on each side of his ribcage and pressed gently.

'Do you feel anything?'

He shook his head. She pressed higher up, her hands working their way up to his armpits.

'Here?'

'Nothing.'

'*Here*?'

'Still nothing.'

'Hold out your arms . . . *slowly*.'

Jay did as she asked.

'Does *that* hurt?'

Jay shook his head.

Madeleine placed two fingers lightly on each of his temples and scrutinized his eyes. 'You don't seem to have any concussion and you don't seem to have broken anything. Do you feel any whiplash?'

'No, I don't think so. My neck's a little sore . . . and my head where it hit the headrest . . .'

'We should get you inside and check you over in the light.'

Madeleine shunted Jay gently to one side and then pulled open the passenger door of the Mamba and lowered him in.

'What about my car?' he asked.

'We can call a tow truck from the house or leave it until tomorrow morning.'

She shut the door, then climbed in behind the wheel and turned the car round.

'What happened?' she asked.

What happened? Good question, Jay thought to himself. Who'd run him off the road? Dan Harrington was the first person that came to mind, but if so: why? Dan may have been a thug as far as everyone else was concerned but their earlier confrontation in the parking lot behind Nicole's surely hadn't goaded him into chasing Jay all the way to Brunswick County before knocking him into the trees? Perhaps Dan *had* recognized Jay from earlier on in the day? But again: was that any motive for what had just happened? Dan didn't know Jay, had never met him before, and certainly had no reason to send him spinning off the road.

'Some car was trying to overtake,' he said, 'clipped me as it went past.'

'Didn't it stop?' Madeleine asked.

'No.'

'Did you get a look at the plates?'

Jay shook his head and told her that he was too busy chomping on the airbag to take down any details. Perhaps the collision *had* been a mistake. Again, the image of a carload of drunken kids or some doddering couple of seniors sweeping him off the road . . . but why had the vehicle's lights suddenly been turned off at the moment of maximum disorientation? The contact between the two vehicles had been more than a glancing blow. And there was also Madeleine's convenient arrival to take into account. Jay accepted that it may have been nothing more than paranoia but he was as suspicious of her appearance moments after the Apache had been pinged off River Road as anything or anyone else.

'It's lucky you came along,' he said. 'I don't think I could have walked anywhere unaided. Where were you headed?'

'I was just heading out to the gas station for some cigarettes.' She glanced across at Jay momentarily. 'I don't really need them. I gave up years ago but started lately after . . .' Madeleine broke off for a moment. 'Anyway, we should check you out first. I can go and get some later.'

'I have some cigarettes.'

Jay pulled out a couple of Spirits and lit them before passing one to her and they drove on in silence for a while, making the turning for the drive to Thackeray after a few minutes, the lights in the ground floor windows coming into view at the end of the tunnel of trees.

'It occurred to me,' she said suddenly, 'that I was unnecessarily rude to you this afternoon. After you'd left, I regretted it. I'd like to apologize.'

'Don't worry about it,' he replied as she brought the Mamba to a crunchy halt on the drive outside the front door of the house.

'How are you feeling?'

'Okay.'

'Can you walk? Do you need help?'

Jay said that he could walk unaided and he unfolded himself gingerly from the car and ascended the nine steps to the front door where he waited while Madeleine punched a security code into the keypad by the doorbell.

'Come in,' she said somewhat formally and then unlocked the door. Jay followed her through the hallway into a kitchen that was about the same size as the ballroom at Willoughby. Madeleine pointed to a stool by a breakfast bar near the appliances.

'Where's your maid?' he asked, letting Madeleine help him off with his jacket before he sat down.

'She lives nearby in Winnabow. Wait here.'

Madeleine left the room and returned with a glass of brandy which she put down in front of him.

'I thought you might need this.'

She again placed two brown fingers lightly on each of his temples and stared into his eyes. 'Hunting for ghosts?' she said (he could feel her breath on his upper lip). 'How did you get into that?'

'I moved to San Francisco a couple of years ago . . .'

'San Francisco? Why there?'

'I had a friend who said I could stay with him. Ironically, I was born there but my parents moved to England a couple of months afterwards. My father was English.'

'And your mother was Japanese?'

'Chinese.'

Madeleine's humid pupils focused on Jay's right eye, then his left, her dark lashes holding steady as she peered at him. 'I think you're okay,' she said and removed her hands from his face, his eyes taking in the cluster of diamonds the size of a brazil nut on her ring-finger and the soft flesh of her upper arms disappearing into the cotton sleeves of her t-shirt.

'So you got to San Francisco and started looking for ghosts?'

'I met this investigator who was looking for an apprentice. When he died, I inherited his business.'

'Is it a good living?'

'Sometimes.'

'And what about Willoughby?' Madeleine smiled. 'You already know what I think. But do *you* really think there's a ghost there?'

Jay shrugged. 'At the moment, I'm not sure. A few things have happened that so far look as if they might defy rational explanation, objects moving in the night and so on.'

'So you actually believe that ghosts exist?' She reached for the brandy she'd poured him and took a sip, her eyes focused on his over the rim of the glass.

'This will sound weird, given that it's how I try to earn my living, but I'm not really sure what I believe.'

'How can you search for something you're not sure exists in the first place?' Her hand touched Jay's leg briefly. (Was she flirting with him?)

'I think it's more the case,' he started, 'that the phenomenon or event you're investigating continually defies your attempts to rationalize it and after a time you find yourself forced at least to accept the *possibility* that something paranormal has happened . . .'

'That ghosts exist? That someone has come back from the dead?'

Jay remembered for a moment the apparition hovering above

General Lockwood's dazed face, and the catalogue of other encounters that he hadn't been able to account for in his two years of investigations: the desperate figure that appeared every night on the recently scrubbed corner of 28th and Judah, on the spot outside the mini-mart where a local man had been stabbed only nights before in a suspected Triad hit; the apparition of a pregnant woman appearing at the top of a staircase at a house on Filbert, stairs down which she'd had fallen to her (and her unborn child's) death; the phantom family that materialized with nightly regularity at the fatal intersection near Lake Elsinore where their winnebago had been sideswiped by a driver who'd nodded off to sleep at the wheel of his logging truck at the worst of all possible moments; the dressing room at the Joseph Peak Theater on Van Ness where Joanna Genthon had slit her wrists minutes before she was due on stage to play Lady Macbeth (the lights there sometimes failed to work, performers felt inexplicably nauseous or claimed to hear a faint whimpering which had been successfully recorded on Jay's sound equipment while the EMF readings plunged); the translucent child that wandered through the corridors of a Market Street department store where a young boy had once been abducted (his remains found later in four separate boxes around the city); the sound of a screaming man reported by clerical staff twenty floors up the Glover Building on Kearny only a block along from Jay's office (was it a bird or the after-presence of a construction worker who'd fallen to his death during the building's construction?).

'Perhaps. I try never to make an explicit connection between a death and an anomalous phenomenon, more try to let any such connection or juxtaposition make itself known to me, even if it's only circumstantial.'

'So how do you work?' Madeleine asked.

'My client's account of what they've witnessed helps me fix an approximate locus for the potential haunting. After that, it's a case of trying to prove that the event or phenomenon is a hoax using cameras and motion detectors to catch the perpetrators, whilst at the same time using a whole bunch of gadgets to measure anomalous fluctuations in a location's temperature, in its electromagnetic field and its humidity and radiation levels. Sometimes these fluctuations seem to be consistent with data from other investigations where the phenomena in question have defied explanation, but they're certainly not a foolproof indicator.'

'Why not?'

'Because what we might broadly call natural phenomena can affect these readings. As a paranormal investigator, I've had to learn to evolve my methods in such a way that takes into account these distorting influences. Does that help you understand better?'

Madeleine stared at Jay, then smiled. 'I'm sorry. I still don't believe you.'

'You think I'm making it all up?'

'No, I think you believe in what you're saying. I just don't think ghosts exist. Death? That's *it* . . . the end. If ghosts existed, someone would have proved it by now.'

Jay didn't bother to contest what Madeleine had said (though it struck him that she'd said the same thing that Zelda had back in San Francisco . . . but so had countless others) and she didn't add any more. But Jay thought he saw a hazy look of sadness in Madeleine's eyes. Like most people when they got on to this subject, even the sceptics, she was probably remembering some grandmother or favourite uncle now dead and buried.

'You're not touching your drink,' she said suddenly. 'Do you want something else?'

Jay shook his head. 'I should be getting back to Willoughby sometime soon.'

'Do you want to call a tow truck?'

'No. I'll do it in the morning. Do you mind driving me back? I could call a cab if you prefer.'

Madeleine replied that it wasn't far and that she would take him and they both stood up, Madeleine picking his jacket up from the chair on the other side of the room and helping him into it, Jay realizing that his arms and shoulders still ached along with his head. He followed her back out of the front door and out to her waiting Mamba. As they funnelled up the drive back to the main road, Jay asked her where she was from. She told him: France.

'Which part?' he asked.

'Menton. It's a small town on the coast near the Italian border.'

'When did you come to America? When you were young?'

'After I left university, I was offered a job in Toronto. Then a job down here in Wilmington.'

'Doing what?' Jay asked, remembering that Madeleine had worked as Frank McKelvy's personal assistant before marrying Wallace.

'Translating for a shipping company. I speak Spanish and German as well as English and French so I've always found it relatively easy to get work.'

'It sounds lonely.'

'What does?'

'Moving around from place to place. You never wanted to settle down?'

'It depends if you like to travel or not. I never wanted to stay at home. And I have settled down, with Wallace . . . or I thought I had.'

Madeleine stopped talking and drove the rest of the way to Willoughby in silence until she had pulled up outside the house.

'We're here.'

'Thanks for coming to my rescue.'

'I hope there isn't too much damage to your car,' she said, 'see you around.'

17

It was a little after eleven thirty by the time Madeleine's tail lights had disappeared from view. Jay circled the outside of the house the same way he had the night before, making an initial assessment of which guests were still up and which guests had gone to bed. Zelda's lights were still visible on the upper floor of the coach house. The only other light on inside was in Toby's bedroom. Should he bother to tell them he was back? Jay decided against it, not least because it would necessitate an explanation of what had happened out on the road: wasn't it better to get on with his work and explain it all in the morning? He moved through the corridors of the house priming his equipment. Thankfully everyone had gone to bed relatively early again rather than staying up drinking and talking in one of Willoughby's drawing rooms. They'd had enough of the house and each other. They'd taken all the drugs they'd brought with them (those that had brought any); they'd got bored of draining Toby's wine cellar (or at least worn themselves out with a day's drinking by nightfall); they'd got bored of the same old conversations and the lack of privacy. What else was there to do but sleep?

First the top floor. Jay initialized the motion detector near to the door of Johnny and Meliza's room and then retreated to the floor below where he checked his equipment and also noticed that Toby had now turned out his lights along with everyone else sleeping on that corridor. Down on the ground floor, Jay fixed himself a cup of coffee in the kitchen where the smell and heat of the evening's cooking still lingered in the air before walking through to the hallway where he opened up the software and then checked the other equipment in the hallway:

the camera, the ion detector, the hydrothermometer and the Geiger counter. Back at the powerpad, Jay scanned the screen. There he was.

00:18:00   Camera 01

Everything was working. Jay then walked under the staircases and through into the main corridor where he settled himself in his seat, telling himself that he would make a circuit of the house at one o'clock and then at ninety minute intervals after that. On with the earpiece. Again, Jay faded down the crossfire of incidental signals until he had a workable baseline, an unrelenting velvety thrum ringing low and deep in his left ear. After that, it was back to the waiting and the watching. *And the wondering* . . . Jay examined the events of the evening for a while, again trying to connect what the day had revealed about the Harringtons, the Kellys and Frank McKelvy. But he came up with nothing new until he considered his earlier suspicion that Madeleine had been flirting with him. Surely he was being ridiculous? And what about his suspicions about her timely arrival at the Apache's crash site? Again, Jay found himself asking why he was testing his picture of how everyone seemed to connect with everyone else . . . was it because he suspected something sinister had happened to Helena (and perhaps also to Wallace)? Why was he being so suspicious? The list of ridiculous thoughts he'd entertained over the last forty-eight hours was getting longer and longer: he'd believed that he'd seen Helena at the marina and then told himself it had been Zelda . . . he'd imagined that Toby had killed Helena and that Madeleine Kelly had been flirting with him and even that Helena had even come to San Francisco to find him. What else could he come up with?

At one o'clock he got up off his seat and tried to unscramble himself, the bones in his spine clicking like the Geiger counter in the hallway beyond as he yawned and stretched. He took the earpiece out for a second and let the silence of the house gradually swell in his ears as the after-echo of the EMF wand faded to nothing. In the hallway, he checked the powerpad. Everything remained the same as it had been three-quarters of an hour before. The same went for the ion detector and the hydrothermometer and the Geiger. The paintings hung on the walls, a moonbeam probing in through one of the windows whose shutters hadn't been fastened properly, a thin streak of light cutting through the darkness and falling across an image of what looked like Sixty Bridge. Jay went back to his seat in the main corridor, picked up the EMF wand and refitted the earpiece. *His suspicions towards Toby — were they based on anything logical?* Besides the linguistic formulation that Jay had pounced on that morning (a line of investigation that now felt increasingly absurd) and the belief that Helena would have been unlikely to abandon her newborn child (he'd reiterated this to himself continually since arriving in North Carolina though, he had to face it, it seemed like a judgment based purely on his assessment of her character, something he had little reason to maintain much faith in), it was only the potential presence of the paranormal in the house, this founded so far *only* in the fact that the paintings had moved, that distinguished Jay's suspicions from rampant and inevitably bitter paranoia. He knew, more than most perhaps, how slender and fragile a link this was, and that it was no basis for anything more substantial than guesswork.

Tommy Cheung had been as confusing about this aspect of paranormal investigation as he had been about many others. The majority of their cases in those early days saw Tommy continually warning Jay against making necessary or automatic connections between the presence of something potentially paranormal and an unresolved, tragic or even violent death. There was the time, for example, when they were hired to investigate a recently recommissioned lighthouse on Point

Lucette a couple of hours down the coast from the city. The coastguard, a newly promoted officer called Lieutenant Maurice Schaffer, had reported to Jay and Tommy a series of strange experiences that had happened to him during his first weeks in charge. He'd listened to the local inhabitants' stories of a ghost haunting the historic building after he first arrived in the area, he'd told them, but dismissed it all as harmless rumour mongering designed to wind up a newcomer to the small town only to find himself hearing echoing footsteps spiralling up and down the tower's steep stairwell most nights as he and his assistants pored over their screens and charts in the swirling light that turned above their heads. Was one of his staff playing tricks on him? It didn't appear so. They'd all be sitting in their eyrie looking out over the roiling Pacific when they'd hear the sound of the old iron door at the foot of the tower slamming shut (when Schaffer went down to check, the door was shut . . . but then everyone had already sworn they'd shut it behind them when they'd arrived for their shift); his juniors reported smelling pipe smoke as they sat out the relief watches in the bleeping dark-light-dark of their long night scanning the scrolling ocean beyond the black window; a figure was sometimes glimpsed on the observation deck at twilight or a shadow spotted on a lower flight of stairs only for the observer to find nothing there when he or she went to take a closer look.

Tommy and Jay had approached the investigation in their usual manner, interviewing all of Lieutenant Schaffer's personnel (there was little doubt that most of the staff were petrified, uneasy at best, nerves now rubbed raw after nights of believing that something uncanny and only semi-visible moved amongst them). And they'd sat up for three nights before their instruments registered an anomalous presence: an ion surge well into the top quartile of the machine's range that corresponded with accompanying peaks in radiation levels and troughs in localized temperature. The microphone recorded footsteps though the camera failed to pick up any trace of their source. And there it was, the stout wooden smell of burning pipe tobacco, discernible in the air behind the thin tang of the smoke rising off Tommy's Deltas.

During the days, camped out in their guesthouse in the nearby town, Tommy and Jay had scanned records detailing the history of the lighthouse and the surrounding area that they'd borrowed from the library in nearby Bixby. Pirates, smugglers and assorted outlaws had notoriously used the local coastline throughout the centuries to dodge swashbuckling Spanish governors intent on their capture and marauding Mexican generals looking to achieve the same. The area had also provided the backdrop for its fair share of genocide and catastrophe, including Miwok uprisings throughout the early nineteenth century (these ruthlessly put down by a succession of colonial forces struggling for possession of California) as well as death *en masse* by way of earthquake, fire and disease.

Looking at the history of the lighthouse specifically, it had been closed in 1909, deemed an unnecessary expense by the state given the proximity of other lighthouses up and down the coast until not much less than a century later when commercial shipping concerns lobbied successfully for its reactivation. There were photos of the building from the old days, moody images of the tower soaring up into the air against a backdrop of sepia skies and sunsets, several technical shots of its construction in 1856 and of the installation of a replacement lens at the turn of the century, shots of workmen hoisting it up the side of the tower's white walls while a crew of supervisors looked on, one of them an old sea dog in an old sea dog's cap and coat with a pipe skewing out of one corner of his clamped lips.

The man's name had been Captain James Hyde-White and Tommy had reported this to his successor the following day.

'He died in his sleep a couple of weeks after the lighthouse was decommissioned, nothing violent, nothing suspicious. Perhaps his spirit, or something we might understand as such, still . . . *lingers* . . . in the building?'

Maurice Schaffer had stared incredulously at Tommy for a moment. 'Are you being serious?' he'd asked.

Tommy had nodded. 'As serious as I can be with the knowledge at my disposal.'

'What am *I* supposed to do?'

Tommy had suggested that the lieutenant did nothing. Was the phenomenon causing him any trouble? Was it stopping him from going about his job? Schaffer's account of his strange experiences and Tommy and Jay's findings suggested that the phenomenon did not interact with his personnel, was merely present in the lighthouse because it had failed (or 'refused', Tommy suggested cautiously) to disengage itself from the site.

'You could try and have it exorcised,' Tommy continued, 'but my hunch is that this would be futile. Probably best to ignore it, think of it like you would a stray cat that you sometimes let roam around your garden or home, sometimes even feed though you're not sure who it belongs to.'

And over the next few months there were other similar instances of benign phenomena and cases where there seemed to be no kind of tragedy at the heart of whatever was taking place. There were cases like The Motel Madame Mystery that saw Jay and Tommy stake out a motorlodge in Miramar where the spectre of Audrey Vanlander, an infamous '49ers era prostitute, was allegedly seen most nights by guests booked into room thirteen even though Madame Vanlander was officially registered as having died peacefully in her sleep aged ninety-nine at the Halcyon Daze Retirement Haven up in tranquil Daris County. There was the time they were hired by cautious civic drones to look into reports that a phantom cop stalked Golden Gate Park, issuing tickets and citations that, when followed up by the motorist, revealed that the issuing officer had been a content grandfather of six at the time of his death a decade or so before.

That the existence of the paranormal didn't *necessarily* seem to equate with tragic or unresolved death had been Tommy's continued assertion. And yet there was a whole array of counter examples. Jay remembered once investigating a branch of Yogurt Yurt in Noe Valley, one of a small chain of Mongolian milk bars dotted around the Bay Area. He and Tommy had been called in by Sunny Andersen, an assistant team leader at the establishment. The store had been suffering a series of unexplainable power failures and other unsettling occurrences.

'The freezers are switching themselves *off*, like, during the night shift an' all. And the yogurt's all curdling, but in, like, super-quick time,' she told Jay. 'Maybe if it, like, happened, like only once, like just one time, you'd have to say that it wasn't so weird. But it's, like, happening all over. And then last night was just too much.'

'Can you say more about that, Miss Andersen?' he asked while Tommy paced around the premises, peering into corners and scratching his beard every so often, Jay unable as always to work out exactly how much of this was showmanship.

'So it was, like, around ten after ten and I was out the front of the store, like *literally* where we're standing right now, and I'm totally desperate to use the bathroom but I'm on my own coz Treena's gone out to the grocery store. Anyways, I end up locking the front door coz I can't leave the counter unattended, and I'm, like, gone only a coupla minutes, like three maybe, or even less, like a *minnit*. And I'm in the bathroom and I hear the door to the store open and close and I'm saying to myself, like, *How come Treena has a key?*

'But when I get back out front it's, like, nobody's there. An' I'm standing there hollering out for Treena but she's, like, not answering so's I go back to the office and she's not there and

I'm shouting out, like, Treena, this is not freaking funny. And it's then that I almost, like, *totally die* because I hear this tapping sound and this small voice crying out my name, like, "Sunny, Sunny, Sunny!" Luckily it was Treena banging on the door yelling at me to let her in.'

'So Treena *didn't* have a key?'

'Like, only assistant team leaders and team leaders get keys to the store.'

'So, you let Treena in. What happened next?'

'So, like, it's at that point I notice that the power's gone off again. And it's then that Treena looks down and, like, screams.'

'Why?' Jay asked her.

'All the yogurt in the counter had gone sour. We run, like, fourteen flavours, and every single one was curdled. Sure, the power had gotten turned off, but like a hundred pints of frozen yogurt does not go off just like that.'

'What time was this, you say?' Tommy asked casually from the other side of the room.

'Just after ten o'clock?'

'At what other times of day do these power failures occur?' he asked.

'Err . . .' Sunny Andersen chewed her lip. 'Like around then?' she said, eyebrows then arching in a modest attempt to be more helpful. 'Maybe?'

The reports by other members of staff, Treena included, replicated Sunny Andersen's account with greater and lesser degrees of correspondence and eventually Tommy and Jay had staked the place out the following night, Jay garbed out in a pistachio *deel* and chocolate *louz*, both emblazoned with the Yogurt Yurt logo, so as not to frighten off any customers who hadn't heard rumours about the possible haunting.

'I look ridiculous,' he'd complained.

'Well, I'm too old so it's got to be you,' Tommy had replied as he reached across and straightened Jay's brown hat. 'People see a mangy old Chinese guy like me dressed like that and think I'm a monk, not honourable employee of Yogurt Yurt.'

'How convenient.'

Tommy had consoled Jay with the suggestion that he view the investigation as a test. 'To see what you have learned. I simply sit back and humbly await your instructions,' he intoned in a wildly overblown *sensei* impression. 'Time for young apprentice to show venerable master how far he has travelled.'

And Tommy did sit back, all night, at one of the low tables circled with cushions at the side of the store, the old timer meditatively spooning blobs of frozen yogurt, vanilla and ground chestnuts into his mouth, these punctuated by pensive nods of his head (and stealthy glances at the small compass placed on the table next to his napkin), while Jay helped Sunny serve the sporadic trickle of customers who strayed into the store, all the time keeping an eye on the machines. As the hour hand on the clock above the door slowly levered itself up towards the ten, Jay noticed Sunny becoming increasingly tense as she hustled back and forth behind the counter. At ten, he glanced over at Tommy who now seemed to be dozing on his cushion, hands clasped loosely in his lap. At ten after ten the lights in the store flickered. Jay looked across at Tommy who raised his head as the lights hiccupped again.

'It's, like, *happening*,' Sunny whispered.

Jay glanced down at the equipment. The EMF detectors and the hydro-thermometer were all virtually useless in the cold, damp and highly electrified environment of Yogurt Yurt. But the ion detector was recording numbers well into the red and when Jay looked back across at Tommy, the old man made a small circular motion with the index finger of his right hand: the compass was spinning.

No one moved. A few cars cruised past outside on 24th, for a moment nothing more than images from the surface of another planet. Inside, Jay primed his ears for the phantom sound of the door opening and closing but only felt a cool flush ripple through his skin. Beside him, he heard Sunny stop breathing. He looked across at her and then saw that she was staring into space, her tongue flopped out on to her lower lip. Jay followed the line of her vision to the centre of the store. There it was, not a figure so much as a mass of condensation or heat haze in the air which remained for a second and then vanished. Suddenly the three of them were all standing there, Jay sweating into his robes (the room was now suddenly and inexplicably hot) while the yogurt lay in clotted slops in its tubs.

'What's your assessment?' Tommy asked, springing to his feet.

'No sound of the door opening and closing this time,' Jay said.

'Can I try something?' Tommy asked.

'Be my guest.'

Sunny was still standing there, eyes voided, mouth slack. Tommy ducked around the side of the counter and gently placed a hand on each of her temples.

'Sunny?' he whispered. 'Sunny, are you okay?'

Sunny blinked.

'Say *yes* or *no* . . .'

'Yes,' she whispered.

'Sunny, how long have you worked in this store?'

'Like, about eight months,' she droned.

'Good,' Tommy whispered back, his left hand pressed against the back of her neck, his right hand held across her forehead. 'Now *trust me*. Do you trust me, Sunny?'

She nodded.

'Close your eyes . . .'

She closed them.

'When did the strange events start occurring?' Tommy asked.

'*Like about three weeks ago, or maybe even a month.*'

'Think back about *three* months. That takes us back to around August. Imagine the leaves on the trees, imagine it's warmer. Imagine you're working the night shift . . . what are you doing?'

'Err . . . I'm, like, in the store and I'm taking a tray out to one of the tables outside and like Treena's behind the cash register and, err . . .'

'Is the store full or empty?'

'There's, like, a few people at the tables inside, and the guys outside and, like, a line of customers at the counter . . . and, like, I'm coming back in with the tray and . . .'

'Who's serving the customers in the line?'

'Treena, and she's, like, pulling faces at me coz she's serving Ernie . . .'

'Who's Ernie?'

'He's, like, this regular who's always coming here, like, every night and he's got, like, this thing for Treena but he's, like, totally gross, like, I don't mean to be mean or nothing but he's, like, rilly heavy and kind of has pee stains on his pants, and maybe he is sad and lonely but, like, Treena's no way gonna go out with him in, like, a gazillion years.'

After they'd dropped Sunny at her apartment in Burlingame, Tommy had driven him and Jay back to the office via the drive-thru window at Sandwich Island on 101 and they'd sipped at triple-shot Konacinos and chewed on Toasted Kahaluu Specials while they'd itemized what they knew so far and stared at a map of the city.

'What have we got?' Tommy asked, patting Marlowe on the head and giving him a piece of tsukemono.

'We've got a recurring anomalous event at around twenty-two ten,' Jay replied, reading from the list he'd scribbled down in the car, 'with simultaneous disturbances to local power sources and electrical appliances, multiple witnesses, timed at around twenty-two ten. We've also got reports of an anomalous auditory event, the opening and closing of the door.'

Tommy pondered the map, marking the location of the store on it with a dot and then drawing a circle around it that stretched as far as 21st to the north, Douglass to the east, 30th to the south and Mission to the east.

'Why the circle?' Jay asked, finally getting round to pulling off the *louz* and *deel*.

'It's the time,' Tommy replied. 'Ten after ten. We've got very little to go on but I suspect that this Ernie character was a creature of relentless habit and left for the store on the hour. Let's start trying to locate him within a ten minute walking radius of the store.'

The next day Tommy and Jay ranged up and down the sidewalks around Sanchez and 24th at the epicentre of the circle Tommy had drawn, asking questions about Ernie. Who knew him? Had people seen him walk past their store? Eventually their search pattern brought them meandering through the streets to a café called Muddy Water on the corner of Valencia and 24th where the staff recognized their description of Ernie but knew little more and suggested that Jay and Tommy ask at the grocery store a couple of blocks up where the manageress apparently 'knew everything'. Five minutes later, they were talking to a six-foot Ethiopian woman called Milly who sat annotating a copy of *L'Etre et Le Néant* in between bagging up her customers' purchases.

'He use to come in the store himself every now and then,' she told them. 'Mostly, my son, Coleman, he makes a weekly delivery to the place. You guys cops?'

Tommy had chuckled and told her no, and they weren't from the IRS either. He presented her with his card, a scaled down version of the advert he ran in the local newspapers printed on it.

'So you guys is *psychics*?'

Tommy shrugged. 'Not exactly . . .'

'Well, you don't look like no troublemakers, especially not the skinny weak-lookin' fella with the nice words and voice . . .'

'Has Ernie been getting his deliveries as usual?' Tommy asked her.

'Now you come to mention it, he hasn't, not this last three weeks, not called once. He must've gone on his vacations or something.'

She'd called out for the boy and he'd ambled in, a blinking black goldfish in a Giants t-shirt and sneakers, a wild afro tumbling around the frames of his milk-bottle glasses. Tommy looked into his huge blinking eyes asked if he could show them where Ernie lived and all four of them drove the couple of blocks to San Jose. There, Tommy had waited in the car with Milly and Coleman while Jay walked across the road, making mental notes for his case report. He walked up the narrow side passage and found the doorway Coleman had described, eighteen twenty-four on the watch, no answer from within, no footsteps, newspapers piled up on the doorstep. Eventually, he'd picked the lock (easy to do on these old Victorians, especially when they were neglected) and pushed his way cautiously into the kitchen on the other side, probing the room with the flash. Something had gone off in the fridge, dirty dishes lined up on the sideboard and stacked up in the sink. Somewhere, a radio fizzled away, not tuned to any particular station. At the entrance to the short corridor leading off to the other rooms in the property, Jay flicked on the EMF wand and scanned the two doorways. The first gave off a low signal and opened to reveal a bathroom in a similar state to the tangled kitchen. Jay then turned to the other, a buzzing rising in his earpiece in concert with the sound of the radio on the other side of the door. The door handle. He turned it. Something was on the bed but he didn't have time to look once the black blind on the window had rippled and then swarmed across the room towards him.

Later, Jay had needed to empty Tommy's reserves of Glen

Achall before he could talk again. The flies had swarmed out, the sensation of being drenched in a buzzing shower of furry black sweetcorn forcing Jay on to the floor (they were in his eyes, his nostrils, his mouth, he was sure of it). Tommy had heard his screaming from the street.

As for Ernie's body, the forensics were immediately able to ascertain that he'd died approximately three to four weeks before. Some time later, Tommy pulled in a favour with a friend at the Coroner's office and had taken a look at the report over Shantung Chicken at The Empress of China. Ernest Frank Arbuthnott, aged thirty-six, suffered a fatal heart attack, most likely while he was sleeping. No one in the area seemed to know much about him except his name, though his size and weight, estimated at around three hundred pounds at the time of his death, had made him a well-known figure in his local neighbourhood. An examination of his home revealed little more, the electronic trail of internet sites in the hard drive of his computer showing that he'd surfed the internet for just under two hundred and ninety hours in the last month of his life constituting the most compelling evidence for his solitary existence.

Was this an example of a paranormal event occurring as a direct result of an unresolved death (and unresolved life)? Tommy would warn Jay that the evidence was incomplete at best, admitting that the kinds of data their machines provided were indicators, sure, but indicators of *what*? 'Imagine a caveman owning a compass, *this* one even,' he'd tell Jay, holding up the antique compass his father had given him back in China when he was a little boy, 'and watching the needle move in increasingly familiar and predictable patterns and wondering what it meant. If one knew absolutely nothing about magnetism or the spherical nature of the planet, I suspect one would have very little idea what the movements of the needle signified even if one could ascertain that they were *consistent*. How long would it take to even register that the sun always rose to the needle's *right* and that it always set to its *left*?'

Sometimes it was easier to remain sceptical, Jay told himself. But cases like Ernie's and many of the others that Jay and Tommy undertook, the alleged roadside hauntings at the scenes of horrendous car accidents, the allegedly haunted hotels that were revealed to be asylums for the unstable and insane at some point in their nascent histories, the potentially haunted battlefields and blood-spattered alleyways and parking lots that had provided the venue for various kinds of violent and hideous death – how many times could one keep on reminding oneself that it could all still be coincidence? The murder of Dana Lockwood was obviously the most potent example that recurred in Jay's mind. But there were others.

And what about Willoughby? Jay reminded himself that the movement of the paintings could have been the product of something paranormal but that this might still have had nothing to do with Helena (or Wallace), nothing at all.

Continuing his clockwork circuit of the house, he penetrated the dark spaces of the two drawing rooms before swinging open the glass doors that gave way to the cold air of the ballroom, the beam of his flashlight tracking the gleaming boards towards their phantom vanishing points, the chandeliers poised like colonies of sleeping crystal bats, and still there was nothing in the earpiece. He shut the door behind him, moved through into the library, splashes of light picking out various objects as he passed them, the spines of books, a handful of pieces scattered across a chess board, the pool balls waiting in an approximation of Cassiopeia on the green baize, an empty glass (a sniff: scotch), the crumpled newspaper lying in the black cradle of the fireplace that Jay knew concealed Helena's face but also the pictures of her staring back at him from the walls and shelves: a photograph of her and Zelda in the kitchen when they were children, perhaps ten years old, a pregnant 'Sourpuss' kneading away with a rolling pin, Zelda watching intently, Helena looking up at the camera with a cluster of star-shaped pastry cutters circling her wrists for bangles; the picture of her on her wedding day, the one that Zelda had picked up on Jay's first night at Willoughby, Helena's veil pulled back from her face (pulled back with those delicate fingertips whose touch Jay had once been foolish enough to believe would be his forever), a younger and leaner Toby in stiff collar and tails with a look of vindicated defiance on his face that reminded Jay of either summit besting mountaineers or murderous colonials; a picture of the two girls sitting on a bench in what looked like the lavender garden, aged around five from the look of their identical clothes and faces (which was which?). Next to this was a black and white photograph of John and Esmerelda Smiling on the front drive, a mustachioed John in a black tuxedo whose gleaming lapels matched his oiled hair, Esmerelda in a silver dress that mimicked the flawless shimmer of her skin, her blonde hair swept back to reveal the virginal slope of her neck (and to condemn Jay to yet another inward crunch of vertiginous longing for her daughter), the ermine stole draped over one arm, a young and spruced Alfred standing by the door of the waiting black Consul to drive them to whatever social gathering it was they were due to attend.

In the hallway, Jay unclipped the wand's earpiece so as not to numb his eardrum with the signal generated by his powerpad and suddenly the darkness at the foot of the main stairs was all Ts: the ticking of the Geiger counter, the tocking of the grandfather clock that sliced the silence into neat segments, the thin whirr of the powerpad's cooling fan. And there was the anaemic glow of the computer's screen and the tenebrous silhouettes of the wilting flowers looming large against the far wall as he passed the beam of the bright flash over the . . . Jay stopped, lungs and ribcage pausing to listen along with his ears. *Something was out there.* This was the first thought to appear in his mind with the fleeting clarity of sheet lightning until he realized that he was spooking himself, it was just the ticking of the clock.

Jay felt the skin on the back of his neck cool as he turned his head towards the shuttered window by the front door. The clock was working again. *The clock was working again?* Jay checked the speed of the ticking. One thousand and *one* . . . one thousand and *two* . . . one thousand and *three* . . . one thousand and *four* . . . as for the window, the shutter was now firmly closed. Hadn't it been left slightly ajar before?

Jay shot a look over his left shoulder, half expecting to see the pale figure of Katherine Smiling or her ancestor, Caroline, or perhaps even the spectre of Helena and Zelda's mother.

Nothing.

Then Jay felt the remote unit in his pocket vibrate at the same time as the screen on his powerpad flickered.

01:46:03   Camera 01
01:49:12   Unit 03

The first entry had been triggered by Jay himself as he'd come out of the library. But something had set off the motion detector he'd placed near the door to John and Meliza's bedroom three minutes later. He fitted the earpiece and stepped quickly down the side corridor past the downstairs office and ascended the stairwell at the other end, slowing down when he got to the top floor. The stairs came out at the end of a corridor between two attic rooms and Jay fired the beam of the flashlight down to the other end of it where he saw his motion detector taped to the ceiling, its electronic eye staring back at him, nothing else visible in the darkness and nothing in his ear. Jay then padded slowly down the corridor. Outside John and Meliza's room, he paused and still heard nothing, no movement from inside nor any sound from the nearby bathroom. Then the remote unit in his pocket vibrated again – *one of the other units had been triggered*. Jay left the bathroom and descended back down the stairwell to the first floor where he took a reading in the main corridor. There it was, a faint signal in his ears that could have been anything. Jay peered past the Remicks' bedroom door from behind his second camera. The doors to all the guest bedrooms were shut and the LED on the motion detector above his head signalled that it remained on stand-by which meant that it had to have been the unit in the hallway that had been triggered. Jay scooted forward along the passage and paused at the top of the stairs leading down to the hallway's half-landing. The hallway itself was empty but the temperature had dropped (when Jay checked the thermometer he saw that it had dropped five points) and when he checked his computer, Jay saw two new file entries.

01:52:55   Camera 01
01:55:33   Camera 02

He was responsible for the second entry. But the first? Something had triggered the camera in the hallway while he'd been on the top floor of the house.

Electronics continued to trill away in his left ear. And now in his right he thought he heard something, a noise coming from the corridor through the archway. Aware of the sound of his footsteps on the floorboards, Jay moved through into the corridor and peered down it. Again, there was a noise from down the far end, a faint glow seeping out into the darkness from the doorway to the kitchen that looked as if was slightly open. Jay now edged slowly down the corridor, the EMF wand trained on the sliver of yellow light, the static rising in his ear with each step. Soon he was at the kitchen door, brandishing the wand in front of him, his heartbeat rattling away inside his chest, the signal in his ear suddenly exploding into a deafening rush of white noise.

18

'Jay?'

Jay ripped out his groaning earpiece. Zelda was crouched down by the open door to the refrigerator (it had sounded like a landslide in his electronic ear).

'Zelda?'

She stood up. 'I'm sorry. I didn't mean to startle you.'

'That's okay,' he replied, switching off the wand and putting it on the counter next to him.

'I've been lying awake for an hour or more now and decided to come get a glass of milk. I looked through the side door to see if you were sitting in your chair. I would have given you some kind of warning if you had been but you weren't there.'

'I was taking a look around. I thought my machines had registered something.'

'Did they?' she asked quickly. Perhaps it was late (perhaps she was disorientated by her insomnia) but it seemed to Jay for a moment that Zelda had sounded as if she'd started to believe in the existence of something paranormal in the house.

'I don't think so,' he replied. 'I'll check over the data more thoroughly in the morning.'

She stood up, a slender silhouette for a brief second against the light of the humming refrigerator, the hem of her cotton rob flaring slightly as she swung the door shut and turned to face him, Jay's eyes taking a snapshot of the smooth skin on the insides of her knees and thighs before she gathered the material back around herself. 'Are you okay?' he asked (he remembered kissing Helena on that exact same spot years before, his lips mid-slide towards their ultimate target, Helena's hips flinching in anticipation, her head thrown back on the pillows while her fingertips churned through his hair).

'Yes,' she replied. She now took a step across the space between them, but then stopped. 'Once I was awake, I couldn't get back to sleep for thinking about Helena. I . . .'

She stopped suddenly and the two of them stood facing each other in the low light

'What were you going to say?' Jay asked.

'I . . .' She pushed a blonde strand of hair from across her face. 'This might sound strange to you but I can't get this feeling out of my head today, this feeling that something is wrong.'

'Wrong?'

Zelda moved a step closer to Jay, her voice almost a whisper.

'I'm scared that something has happened to Helena. I know what I'm saying sounds ridiculous but I haven't been able to shake the feeling all day.'

Jay could smell the biscuity warmth of sleep coming off her skin and hair. 'Zelda,' he asked, 'I once asked Helena if she believed in twins' intuition. She said that she didn't believe that there was a bond between the two of you in that way. What do *you* think?'

'I think maybe she's right. Helena and I are very different compared to a lot of identical twins, especially female identicals . . . always have been, ever since we were small girls. And to be honest, the idea that there *is* a bond between us is something I've always tried ignore.' She came and leaned against the counter next to where Jay was standing. 'But there have been a lot of times when it's been hard *not* to believe in some kind of . . . *connection*. Helena and I stopped giving each other Christmas presents when we were eighteen. We'd already chosen the same thing for each other four years in a row and couldn't see the point. When I had my ears pierced, Helena's swelled up and went red even though she was on the other side of the county. Back in January, I got stomach cramps so bad that I had to stop work and lie down for six hours. When I could get up again, I rang here and found out that Helena had just given birth to Jacob. And there are all the other little coincidences: the times we've picked up the telephone to call each other and found the line engaged because we were trying to call each other at the same time; the times we've read the same book simultaneously even though we were on different sides of the world; the times we've dreamt the same things on the same nights. That kind of thing just doesn't happen to other sisters in the same way.'

'And what do you feel now?' Jay asked slowly.

'I don't know.' Zelda's hands moved nervously to the necklace lying below her throat. It flashed between her fingertips. Then she took a pace away from the counter and turned to face Jay. 'What time did you get back?' she asked.

'Some time just before half eleven. I had an accident with the car.'

'What happened?'

'Another car collided with me and I skidded off the side of the road.'

'Are you okay? Do you want me to check you over?'

Jay said that he was fine.

'And how did you get back? You should have called the house. We could have come and got you.'

'Madeleine Kelly happened to be driving past. She gave me a ride back here.'

'Madeleine Kelly?' Jay noticed an unreadable look in Zelda's eyes. 'Well, I'm glad you're not hurt,' she said moving towards the door. 'I'm sorry again for startling you. How long are you staying up for?'

'Until five or six.'

'Well, I'll see you tomorrow then. Goodnight.'

Zelda was about to walk through the door in the corridor outside when Jay spoke again.

'Zelda, before you go . . .'
'What is it?'
'Did you happen to go into the hallway just now?'
She shook her head.
'No. Why?'
Jay said that he thought he'd heard something.
'Did anything figure on your machines?'
He shook his head.
'Goodnight then.'
'Goodnight.'

Zelda paused for a moment longer and then walked out into the corridor, the side door to the house squeaking quietly open on its hinges and shutting just as quietly behind her.

The sound of a car on the drive outside. 'That'll be the girls back from lunch,' you say, getting up from the sofa and walking out of the room to take a look, the tone of your voice making it impossible to know whether you feel we're about to be caught doing something we shouldn't. There's the sound of voices, two of the French girls (Marie-Antoine and Marie-Elisabète?) and two male American voices.

'Jay has just been refuelling the generator,' I hear you say out in the hallway and I'm on my feet washing my hands in the kitchen sink by the time you re-enter the room with the others.

●

Back at the mansion a few minutes later, I walk up to the roof, wondering if I'm being ridiculous. Weren't we just seconds away . . . I can't finish the sentence in my head, stunned by the memory of the light glancing off the hot, humid pulp of your lips as they'd hovered near mine.

●

I spend most of the following night and the entirety of the following day up on my roof terrace. In the morning, I turn the area around the telescope into a kind of surveillance HQ, putting a cooler full of beers, bottles of Fanta and chocolate bars up there as well as an ashtray and a cardboard box for stowing my empties. Also, I give up wasting time eating at the Restaurante S'Illot where I've previously taken most of my meals (since I've started working for Pepé, his daughters, sisters, aunts and nieces all seem happy enough to hand me a plate of steaming leftovers at least once a day). Instead, I ask for a box of sandwiches and munch methodically through its contents while I stare at Can Jazmín.

●

How much bread, cheese and ham can one guy eat?

•

And what about the villa? During the first view days of my stakeout, I'd only seen you that first time, that first evening as you'd fought with Jean-Marc. Now you're a perpetual figure in the round frame of the telescope: in the morning you swim lengths of the pool and then lounge on a white towel at the water's edge in a gold bikini, a cigarette smoking away between your lips, your arms stretched out loosely behind your head (even your armpits and elbows look impossibly sexual); in the afternoon, you climb into the Silentium with Jean-Marc and one of the girls and go through the same ritual as before with your necklace, taking it from your neck and hooking it around the rearview mirror before starting the engine and getting the jeep into second before you've made it to the first bend, sunglasses pressed against your eyes, the golden pennant of hair flying out behind you; that evening, out on the veranda, you flank Jean-Marc at the dinner table, a hand stroking his thigh as you laugh at his jokes and fill his glass. Around ten o'clock, I watch as the two of you slip away into the kitchen before disappearing from view, reappearing moments later in an upstairs window where for a brief instant I see you step out of the halo of your fallen skirt before you both disappear again from sight. At least I know which room is your bedroom (the last room at the far end of the first floor). You both reappear on the veranda ten minutes later, Jean-Marc leading the way back to your seats, you trailing behind him, your index finger hooked around his. No one seems to have noticed, your absence, or no one makes any reference to it at least, but then the two of you don't look like either of you would care if they did. A bottle of Sambuca gets opened and makes the first of a series of slow half-hourly orbits around the table. Then another. I watch as the entire complement of people around the table applauds as you light the trapped vapour in your mouth (for a few petulant seconds, your lips are a burning ring of blue fire). Later, around one, the whole group gets up and drives off in the fleet of cars, bound for one of the island's thousand parties. You probably won't be back for hours and I climb out of the chair and flop down on the cheap vinyl lilo I've thrown into the corner of the terrace where I smoke a joint down to the roach and stare up at the stars.

•

Jean-Marc calls me on my mobile the next day.

'Jay,' he says (almost pronouncing it 'Ché'), 'it's Jean-Marc. *Bonjour.*'

'Hi. How're you doing?'

'I'm good.'

No mention that I spent the previous afternoon lounging around his villa with his girlfriend. I've been waiting for thirty-six hours to speak to Jean-Marc, to see if you've told him – it doesn't seem as if you have.

'Could you come to the villa some time today?' he asks. 'Nothing serious. I just need to talk to you about something.'

I say I'll drop by in a few hours.

•

I run errands around the island for Pepé, letting some tenants into his villa near Can Tumas (a stag party of six London stockbrokers dressed like a boy band), delivering a load of supplies to Cala Grassió and fixing a pool filter at a villa in nearby Cap Negret while the exophthalmic German family occupying the place watch my every move. Then I drive up to Can Jazmín and this time it's Jean-Marc's Kodiak that's the only vehicle in the driveway. As before, the inside of the villa is empty, the kitchen, the veranda, the pool, the downstairs rooms and hallway. I call out Jean-Marc's name but there's no reply, just the hum of the fridge, the slow grumble of the generator, the teeming hillside.

'Hello?'

I scuttle up the main stairs on to the first floor corridor to see if there's anyone up there and it's then that I hear the sounds of two people grunting. The door at the end of the corridor is slightly ajar and I sidle towards it, allowing my steps to fall in time with your breathing (I thought I already knew what you tasted like, how your tongue moved, what your fingertips felt like, but I realized that I had no idea when I imagined you with Jean-Marc in the room beyond). Eventually I'm near enough so that I can gaze through the strip between the frame and the doorjamb and I peer in, moving only as fast as the motes of dust suspended in the air around me . . . in a second, I see that Jean-Marc's kneeling on the bed, his shorts around his thighs, his buttocks clenching in time with the painted toes curled around his ears. They aren't your toes. They aren't your thighs crushed against his chest. It isn't your housecoat that lies in a puddle on the floor beside the bed.

•

I tiptoe away, eventually walking back out on to the driveway and driving to the mansion where I wait until I see Alondra, one of Pepé's flock of cleaners, drive off on her scooter (it was propped up against a hedge in plain sight all along, I just hadn't seen it). Once she's gone, I watch as Jean-Marc comes out to the pool and throws himself in before collapsing on to a lounger. He lies there, basking in the last of the afternoon's heat, and is still there when you and three of the other girls pile out of your Silentium, the rainbow of bags suggesting a return from a shopping trip in Ibiza Town. You step down to the pool area where you shake Jean-Marc awake and kiss him before peeling off your sarong and jumping into the water yourself.

•

And what did Jean-Marc want to talk to me about? I drive back around the bay a few minutes later and sit with him as he tells me about his party, only half paying attention (over his shoulder, you score lines through the water).

'So, I have everything organized,' he says, 'the bar, a DJ and also a sound system. But I was wondering if you could help me get hold of some coke.' (Behind him, you continue to slide from one end of the pool to the other, now swimming backstroke, shoulders churning, your eyes meeting mine for a second before zoning back into the whirring rotations of your limbs.)

'We've been buying stuff off guys in clubs since we've got here and . . .' He shrugs. 'But you can't expect to buy good coke in clubs. I was thinking that maybe you could get us something *better*?'

'How much do you want?' I ask.

'An ounce? How much would that cost?'

'I'll have to make a few enquiries.' Now you come to a stop at the far end of the pool, climb out and look around for your towel. It's lying on the lounger next to where Jean-Marc and I are sitting, and I watch as you come towards us, twilight dripping off your skin, Jean-Marc twisting to gather your wet legs towards him with a scything arm.

'Jay says he's going to help me,' he tells you as you reach across for the towel and the bushes whisper jasmine-scented secrets to each other in the evening air.

•

The party at the villa is scheduled for the following Friday night and I monitor some of the preparation first-hand, some of it from across the bay. Throughout the next few days, a dusty procession of vans trundles up the camino, unloading crates of limes and lemons and oranges, sacks of ice, a felled jungle of mint. Bottles of spirits and gallon containers of juice follow, the flotilla of Can Jazmín 4x4s running back and forth between the villa and the supermarket in San Juan, negotiating for space on the driveway with the van delivering the sound system and the lights that are soon strung throughout the ivy and along the trelliswork and stucco down by the pool. Jean-Marc is at the centre of it all, directing the delivery boys, handing out beers and bottles of water to anyone who wants one and dispensing wads of money in every direction like handshakes.

•

By eight on the Friday, everything at Can Jazmín is ready. Down by the pool, I find Jean-Marc in a white suit, his shirt already translucent in the humid air. He seems strangely distant when I approach, not so much formal as preoccupied.

'Ça va?'

'I'm good.'

Have you had a fight? Have you found out that he's been sleeping with the maid? I give him the ounce of coke I've got for him as well as a pile of cash that I haven't used and he pockets it except for a hundred pesetas that he proffers in my direction. I wave it away.

'It's okay,' I say. 'Call it a favour.'

•

Later on, standing by the turntables, I watch as the guests start to arrive. The English first, appearing in orderly waves, forming polite queues to kiss each other and shake hands, the atmosphere that surrounds them best described as *cheerful* though there is the inevitable clutch of drunk buffoons and confident hustlers amongst them. Later on, around ten o'clock, Spanish kids appear, a steady stream of them, the boys often content to wear vests and sports clothes while their English counterparts stand around in designer shirts and jeans, the Spanish girls more eager to expose tanned skin, tattoos, piercings and underwear. The Spanish kids always seem as if they're just passing through (though many of them stay for hours) whereas the English act as if they're under siege. And there are the random groups of Americans, telling everyone which DJs they've seen in obsessive detail, and the intent packs of beetroot-faced Celts swigging lager and sweltering away in the sticky night air and the German voices rising above the chatter every so often and the French girls standing to one side and staring at it all with remote distaste while the French boys stand nearby, staring at their French girlfriends or whatever it is their French girlfriends are staring at. Jean-Marc holds court at one end of the pool and you spend a lot of the evening sitting by him, part of a circle of loud men and deft blondes, mainly American and English, who talk a lot about the quality of the coke (opinions vary, but then they always do, always did and always will), or else the quality of the restaurants on the island or the villas they've rented. At other times, I glimpse you weaving through the crowds of dancing bodies, always with a bottle of champagne swinging from your fingers, stopping here and there to listen to the end of a joke, to compliment a girl on her dress, the centre of attention as you move from group to group, even with people you don't know, then twirling on through the parting waves of faces and candlelight to penetrate another circle of guests to borrow a joint for a couple of drags, to fill an empty glass, to introduce yourself, sometimes pointing over to Jean-Marc on the other side of the garden, sometimes not.

•

At some point, I'm aware of a presence beside my right shoulder.

'You don't seem to know many people here either.'

An American accent. I turn to see a hamster-faced woman also staring at your performance on the veranda.

'Pardon me?'

'You've been standing here on your own for ages.'

She offers her damp hand.

'Hi, I'm Elizabeth Stevlingson, a friend of Helena's from North Carolina. Call me Bessie.'

'Jay,' I say but decide not to elaborate. 'You aren't one of the guests staying here are you?' I ask. I haven't seen her before, in the telescope or otherwise.

'No,' she replies. 'Or, at least, not until today. Some of the others are going back to France this weekend so Helena invited me to come and stay with her and Jean-Marc for a week. It's nice to see her and it'll be good to get a proper look at him.' Bessie stops to light a cigarette. 'I've heard a lot about him but this is the first time I've met him.'

'When was the last time you saw Helena?' I ask.

'A year ago. I met her in Amsterdam when I was in Europe on business.'

•

Amsterdam? You'd been in Amsterdam? I wonder if I passed you in the street there, scanning the appropriate memory banks but coming up with nothing. Surely I would have noticed you?

•

Bessie looks around the sparkling garden and the flow and contraflow of people moving from tier to tier, everyone glistening in the dense air. There's a scrum of bodies in the kitchen, couples talking at each of the windows on the upper floors of the villa. And even a crowd of boys up on the roof swigging from vodka bottles and driving golf balls out and over the sea, cheering each time one of their miniature moons speeds its way towards its mother in the sky.

'It's pretty serious between them,' I say as casually as I can.

'I think *he's* pretty serious,' Bessie replies. 'But you can never tell with Helena. Since she was sixteen, she's managed to convince an army of men that "it's serious" but it never has been. I'm sure Jean-Marc thinks he's got what it takes . . . we'll see. What about you, Jay? Got a girlfriend?'

'No,' I reply.

'Aren't you the lucky one. Look what I have to put up with.' Bessie nods towards the centre of the veranda where a sweaty man dodges and bucks among a crowd of girls I recognize as waitresses from Pepé's restaurant in San Carles.

'Ed, my husband. Allegedly.'

•

Bessie and I loiter at the veranda's edge for a little while longer. It's around three o'clock and the pressure in the air has continued to thicken and jangles with electric potential. I haven't seen you or Jean-Marc for a while (my eyes keep shifting up to your bedroom window but it's full of people each time I look) and I scan the crowd and finally spot the two of you coming through the crush of bodies on the dancefloor hand-in-hand. Jean-Marc leans over the turntables and says something to the DJ (you don't look in my direction, not once) who stops the record, exposing a crossfire of chatter that takes a few moments to fade into silence. Eventually everyone's turned to face Jean-Marc. Looking down at your left hand, I see the diamond dangling from your third finger.

'*Je vous remercie d'être venus tous aujourd'hui. C'est un grand plaisir de vous accueillir et j'espère que jusque-là vous vous êtes amusés. Maintenant, j'ai une annonce à faire . . .*'

He pauses.

'*Je suis sûr que certains d'entre vous sont au courant que je ne connais Helena que depuis Noël, mais également que je pense d'elle toute le bien du monde. J'espère que vous ne serez pas trop choqués d'apprendre que j'elle ai demandé sa main . . .*'

Another pause.

'. . . *et qu'elle a dit "oui"!*'

Helena holds her left hand aloft and twirls on the spot like a victorious pageant queen while the ranks of guests clap and cheer from every corner of Can Jazmín. As if disturbed by this sudden outburst of noise, the sky tenses somewhere up above. And then rain comes spiralling down. A scream goes up, people initially streaking towards cover, scrabbling for drinks and wraps of coke and half-rolled joints before they're washed away. But then enough people start to realize that the temporary bar is under a couple of tarpaulins (as are the decks and the speaker stack) and that there probably isn't enough shelter for everybody in the house and that the storm might be a short one anyway. Soon the music's back on and the more confident girls are dancing, clothes plastered to their bodies, Jean-Marc amongst them, his wet hair raked back across the top of his head. At some point you swoon off the dancefloor, arms slick with rain, and grab hold of Bessie's arm before spinning back towards him, your eyes catching mine for a second before you and Bessie start talking and she gives you a hug. I let myself watch you for a few seconds longer and then slip quietly away, through the hot mouth of the crammed kitchen, through the bottleneck of bodies in the hallway (I find a bag of golf clubs leaning against the wall and pull out an umbrella from a side pocket . . . I'll be needing it up on the roof of the mansion) and out into the rain. Walking down the sodden camino, I stop and join a crowd gathered to watch an argument between two men whose cars have collided on the slick ground. They're both drunk, clearly about to fight, both girlfriends yelling that their boyfriend's opponent 'isn't worth it' over and over again in a strange staggered set of echoes. Then I leave them to it and walk on to where I've parked my Scout at the bottom of the hill.

•

Up on the roof. I scan the battlements of Can Jazmín under the beating drumskin of the umbrella but soon give up. The whole place is a haze of misty reflections and liquid glare and I let go of the telescope and sit back in my chair.

•

It's then that I think I hear a noise downstairs. *Did I hear something?* Or is it simply a freak acoustic from across the bay or something on the hillside shifted by the rain or just my imagination?

I get up out of my chair and enter the shadows of the mansion, trying to ignore a thought that I should turn on a light (or maybe that I shouldn't), and end up in the hallway. The darkness is full of drips and squeaks and splashes, the rain keeping up its distant soundtrack as does the beating pulse of the music at Can Jazmín. I peer into the kitchen and then into the dining room.

Nothing.

I laugh off my paranoia and wander back up to the top of the building to grab a final beer from the cooler and it's then that I see you standing there gazing out across the bay, the umbrella in one hand, the telescope's eyepiece in the other. You turn, your arms cradling your shoes, your hair wet, the twirling rim of the umbrella spraying a swirl of silver raindrops out into the darkness. *I followed you*, you say, allowing me to close in slowly, *I noticed you'd gone and came after you. If you hadn't stopped in the driveway, I'd have lost you, I wouldn't have known where to come . . .*

The shoes clatter to the ground and you let the wind carry the umbrella away into the night, hands loose by your hips, eyes staring back at me. I take another step. What will you say about the telescope? Nothing? Your left hand moves towards me, evolution slow, as if each of your fingertips were stalking gravity itself and trying to outsmart it, and eventually finds the skin on the side of my neck. The wind blows a stray twist of gold across your forehead and I brush it back from your eyelashes, the touch of my hand turning your eyelids into butterflies and your mouth into a quivering animal that needs pinning down and devouring. And still I resist plunging towards you, deferring the collision for one more moment, knowing that every cell in my body is about to undergo beautiful and irrevocable change.

•

'Is this the point where we kiss?'

•

You look strangely at me for a second, then dip your head towards mine, your breath like a force field surrounding your face (once I'm in its maniacal grip, I will never be the same again).

•

Then first contact. Immediately your mouth becomes a blind spot, my consciousness flooding with any sensation other than that of the radiant void at the end of my nose, your wet hands pulling me towards you, your wet hair in my fist (my other hand ghosts your glistening hips, not quite daring to touch them, not yet), the rain coming down harder around us.

•

Then my world inverts and nothing exists except the G-forces in the whirling vortices of your mouth, the milkshake foam of your kisses, the caress of your tongue somewhere amongst your teeth and merciless lips. At some point I slide my mouth down the sides of your neck and feel the impenitent bite of eight fingernails in my back. And when I push the silver strap of your dress away, I discover in the thin strip of bare shoulder a whole star-map of light freckles and moles (I want to hurtle through it, a lost astronaut held in suspended animation forever, right there in the infinity of your skin). Then I'm peeling your dress away from your breasts, the trusting immobility of your body causing me to shudder, your nipples like the petals of some mysterious and carnivorous plant, expanding and blushing at the touch of my fingers and teeth, your hand like a drugged tarantula on the back of my head. I drop to my knees, my face traversing your stomach until it comes to rest against your left hip, a hand sliding simultaneously up over your shimmering calves and the backs of your knees and taking the hem of your dress with it as it climbs your thighs. Your dragon tattoo rears up in front of my eyes and I let my mouth follow the long looping line of its tongue to the blonde cleft between your legs where it searches out your gentle moans as if each one were the goal of its own sublime and perilous quest. Then you fall on me, your lips suddenly everywhere all at once, and I'm nothing more than the plaything of your swerving pelvis. At some point my ears hear you begging me to stop but the frenzied grip of your fingers tells me you don't mean it. At some point you lose all traction on reality (you grab hold of me with all four limbs but it won't save you) and I'm skidding towards my own oblivion on your splayed, helpless body, surfing a wave of skin and hair, pounding the rip in your smooth peach-goddess skin. Summer winds. Rainstorms.

19

Jay awoke the next day around ten and found himself sprawled on top of his bed in his clothes and sneakers, his mouth sour, his blood like quicksand. After getting himself vertical, he drifted through a series of random encounters with various objects (door handles, water, clean clothes) that seemed more like a puzzle he needed to solve for its own sake than anything corresponding with physical reality. After that, he stumbled downstairs and found himself connecting his mouth with a cup of coffee that didn't feel like the first of the day so much as the next in a sequence that had started somewhere in his vague past and eventually managed to clear his mind sufficiently to drink another while he checked over his computer log.

01:52:55   Camera 01

There it was, the unaccountable entry from the night before. Zelda had told him in the kitchen that she hadn't entered the hallway so what had triggered the camera? Jay opened up the file and scanned through it but saw nothing out of the ordinary appear until he himself showed up on the half-landing at the top of the two sets of stairs after approximately four minutes. After that, there was little else to do but take a look at the clock by the door to the library (it had stopped again) and then go looking for Toby. Jay eventually found both him and Zelda in the nursery on the top floor of the house, Toby unsuccessfully attempting to goad Jacob into drinking a bottle of milk while Zelda watched from an armchair by the window on the far side of the room.

'Good morning.'

'Good morning,' Zelda replied. Toby didn't say anything and continued to thrust the teat of the bottle towards the baby's mouth for a few moments more before giving up.

'He seems to have had enough,' he grunted to neither of them in particular before putting the child down on its playmat and turning to face Jay. He was in Jay's presence without a drink or cigarette for the first time since Jay's arrival. But he looked like he was desperate for both, his recently shaved face looking all the more raw and exposed for having nothing smoking away in front of it. The skin under his bloodshot eyes was mottled with insomniac shadows and he looked as if he was aging a decade a night. Jay guessed that there was still no news from Helena.

'So,' Toby started. 'What have you got to tell me?'

Jay took a moment to look across at Zelda. Morning light streamed in through the window behind her.

'So far, very little,' he replied.

'What a surprise,' Toby scoffed. Jay half expected Zelda to say something, but she let Toby's interruption pass.

'My equipment on the top floor of the house registered some movement at one forty-nine,' he continued, 'but nothing extraordinary seemed to be happening up there when I went to investigate first-hand . . .'

'What do you think set it off then?' Toby challenged.

'I don't know,' Jay replied. 'The equipment isn't foolproof – and anything can set off a motion detector, pets or mice or rats . . .'

'Are you saying I have rats in my house?'

'No, I'm saying that a motion detector was triggered in the middle of the night but that I don't think that it was caused by anything potentially paranormal. One of your guests could have got up in the night to go to the bathroom or get a glass of water . . .'

'Johnny and Meliza's room doesn't have it's own bathroom does it,' Zelda interrupted.

Toby agreed that it didn't.

'So there's immediately one possibility,' Jay added. He looked again at Zelda who sat there watching Toby intently. 'Something else *did* happen last night that I can't be as sure about,' he continued.

'Which was?' Toby asked.

'Do you remember we were all standing in the hallway discussing the paintings two nights ago when we realized that the clock there had stopped working?'

'How can I forget?'

'What you remember is what I'm interested in,' Jay replied as neutrally as possible. 'What time was the clock telling at the point that it stopped?'

Toby waved his hands in the air in a vague gesture. 'How should I know? It was about half-past four or something like that.'

'The clock was stuck at twenty-eight minutes after four.' Jay looked at Toby, waiting for his reaction. 'Four twenty-eight. If you take a look at the clock *now*, it's frozen at one minute after five. It started working at some point in the night, for thirty-three minutes, and then it stopped working again.'

Toby looked back at Jay, his eyes loaded with hesitation. Zelda, he noticed, continued to observe Toby.

'Go and take a look if you don't believe me.'

Toby didn't move. Nor did Zelda.

'Of course, it may be that the clock started functioning again,' Jay continued, 'if only temporarily, because of mechanical reasons. I'm not really qualified to say anything more about that. Have you contacted a specialist to have the clock examined?'

'No,' Toby replied, 'nor am I going to for the moment. Someone could have tampered with it. Maybe it just started working for a while before whatever's wrong with it just . . .' Toby again waved a hand vaguely in the air.

'Yes, somebody *could* have sneaked through the house and started up the clock,' Jay replied, 'and then come back thirty-three minutes later and tampered with it again, just as somebody *could* have moved all the paintings in the middle of the night. I'm not saying that I know what's going on, just telling you what I've discovered so far.'

Jay decided not to mention that the shutter in the hallway had closed inexplicably while he'd made his tour of the house, and also decided to keep from Toby the fact that he'd come across Zelda in the kitchen.

'Which basically amounts to nothing,' Toby replied. Jay didn't bother to dispute this.

'Jay, what about your cameras?' Zelda asked. 'You have one in the hallway don't you?'

Jay nodded. 'That's right.'

'Did it record anything last night?'

'No. I checked the files this morning. There were some curious fluctuations in both radiation levels and temperature readings, but nothing more conclusive than that at the moment.'

'Anything else?' Toby asked.

'I researched the history of the house yesterday at the library in Wilmington,' Jay replied. 'A couple of ghost stories have been connected with the house but that's not really surprising given its age and the history of the local area.'

'What kind of stories?' Toby asked.

Jay told him about Caroline von Smiling, Jan Hendricks and Katherine Smiling. 'At the moment,' he concluded, 'I think it's worth keeping this secondary data in mind. But until we get some more evidence, we shouldn't take it any more seriously than anything else we've considered so far.'

'So what happens next?' Zelda asked.

'Well, I'll see if the machines keep throwing out these anomalous readings. In the meantime, let's see if the cameras pick up anything over the next few nights.'

'And what if your cameras fail to spot anything night after night?' Toby asked.

'Like I said, Toby, if I find nothing, I pack up my bags and go back to San Francisco . . .'

'You've got three days,' interrupted Toby.

'Three days?'

'You heard me. If that's everything?'

Toby walked out the room, presumably headed for his study where he could smoke and drink. Jay looked across at Zelda once he'd gone. 'Three days might not be enough to find out anything conclusive.'

'It's up to him,' Zelda replied. 'There's not much more I can do.'

'Obviously there's been no word from Helena this morning.'

'No. How are you feeling?'

'Okay.'

'Do you feel sore anywhere?' She got up from her chair and moved towards him. 'Often the body initially tenses itself against a muscular injury and the pain appears later when it relaxes.'

'I've felt better. But I'm okay, really. I've got to call a tow company and sort my car out. And I should probably call the rental company. I guess that's the excess gone.'

'How much money have you got left?'

Jay did a quick calculation in his head and told her: a little over fifteen hundred dollars.

'Tell me if you run out of money. And tell the tow company to send their bill here and I'll pay it.'

'Zelda, thanks. And I'm sorry . . .'

Zelda raised a hand and stopped him. 'Let's just not mention it to Toby. I'll get a number for you in a while and leave it on the table in the kitchen.'

Jay left her in the nursery with Jacob and went downstairs and out on to the loggia where the garden was all Ys, the birds yakking and yawping at each other in the treetops and the yolk of the sun the only thing up there in the cloudless yantra of the sky. Jay yawned, pulled out his cell and called the office back in San Francisco:

'Penny 'n' Richards Paranormal Investigations. We ain't in right now but if you leave your details, we'll be gettin' straight back to you. You all have a nice day . . .'

The bleep.

'Mike, it's Jay. I'm just calling to ask if you can do something for me. Do you still have any contacts in the tri-state area? I need to find out as much as I can about a guy called Buck Harrington . . .' He spelled it out. '. . . rumour has it that he used to be involved in organized crime in Chicago back in the late seventies and early eighties. I'm not quite sure how much truth there is to that but it's a starting point anyway. Hope things are going well at your end. I'll be in touch.'

After he he'd hung up, Jay dialled Lara's cell. She picked up after four rings.

'Lara, it's Jay.'

'Jay.' Her tone was flat.

'I rang to see if you're okay after last night. Did Dan give you any trouble when he came back inside?'

'Did Dan give me any trouble? Yeah, he fired my ass at the end of the shift.'

'I'm sorry . . .'

'Forget about it, Jay, it's not your fault,' she interrupted. 'So, anyways, I'm guessin' you need a ride?'

'How do you know?'

'I saw an Apache on the side of River Road when I was comin' home last night. I guessed it was yours. What the fuck happened to you?'

'I got knocked off the road by another car. They didn't stop. I need to get it towed. Can you drive me up River Road?'

Lara said that she would and Jay went back inside and found

the number Zelda had left on the kitchen table and dialled it, arranging to rendezvous with the tow truck before going upstairs to his room where he rolled a joint and gathered a few things. Lara's Gazelle was waiting for him by the old coach house when he eventually went back outside and as they picked up speed down the drive, she tuned the radio to a teen-rock station.

'I just want to tell you again that I'm sorry for my part in what happened last night,' Jay said, pulling three tens from his wallet and handing them to her.

'Like I said, forget about it. It's my fault as much as it is yours.'

'Did you tell your mother?'

Lara sneaked a sideways glance at him.

'Are you fuckin' kidding me? No way is she findin' out before I've got another job.'

Jay asked what she was going to do for work. Lara didn't know. She had enough saved not to have to worry about it for a few months. But it meant that she couldn't move out of home or travel to Europe for a while longer, the reasons why she'd saved some money in the first place.

'You said you got hit by another car. Do you know what kind of car it was?' Lara asked.

'Not really. Something big, like a Searcher maybe, or a Cruiser.'

Jay considered questioning her as to Dan's movements after she'd gone back inside the restaurant. Earlier she'd said that Dan had fired her at the *end* of her shift. That still left Dan a window in which he could have trailed Jay back over the river. Jay remembered that Lara had said that Dan drove a Firefly (that was the car she'd seen Dan and Helena in together) – there was no way the vehicle that had knocked him into the fence at the side of River Road had been a Firefly with its racing lines and flattened flexure (just as there was no way it could have been Madeleine's sporty little Mamba). Perhaps Dan had other cars. It was almost a certainty that he did. Also, Jay had driven away from Nicole's and not stopped until he reached the gas station. If it had been Dan who'd followed him, he would have needed to have done so immediately (and parked unseen across the street while Jay had stopped to buy cigarettes).

'Lara, you said Dan fired you at the end of your shift last night.'
'That's right.'
'Did he follow you back inside the restaurant?'
'Yeah. He bawled me out in the kitchen and then sent me back to work. Why? You think it was *him* that smacked into you?'
Jay shrugged.
'What reason would he have?'
'I don't know. But it can't have been him so it doesn't matter.'

Eventually they reached the stricken Apache and got out to take a closer look, passing the joint and a bottle of water between them and examining the point where the other vehicle had struck Jay's car as well as the point where it had struck the fence at the side of the road, Jay noticing that there was dark green paint scraped against his rear right fender before they both took shelter in the shade. It was just after midday when the tow truck came into view, lumbering along the road towards them through the heat-haze and the fleeing mirages. The driver lowered his window.

'You Jay Richards?' he called out.

Jay nodded and the driver swung out of his cab and inspected the Apache, examining both the buckled metal of the impact point and the gap between the chassis and the ground before telling Jay that he was going to have to lift the whole thing on to the bed of his truck.

'Get anything you want to take with you and then leave it to me,' he told Jay, rubbing his damp hands on his overalls.

Jay nodded and got his Lester Young discs from out the front of the car before handing the keys over and asking for the bill to be sent to Willoughby. After that, Lara drove them both back to the house. 'What you gonna do for transportation?' she asked as she came to a stop outside the coach house. Jay said that he didn't know and she told him that he could borrow her car if he needed it.

'I've got to work here at the house for a few days anyway so it's not like I'm going anywhere. Just replace whatever gas you use.'

It turned out that Jay needed the car sooner than he'd planned. Back inside the cool hallway (silent clock, paintings where they were when he'd left an hour or so before), Jay heard Zelda's voice floating along the side corridor from the downstairs office.

'Hello. Could I speak to Mrs Kelly please? It's Zelda, Zelda Smiling.' There was a pause.

'Hello? Mrs Kelly? Madeleine, it's Zelda Smiling . . . I'm fine thank you. How are you? Good . . . I've rung to ask if your husband has been in contact with you yet. No? Nothing yet. I see . . . no, nothing from my sister so far. If I hear anything from her I'll be in touch immediately . . . no, it's no problem at all . . . goodbye.'

'No word from Wallace Kelly either?' Jay asked when Zelda came out into the hallway.

She shook her head. 'Did you get your car towed?' she asked.

'Yes. I called that number you gave me. They've taken it back to their yard. I've got to call the rental office at some point today to let them know what's happened.'

'That's a pity.'

'What's the matter?'

'I need a ride to Parton.'

Moments later, Jay and Zelda were in Lara's Gazelle, heading for Buck Harrington's ranch.

'I forgot to ask this morning,' Jay said, 'are you feeling better today?'

'Not really,' Zelda replied. 'But I'm sorry if I sounded alarmist last night. I'd been lying awake for hours with nothing to think about except what's been going on. I think I was just angry, that's all.'

'What about?'

'Helena's selfishness, I guess. How many times have she and Toby put everybody through this? What will Jacob make of it all when he's older? Helena and Toby are worse parents than my mother and father.'

Jay was surprised at the tone of her voice. In Ibiza, when he and Helena had talked about her and Zelda's parents, she'd never criticized them openly, not once. Of course, the differences between Zelda and Helena seemed as if they were never more exposed than when it came to the subject of the Smiling family and Willoughby. Jay looked across the car at her. Both had left Willoughby as soon as they were adults – but Helena had returned, got married and given birth to a child there while Zelda had gone off to work in the typhus-infested mud of the Balkans.

'I'm presuming that you know about Buck's . . . about his *interest* in Helena?' Jay asked, changing the subject.

'Yes. How do *you* know?'

Jay said that Madeleine Kelly had mentioned it. 'Do you think it's likely that Helena will have contacted him?'

'Not really. But there's no harm in asking,' Zelda said and then pointed to a turning that was drawing up on their right.

'This is it.'

The turning led to a gate in a brick wall that was eight feet high and stretched away along the treeline of a wood in both directions. When they got out and peered through the black spears of the gate itself, they saw the ranch house in the distance beyond a small orchard, a training field to one side of the house, horses tumbling back and forth across the grass. There was a buzzer attached to the brickwork and a security camera perched on top of one of the gate posts.

'I guess we ring and let them know we're here,' Jay said, turning to look first at the camera and then at Zelda. She nodded and he held the button down for a few seconds before releasing it. '*Yeah?*' the speaker grunted back at them a minute later. Jay leaned towards it.

'It's Jay Richards and Zelda Smiling . . . from Willoughby. We were looking to speak with Mr Harrington. With *Buck* Harrington. He isn't expecting us but we'd appreciate ten minutes of his time.'

'*I'll go take a look and see if he's in.*'

Jay and Zelda waited by the speaker, neither of them saying a word. Then the bars of the gate vibrated before starting to swing slowly inwards and the two of them climbed back into the Gazelle and drove through, the car coming out into open ground, the trees giving way to flat land that rolled uninterrupted up to the ranch in the distance and the horizon on the other side.

'I guess you know the rumours about this guy,' Jay said, staring at a pair of horses cantering past Zelda's window on the other side of a low fence.

'Yes,' she said simply. 'And I've heard about his son.'

The drive eventually came to an end by a stable block, the two-storey ranch house glinting in the sunlight. A man was waiting for them and approached the driver's side before Jay had brought the car to a standstill, gesturing with his hands that Jay should lower his window. Jay noticed a scar running horizontally across the face of his raised palm.

'Good afternoon,' the man said, peering first at Jay and then across at Zelda.

'Good afternoon,' Zelda replied. 'I'm Zelda Smiling. Was it you we spoke to moments ago?'

The man shook his head. 'No lady, that was somebody else. But he relayed your message to me. My name's Freddy Graham and I'm here to tell you that Mr Harrington ain't around right now to meet with you.'

Graham's voice sounded like a kitchen knife being sharpened, Jay thought to himself, his head like a bullet with the tip filed off.

'Will he be in later?' Zelda asked.

'I ain't too sure at this moment in time,' Graham replied. 'But I'll be sure to tell him that you came by, Miss Smiling and . . .'

His gaze shifted in my direction.

'This is Jay Richards,' Zelda said. 'He's working for me.'

'Well, I'll let the boss know that you both came by. I thought you'd like to be told in person which is why I buzzed you in through the gate. I'm sure Mr Harrington will be in touch with you as soon as he can.'

20

I just got off the phone with an old buddy. Turns out your man is somethin' of a notorious figure in the Chicago underworld, or he used to be anyway . . .

Back at Willoughby, Zelda had gone to check on the great-aunts and Jacob whose crying could be heard echoing down through the house's corridors and Jay had gone upstairs to sleep for a few hours, Sara Taft knocking on his door and waking him just before seven, her face appearing at the doorjamb to tell him that dinner was being served in an hour.

. . . apparently the guy first showed up on the radar back in seventy-three, maybe seventy-four, workin' for the Italian mob. The city has always ultimately been run by the Italians but other gangs sometimes rise to prominence and threaten to interfere with the smooth runnin' of their operations. For example, you got your Latino Kings on the South side. The Italians ain't so worried about them because they mainly keeps themselves to themselves. The black gangs are a different story . . .

Dinner had been a laborious affair, with no news from the cops and no new arrival to shake things up. Jay had sat next to Molly Remick and interrogated her unrelentingly about her children to keep her off the subject of the paranormal while her husband and Tony talked about tech stocks for almost the entire meal. Nina and Bessie seemed to be having a faltering discussion with Will about his work while Meliza and Toby said very little. Zelda herself failed to appear altogether, as she had done two nights before.

. . . apparently the only thing stopping the black gangs from mountin' any serious kind of threat to the Italians was the fact that they couldn't stop fightin' with each other . . .

At some point, Molly had noticed that Jay was placing his food (boiled ham, semi-formless vegetables) between pieces of bread and eating it with his hands and had asked him about it. When he'd replied that he only ate 'sandwiches and certain kinds of dim sum and compact breakfast patisserie', she'd looked at him as if he were a helpless child.

. . . your main players in this case were your Blackstone Rangers and your Lords and your Disciples. The Italians figured that if they kept them all in a stalemate, then they wouldn't be a problem and that's where Buck Harrington comes in. The Italians needed someone who wasn't Italian to come in and sell guns and drugs to the black gangs. Buck had a free licence to run his operation how he wanted and to make as much money as he could. It wasn't hard, sellin' goods subsidized by the mob to every gang-banger in the city. And every time one of the gangs got a stranglehold on their local drug market, Buck would arrange for some cheap product and cheap guns to fall into the hands of the competition . . .

When the meal had come to an end, Meliza had gone straight to bed, Bessie following her upstairs to look in on the baby. Toby retreated to his study as usual while the couples left Johnny and Will to get drunk in the den and Jay set about priming his equipment. His cell had rung just as they too had stumbled upstairs to their rooms.

. . . not the prettiest line of work. By the end of it all, there were several disgruntled brothers lookin' for Buck's scalp. Accordin' to my buddy, this Harrington character's got into more than his fair share of scrapes until he dropped out of the circuit about five years ago as you told me in your message. Guess that's when he moved back to North Carolina. Anyway, if you want anythin' more specific, you give me a call and I'll see what I can come up with.'

Sitting there in the main corridor of the house, Jay was still trying to piece it all together hours later. So Buck really did have a violent and criminal history . . . could this knowledge be applied to Helena's disappearance? Had Buck become jealous of Wallace and Helena's affair? And if so, what was it *exactly* that Jay was proposing he'd done about it? That he'd abducted the two of them? That he'd killed them? If this was the case, Buck could hardly have gone about it with less subtlety, crashing the anniversary party with his henchman (presumably the Graham guy that had spoken to him and Zelda earlier that day) in tow as Bessie had described. It was hardly worth considering. Jay yawned and then got up out of his chair and walked down the corridor to the kitchen. He'd fix himself a cup of coffee and then make a tour of the house. Inside the kitchen, waiting for the kettle to boil, he remembered Zelda the night before, backlit by the fridge (the light catching the faint hairs on her arms, the scent of some jasmine lotion or soap reaching his nostrils). Zelda had been anxious. Did she too wonder if her sister was . . . the remote unit in Jay's pocket vibrated. He plugged his earpiece back in and moved down the corridor and through to the hallway, scanning the darkness with the EMF wand, the light of the flash gliding over the shutters (they were closed tight) and the silent clock, the banisters' shadows above him moving across the walls like the silhouettes of dominoes toppling in slow motion as he walked up to his powerpad.

01:01:49	Camera 02
01:02:30	Camera 01

Jay brought the two files up on to the screen. The second showed him entering the hallway, the beam of the flashlight whirling bright figures of eight through the murky light. He closed it and then clicked on the other. *The file was still active* . . . he squinted down at the picture, the first-floor corridor stretching away from the camera's eye, the timecode moving in the bottom right-hand corner, the door to the Remick's bedroom flush against the left side of the frame, the door to the Shipmans' room beyond it, the door to Toby's room nearly invisible amongst the shadows at the far end. If the motion detector received no further signal within five minutes, both it and the camera would switch back to stand-by mode and log the file as complete. Jay waited, watching the timecode blur through its staggered cycles, each number the lumbering cousin of the one to its right. The first-floor corridor stayed empty. No sleepwalking guest. No Will Hooper or Johnny Fulton skulking through the shadows.

01:04:00:000

Jay focused on the third digit from the right and its slow arithmetic evolution, aware of the Geiger counter clicking behind him, aware of the first snowflakes of anticipation settling on his forearms.

01:06:49:123

And still the numbers kept moving. Jay took seven breaths and told himself to calm down: something was moving up there, according to the machinery anyway . . . there was a light blur at the edge of his peripheral vision and he glanced towards the half-landing and the entrance into the first-floor corridor beyond it . . . *something had drifted past, moving right to left* . . . or was it just the glare of the computer glancing off the chandelier? He looked back at the camera shot of the corridor on the screen: nothing or, at least, nothing he could see. Moving as quickly as he could without turning his flashlight back on, Jay padded round the bottom of the house to the stairwell by the kitchen and ascended through faint echoing clips of his footsteps to the first floor where he crouched down beside his second camera but saw nothing in the corridor and got nothing in his earpiece but the fat round hum of black background signal as he crept beyond it, one hand against the wall to steady himself (he glanced at his watch, he would appear in the file at around eight minutes after one). He came to another stop a couple of feet from the door to the Shipmans' bedroom, the first-floor archway that led down to the hallway just in front of him to his right, and pulled out the compass from his pocket. He flipped open the lid and watched as the needle settled in the half-light. After a moment, it found its equilibrium, describing a line that ran the length of the corridor, north to south, south to north.

And then there was a noise, a knocking sound, just one. It could have been anything, Jay told himself, but then he heard it again. By the time he heard a third and fourth beat down at the other end of the corridor where it bent round past Toby's study and continued on to Will Hooper's room, he realized he was listening to a slow procession of footsteps. For a moment, he wondered if it was Will himself, banging some kind of walking stick on the wooden floorboards in an attempt to scare him. Jay would approach and Will and Johnny would leap out of the darkness at him and laugh about it unceasingly until Sheriff Bryar allowed them to go home. And still the footsteps continued to sound out along the corridor.

'*Will?*' he hissed.

Silence. Then Jay heard something like a moan in his right ear. It had come from behind him (from the direction of the passage leading to Clemmy and Lobelia's bedroom?). There it was again, a faint mewling in the darkness . . . *the sound of a woman crying*? Jay couldn't be sure, the sound drifting in and out of existence in the space of a moment . . . he checked his compass and saw that the needle remained perfectly still and flipped the lid shut only for a gong to burst in his earpiece at that exact moment, a flood of golden signal spilling across a glistening black floor towards him as he saw his breath condense in front of his face and felt a burning in his lungs as if he'd just run a mile and suddenly come to a dazed halt.

It was gone as quickly as it had arrived, Jay's stunned skin suddenly burning with the return of the heat of the night air. He looked behind him: nothing between him and the camera and the motion detector whose green LED confirmed that it still had him in its sights; nothing between him and Toby's bedroom door at the other end of the corridor. Jay sidled up to the archway that led to the half-landing and peered down into the hallway. Again, nothing. He moved down the stairs, looking through the banisters to see if anything appeared, the remote unit in his pocket reminding him that he'd just triggered more footage of himself skulking around, and detached the earpiece as he approached his computer.

01:09:13   Camera 01

Jay stared down at the computer image of himself staring down at his own computer image and then moved to close the file when he heard the clicking of the Geiger counter accelerate behind him. His right hand froze where it was (though he couldn't stop it from shaking), the idea that someone was standing behind him materializing in his mind, the sensation of someone watching him from a few feet behind him materializing between his shoulder blades. He heard breathing, a second set of inhalations and exhalations phasing in and out of time with his own. *He should turn around*, he told himself, *he should turn around* . . . but the air around him seemed suddenly to close in on him and his breath again appeared in front of his face. He stared down at the screen, focusing on the space behind his digital image where black pixels danced with white pixels in amongst the miniature implosions of static and interference. Then he slowly turned on the spot.

Nothing. The Geiger counter clicked away, back at its normal rate. The hallway was empty. Jay turned back to his computer but then noticed the flowers in the vase beside it. He reached a hand out towards one of the white petals and it crumbled on contact. Then he heard something and stopped breathing for a moment. The sound was coming from the library, no, from beyond it perhaps . . . *the ballroom?* Twisting the door handle as silently as he could, Jay pushed through into the library, reminding himself that the sensation of cooler air on his skin might simply have been the product of natural atmospherics (but what about the desiccated flowers in the vase?) as he concentrated on the faint sound of a piano coming in through the open doorway on the other side of the library. Someone (or something) was in the ballroom. He crept across the library, swerving past the armchairs and glancing through into the drawing room on the other side. It was as empty as the library and the hallway. But the door to the ballroom had also been left open and the sound of someone playing the piano floated in from the black space beyond. Jay moved forwards, fitting the earpiece and firing up the wand. At the ballroom door, he made a sweep but got nothing in his ear, just the sound of the piano floating through the air above the sprung floorboards towards him, the tune vaguely familiar though he couldn't place it exactly. He pulled out his compass (nothing) and took another few paces and it was then he got a blast of scratchy static from the far end of the room. He peered into the darkness, saw nothing and then took a deep breath before aiming his flashlight across the wide dancefloor and pressing the button. The signal in the earpiece immediately shrank down to a mere hum and Jay was suddenly aware that he was listening to a loop of faint music repeating itself over and over again.

> *. . . need that person much worse'n just bad, I'm half alive and it's drivin' me mad . . .*
>
> *. . . need that person much worse'n just bad, I'm half alive and it's drivin' me mad . . .*

. . . need that person much worse'n just bad, I'm half alive and it's drivin' me mad . . .

On the far side of the ballroom, he found a stereo playing a Billie Holiday record, the volume low, the needle caught in a scratch that flicked it back a few grooves to the beginning of the line. 'I Must Have That Man.' Esmerelda Smiling's favourite song. Jay pressed the stop button on the turntable (he knew how the rest went) and looked around the silent ballroom, again wondering if Helena and Zelda's mother was about to appear. The sounds from outside slowly filtered back into being, the bullfrogs burping into the darkness, the vibrating of the cicadas . . . *then the sound of someone moving beyond the sashed window on the east side of the room* . . . Jay stopped breathing and listened . . . someone was moving around *outside* the ballroom? He went over to a window and peered out from behind one of the thick drapes, looking out over the terrace behind the house. A figure came into view, gliding down the terrace steps and through the southern cherry grove towards the Italian garden just as a cloud passed in front of the moon. Jay raced back through the house, along the ground-floor corridor and out through the side door where he slowed to a shuffle, moving silently across the terrace itself, then faster across the grass. Where was the figure? Seconds earlier, it looked as if it had been heading north-east towards the parkland and river beyond and Jay accordingly followed in what seemed like the best direction until he came to a stop at the far edge of the northern cherry grove and surveyed the garden in front of him. The moon covered everything with silver light but he couldn't see the figure anywhere and continued on towards the treeline and the path that he'd taken down to the lake the previous afternoon. The trees around him leered in as he picked his way between them, the faces of unshaven drunks at closing time, their branches thick with leaves and Spanish moss. And there was still no sight of whatever it was he'd seen as he crept along the path to Willoughby Lake and stopped at the water's edge. Would he see Katherine Smiling down there or the beheaded pirate wandering through the forest? Suddenly, a cigarette lighter blazed on the other side of the water, a man's silhouette visible for an instant before it disappeared again. Toby Charteris? Someone else? Certainly nothing paranormal. Jay squinted at the far bank and eventually located the figure. It had started tracking its way around the edge of the water before turning up a path and foraging its way back into a dark mass of the pitch-black pines. Jay followed, pulling out his compass to track his direction in the bewildering darkness – north-north-west – and doing his best to avoid low or fallen branches and trying to keep his distance but not lose sight of the figure at the same time. There was barely any light yet the figure moved confidently through the trees without a flashlight and Jay was certain it might disappear at any moment. This eventually happened ten minutes later. The figure up ahead turned left and vanished. Jay hurried forwards as quickly as he could, wondering if he'd been rumbled, wondering if the figure would still be visible when he got to the spot where he'd last seen it, wondering if the person (whoever it was) would jump out at him when he got there. In fact, the path opened out on to a small stream and Jay could see the figure picking its way along the near bank and heading west. Jay did the same, following it as far as the Sixty Bridge (the sign on this side was missing the 'x', he noticed, and read 'Si ty Bridge') where it paused before crossing the water and moving back into the dense vegetal darkness on the other side. As for being spotted, Jay felt confident that he remained undetected – whoever it was up ahead had ignored the obvious opportunities to slip off the path and make himself invisible and instead continued to move west along the north bank of Willoughby Pond.

Who was it?

Jay resisted the temptation to assume it was Toby. But who else could it be? One of the other men in the house? And where was it heading? Jay reminded himself that the figure was heading nearer and nearer Thackeray. Was whoever it was on their way to meet Madeleine Kelly? Five minutes later it seemed as if Jay might never find out because he lost sight of the figure again. He scanned the darkness in front of him but couldn't see it anywhere and decided that there was nothing else he could do but continue along the bank, the path eventually veering away from the water before opening out on to a small track, one wide enough for a couple of vehicles to pass each other. Jay still couldn't see the figure ahead of him but soon came across a short driveway leading left off the lane and back towards the water. He crept along it and at the end of it found a small clearing in which sat a decrepit cabin with a short jetty sticking out into Willoughby Pond. Jay gazed across the area but couldn't see any movement. Then he pulled the EMF wand out of his pocket, plugged in the earpiece and scanned the house: nothing as far as he could tell, no human beings, no paranormal entities, no deer, no stray cats nor any electrical appliances. He allowed himself to have a closer look and took in the corpses of two motor boats half-submerged at the end of the jetty ('Eurydice' painted in dirty white letters across the back-board of one, 'Orpheus' painted across the other), the rusty triangular frame of an old swing standing in the small yard, the windows on the upper storey of the shack boarded up, the front door hanging open on its hinges between two smashed downstairs windows like a broken nose between two cracked spectacle lenses. Another fifty yards along the lane, he found another driveway which led to another cabin in a similar state of neglect. Whoever had previously used these fishing shacks hadn't done so for a while. The next one had an old Torpedo sitting in the driveway, the grass thrusting up through the charred chassis and out through the hole where the windshield used to be, a sofa on the porch that looked as if it had been savaged by a wild animal and an old barbecue set rusting away in the yard.

Jay moved on, the night mist swirling around his ankles. Further along the track, he came across another cabin. The yard was as overgrown as the others but light was visible at the sides of ground-floor windows that were hidden behind shutters rather than boarded-up or broken. Jay waited, crouched down in the undergrowth, checking that no one had heard him approach. Then he moved closer. Twenty feet from the shack, he almost crashed into a low wire fence, only seeing it at the last moment, he'd been concentrating so much on the building itself. After that, he stepped more slowly across the ground, picking his feet up as he moved so that they didn't swish through the long grass, and soon he was right up against one of the wooden side walls. He heard voices from the other side — two voices, a man's and a woman's — but couldn't make out what they were saying and circled around to the side of the cabin facing out over Willoughby Pond. Here he found a couple more windows but they were both closed off behind more shutters. Eventually, in the snatches of moonlight that threw shadows all around him like blue-black zebra stripes, Jay found a shutter on the other side of the cabin that had been left open a couple of inches and he looked through it, reminding himself that he only had a second to take in as much as he could. Madeleine Kelly sat on a sofa, smoking a cigarette and talking to someone who Jay didn't get a chance to see before he ducked back down again.

'Are you sure no one saw you leave the house? What about the English guy?'

'Don't worry about it,' a voice replied. 'I used the secret passage. He's still sitting in the hallway pointing his gadgets at cobwebs.'

It was Toby.

'There's still no word from Helena or Wallace yet?'

'No. Not yet. Zelda hasn't heard anything either, or that's what she's saying at least.'

'When do you think they'll come back?'

'How the hell should I know?'

'And what's *she* doing here?'

'Zelda?'

'Yes. You've always told me that she takes no part in your relationship with Helena.'

'She doesn't usually . . .'

'So why's she here?'

'I haven't the faintest idea. I've always notified her when Helena's run off and she's never shown the slightest bit of interest before now. This time she shows up. Maybe she's worried about Jacob?'

Madeleine didn't reply but Jay guessed that she wasn't convinced by Toby's answer.

'Do you think I like having her around the house?' he heard Toby ask. 'Or that fool she's hired?'

'That's exactly what I mean. First, the fact that she's come back to Willoughby at all is suspicious. And now she's hired this man to come all the way from California to sneak around Willoughby with cameras and recording equipment.'

'It's like I told you, Zelda and some of the others believe that there's a ghost in the house . . . of Helena's mother or something ridiculous like that. Zelda's taken it upon herself to hire him and I can't really stop her. Apparently he once worked with the police in San Francisco and she thinks he's reputable.'

'What do you mean "you can't really stop her"? Is it *your* house or *her* house?'

'You know the answer to that,' Toby replied.

Neither of them said anything for a moment. Then Jay heard Toby speak again. 'So, what did you find out about him last night?' he asked. 'Did it all go to plan?'

'Yes it did. But I didn't learn very much. He didn't mention any previous connection with Helena . . .'

'What about Zelda?'

'Nor her. I couldn't tell whether he was lying but I don't think he was.'

'What did he do? Where did he go?'

'I followed him all night. He drove into Wilmington and met that girl, the daughter of your housekeeper. They sat in his car talking for a while and then Dan Harrington showed up and hauled the girl back into the restaurant.'

'And did Harrington speak to Jay?'

'Yes.'

'How did they seem together?' The answer to this especially seemed to matter to Toby.

'Dan seemed to threaten the English guy who then drove away. It didn't look like they were working together.' Madeleine paused. 'How do things stand with Dan Harrington?'

'Not good. I'm running out of time.'

Jay heard Madeleine light another cigarette. 'What are we going to do?' she asked. There was a slender scent of vulnerability in her voice.

'You know what we're going to do: nothing. Let's just wait till the house is empty again and the police have let everyone go home. By that time, maybe we'll know where the hell Helena and Wallace are and know what to do next. I think I can keep Dan off my back for a little while longer.'

A silence followed this and Jay risked another quick look through the gap between the shutter and the window frame. Madeleine had got up and sat down next to Toby, one hand lazily stroking his ear.

'If it comes to it, I can try and get you the money,' he heard her say, 'I know it's a lot – but there must be a way . . .'

'Let's just wait and see where Wallace and Helena are,' Toby replied. 'Until then, its useless to plan too far ahead. In the meantime, I'm also going to keep looking for Santina.'

Jay waited there in the moist darkness, waiting for one of

them to speak again. Who or what was 'Santina'? But neither of them said anything and after a minute Jay allowed himself one more brief glance over the bottom lip of the window. Inside, Madeleine and Toby were kissing on the sofa, Toby massaging her left breast as if he were crunching the juice from a ripe lemon while his mouth chewed on hers, two cigarettes smoking away in the ashtray on the table beside them.

21

Lying back on the bench in the lavender garden with a small joint between his fingers (he'd got out of the house as soon as he could so as not to be disturbed by the other guests), Jay blew smoke at the blue sky as he went through it all one more time. He'd repeated Toby and Madeleine's conversation back to himself more or less continuously since he'd crept away from the shack and back to Willoughby, thought about it as he'd checked his equipment on his return (nothing had happened in the house since he'd scuttled out into the garden), thought about it as he sat on his chair in the corridor and then later as he'd fallen asleep upstairs in his room. And still his head was all Ps and Qs, full of propositions and the questions they entailed.

Toby and Madeleine were having an affair, he told himself. The reality of this hadn't changed with the arrival of bright morning light. Nor had the reality of another certain proposition, that it was Madeleine who'd run him off the road, a plan that she'd cooked up with Toby. Presumably she'd followed Jay back from Wilmington, pushed him into the fence and then driven on to Thackeray where she'd switched cars and driven back towards him ... *why*? What reason did Toby and Madeleine have to be suspicious of him? Of being complicit with Zelda over ... over *what*? Jay had no idea. Again, he wondered if Helena was dead, if Toby had killed her and Wallace, possibly with Madeleine's help. *That* would be something for him to be paranoid about (and both would have a tremendous amount to gain from doing away with their spouses).

But then Jay came across the same problem that he'd encountered when thinking about Buck Harrington the previous day.

Toby and Madeleine had hardly acted like murderers (murdering their spouses while there were two hundred potential witnesses around just didn't make sense). It was still possible that Helena and Wallace had simply run off together (and now Jay wondered when Toby and Madeleine's clandestine affair had started: before Wallace and Helena's or afterwards?). Certainly, from what they'd said, it seemed reasonable to believe that both Toby and Madeleine didn't know where their absent spouses were, even if they expected them to return home at some point like everyone else.

Jay took a drag on the joint. There were two other things that also remained unaccounted for. Who or what was 'Santina'? And how did Dan Harrington fit into the puzzle? He'd distinctly heard Toby and Madeleine discuss him. The connection between the two men, whatever it was, involved *money* and *time*. Jay also remembered that Toby had been as suspicious of any hidden connection between him and Dan as he and Madeleine were of one between him and Zelda.

Turning to the details of his investigation of the house the night before, it seemed again as if all Jay had were a set of leads flapping wildly in the wind, a mass of facts that wouldn't snap together to form any kind of meaningful shape. He walked back to the house and through the dining room into the hallway where he picked up his powerpad, took it up to his room and opened up the log for the night before. Up on the first-floor corridor, he'd encountered some kind of anomalous phenomenon, if only transiently. He looked up the file for Camera 02 and scanned through it in slow motion, his own figure appearing in the frame around eight minutes after one and crawling away from the camera until it came to a stop outside the Remicks' bedroom door. Jay watched his digital self pull out the compass, flip its lid and wait. Then he watched as his own image flipped it shut moments later . . . *that had been the moment when* . . . the digital picture flickered for a few seconds and by the time it was intelligible again, Jay was poised at the top of the stairs leading down into the hallway.

Jay closed and archived the file and then opened up the file Camera 01 had logged a minute later. There he was, coming down the stairs one frame at a time, the beam of the flash like a frozen tube of light in front of him as he traversed the dark floorboards and bent down towards the screen of his computer. Jay saw the image that he'd stared at live the night before, the white cloud of pixels coagulating in the air behind him. It could just have been interference, static . . . but what about the music in the ballroom, Esmerelda Smiling's favourite song spinning on the record player? And what about the figure that Jay had seen floating across the garden? Sure, he'd eventually come across Toby by the lake and followed him to the fishing shack by Willoughby Pond. But something about the speed and momentum of the figure's movement earlier on through the cherry grove had Jay wondering whether he'd been looking at that point at something different altogether, something paranormal, something (and now he couldn't stop himself following his thoughts to their natural conclusion) that had *led* him to Toby out there in the forest?

There was the sound of a car coming up the drive and Jay went to the window and saw Sheriff Bryar pull up at the front of the house, hitching his belt and straightening his hat before approaching the front door, flanked as before by his gangling deputy. Jay scurried out of his room and round to the main corridor on the first floor in time to hear Sara Taft usher the two into the library, their boots clicking across the floorboards. Then Jay heard Bryar acknowledge Toby before the door closed again and he heard Sara walk across the hallway and down the corridor towards the kitchen.

'The Sheriff is here,' she told him when he entered a second later.

'Is he?'

Sara moved around the kitchen, straightening objects and wiping the counters even though they were already clean while Jay poured a coffee which he took out into the Italian garden, too tired to anticipate what news it was that Bryar had brought with him. Perhaps he'd only dropped by to tell Toby that nothing had changed.

Half an hour later, he saw Zelda coming through the cherry trees.

'Toby's just been speaking with Sheriff Bryar.'

'What did he have to say?'

Zelda sat down across from Jay, dressed in a pair of loose trousers and a loose white shirt with the cuffs rolled up to the wrist. Was it his imagination or did she seem to have a little more colour in her face and neck? When her blue eyes locked on his, Jay also wondered if they were a shade lighter than her sister's. He couldn't say for sure.

'He came to tell Toby that Helena and Wallace have been taken off the Missing Persons' list,' she continued.

Jay asked if they'd been seen or if they'd made contact with anyone. Zelda shook her head. 'The police have been examining Helena and Wallace's financial records. A couple of weeks ago, Helena bought a flight from Mexico City to Buenos Aires on the first of September . . .'

'In four days' time?'

'. . . Wallace has done the same. He's also transferred money to an account that he only opened a couple of months back, an account his wife didn't know about.'

'How much money?' Jay asked.

'Sheriff Bryar wouldn't say. But he suggested that it was a lot.'

Jay asked if the Sheriff had been to Thackeray and Zelda said that he had. 'As far as the police are concerned, the matter's resolved. Helena and Wallace's passports have been missing from the start as have items of their clothes and luggage.'

'And the guests here at the house are free to go home?'

'Yes. They've all started packing. Toby's thinking about flying to Mexico to confront Helena at the airport.'

Jay wondered if Madeleine would go with him. And should he confide in Zelda what he'd learned the night before? Before he could think about it, Bessie appeared on the terrace.

'I've just come from my mother's,' she said as she walked towards them. 'They've found a dead body floating in the water down in Southport.'

'Where?' Zelda asked.

'Down near Lookout Point a little way along from the ferry terminal.'

'Did you see it?' Zelda asked.

'According to the news report I heard on the radio, a fishing boat found the body of a man tangled up in one of its nets and called the police on shore. The fishermen didn't want to touch it. Quite a large crowd's gathered, waiting for the coast-guards to bring it in.'

Ten minutes later, Jay and Zelda were in Lara's car heading for Southport. They drove through Parton, passing by the gate to Buck's ranch on their right, the naval base somewhere beyond the towering trees to their left. Jay noticed that Zelda stared out through her window and bit on a fingernail the same way Helena had years before when she was perplexed by something.

'What are you worried about?' he asked. 'You think the body in the water might be Wallace's? Sheriff Bryar wouldn't have come to the house and let everyone leave if that was the case.'

'The body wasn't discovered until *after* Bryar left,' Zelda insisted.

'The cops would have had time to call Willoughby before we left if they'd needed to,' he replied, though he wasn't entirely sure if he believed it himself. When they reached Southport, Jay let Zelda direct him through the maze of residential streets until they came to a bluff overlooking a small marina and the mouth of the Cape beyond it, a bulky ferry chugging its way through the scatter of lighter vessels bobbing towards the low islands on the horizon. Cordoned away from the jetties of the marina itself was the crowd that Bessie had described, clusters of people between the road and the edge of the low headland pointing video cameras at the launch that had pulled alongside a fishing boat about two hundred metres out to sea. A news crew waited on one of the jetties below, a reporter updating the camera lens as to what had happened so far. In the meantime deputies attempted to keep the line of bystanders in place, trying to stop people both from getting run over or from falling down the rock face.

'Can you see anything?' Zelda asked as she followed Jay through the crowds.

'No,' Jay replied. As they passed through a crush of bodies congregated around a hot dog van, Jay reached his hand back and she took it until they'd squeezed their way through. On the other side they moved further along the crowd until they found a space next to a family, a mother and father and three blond boys in matching t-shirts and shorts, the father relaying a vague commentary about what was going on to the others. *'They just sent a coupla divers into the water . . . looks like they're gonna have to cut him outta the net.'*

What if it was Wallace floating out there? Was Helena's body about to bob suddenly to the surface, bleached, bloated and barely recognizable?

'Jay?' Zelda's voice in his ear, her hand in his. Her voice was lowered.

'What is it?' he asked, tilting his head towards her.

'Is that Madeleine Kelly over there?'

'Where?'

Zelda pointed. Madeleine Kelly stood twenty metres along the bluff, staring at the boats through a pair of sunglasses, a cigarette burning between her fingers.

'I need to go and talk to her.'

Before Jay could answer, Zelda was moving along the line towards her and all he could do was follow behind.

'Mrs Kelly,' Zelda called out. '*Madeleine.*'

Madeleine turned.

'Zelda Smiling?' she asked slowly (smitten by Zelda's physical resemblance to her sister, Jay concluded, watching Madeleine's unblinking eyes assess Zelda as she approached).

'Yes, that's right. When I saw you standing here, I thought it was a chance to come over and introduce myself.'

The two women faced each other for a moment.

'You've met Jay, of course,' Zelda continued.

'Yes, I have,' Madeleine replied. 'How are you, Jay?'

'Better. Thank you for coming to my rescue the other night.'

'It was nothing.' Madeleine turned back to Zelda. 'Zelda, I'm presuming that Sheriff Bryar visited Willoughby this morning.'

'Yes, after he called on you apparently. Toby and Helena's guests are all packing up now that they're free to leave.'

'They should never have been forced to stay in the first place,' Madeleine replied, Jay staring at her face and remembering her burying it into Toby's neck the night before as he'd unbuttoned her shirt in the dim light. 'How is Toby taking the news?' she asked.

'Obviously you know all about the flights the police have discovered,' Zelda replied. 'Toby's thinking of flying to Mexico City and confronting Helena at the airport.'

'Is he?'

Madeleine's face was inscrutable.

'You sound dismissive.'

'Zelda, we've only just met. And I know Helena is your sister. But do you honestly believe that Toby's going to Mexico will achieve anything?'

Zelda stared back at her. 'No. I'm guessing that this might

finally be the end of Helena and Toby's rather unfortunate story.'

'Well, it's a pity she had to choose my husband as a means of ending it,' Madeleine replied. 'It's good to have finally met you, Zelda. My husband has mentioned you to me and has always spoken fondly of you. Goodbye, Jay.'

Madeleine walked away, presumably to wherever her car was parked.

'She seems bitter about everything,' Zelda said. 'I guess that's not so surprising though I'm sure a slice of the Kelly millions will give her something to wipe away the tears.'

Jay was about to reply when a voice nearby shouted out that the coastguards were finally hauling the body out of the water. A man in his sixties standing next to them raised his binoculars to the brow of his USS ENTERPRISE cap and muttered answers to his wife's enfilade of questions.

'Can you see something?'

'Sure, I can see something!'

'What can you see?'

'It's a guy.'

'What kind of guy?'

'How should I know what kind of guy?'

Well, like how big is he?'

'I dunno . . . I can only see his head and neck . . . wait, they're pulling him out now! Sheesh . . . !'

'What is it?'

'Some guy, looks kind of middle aged though it's hard to tell. But he's been stripped naked . . .'

'Naked?'

'Yeah, naked . . . looks like some sicko pervert stripped the poor son of a bitch.'

'Excuse me sir?' Jay tapped the man on the shoulder. He took his eyes away from the binoculars and squinted back.

'Can I help you?' he asked.

'Would you mind lending me your binoculars for a second?

I just need to take a quick look at what's going on out there.' The man was about to say something but Jay pressed on. 'My girlfriend . . .' He pointed at Zelda '. . . *her* sister and her sister's boyfriend went missing a little while ago. She's scared that the body out there might be his.'

The man looked sceptical but his wife seemed to believe him.

'Of course,' she said, poking her husband in the ribs. 'Give the nice gentleman the binoculars.'

The man handed them over and Jay thanked him again before taking a look out across the water. Eventually he was focused on the men leaning over the bulwark of their launch, frogmen in the water hoisting the body up towards them. As for the body itself, Jay glimpsed it only briefly and didn't learn much about it. The flesh had bloated and turned the colour of old bacon fat. Some parts of the body seemed to have been completely lost, either to putrefaction or the mauling of the fish.

'You take a look,' he said to Zelda. 'I don't know what Wallace looks like.'

Zelda took the binoculars from him and scanned the boats.

'No, it doesn't look like Wallace.' She handed the binoculars back to the couple and turned to Jay. 'Shall we go back to the house? We aren't going to find out anything more here.'

The old couple smiled at Zelda and Jay. 'I hope your sister and her boyfriend turn up,' the woman said.

'I'm sure they will,' Jay replied as they walked off. He led the way, again letting Zelda take his hand as he pushed through the shifting gaps in the huddle in front of them, eventually arriving at the side of Lara's battered Gazelle only for three men to suddenly appear beside them, two guys in their late thirties next to Jay, an older man in his fifties next to Zelda, the same guy who'd come to the car to meet them the previous afternoon. Freddy Graham.

'Miss Smiling?' he said.

'Yes?'

'I'm here to invite you to Mr Harrington's ranch.'

Graham glanced over at Jay who sensed his two accomplices breathing down either side of his neck. They were all wearing slacks and golf shirts and looked like a trio of Wilmington dentists on their way to Windy Point for eighteen holes.

'He would very much like the pleasure of your company. And that of your friend.'

'That's very kind of *you*,' Zelda replied coolly, 'and *him*'.

'If you lead the way, we'll follow.'

'Like I said to you before, to start with, it was always me and Zelda. I hardly have a memory from the early part of my life that doesn't include her.'

•

'The only thing to say about my father is that I don't understand him. Not *knowing* him? That I can take. I can accept that given that I never had a conversation with him in my life. But not *understanding* him? It's another reason to wonder what our lives would have been like if they'd both lived.' I tell you this as we smoke joints in my bedroom at the mansion and stare at the volume of my father's notes that I keep under my bed with my other possessions. It isn't a representative selection of his work, more a random one. You read the first paragraph on the first page out loud. *Recently I have reported convincing empirical indications of the considerable role of hidden matter in the dynamics of single and double galaxies. It seems as if this matter is concentrated around massive galaxies, forming their coronas. The total mass of galaxies is about one order of magnitude greater than the mass of their visible parts.* We can keep up only for a short time. It's fine when he's tossing out such scientific small change as '*massive galaxies like our own galaxy or the Andromeda galaxy, M31, are surrounded by clusters of small companion galaxies*' or '*there remains the suspicion that the only agent capable of producing the interaction of the galaxies studied is intergalactic matter surrounding massive galaxies*'. There's a kind of inclusive mystical quality about the language that overrides any sense of intellectual vertigo. Within a few lines however, my father loses us in a haze of mathematical dust.

The companion galaxy has a chance to preserve its gas

only when the gravitational binding of this gas with the companion is stronger than the pressure of the coronal wind. The gravitational binding energy can be expressed by the formula

$$U = -G\rho_g M_s R_s^{-1}$$

where G is the gravitational constant, ρ_g the mean gas density of the companion galaxy, M and R its mass and radius respectively.

Elsewhere, he helpfully adds:

The expression for the force of the coronal wind is

$$p = \rho_c V^2$$

•

'We were born in 1973. Father married Mother when she was nineteen and they had us soon after, when Mother was only a little younger than we are now. Their families had done a lot of business together for generations. Mother was one of the Montgomery County Candors who owned a lot of timber and used to transport it around the world using my grandfather's ships. Anyway, when Grandpa Wesley died, our mother was left on her own . . . our father fell in love with her at the funeral and proposed to her a week later. They were married within six months and lived at Willoughby. According to everyone I've met who ever knew them, they were one of the most glamourous couples in the whole state.'

•

Lying there in bed, I tell you about how I'd gone through a particularly glum patch back when I was seventeen about 'not understanding him'. To be entirely accurate, it was a constituent part of a larger and more generalized 'down' phase about the whole issue of having very few memories of *them*. I had a small archive of images that I pondered every so often, not stills exactly, rather brief looping quanta of light, time and movement, images of my mother bending down over a table or arriving in the hallway carrying bags of shopping, my father taking me to nursery school. But that's about it and I can't tell if I've made them all up, composed them out of a scant pool of family photographs and augmented everything with a touch of Hollywood wistfulness. I remember more about my childhood dreams than I do details of my childhood reality, some of them the standard edge-of-oblivion stuff that everyone gets their fair share of, some that felt a little bit more *personal* than that. There was the recurring freefall of a Futile Suicide Leap, futile because there was nothing out there, nothing to break the fall, and who knew what (or where) I'd jumped from in the first place? There were the Giant Falling Numbers, the Endless Swinging Sensation and Imprisonment In The Egyptian Tomb (perhaps this one came later, a kind of afterworld torment where I was forced to read a boundless wall of crumbling hieroglyphs under the yoke of some shapeless malevolence).

•

'I'm probably giving you the wrong idea about them, like they were this perfect couple. I suppose there are a few happy memories in there amongst it all, the four of us playing in the garden or the two of them putting us to bed, vaguer memories of a trip to New York one Christmas to buy presents and have tea at Klipspringer's. Zelda and I were allowed to order for ourselves, maybe for the first time, and though we ordered the same thing as usual, for once it was funny and they thought it was the sweetest thing they'd ever seen and let us each have a sip of champagne.'

•

I sometimes wonder what it would have been like if my father had been a movie star. I'd probably be sitting around some Malibu beach palace watching his entire oeuvre over and over again, coked up and crying into the bleached curls of some starlet or groupie about how I never knew him. But at least I'd *understand* him. He'd be up there, in a cowboy hat, 'A gun is a tool . . . no better or no worse than any other tool, an axe, a shovel or anything . . . a gun is as good or as bad as the man using it,' he'd say and I'd know exactly what he'd mean. As it is, I can walk up to any computer in the world, type 'Julian Richards' into the browser, find myself bombarded with a flood of information about him including helpful titles such as *Runaway Stars and the Pulsars Near the Crab Nebula* or *Galactic Evolution (pt2): Disc Galaxies with Massive Halos* or *Gravitational Radiation from Stellar Collapse* and none of it means a thing to me.

•

'But mostly I remember the tense silences and the terrible arguments. Some evenings at the house, Zelda and I would be playing in the garden and suddenly the housekeeper, this local woman called Mrs Taft, she'd be dragging us up the stairs and into the nursery. Their voices would fade slightly but we'd still be able to hear them through the walls, on the stairs, along the corridors. Did we ever hear anything specific? Not really, just general stuff, random parts of arguments. Mainly it was our father who did the screaming but there were a few times when it was the other way around. More than a few times, my mother would get as far as calling a cab to take her away and we'd wait at the top of the stairs, out of sight, listening to Father begging her not to leave.'

•

After he died, my father's 'intellectual estate' was bequeathed to Cambridge University, more specifically to a cabal of intellectual heavyweights there called the Rutherford Institute. (Did I have any say in the matter? Yes, theoretically, I suppose, though no one asked me about it at the time.) As I understood it, besides his published work, between hard covers and in the pages of scientific journals, my father had also built up an archive of personal notes, unconsidered jottings and theoretical musings deemed important enough for scientists there to have spent a decade sifting through them all.

•

'They got divorced when we were five, or at least they first separated around then. There was a period of Mother coming and going from the house. She'd come and see us and tell us she was taking another vacation though we knew that something else was going on and that we wouldn't be seeing her for a while. Around that period I also remember her sleeping in different rooms in the house when she *was* there, sometimes back in the main bedroom with Father, sometimes on the top floor with us, but it's hard to know exactly when that was. And I can't remember the moment when she finally left the house and never came back. I can't picture the scene where they're breaking the news to us, no "Children, there's something we have to tell you" speech, and no moment when Mother officially says goodbye and heads off down the driveway in a taxi for the airport. She just disappeared. Oh yes, we saw her again. Eventually. For a while, I don't know how long – Zelda thinks it's only a year and pretends that she's sure – we can't have seen her at all. And then we both started at St Ada's in Charlotte and we didn't see much of either of them. We'd stay at Willoughby during the vacations and stay with Mother during midterm break.'

•

When I was eleven, the Rutherford Institute made a big thing of inviting me to spend a day with a member of faculty and I remember walking around a large number of colourless laboratories with the terribly posh Professor Endicott who seemed to *love* my father in spite of having had about as much real contact with him as I had.

'He had that kind of mind,' he told me at one point, struggling to match his own admiration with what he perceived mine to be as we lingered by a small, muddy and inconclusive oil painting of the old man in some dusty nook of the university library, 'that could combine the rigours of scholarship with a bold romantic streak.'

After taking in some other historical Cambridge sights, we eventually returned to his study, a spartan bunker of charts and notes, where the torture continued.

'What do you *know* . . .' Professor Endicott almost *blew* the word at me. '. . . about your father's work?'

'Very little,' I said, burrowing deeper into an avalanche of ginger biscuits armed only with a gallon jug of tepid barley water and a Duralex tumbler.

'I see,' he hissed, sipping up some of his pale liquid.

According to Endicott, Dad wasn't 'with all due respect, a big hitter in the world of theoretical physics, not a Newton nor an Einstein nor a Planck'.

'*But*,' he continued, 'he has a hell of a lot to say that helps people like me understand people like them as well as forcing us to ask some interesting questions about things we previously took for granted . . .'

Endicott sounded as if was summing up someone's batting career, I thought, as I looked around the room and shuddered: skeletal chains of equations stretching for yards across pieces of typing paper that had been taped or glued together, sometimes scaling the walls from floor to ceiling.

'. . . so, we've been analysing his notes. It took a quite a while just to get them in order, I can tell you. Your father wasn't very good at putting dates on things and we've had to look at the content of the notes themselves and piece them together *that* way before we could get them into something vaguely resembling a correct historical sequence. Actually proved to be quite a timesaver in the long run, helped us progress *miles* further in terms of understanding his work, and that of other people, the *thing* I was saying just now.'

•

'I say we "stayed" with Mother as if she had a home that we used to go to. She probably did . . . *somewhere* . . . but we don't have any memories of it, or if we do, they're all blurred up with memories of everywhere else. No, our weekends with Mother always seemed to take place at some large country house in the Hamptons or Cape Cod, or else some sprawling set of apartments on the Upper East Side of Manhattan. We got used to picking out the drivers waiting for us at Grand Central or Kennedy and driving us to wherever it was Mother was waiting. A lot of my memories of her are images of her standing in the lobbies of various apartment blocks and hotels waiting to twirl "her princesses" up in her arms. We'd be "her girls" by the time we met whoever it was whose driver had been sent to collect us. The names Jean-Claude, Faisal and Nicandros seem to recur – but there were others – and there were the different housekeepers and cooks and maids to get to know and forget . . .' (I imagine you waving goodbye to the fluttering tail of your mother's ball-gown as she moved beyond the stranger's front door into the throbbing night and the waiting limousine) '. . . the different kitchens we used to eat our meals in, the different spare rooms we slept in, some of which became more familiar, some which didn't. At Willoughby, during vacations, our father would never ask us about these trips but there would always be one point during the weekends themselves where we'd be summoned to the telephone by our mother and he'd be on the other end of the line. The conversation would always go the same way: how were we? We were fine? Good. And that was it. The rest of the time, he used to act as if we hadn't left the confines of St Ada's since he'd last seen us.'

•

Professor Endicott was still there six years later. He'd sent me Christmas cards and the occasional Institute newsletter in the interim. Also, I'd realized by then that I received two cheques every October from the university, one a donation in return for the loan of my father's notes and another for the royalties from the sale of his published work (it amounted to a little over six thousand pounds a year in total, a sum that my uncle had demanded be used to pay for my upkeep and education as a child, a sum that frittered itself away easily enough without much effort on my part once I was deemed old enough to take responsibility for it). But we'd never spoken and I'd never been back to Cambridge. Then, a little while after I turned seventeen, there came the blue period I've already mentioned and I'd rung up the Rutherford and made an appointment.

•

'The midterm break in the spring of our second year at St Ada's, Mother actually came to collect us. She was taking us for a weekend in Miami. Her "friend" this time was a man called Ignacio and he was "treating us" to a stay at the Deauville. We flew from Charlotte and landed in the middle of a thunderstorm and took a cab to the hotel where Zelda and I had a suite to ourselves. "Only ever stay in the Deauville when you visit Miami, my princesses," she told us in the dining room later. For once, it was just the three of us having dinner together on a Friday night, me and Zelda still in our school uniforms. After that, we spent the rest of the evening watching the television in our room. You see this necklace? It was *that* night she gave it to me and an identical one to Zelda. She told us that we could have them if we promised never to lose them.

'And then the next day she asked us to stay in our suite while she went out. She was gone a couple of hours and when she returned she told us she was going to lie down for a while. Zelda asked her if she was okay and she said she was fine but that she was tired. "The excitement of having my princesses to stay," she said, standing in the doorway to our room, "has worn me out." She was going to rest in her room and told us to stay inside ours and not to go anywhere. We could order anything we wanted from room service. "No champagne darlings," she joked, "but anything else you want, anything". There was only one condition: we mustn't leave the room.'

•

This time we had lunch in the pub. Endicott hadn't changed much, become a little leaner around the cheeks and jaw perhaps, his lobes a little droopier, his hair a little thinner and a little more windblown (if only from preoccupation) and he made an effort to let me know about the progress he'd made during the past few years as we munched our way through a stolid Ploughman's on Silver Street. After that, he asked me what I was 'doing with myself' as we drained our pints and stared at me with a mildly mystified expression as I gave him the polite version. I told him about leaving school, leaving home, moving to London and setting up the stall in Kensington Market and I didn't know what he found more puzzling, that a world of Ramones t-shirts and studded leatherette belts and cheap plastic sunglasses and marijuana-leaf necklaces *existed* outside Cambridge's cloisters, or that the son of his hero should have left school at sixteen to pursue a life selling such items to kids who, equally as mystifying, considered such objects valuable enough to spend money on.

And then we came to the crunch. My father's notes: *could I take some as souvenir?*

I'd anticipated the possibility of Endicott suddenly getting possessive about them, remembering his earlier reverence for my father, and added: 'I don't want a lot, perhaps just a handful of papers, not anything that *matters*.' But old Endicott seemed to understand my request and he took me over to the Institute and showed me the archive of my father's work, two rooms of papers in cardboard boxes with dates and reference codes written on them with black board marker.

'This is approximately half of it,' he said, hands behind his back. I asked Endicott if I could look in one of the boxes and he nodded. Inside was a stack of yellow pieces of notepaper. I pulled out a sheaf and stared at the top sheet. *Recently I have reported convincing empirical indications of the considerable role of hidden matter . . .*

•

'It's funny. Every time I think back to the moment she closed the door behind her, all I can see is the design of the door, the white wood panelling, a list that must have been the hotel regulations hanging on a hook, the gilt, the golden doorknob, never her face. Or if I imagine her face, it's an image I know I've made up. I can remember Zelda's face, I can remember exactly how *she* looked, but I can never remember Mother's.'

•

Endicott had cast an eye over my selection and seemed satisfied that I wasn't likely to be walking off with The Secrets To The Universe. And a parcel duly arrived on my doorstep a week later, the thirty or so pages of notes and equations bound in leather and tied shut with a turquoise ribbon. I took it to the stall with me and sat reading through it, not understanding much of it until I came across a single typed sheet of paper right at the end that didn't match up with the one before it and seemed to have been included as randomly as the others. At the top, there was a heading and a page number:

Superforces and the Universe (Miracle, Accident or Design?) – 11

Was it a sketched endnote to a short essay or the concluding words of an introductory chapter of a longer piece of work? Below this line, there were a couple of paragraphs:

The universe is comprised of a vast array of deeply textured hierarchies of complex processes that reveal themselves to the intrepid scientist who assumes the role of cosmic code-breaker or detective in a universal mystery.

That these hidden truths of the universe, once exposed, consistently show a tendency towards increasing complexity is fascinating. That they also point to the fact that the potentially infinite range of the cosmos is unified by a series of elegantly interconnecting mathematical relationships is profoundly awe-inspring and deserves the kind of human commitment that in previous ages was expended on religious activity.

(March 18th, 1975)

It was longest passage of my father's writing that I had understood. Looking at the date, it was also likely to be one of the last things he'd written before he died.

•

'So Zelda and I stayed there for the whole day. We were used to Mother's afternoon naps, her dizzy spells and her early nights. And we knew never to disturb her in her bedroom. One time in Manhattan, I'd had a nightmare and walked in on her and one of her men. She'd been furious with me and after that we'd never disturbed her again, not for any reason. So Zelda and I remained in our room and played with our dolls and read what books we had with us. We ordered chicken sandwiches, and juice and cakes, and stared out at the sea and in the evening we turned on the television even though we hadn't asked permission and watched it until midnight when Zelda said that we should both go to sleep.

'The next day, we ordered breakfast – scrambled eggs and toast – and when we'd finished it we sat there on our beds, washed and ready to leave. We expected Mother to walk into the room at any moment but she still hadn't showed by ten. By eleven, Zelda was restless and wanted to sneak out but I told her to be patient. By twelve, she was going on at me again.

I said that we could call room service and ask them to bring us some lunch. "By the time we've finished, Mother will be here," I told her.'

•

What else? Details. Facts.

Marilyn, my mother, was a Chinese-American woman originally born in Hong Kong. She moved to America as a student and met my father when they were both attached to the physics department at Berkeley. A little while later, I was born in San Francisco General and we all lived in the city for the first three months of my life until my father took up a post at Cambridge. Flight CA1109 crashed into the mountains of Fujian three years later. My father was travelling to a conference of physicists in Shanghai, the first western scientist to lecture in China for twelve years, and my mother went with him, in her usual role as his assistant, but also in a new one as his translator. I was left with my Aunt June in Swanley where I stayed until I was sixteen, at the house she lived in with her husband, Harold.

•

'Zelda told me that she wasn't hungry, that she was sick of sandwiches and TV. So we sat there and did nothing. Hours passed and even now, I can remember precise details from around that hotel room – the shape of a glass, the way the curtains hung, a patch of wallpaper – and not just because of what happened next, but because I was so bored. *All those hours spent waiting*. Eventually Zelda said that we should knock on the door. "We'll just knock on the door and stand there, she said, "but we won't go in." But we were still there in our room by the time it got dark again, the two of us now just sitting at the end of our beds. For some reason, we'd both packed and our matching suitcases sat on the beds behind us. Then I remember starting to cry and Zelda coming over to me and giving me a hug before saying that she was going to get Mother. I begged her not to, even though I was in tears, but that didn't stop her. And then she was gone. The next time I saw her was thirty-minutes later, the hotel manger behind her followed by a chambermaid and a cop.

•

Harold Lewis. The creator of Lord Henry Lentaigne, the celebrated and aristocratic Interpol sleuth who also maintained a top six world ranking at chess, was one of the worlds 'finest connoisseurs' of classical ballet ('the choreography of the dancers on the stage reminded Lentaigne of the movement of chess pieces on a board,' my uncle is often quoted as writing, though not usually in a way that is complimentary) and the protagonist of such bestsellers as *Alibi Declined* (one Grand Master is accused of assassinating another 'but did he do it?'), *Black Square Bishop* (an unbelievable piece of tosh about skullduggery in the higher echelons of the Anglican church and a plot to assassinate a visiting African clergyman) and *The Corbomite Manoeuvre*. It was hard not to imagine that *he* was my father's sibling (rather than my aunt who seemed too vague to bear a resemblance to anyone) for he sat alone at his typewriter from seven in the morning until nine at night when he emerged and placed himself in front of the BBC news and silently abused the screen for half an hour, his lips moving as if he were chewing the air out of his words before they could find any audible life. The only other times he came out were when he relieved himself noisily in the toilet next to his study and when he expected his meals to be on the table (lunch always at one, a plate of grilled cheese on toast with a pickled onion on the side along with a tomato cut into four crescents; dinner always at six, a bleached piece of meat and a sludge of vegetables). Aunt June would appear with a small tray of tea and biscuits at precisely ten thirty, at three forty-five and at a quarter past seven every evening after he'd sat down for another couple of hours of work. The house, a large suburban hutch (functional, thin-walled) in the middle of market-garden Kent was a temple to silence, to his *concentration*. It took some time to get used to this and for a while I could only meet my aunt's occasional insistence that I 'talk more quietly' with a bewildered incomprehension. 'Why?' I wanted to ask. I soon realized that if I was noisy he'd not say anything to me but take it out on her later on and I quickly learned to keep my head down.

•

'She'd died the day before. They found her lying on her bed with the tablets and the telegram from Ignacio. Mother had originally persuaded him to take us in his yacht to Brazil where he'd promised we could all live together with him but he'd backed out of the deal at the last minute . . . anyway, the hotel manager's wife stayed in our room with us until Father arrived with Mrs Taft the following day and took us back to Willoughby on the next available flight. I remember just a few things after that. I remember that we slept most of the flight back to North Carolina, Father and Mrs Taft sitting in the row in front of us, Zelda in the aisle seat next to me. At some point I remember waking up for a moment and staring through the plane window and catching sight of the sun falling into the sea below us. It's still the most beautiful sunset I've ever seen and I remember looking across at Zelda who was asleep and feeling sad that she hadn't seen what I'd seen, but also thinking that it could have been *me* asleep and *her* looking out the plane, that it could have been *her* watching the night close in and thinking about Mother.'

•

Two more things about Uncle Harold. He was infertile and he was a racist. To deal with the second thing first, it was there in his writing, chortling away nastily in the background. In one of his minor hits, *The King of Kenya*, Lentaigne is about to board a plane bound for the art galleries of Florence when he is propositioned by a delegation from the Kenyan government in the departure lounge at Charles de Gaulle. As Lentaigne proceeds to solve the mystery of the murder of the crown prince as a personal favour to an ageing African monarch with whom he once shared rooms at Eton, my uncle reverts to a descriptive palette that includes such smoky treats as the 'untutored savagery' that 'burns' away in the faces of suspicious courtesans 'like a bushfire' as well as references to characters' 'primitive incomprehension' and 'animalistic urges'. And it was there in his real life as well. Nothing set his lips quivering so much as images of racial unrest, images of burning cars and brick-hurling skirmish lines on the streets of Liverpool and London.

As for his *other problem*, it might never have been an issue in his life had my pallid aunt not insisted that she be the one to raise me. He certainly never cared about what my aunt felt about anything (he only cared about his writing) and was almost certainly too arrogant to have even mentioned the subject once its truth had been ascertained. But there I was, a continual reminder of his limitations, and a little half-Chinese reminder at that.

•

'After that, I remember trying to fall back to sleep with the smell of Father's cigarettes all around me, Mrs Taft awake but silent in the seat next to him, and all I could think about was our second day in the hotel. How long would I have been prepared to sit there if I hadn't had Zelda with me?'

•

No wonder Uncle Harold tried to get me out of the house as soon as he could. There was the initial attempt after I turned seven to dump me in a boarding school, a tremendously pretentious place called The Fount that tried to pass itself off as a hallowed seat of traditional learning though it never ceased to resemble the Chobham Golf Club it had previously been. But I'd barely completed two weeks at the place before I'd been expelled. *Why?* I simply hadn't turned up to anything. Then, when I was assigned various duties and gruelling chores as punishments for not turning up to anything (lessons, chapel, roll-calls and so on), either by the masters or by the senior boys who were still wearing cricket jumpers in September, I failed to turn up for *them* or any of the punishment details that were subsequently added to those that were already outstanding. Within a week, I'd accumulated enough hours of detention to keep me occupied until well past Christmas and the headmaster sent me back to Kent with the standard documentation.

•

'Mother was buried up in the family plot near Grandpa Wesley's house a week after we got back to Willoughby. After that, we were taken out of St Ada's and sent to the local high school. I started travelling when I left. Zelda's at Chapel Hill where she's training to be a doctor, says she wants to go and work in Africa.'

•

After that, it was the local school and local kids with their shorn heads and their facial piercings and their propensities for random and whimsical violence. I stayed out of harm's way, largely by staying away from school altogether (the new place was much more obliging about non-attendance than The Fount, as were my Uncle Harold and Aunt June as long as the school didn't involve them), scraped together some GCSEs (I sat the first year of these and the government seemed more than happy to deem turning up and marking the paper with ink the sole condition for receiving a formal 'pass' grade). After that, it's London. This part of the story feels more complicated but is probably more simple (if also more involved) and largely centres around selling weed, pills and cocaine from the stall in Kensington Market, a short period messing around with moody money, with counterfeit cash, and getting burned by a girl called Zoë. Then comes Amsterdam and after that there's Ibiza and Pepé and life on the roof of the mansion that formerly belonged to the French former ambassador to Cuba.

22

Buck Harrington's living room was all Cs: the central section was sunk into the ground, three cream sofas arranged around a chestnut coffee table and a cream rug in front of a broad chimneypiece, copies of *National Geographic* on the table as well as a book of photographs of Cape Fear and Cape Hatteras up the coast, logs stacked to one side in neat clusters, unlit candles on sconces stuck into the brickwork on each side of the fireplace. Around this area ran a raised section: pale sea-grass on the floor, a cabinet full of bottles of liquor, shelves with a few books and other items. There was the huge gulping u-bend of a tenor sax in a glass case with the inscription 'John Coltrane: 1926–1967' painted along the front of the base in copper capitals (did Buck Harrington *really* own one of Coltrane's horns?), a ship's compass the size of a dinner plate, an antique cross-staff on the same shelf (from the same ship?), Civil War memorabilia including a cannonball from 'The Battle of Monroe's Cross' mounted on a wooden plinth, a pen-and-ink illustration of the *Chameleon*, an old Confederate blockade-runner, and a pair of maps of Cumberland County dated 1843. One wall of the room was given up entirely to monochrome photographs of Chicago. There was Wrigley Field after a snowstorm, the offices of the *Chicago Tribune*, Burnham Park in the autumn and a shot of a catamaran skimming across the surface of Lake Michigan at either dawn or dusk (the sun poised at the point the vessel's skids cut through the swell – which way was it travelling?). On two occasions, a telephone bleeped quietly in the corner and was picked up after a few rings.

'What do you think he wants to talk to us about?' Jay asked Zelda. It was clear that Freddy Graham and his accomplices had followed them all the way to Southport from Willoughby and hadn't simply spotted them by chance down on the bluff. 'Do you think Helena's contacted him?'

'Maybe,' Zelda answered. 'Who knows? Perhaps he just wants to know why we called at the ranch yesterday. Either way, we're here now.'

At that point, the door opened.

'Zelda?' A man stood in the doorway in a denim shirt and jeans. Jay watched him as he stepped down into the sunken section of the room. 'I'm Buck Harrington,' he said. 'Thank you for accepting my invitation.' No apology for his goons accosting them in Southport or for keeping them waiting for almost half an hour. Buck stood in front of Zelda and offered her his hand.

'That's our pleasure,' Zelda replied as she shook it. Jay noticed that Buck's eyes clung to her. Was he attracted to her (as he had possibly been to her sister)? Jay took a look at the rest of him. He was three or more inches over six foot tall, broad chested with wrists like baseball bats and hands like baseball mitts. There was a resemblance to his son Dan, Jay thought, in the cheekbones and forehead. But Dan's eyes were brown whereas his father's were the colour of arctic water. For some reason their colour made it a little hard to tell how old he was, as did his hair which was cropped close to his scalp, but Jay guessed that he was somewhere in his early fifties, perhaps a little younger than Alfred Taft back at Willoughby. And he remembered what Mike had told him on the phone. Buck was dangerous . . . yet for all the authority in his voice and manner, the man's blue eyes seemed as if they were melting.

'This is Jay Richards,' Zelda continued.

'Please . . .' Buck said, gesturing towards the sofas. They took one each, Buck noticing that they didn't have any drinks and asking Zelda if she would like anything. She shook her head.

'You?' he asked Jay.

'No, thank you.'

'In that case, I'll say what I've got to say,' Buck replied, Jay noticed that he still couldn't take his eyes off Zelda. 'First of all,' he started, 'I'd like to apologize for not being free to talk to you yesterday. It was unavoidable.'

'That's quite okay. We called without having made an appointment,' Zelda said calmly.

'Not at all. Anyway, perhaps you'd like to tell me why you called?'

Zelda paused for a moment. 'I understand that you've become friendly with my sister this past year.'

Jay watched Buck's face, wondering how he'd react. He simply stared back at Zelda, completely focused on her and Jay wondered if he was fascinated by her resemblance to her sister just as Madeleine Kelly had been earlier on.

'As you will probably know already,' Zelda continued, 'she's gone missing along with Wallace Kelly. It doesn't seem to be any kind of secret that they were having an affair. Anyway, I wanted to ask you if you'd heard anything from Helena in the last two weeks. To make things more complicated, Sheriff Bryar came to Willoughby today to let us know that Wallace and Helena have booked tickets to fly from Mexico City to Buenos Aires in a few days time . . .'

'Why would they get on a plane in *Mexico City*?' Buck interrupted.

'The police have a theory that Helena and Wallace are currently driving to Mexico in order to avoid detection by either Madeleine or Toby. Apparently it's easier to trace a person's movements if they use a domestic airport and it seems as if Helena and Wallace are going to some lengths to ensure that Madeleine and Toby don't find them. Anyway, my sister hasn't contacted anyone in her family or any of her friends, at least as far as we know, and we're getting a little worried. Even though we know she's due in Mexico City on the first, we'd like to speak to her before then if possible, just to check that she's safe. Also, we don't know what she's planning to do once she and Wallace get to Argentina. If you know anything about any of this, or if my sister has been in contact with you in any way, I'd appreciate you sharing it with me. Perhaps she's called or written to you? Perhaps she talked some of this over with you before she left? Perhaps you've even helped in her some way?'

'Why are you worried about her safety?' Buck asked calmly. 'Do you think Kelly will harm her?'

'No, not at all. I'd just feel safer if I could contact her.'

'That's understandable,' Buck said. 'But I'm sorry – I can't help you. Your sister hasn't phoned me or contacted me in any other way. If she does, I will call you at Willoughby immediately, you have my word.'

'I see,' Zelda replied. 'Thank you. I'm sure you're very busy so we'll leave you . . .'

Buck raised his hand and stopped her.

'Before you go, Zelda, I need to ask *you* a small favour.'

'What is it?' she asked.

'I'm right in understanding that Mr Richards here is currently employed by you?'

Zelda nodded.

'That's right.'

'I'd like to have a word with him alone. With your permission . . . and *his*, of course.'

Zelda looked across at Jay. 'I'm sure that will be fine, Buck.'

'If you go out into the hallway and take a left out the back of the ranch, it'll bring you out to the paddock where you can take a look at some of our horses. If you'd like any kind of refreshment, Freddy should be somewhere nearby and he can arrange it for you. We'll be done in ten minutes.'

Zelda got up and Buck escorted her to the door and shut

it behind her before walking back to his sofa. What did he want to talk about? Was this something to do with Dan? Once Buck was seated again, he stared at Jay but didn't say anything and suddenly Jay knew what was coming next. He almost breathed a sigh of relief.

'What's the nature of the work you do for Zelda?'

'I'm a paranormal investigator. She's hired me to investigate certain kinds of events that have been taking place at Willoughby over the last ten days . . .'

'What kind of events?'

'I'm not sure I can say without Zelda's permission. It's her private business . . .'

'Don't come clever with me,' Buck said quietly.

'I'm not being clever,' Jay replied, trying to keep control of his voice. 'I just can't talk about details of her case with you unless I get her permission.'

'You want me to drag her back here?' Buck asked.

'No.' Jay thought for a second. 'Perhaps I can describe what I do more generally?'

'Why don't you give it a shot?'

'As a paranormal investigator, I'm called in by people who think they may have encountered some kind of paranormal or what you might call "supernatural" activity. They've seen what they think is a ghost in their home or place of work, or experienced what they think is a poltergeist or something similar. I go and investigate and try and work out whether what they've witnessed is attributable to some other kind of explanation.'

'Like what?'

'I try and find out whether something natural is behind the alleged paranormal activity or whether someone is playing a hoax on my client or, in some cases, if my client is playing a hoax on me. Yes, I know it's hard to believe but there are people out there who have nothing better to do.'

'What if you don't find one of these *natural* explanations?' Buck asked.

'That's more complicated.'

'How?'

Jay took a breath. 'It depends on what's going on. Sometimes nothing happens. No natural explanation suggests itself but also no further alleged paranormal activity neither. Sometimes the client and I are left with a near certainty that we've witnessed something that we can't explain. At that point, I've usually helped the client all I can. People try all sorts of avenues at that point, exorcism, coexistence, moving house altogether . . .'

'So you've seen a ghost before?' Buck interrupted.

'Mr Harrington, I don't really like the word *ghost*. But if you're asking me if I've seen things whose existence and activity I find hard to rationalize by conventional means, then I'd say "yes". I've seen objects move for no apparent nor logical reason, apparitions that at some level *resemble* people who've been dead from anything like a few hours to a few centuries, taken digital sound recordings of footsteps and disembodied voices that seem to have no visible source, or none that can be seen by either my cameras or by direct observation. Are these phenomena connected in some way to people who've died? I don't know. There's only ever circumstantial evidence to work with and it's simply something I can't prove indubitably at this point. I have reasons to believe that it *might* be true and that's good enough for me for now.'

Jay sat back in his seat and wondered how Buck would react.

'Is it enough for most of your clients?' the man asked simply.

'No, not usually. How easy they find it to learn to live with a certain amount of uncertainty is up to them.'

That seemed to silence Buck for a moment. He stared at the fireplace for a while, puffing on his cigar.

'Last night, maybe sometime after one thirty, I was in this room. I was sitting where you're sitting now. *Something came to me* . . .'

'What happened?' Jay asked quietly.

'I'm not going to say just yet.'

Jay was confused. 'Why not?' he asked, 'I don't get it.'

'I want to hire you Jay. I'll be clear about that . . .'

'But you're not going to tell me why?'

'What I saw stays with me for now. You've told me that you spend your time looking for things you're uncertain exist in the first place. This is no different.'

That silenced Jay for a moment.

'We'll have to ask Zelda. I'm currently employed by her,' he said eventually.

'Let's go ask her then,' Buck replied, climbing to his feet.

23

As Jay and Zelda approached Willoughby, they passed the Remicks in a cab on the drive and when they pulled up outside the front of the house, it seemed clear that everyone else was in the process of leaving. Sara and Lara Taft were helping ferry luggage out on to the gravel and Jay almost collided with Alfred who came bundling through the front door with two suitcases, one in each giant hand.

'Who else has left?' Jay asked Bessie who had just waved the Remicks off.

'No one yet. Will, Johnny and Meliza leave for the airport in three hours. The Shipmans are going in half an hour – they're upstairs doing the last of their packing. Molly tried to hang around to say goodbye to you but eventually she couldn't wait any longer or she and Jim would have missed their flight.'

They found Toby upstairs in his study.

'Where have you been?'

He was clearly drunk and Jay wondered how long it had been since the Sheriff had left. Four hours? Five hours? Toby had probably been sitting there ever since. 'Your cousin's been waiting to say goodbye to you.'

'I'm sorry, Toby,' Zelda replied. 'We got held up by something unavoidable.' Toby didn't seem to care but she continued anyway. 'I thought I'd let you know that Jay will be working over at Buck Harrington's ranch tonight.'

'Why? Is he seeing ghosts too?' Toby scoffed.

'Apparently,' Zelda replied.

'This is a pretty good line of work for you isn't it?' Toby sneered at Jay. 'All of these people paying you to tell them want they want to hear.'

'I'll still be leaving some of my equipment in the hall,' Jay said smoothly. 'I know I haven't come up with much so far but there's still little explanation for why the pictures moved. That all your guests will have left by this evening makes my job a lot simpler. If anything out of the ordinary happens in the house tonight, my equipment should pick it up and record the data even though I'm not here . . .'

'Also,' Zelda cut in, 'while Jay is in Parton with his hand-held equipment, I'll be in the house watching for signs of anything strange. I'll sit by the computer. If anything happens, I'll call him at the ranch and he can come back and take a closer look.'

Toby looked at the two of them from behind a screen of cigarette smoke. 'Very *cute*, the two of you clowning around looking for spooks together.'

'So you don't mind?' Zelda asked.

'Why on earth should I mind?' he replied. 'You've made it perfectly clear that Jay's here because of you. I've made it perfectly clear that I think that the idea of a ghost haunting Willoughby is nothing more than laughable nonsense and that Jay is out of here the day after tomorrow. Why should I care if Buck Harrington wants a piece of the action?'

After they'd finished speaking with Toby, Zelda went to say goodbye to the Shipmans and Jay went and found his flashlight before walking out through the loggia and through the Italian garden to the parkland beyond it. There he found a statue of a nymph, six feet tall, her right arm stretching out towards the house (was she reaching towards it or waving goodbye?), her name engraved on the pedestal beneath her almond toenails.

$$\Theta\varepsilon\iota\alpha$$

Jay sat himself down with his back against the inscription and rolled a joint. Were Helena and Wallace at that moment driving across country to Mexico on their way to Buenos Aires and the planet beyond? Jay imagined them speeding through the swelter of the Gulf Coast, booked into a series of luxurious billets in Tallahassee and Mobile and New Orleans along the side of the satin-smooth freeway. No MotorCourts or TravelChalets or AutoCabins (with their synthetic sheets and sewerish bathtubs and rusty bottle openers screwed into the wall by the bedside light) for 'Mr and Mrs Smith' starting a new life together. And what would happen if Toby confronted them at Juarez International?

As for his investigation, Jay wondered what it was that Buck might have seen. It could have been anything. The man wouldn't say. Why? To ensure that Jay wouldn't attempt to hoax him? No, it seemed more like the ultimate form of scepticism. Jay let a creamy exhalation flood out over his tongue and lower lip while he considered this last point. In the end it didn't matter, he told himself. Zelda, Buck and Jay had agreed by the paddock that Jay would monitor the ranch with Buck while Zelda watched over the equipment at Willoughby, calling him if anything happened. Would she encounter the same phenomena that Jay had encountered the night before?

There was also the issue of the secret passage that Toby had said he used to get out of Willoughby undetected. Jay pushed himself up from the ground and walked through the cherry trees towards the woods and retraced the route he'd taken the night before (again flirting with the idea that whatever he'd followed across the garden the previous night had *led* him to the lake ... *was it possible?*). He'd first seen Toby appear by the cupola at the edge of the water. That didn't necessarily mean that the passage had come out there but it was as good a place to start looking as any. Jay slipped through the trees and soon found himself skirting the morbid calm of the water and stepping up on to the stone platform. Where could the entrance to a tunnel be? He checked the stone columns – nothing – and then examined the floor of the platform itself. Nothing stood out. And yet there was still something about the previous night that he kept returning to . . . he went and stood on the spot where he'd first seen Toby appear and pictured again the moment he'd lit his cigarette and shaken out a match . . . Jay looked down at his feet and let his eyes flit over the surrounding ground behind the platform itself and eventually saw the burnt match on the grass. He bent down to pick it up and then prodded and kicked at the area around it until he found a metal ring and then the hatch to which it was attached. It looked innocuous enough, hidden under a few scattered leaves (to a disinterested passerby, it would have looked like a cover to an old drain – if they'd seen it at all). Jay took out his compass and gauged the exact direction the house lay in – south-south-east – and then took a deep breath before he locked a finger around the metal ring and pulled. The metal hatch lifted up easily and silently enough and Jay stared down at the dark shaft sunk between ten and fifteen metres into ground, metal rungs driven into the wall serving as a ladder. Jay placed his foot on the first of these and then lowered himself into the hole. At the bottom, he turned on his flashlight and saw that the passage was over six or seven feet high and had a stone floor and a brick ceiling and walls, wooden cross beams supporting the roof as it ran back in the direction of the house. When had it been built? Who'd built it? Standing there in its cold damp reality, Jay realized that any of the Smiling patriarchs of the past could have ordered its construction, a costly but entirely feasible contingency against a slave uprising or Unionist aggressors. How had Toby come to know about it, Jay wondered, and had Helena also known about it? Zelda certainly didn't seem to have any knowledge of its existence otherwise she would have mentioned it to him. Perhaps John Smiling had known about it but had died before he was able pass on the knowledge to his daughters and Toby had stumbled across it by accident a few years later?

Jay started moving along the passage, all the time trying to imagine the landscape above and keeping an eye on his compass in case the direction of the passage changed radically in any way. After a minute or two, he guessed he was under the maze of interlocking gardens, and then the ballroom, and then either the second drawing room or the library after that. Every so often, he stopped, held his breath and tried to listen for sounds from the house above but the cold air of the passage remained silent. Then the passageway came to an end. Jay let the beam of his flashlight trace the path of another set of metal rungs up the brickwork, the shaft looking as if it came to an end twenty metres or so above where he stood. Then he started climbing. He paused after travelling half the distance . . . he'd heard a noise. He again held his breath and listened, the sound of footsteps, then muffled voices. He must be somewhere adjacent to the main staircase in the hallway he told himself before starting to climb again. Another ten metres or so and he reached the end of the shaft. It gave way to a little ledge. On the other side was a wooden panel. Was it the back to a secret door? If so, where in the house was it? It was then that Jay heard Toby.

'Yes, I understand that . . .'

Toby's voice was faint and in order to hear everything he was saying, Jay had to press his left ear up against the wood. Who was Toby speaking to? Madeleine?

'This isn't what we agreed. I've already conceded that . . .'

The passage originated somewhere in Toby's study, perhaps behind one of the bookshelves.

'I'm just asking for a little more time . . .'

Toby sounded agitated and whatever he heard next hit an exposed nerve of some kind because he suddenly exploded.

'I've told you before: that will never happen. Do you think I was born yesterday? Do you think I don't know what you're trying to . . .'

Toby suddenly went quiet and Jay guessed he'd been

interrupted. Then Toby put the phone down and a few seconds passed before Jay heard him speak again.

'It's me . . . we need to talk . . . no, not now . . . tonight, half-past midnight . . . I don't care if it's risky, I need to talk to you . . . yes, everyone's left except Zelda and Richards . . . he's spending the night at Buck Harrington's place so he'll be out of the way . . . no, I still don't buy it, but at the moment I've got bigger problems . . . okay . . . yes . . . I'll see you there, twelve thirty.'

24

Sitting in the same room as before at Buck's ranch, Jay couldn't take his eyes off the clock on the wall by the liquor cabinet. Eleven thirty. All he could do was picture what was happening at Willoughby, Zelda sitting downstairs by his powerpad waiting to see if anything happened, Toby upstairs in his study waiting until it was time to enter the secret passage and head off for his rendezvous with Madeleine Kelly. Who had he been speaking to before her – Dan Harrington? Again, the issue of *time* seemed to be at the heart of whatever connected Toby to whomever it was he was speaking. Besides that, Jay had learned little more, except that Toby and Madeleine were due to meet in an hour.

Jay looked across at Buck. The man had already known about Jay's role as a paranormal investigator before he'd questioned him earlier that day (just as Freddy and the other two had waited for him and Zelda to leave the house and followed them to Southport). Who'd told him? Did he have a source inside Willoughby? And if so, who was it? Jay considered for a moment the strange possibility that Buck Harrington and Toby shared some kind of secret agenda. After all, he still didn't trust the man's claim that he'd seem something potentially paranormal the night before and he wondered if Buck's hiring of his services was a convenient way of keeping him out of Willoughby while Toby got on with . . . with *what*? Jay already knew that he was planning to meet Madeleine (and Toby had no reason yet to believe that anyone, let alone Jay, had discovered these trysts). Yet if any of this were true, then what were the terms of such an alliance? Being suspicious of Buck didn't necessarily place him in any kind of alignment with Toby. Whatever the exact truth of the situation, Jay told himself, there they both were, him and Buck, waiting for something to appear though only Buck who knew what it was they were hoping to see, hear or experience. And whatever the truth, it was serious enough for Buck to come clean up to a point with Jay and Zelda whom he hardly knew, enough to ask Freddy Graham to leave him and Jay alone that night, a request to which Freddy had acquiesced only after a short protest.

Buck sat across from Jay, thumbing through one of the magazines from the table while Jay continued to let everything he knew shuffle around inside his head: there was the truth about Dan and Helena's affair but also the existence of the secret passage and the revelations that Madeleine and Toby had conspired to run him off the road, that the two of them were having an affair and that they were meeting to discuss something that involved Dan in less than hour . . . by a quarter to twelve Jay still hadn't been able to piece it all together and he was also unable any longer to avoid concluding that the chance of definitely finding out something at the shack by Willoughby Pond seemed more valuable than the possibility of discovering something paranormal at the ranch. And yet he was stuck in Parton and would stay trapped there unless he did something about it.

'Buck?'

'What?'

The man put down his magazine and Jay waited until he had his complete attention.

'Does the name "Santina" mean anything to you?'

Jay watched Buck's face. Buck stared back at Jay as if he himself was the issue at hand, not the question he'd asked, and that was enough for Jay who sat there in silence, waiting for the man to answer him.

'What does it mean to *you*?' Buck asked eventually.

Okay, so it was up to Jay to decide how much he was going to share. 'I overheard Madeleine Kelly and Toby discussing it,' he replied, 'last night.'

'Last night? Where?'

'Down by Willoughby Pond. There's a set of fishing shacks there. Most of them are abandoned but I overheard Madeleine and Toby talking in one of them at around two o'clock this morning. I heard them talk about Santina. And some other things too.'

Jay knew that if he was going to get Buck to open up, he'd almost certainly have to present what he knew to the old man first, possibly in its entirety. As expected, Buck didn't say anything and instead pulled out a cigar which he clipped and lit, patiently revolving its tip in the flame of a cluster of matches which he then threw into the fireplace.

'What were you doing down there?' he asked.

'I was monitoring Willoughby late last night, just like we're doing now. I happened to spot Toby creeping through the garden,' Jay replied economically (there was no point giving everything away all at once), 'I followed him to Willoughby Pond through the forest.'

'So Madeleine and Toby are sleeping with each other in secret?'

'Yes.'

'Why haven't you gone to the police? Don't you think that it's a little suspicious, Helena and Wallace disappearing at the same time as Madeleine and Toby are having an affair?'

'Yes, I do think it's suspicious. But I don't know what to do with my suspicions. There's every indication that Wallace and Helena are right now in a four star honeymoon suite somewhere between here and the Mexican border. Just because their spouses are locked away in their own little love nest at the same time doesn't mean anything illegal's happened. To be honest, I haven't really had a chance to get it all straight in my mind, let alone talk to the police. Do you think I should call them?'

They both knew what Buck's answer would be to that.

'What I *do* know,' Jay continued, 'is that Madeleine and Toby are planning to meet again tonight. I overheard Toby arrange it with her on the phone this afternoon.'

'What time?'

'Twelve-thirty.'

'And where did you say this fishing shack is?'

Jay described its location to Buck before the man got up and left the room, to talk to Freddy, Jay presumed, also noting that Buck hadn't yet answered his initial question about Santina even though the name clearly meant something to him.

Buck returned ten minutes later with his henchman in tow. 'Okay, listen up, here's the plan. I am going to take a drive over to this fishing shack and wait for Madeleine and Toby to appear. Then I'm going to hang around and listen to what it is they've got to talk about. In the meantime, Freddy here is going to drive over to Thackeray and see if he can turn up anything out of the ordinary over there while Madeleine is busy with Toby.'

'What am I doing?'

'You're going to stay here.'

'I should go with Freddy . . .'

'I said you're going to stay here.'

'There's a numerical keypad by the door that deactivates the alarm. I saw Madeleine use it two nights ago.'

'And you know the code?'

Jay said that he did though he realized that he'd only seen Madeleine's hand at the keypad for a short moment.

'Are you sure?'

He nodded.

Ten minutes later, the three of them were assembled outside the ranch, the night all Vs as a thin voile of grey clouds volleyed across the violet velour sky and the vacuum in Jay's gut persisted in spite of his repeated mantra that it was too late for him to turn back. Freddy Graham asked Buck if he was sure he didn't want him to check out Thackeray on his own, his vesicated face devoid of expression although the tone of his voice had

Jay expecting him to pull out a knife and start using it as a toothpick.

'No, take him with you,' Buck replied, 'and call me if you find out anything.'

Buck then climbed into his huge black Orca and pulled away towards the gates and River Road, Freddy and Jay climbing into Freddy's Caesar and following his tail lights. Eventually they passed him, after he'd pulled over a few minutes down the road, and continued on towards Thackeray until they too were killing the lights and turning away down a small track and climbing out into the verdant air.

'No flashlights,' Freddy grunted. 'Follow me, keep up and don't make no noise.' He moved off and Jay slipped through the trees behind him, the two of them picking their way through the rustling undergrowth until they'd reached Thackeray. It sat there on the other side of the drive, moonlight streaking through the whispering treetops and across its silver parapets, no lights on in the windows beneath.

'You sure the maid isn't inside?' Freddy asked.

'She lives some place nearby called Winnabow. Madeleine told me the other night.'

'Then let's do this. Don't run. Just follow me. If anyone shows up while we're inside, don't panic. We just slip away and don't make a big deal about it. Shouldn't be too much of a problem in a house this big. You got all that?'

Jay nodded.

Freddy took out two pairs of plastic gloves and handed one set to Jay. After they'd pulled them on, they stepped out into the open and across the drive, climbing the nine steps and coming to a stop under the portico by the front door.

'Okay, enter the code and I'll do the lock.'

Jay nodded but then stared at the keypad and felt his mind blur with panic. When he'd said that he knew the code for the alarm system, he'd pictured the buttons arranged in a three-by-three square with a tenth extra button sitting below the one in the middle of the bottom row:

```
1   2   3
4   5   6
7   8   9
    0
```

Now that Jay stared at the keypad, he realized that he'd been mistaken. The keypad had three rows of four buttons, a star and hash key along with the ten digits:

```
1   2   3   4
5   6   7   8
*   9   0   #
```

Now what? Originally he'd told himself that the code had been 2-4-6-0, the points of the Southern Cross (gamma, beta, delta, alpha) but his mistaken assumption about the format of the keypad now rendered this theory little better than useless. The second and third digits of the code were still 5 and 8, he was certain of that, but the first digit could have been either a 2 or a 3 while the last digit could have been either a 9 or an 0.

'What's the hold up?' Freddy whispered in his ear.

Jay didn't reply but stared at the grid of numbers in front of him for a second longer. As he reached a finger out towards the buttons, he tried to calculate the probability of his getting it right. It was a one-in-eight chance if he had the 5 and the 8 in the right place (and was he *really* certain about them?).

And what if he got it wrong? Would the whole place light up, security floods blazing on, an alarm sounding out into the night? What if it was one of those systems that relayed a silent signal direct to Sheriff Bryar and his cronies who would encircle the house minutes later while Freddy and Jay were still inside?

Perhaps they could use his EMF detector to locate the power source of the alarm system and deactivate it?

One more breath, then Jay pressed the buttons.

	2		
5	-	-	8
-	-	0	-

Nothing happened for a slow, painful moment. Then a green LED winked at him briefly and he nodded and tried not to look too relieved while Freddy's hands scurried in the darkness at the lock of the door.

'Okay, we're in. Like I said, no flashlights unless it's absolutely necessary.'

They both walked through into the hall, the main staircase rising up to the floor above, a corridor leading off both to the left and to the right.

'What do we do now?' Jay asked.

'We check the whole place over – what's down here?'

'The kitchen is off the left. There's a drawing room straight ahead. That's all I know.'

They worked through the first wing of the house together. Jay was sure they were about to see red and blue lights streaming in through the windows at any moment, wheels skidding in the gravel, the vehement loudhailered warning above it all in the clear night air. But this didn't seem to be a possibility that bothered Freddy as he took the left corridor first, moving from the kitchen where Madeleine had bandaged Jay's hand two nights before into a long narrow dining room next to it. They also looked in on a downstairs bathroom, a laundry room and a conservatory before Freddy found and unlocked a side door which he discovered in a scullery between the kitchen and a utility room. 'If someone shows up out front,' he told Jay, 'remember that you can get out *here*.'

Jay nodded. Then they returned to the hallway where Freddy pointed up the stairs.

'You go take a look up there. Go look for her bedroom.'

'What am I looking for?'

'Anything. Diaries, letters, notebooks, personal journals, bank statements, credit card bills – if you see a phone, check the messages. If you see a computer, check the emails and the file history. If you find a desk, open the drawers. Just be careful what you touch. If you're not sure about anythin', you come and find me. That clear?'

Freddy went off to check through the other wing of the house and Jay went up a floor and found himself in the blue light of another wide corridor, everything (the walls, the circular rug, the moonlight on the ceiling) the same colour as the eyes of a Persian cat. Which way now? He turned left and walked along the corridor. The first door on his left gave way to a guest bedroom, the second to another. On the other side of the corridor, he found what he assumed was Madeleine and Wallace's room. It was the size of both the two rooms he'd just looked into added together, a triple-sized bed against the far wall between two sets of sashed windows, an eye-mask sprawled across one of the blue-white pillows on the rumpled blue-white comforter, the usual objects on top of the small sets of drawers on each side of the bed (a glass of water, a dirty ashtray, a clock, a box of tissues, a collection of bottles of various skin lotions, a telephone, a small vase of flowers). There were a pair of tallboys against another wall, standing either side of a set of sliding doors. Next to these were an armchair and a sofa next to a low table (nothing on the table except a clean ashtray). Along the wall directly to his left stood two sets of dressers and then a doorway that looked as if it led through into a bathroom.

Jay worked methodically through it all, starting with the drawers to his left that seemed to contain only Wallace's shirts, neat right-angled stacks of them laid out on crisp tissue paper like the perfect bricks of money one saw in movies, usually in leather briefcases opened up in the back of some hood's Ultrastretch. On top of one of the dressers stood a photograph of Wallace and Madeleine. Jay realized that he still didn't know what the man looked like and allowed himself a blast with the flashlight as he bent down to take a closer look. The two of them were on a beach, Madeleine's eyes and hair dark against her white dress and the tiers of aquamarine banking up behind her, the blue-white surf, the sea, the sky, strata of translucent clouds. Next to her, Wallace stood in a white cotton suit and brown leather sandals, an arm around his new bride, brown hair (what there was of it) pushed back over his scalp, the pensive eyes underneath with their dinner-plate pupils reminding Jay of a bloodhound, a negligible set of nose, lips and chin beneath these.

He turned off the flash and walked across to the bedside drawers which contained very little. One appeared to be Wallace's: a few watches, two boxes of cufflinks, a fountain pen, some coins (two nickels, a dime and a penny). The other seemed to be Madeleine's: more make-up, more tissues, a notebook (empty), a rosary (black beads and a simple wooden cross), a diary (again empty, January through December). Jay moved across to the tallboys which contained variously Madeleine's underwear, Wallace's underwear, spare bedlinen, more of Wallace's shirts and some cream handkerchiefs monogrammed with 'W.F.K.' in Indian indigo. The sliding doors themselves opened to reveal a walk-in dressing room. One side of it was taken up by two rails of Wallace's jackets and suits, his shoes kept in a neat orderly grid of cubbyholes underneath with more shelves (full of more shirts, more cufflinks, more watches) to one side. The opposite side of the room was given over to Madeleine's clothes, rails of dresses and skirts and suits, shoes in cubbyholes but also in boxes stacked up on the floor. There were drawers on her side of the room too, but they contained jewellery and nothing else or at least nothing of any interest to Jay and it was as he was fingering though the last of these that he heard Freddy coming along the corridor.

'Freddy,' he called out, 'There isn't much in here. Did you find an office?'

The footsteps continued.

'Freddy?'

Jay walked out into the corridor and looked back towards the main landing at the top of the stairs. It was empty except for the blue moonbeam angling in from an upper skylight. Slowly, Jay reached into his pocket and pulled out the EMF wand, fitting the earpiece and pulling out his compass in a single fluid movement. His thumb nudged the power switch and he heard the machine hum into his ear as it settled on its baseline reading.

'Freddy?'

Was something moving beyond the moonbeam at the top of the stairs? Jay stepped forward, wand pointed out towards the shadows. Again, something seemed to stir out there, a signal appearing in Jay's ear like a flock of distant white seagulls suspended over a dark ocean before it filtered away. Then a noise behind him. Jay wheeled on the spot and listened. Someone or something was moving around in Wallace and Madeleine's room. He approached the door and peered round. There was a figure in the dressing room. It turned and though it didn't have any eyes, Jay still sensed that it was looking at him (the wand brayed in his ear but Jay couldn't move).

Then it disappeared.

Jay?

Jay was vaguely aware of a voice behind him, then Freddy appearing by his shoulder.

'What the fuck are you making so much noise for?'

Jay switched off the wand but couldn't speak for a moment, his breath unable to clear his windpipe . . .

'I could hear you all the way down on the ground floor . . .'

'You f-find anything?' Jay asked eventually.

'I found an office but I turned up nothing. Nothing that connects her with Charteris anyway. What about you?' Freddy looked around the bedroom. 'What the fuck have you done *here?*'

Jay looked where the man pointed. Some of the drawers containing Madeleine's jewelry were scattered on the carpet.

'You take any of this?' Freddy asked him.

'No, of course not. I . . .'

'You break something? I thought I heard something smash.'

It was then that Freddy's cell bleeped in his pocket. He pulled it out and stared at the screen. 'It's the boss,' he said. 'While I talk to him, you put all this shit back where you found it.'

Jay went over to the dressing room. No sign of the apparition that had been standing there moments earlier. Behind him he heard Freddy talking to Buck. It sounded as if Madeleine Kelly was on her way back to the house and there was no time to take any more EMF readings. Jay quickly started picking the drawers off the floor and sliding them back in the empty slots in the wall. Was he putting them back in the right holes? Probably not. But he couldn't remember their sequence (he'd only glanced inside each of them briefly, looking for anything *other* than jewellery) and there wasn't time for more than random guesswork. Finally there was one drawer left to pick up and Jay stooped down to grab it only to see that it contained no jewellery. Instead, there was a ziploc bag and a small wooden box.

'What's taking you so long in there?' Freddy called out across the room. 'We've got one minute.'

Inside the box, Jay found a newspaper clipping written in Spanish, a colour snapshot of two dark-haired girls sitting on a pair of swings in a park (they looked between ten and twelve years old, both potentially a young Madeleine) and two plastic earrings in the shape of pink butterflies. The ziploc bag contained a wad of passports. Jay pulled out the first one, an American passport, and opened it, ready for Helena's face to stare back at him but instead finding Madeleine's image there but also the name 'Jordan Hinkley' in place of her own. When he rooted through the rest of the bag, he found three more passports (Argentina, Britain, Canada), Madeleine's photograph in each of them but not her name, and quickly stuffed them along with the box into the pockets of his jacket before replacing the last of the drawers. After that he pulled the sliding doors together, turned to leave the room but stopped when he noticed that the glass protecting the photograph of Madeleine and Wallace Kelly had shattered in its frame.

'*Twenty seconds* . . .' Freddy's voice from along the corridor. Jay took one last look at the jagged web of fractures cracked across the face of the photo (the impact point of some invisible fist?), then stepped into the corridor and followed Freddy down to the front door.

'Type in the code,' he whispered once they were outside. Jay tapped in 2-5-8-0.

'Right, let's get outta here.'

So much for not panicking. Freddy sprinted across the gravel towards the undergrowth and Jay followed him, only making it to the cover of the trees and tall grass seconds before the Mamba swung into view, lights off, Madeleine alone behind the wheel.

'We left the side door unlocked,' Jay whispered. 'She'll definitely know that someone's been inside.'

'You trashed her closet. You think she wasn't going to notice?'

After they'd watched Madeleine let herself inside, Jay tried to make sense of what had just happened in her bedroom as he trailed Freddy back to the Caesar. A figure had appeared there and it had led Jay to the objects sitting in his pockets just as a figure had led him to Toby and Madeleine the night before. He wondered if Zelda had encountered anything back at

Willoughby or if something paranormal had occurred at Buck's ranch while they were out . . . Jay looked around: he'd lost sight of Freddy. Where was he? Jay looked for the man in the murk but couldn't see him. Then he stumbled forwards a few paces, eventually slipping down into a narrow ditch and reaching out towards a nearby clump of trees for support only for his hand to come into contact with something cold, smooth and artificial. He scrabbled his way up the bank and brushed himself off before taking a look at what he'd come across. It was a car, some kind of jeep or SUV under a thin tarpaulin. He walked around to the back of the vehicle, bent down to grab hold of the lip of the covering and pulled it up. Then he took out his flashlight and aimed it at the green paintwork.

Searcher Elite

It was the car that had run him off the road, he was certain of it. Jay was about to aim the beam of the flashlight into the Searcher's interior when he heard Freddy calling out to him through the trees.

'What the fuck are you doing?'

'I'm over here.'

Jay showed Freddy what he'd found.

'There anything inside?'

'I was just about to take a look.'

They scanned the interior, Jay sure that he was about to see Helena's pale and lifeless face at any moment. But the car was empty.

Back at the ranch in Parton twenty minutes later, Jay, Freddy and Buck stood around the kitchen table with mugs of hot coffee. 'You say that it's only a matter of time before she realizes that someone was in her house?' Buck asked Freddy. Freddy nodded.

'Thanks to the boy wonder here.'

'What were you playing at?' Buck asked him.

Jay decided not to mention the figure that had appeared to him but pulled out the contents of his pockets.

'I found this stuff in her dressing room. I was in too much of a hurry to ask whether I should leave it or not. So here it is.'

He laid it out on the table in front of them all, the four passports, the photograph of the two girls, the plastic earrings and the newspaper clipping.

'It's in Spanish,' Buck said taking a look at it. 'It seems to be about a girl called "Chica Valdez" but I can't work out any more than that. What about the names in the passports?'

They opened them up.

Argentina: Angelica Casares
Britain: Julia Everett
Canada: Marie Fontaine
United States: Jordan Hinkley

'No *Madeleine Kelly*. No *Chica Valdez*,' Buck observed, picking up the photograph. 'Either of these girls could be Madeleine.'

'I agree,' Jay replied.

Buck puffed on his cigar and said that he was going to have the article translated first thing in the morning. He also had some contacts in the FBI who could track the names in the fake passports and see where they showed up. 'We can see if they figure in any credit histories or address registers of police arrest records.'

Freddy reminded him that Madeleine was going to know that the things were missing.

'Yeah. You'll need to get back over to the house and watch it. If it looks like she's found out we've been inside, see what she does, where she goes, who she talks to and so on. Go wake either Larry or Pete and take him with you.'

Buck turned to Jay once Freddy had left the room. 'Where did you find this stuff?' he asked.

'Amongst Madeleine Kelly's jewellery.'

'You just stumble across it by accident?'

'Something like that.'

'I'm not convinced.'

Jay stared at Buck. 'If I said that something appeared in Wallace's bedroom and led me to it all, would you believe me?' he asked, knowing that Buck had also claimed that he'd seen something possibly paranormal in the last few nights. As expected, Buck couldn't answer him immediately and Jay looked down at the objects at the table and repeated his own proposition back to himself . . . *something had appeared in Wallace's bedroom and led him to them* . . . the apparition had wanted him to find these things. Why? He picked up the photo of the two girls and stared at it, examining details in the background of the image that might identify where it had been taken. But there was nothing there to help him, no signs or any other kind of distinguishing element. Again, the same old question: *why*?

It was then that Jay's cell vibrated on the table. It was Zelda.

25

Jay and Buck plunged through the night towards Willoughby in the Orca, Buck cutting the lights and engine when they were halfway down the drive and freewheeling to a standstill as the moonlit house came into view around the last bend.

'This is as far as I go,' Buck said, preparing to turn around.

'Let's talk in the morning,' Jay said and Buck nodded.

'Jay,' he added before Jay climbed out, 'don't mention what we've been doing or what we've found to Zelda. Do you understand me?'

Buck's tone was indisputable and Jay nodded before he watched the man drive away. Then Jay turned and walked the rest of the way down the drive towards the house, wondering if Toby was still awake in his room, wondering what Zelda had seen, wondering about pretty much everything and aware that Buck still hadn't told him either what he knew about Santina or what had taken place at Madeleine and Toby's cabin. As he approached the house, he saw Zelda appear at the head of the side passage that ran between the house and the old stable block.

'Zelda, what happened?' he asked when he reached her, ushering her back into the shadows of the passage. For some reason, he felt exposed standing out on the drive in plain sight.

'I saw something,' she breathed at him. Her voice betrayed how nervous she was as did her pupils which darted back and forth like a pair of the dark swallows that zigged and zagged around the eaves of the house at twilight.

'Where? Out here?' Jay asked.

'No. Inside the house.'

Jay asked her what had happened and she told him that she'd seen the powerpad register activity up on the top floor of the house.

'I thought it might be Toby or Bessie checking on Jacob so I went to take a look and it was then that I thought I heard someone moving about in the baby's room. I called out. No one answered. It was then that I suddenly heard something else.'

'What did you hear?'

'Jay, I heard a woman's voice . . . she was singing a lullaby. For a minute I thought I was imagining it.' Her trembling hand reached out for his. 'Jay, it was my mother's voice.'

They stood there for a moment.

'Are you sure?'

Zelda nodded. 'She was singing the nursery rhyme she sang to me and Helena when we were younger. "*Sweetest little angel that anybody knows, don't know what to call her but she's pretty like a rose . . . Looking for her mother with eyes so shiny blue, makes you think that heaven is coming close to you . . .*" I couldn't be more certain.'

Jay recognized the melody, remembering how he'd lain in bed and listened through the open door to Helena humming the tune to herself as she sat in the bath getting ready to go back to Can Jazmín.

'What happened next?'

'I pushed open the door to Jacob's room,' she told him, 'and peered in, half expecting to see my mother's ghost standing there. But the room was empty except for Jacob sleeping in his cot.'

'Then what?'

'I stood there for a moment . . . and then suddenly the air in the room turned cold.'

'Are you sure?'

Zelda nodded.

'How long did it last, this temperature change?'

'I don't know. Ten seconds? Half a minute? I couldn't tell you for sure.'

Jay could see she was scared.

'Should we wake Toby?' she asked.

'No,' Jay said, almost too quickly. He slowed down and tried to sound as calm as he could, 'I'm going to go inside and take a look. Why don't you wait here . . .'

Zelda shook her head. 'No, I'm coming with you.'

Jay thought about trying to dissuade her but knew she'd never let him. 'Okay,' he said. 'Follow a few feet behind me.' They entered the house through the side door, Jay twisting the doorknob as quietly as he could and holding the door for Zelda who brushed past him, her white cotton shirt turning blue-grey to grey-blue as she entered the shadows of the house, a final moonbeam catching her slender arms.

'Which way?' she asked.

'Wait here for a moment,' Jay replied. 'I'm going to check my computer and see what the equipment's picked up. I'll be back.'

Zelda nodded and Jay slipped away down the corridor and into the hall where he scanned the screen of his powerpad but found no other entries after the one that Zelda had observed and investigated. The motion detectors hadn't picked up anything moving around the house in the ten minutes or so since, not on the top floor, not on the first floor nor in the hallway. Back outside the kitchen door, Jay found Zelda where he'd left her and told her that he was going to go up and take a reading in Jacob's room.

'Are you sure you want to come with me?' he asked. Zelda nodded.

'We're going to take the stairwell all the way to the top floor,' he said and then turned and began moving up through the house. At the top, he turned to check that Zelda was behind him and he found her right on his shoulder, eyes wide and expectant. 'Stay behind me,' he whispered to her, 'I want to get a clear reading.'

Zelda nodded again while Jay fitted the earpiece. Then they moved down the corridor, Jay scanning the area in front of him with the EMF wand as he passed the doors to the store cupboards and attic rooms and the room Johnny and Meliza had been using, the remote unit vibrating in his pocket as he and Zelda triggered the motion detector taped high up on the wall at the far end. They followed the corridor round to the left and eventually stopped outside the door to Zelda's old bedroom. Jay whispered back at her that he was going to go inside and that she should stay where she was. Then he pushed open the door and walked inside, probing the darkness with the point of the wand. The background signal droned in his left ear, dark clouds of noise drifting across a dark sky, flecks of signal appearing here and there like vague and distant stars. Nothing out of the ordinary in there, as far as Jay could tell. To his right, the door that led to the short adjoining corridor between Zelda's and Jacob's room lay ajar and he walked slowly across the room towards it, taking a quick look back at Zelda who waited at the doorway, one palm pressed flat against the doorframe. In the corridor itself, Jay paused and took a scan of the small bathroom that lay off to the right – nothing – and then moved towards the door to Jacob's room and pushed it open. On the other side, he could see the child's cot against the far wall, a table to one side with various objects on it, a packet of diapers, an empty bottle, a changing mat propped up against one of the legs. Jay then swept the silent room with the wand, starting with the far left corner and moving towards the middle, a bright buzz of static growing in his ear. Was something in there? Perhaps the signal was generated by Jacob himself? Jay fixed the searching eye of the wand on the centre of what seemed the source of the disturbance and considered the LED readouts. The signal was almost certainly too high to be the baby's. At a couple of hundred milliguass above the normal, it might have belonged to an electrical appliance if the appliance was turned on. But nothing seemed to be switched on in the room. Jay moved forwards, one step at a time, the signal in his ear becoming clearer and clearer, and he was soon by the cot itself, looking down at Jacob who lay sleeping on his front, the soft skin of his eyelids pressed shut, his mouth slightly open, his fingers curled against the comforter, the signal in Jay's left ear now buzzing high and taut. *Where was it coming from?* Jay looked around the room and then back at Jacob. And then he saw it, the dot of red light peeking out from behind Jacob's pillow. The mike unit for the intercom . . . Jay breathed out and took one last look at the sleeping baby, then snapped off the wand and returned to the doorway to Zelda's room.

'Is Jacob alright? What did you find?' Zelda whispered

'Jacob's fine,' Jay whispered back. 'I didn't find anything.'

They looked at each other across the space of a few inches, noses almost touching, something sweet and creamy in Zelda's breath that reminded Jay of Helena, the same sparse and isolated spray of light freckles across her nose and cheekbones, the cold dark matter of her gleaming pupils. Her lips moved, flared, pulsed shut, a tongue lashing over the fulcrum of her teeth, and it took Jay a moment to realize that she was asking him something. *What do you think it was?* she asked, Jay watching her hand move to her throat and feeling a sudden urge to take it and hold it in his own. As, if reading his mind, he felt her other hand slide between his fingers.

'I'm not sure,' he whispered. 'Maybe you heard the intercom-unit feed back on itself? Maybe you heard Toby moving around downstairs?'

'But . . . my mother's voice?'

There was nothing defensive about her tone but no certainty there either – it was simply a question. Jay squeezed her hand.

'There was nothing there when I checked. But we can stay up here and monitor the room for the rest of the . . .'

Jay broke off. The remote unit had buzzed in his pocket.

'What's the matter?' Zelda asked.

'Something's triggered one of the other motion detectors.'

'Which one?'

'I don't know.'

Moving past Zelda, he gestured for her to follow him and then moved back through the corridor to the point outside Johnny and Meliza's room. He peered down the corridor, sensing Zelda coming to a stop just behind him. 'Can you see anything?' she asked, her breath on his neck.

'Nothing.' He glanced up at the motion detector and saw that the small light on the side of the unit was red and that it had reverted back to stand-by mode. *It must have been one of the others that had been activated* . . . they walked back to the stairwell and down to the first floor, Jay remembering what he'd seen and felt two nights earlier, the cold spot on the main corridor there, the figure he'd felt behind him in the hallway and then seen out in the garden (after his encounter in Wallace and Madeleine Kelly's bedroom, he was sure that it had been an apparition that had led him from the house down to the lake). Again, the LED on the side of the motion detector outside the door to what had been the Remicks' room remained red. So something had moved in the hallway downstairs . . . he moved forward down the corridor, triggering the motion detector as he passed it, Zelda close behind him, Jay glancing through the open doors into the empty bedrooms.

'Can you see anything?' Zelda whispered, again slipping her fingers between his as they paused at the top of the stairs, her cold fingertips nervously squeezing his knuckles.

'Not yet,' he whispered back, 'stay here for a second.' Jay edged his way down the steps, earpiece plugged back into his ear, thumb poised over the wand's power switch as he sank down to a crouch on the carpeted half-landing (the click of his knee joints boomed out into the darkness) and shivered. Staring down through the spokes of the wooden balustrade, Jay could see a figure standing in the middle of the hallway, the Geiger counter rumbling away in the corner behind it. He turned on the wand and pointed it at the translucent body of light and got a high blast of signal back in return before he switched it off again. Then he turned and looked over his shoulder at Zelda. Before he could say anything or nod, she was coming down through the shadows towards him.

'It's freezing – what can you see?' she asked, curling her body in tight around his and whispering in his ear. He whispered back, aware that his lips brushed against her ears and that his nose had now penetrated the aura of her warm hair. 'There's something down there. Look . . .'

'I can't see anything . . .'

'There, by the door.'

She tilted her head. 'I see it,' she whispered (her hair moved, brushing against Jay's eyelids). Jay took another look through the balustrade and tried to start making mental notes. *A white humanoid apparition . . . maybe as much as six-feet tall* (like the figure he'd seen at Thackeray an hour or so earlier though it was hard to be precise from that angle) . . . *indistinct features* (again, like the figure he'd seen at Thackeray) . . . he inhaled, let the air slowly out again and then crept down the right-hand branch of the staircase, vaguely aware of Zelda following behind him as he kept his eyes on the figure. Halfway down, he stopped: the figure seemed to be moving too. Or was it just his imagination? He glanced at Zelda – she'd seen it too – and they both watched as the figure glided towards the door to the library and then disappeared.

Jay shone the flashlight at the door. It was shut.

'It passed through . . .' Zelda's voice broke off.

'Zelda, are you okay?'

She nodded.

'I'm going to try and follow it. Do you want to stay here?'

She shook her head and Jay took her hand before leading her down the remaining steps and across the hallway to his equipment where he saw that the apparition had redlined all the sensors and shorted out the Geiger counter completely. After that he moved to the library door and pressed his ears against it (nothing but silence on the other side) before twisting the handle and pushing through into the library where he saw the figure drift through the open doorway on the other side of the room, moving slightly quicker now through the first drawing room and then the next after that, Jay following, Zelda following, the sound of something fragile smashing somewhere in the darkness (was it Zelda? Was it him? Was it the figure?), Jay increasingly feeling as if he was underwater and swimming through the shifting and folding of deep-sea currents. The figure floated through the dining room ahead of them and into the kitchen where it stopped and Jay and Zelda peered at it across the bare table. Jay again felt that the figure observed him with its eyeless face for a few seconds before vanishing.

'Did you see that?'

'Yes I did.'

He felt Zelda's hand in his. It was trembling. He swivelled round and put an arm on hers.

'You're petrified.'

'No, I'm . . .'

'. . . you're shaking all over.'

They stood facing each other, the house around them all Ns: the kitchen and the noiseless corridors flushed through with nebulous blue-pink anti-twilight, no sounds inside or outside the house and silence outside in the garden too (if one negated the seething rustle of the insects), a silence that seemed poised to explode with birdsong the moment the sun broke the horizon. Now that the adrenal rush of chasing the figure through the house was little more than a faded dream, Jay felt his fatigue as a numbness in his temples, felt it as a low innervated throbbing in the plates of his skull and something like emptiness in his nerve endings. Six nights of negligible sleep. Zelda looked as if she was about to collapse too.

'You need to go back to bed,' he told her.

'Yes, you're right,' she replied but still didn't move. Jay stared at her, she back at him, and he had a sudden flash of memory of the night they'd met in San Francisco, the two of them standing there and Jay dying inside while the sky melted above them (for a brief and elusive moment he'd managed to pretend that she was Helena and that she'd come back to claim him before cynical reality had reasserted its grip on the world).

'What about you?' she asked, 'Are you going to stay up the rest of the night? The sun will be up in less than an hour.'

'I'll probably make one last sweep of the house and then go to bed.'

Zelda nodded, then smiled. 'Get some sleep Jay, you look terrible.'

She moved past him towards the door of the kitchen, letting a hand come to rest on his shoulder momentarily, and he almost reached out to pull her towards him. Then she was gone, steps echoing behind her, and it was too late anyway. Jay stood there in the silence for a moment, the light growing around him, and then trudged into the hallway where he shut down his powerpad before going up the main stairs to his own room. The computer could wait until tomorrow. He'd examine the files and consider his options in the morning. Now all he wanted was sleep.

Up on the first floor, he lay down on his bed and rolled a joint from the last of the schwag he'd bought from Lara, unable to think about anything else except Zelda taking off her clothes, climbing into bed and settling her face on her pillow. Searching for his lighter, he also found that he'd pocketed the photo he'd discovered in Madeleine's bedroom and took it out to examine it one more time: two girls sitting on a pair of swings either or neither of them potentially Madeleine . . . he was getting nowhere, he told himself and put the picture on the nightstand, dropped the roach of the joint into the glass next to it and kicked off his clothes. If he fell asleep, he didn't realize it. He lay there, thinking back (or was he dreaming?) to the week that followed his journey to Scotland with Tommy's ashes. He hadn't felt like going to the office and had instead spent his mornings down on the beach with Marlowe and the old man's kite. Marlowe had sat on the sand a few metres away (Jay knew the dog still had reservations about him) and watched as Jay had launched the cherry-red triangle up into the salty light where he'd let it hang all morning. Then came the seventh morning. Jay had let it hang up there in the sky from sunup to sundown, perfect conditions, perfect enough for him to be able to tether the kite to a railing and dip inside Café Judah to use the bathroom or procure his and Marlowe's rations and come out to find it still eddying around the same spot in the sky. Then, as the sun set, Jay had untied the kite, let it go and trudged back to his Apache, Marlowe taking one last look up at the massing clouds before trotting back to the car too, leaving a parallel set of footprints in the sand next to Jay's.

Jay?

Jay twisted on to his back and found Zelda sitting on his bed. He must have fallen asleep because he hadn't heard her come in.

'Jay? Sorry to wake you . . .'

Jay hoisted himself upright. 'What is it?' he asked, 'have you heard something?'

'No. I can't sleep, that's all.'

'Are you scared?'

'No.'

'What then?'

'It's almost as if I'm too tired to sleep. I know that sounds stupid.' She looked across at him, her nightdress leaving her shoulders and arms bare, the diamond hanging there between her breasts. For a second, he pictured her, seven years old, opening the door to her mother's hotel room and seeing her body sprawled across the bed. 'I don't think I can sleep alone tonight.' Without waiting for him to reply, she pulled back the bedclothes and Jay felt the cool soft skin of her foot graze against his leg as she slid in next to him.

'Do you want to talk?' he asked quietly, aware of her arm wrapping itself around his waist.

'I don't think so,' she murmured from the pillow. 'I just want to sleep. Do you mind?'

Jay stared down at her (Zelda's eyes were already closed, her pale lips pressed together) and wanted to stroke her hair while he watched her sleep. But he also wanted to bend his head down towards her neck: would there be the same magical spot as on Helena's where the faintest pressure of his lips could start a chain reaction of caresses that ended with her coming at him with raw, open-mouthed hunger? Zelda lay motionless beside him in the bed. 'What are you thinking, Jay?' she murmured sleepily.

'Nothing,' he replied.

'Then lie down and go to sleep.'

Jay hesitated, didn't move for a second, and then slid himself down into the warmth of the bed, the way Zelda seemed instinctively to gather his body towards her again placing an image in his mind of her writhing beneath him on the silver sheet, her hands hooked around his neck as if it was the only thing keeping her from being swept away. He almost fell on her at that point, reaching some kind of precipice over which he seemed prepared to throw himself. But her hand guided him down on to his side and then drew his back towards her until he could feel her forehead against his neck and her knees gathered up behind his, her hand resting on top of his, a thumb traversing the ridgeline of his knuckles before coming to a standstill. If he closed his eyes, Jay was sure he would fall asleep in seconds and the idea of turning over and pulling Zelda's white nightdress up over her head would fade from his thoughts. But instead he lay there, eyes open, the presence of her body against his making it impossible to do anything else except endure his uneasy heartbeat that threatened to stampede at any moment, to feel the hot cells of his tongue burn up with longing. *I just want to sleep* . . . Jay tried to lock on to the rise and fall of his own breathing but could only attach his mind to hers, her breasts pressed against his back, one of her naked feet clasped between his own.

'Jay?'

He felt her breath on the skin of his back.

'What is it?'

'Are you still in love with my sister?'

'What?'

She repeated the question.

'Are you still in love with my sister?'

Jay didn't answer.

'Don't worry about it,' she said eventually. 'I'm just tired. See you in the morning.'

After we make love a second time in my bedroom inside the mansion, the idea of sleeping there again without you is only ever a possibility at best, a fiction, a meaningless and absurd fantasy. You leave after an hour that first night and maroon me on my bed with only the impossible beauty of the soft skin between your shoulder blades to think about, leave me there with hands that are still feverish with the cell memory of the hollows at either side of the base of your spine (two diagonal dimples in the flesh, one above each taut buttock, implying the spread wingtips of a butterfly), with the ghost of you still straddling my thighs, your slotted eyes still looking down at me through the twists of golden hair plastered against your face and neck and the perfect pink triangle of your lips.

•

Sometimes you arrange things so that you don't have to hurry back to Jean-Marc and we get to spend the afternoon in my bedroom's premature dusk, breathing the same sweet and sleepy air in unison as we lie exhausted in my bed, the black stardust of your eyeliner smudged and scattered across your perfect cheeks.

•

When you're not there, I carry around a demented impatience to kiss you on your eyelids (your breasts would shift position against my chest, your breathing break its rhythm for a second). It beats away inside of me when I'm driving around the island, when I'm lying awake at night, when I'm listening to you walk down the stairs at the mansion as you begin your short journey back to Can Jazmín, when I'm trawling the leaves out of the pool there and you're sitting metres behind me, Jean-Marc snoozing peacefully by your side.

•

On the rare occasions we get to spend more than a few hours together at the mansion, we also talk. About me. About you. One of the first things I notice is the way you talk about Willoughby. You rarely call the place 'home' – it's always 'the house' or just 'Willoughby' and to begin with, I wonder if this is a way of keeping the place at an emotional distance, as if your memories of it are haunted by too many images of heartbreak and ghostly reminders of your mother for you to be able to think of it with any kind of intimacy or happiness. Soon I realize that the opposite is true. You look on Willoughby in the same way that another person might indulge a revered and ancient grandmother, pampering her with flawless respect and wilful idealization.

•

It's not possible to get a more detached view of what Willoughby is really like. And the same goes for your parents. There's plainly a great deal of wilful idealization in your description of your father too, about as much of that as there is resentment, and your descriptions of your mother are subject to similar distortions. One day you show me a picture of her, the photograph that you'd hidden from me the first time we were alone together. It's a black and white portrait, professionally taken, an erotic tussle between gleaming bone structure and murky penumbra, her platinum hair marshalled around her head and shoulders in breaking waves of light. There are diamond teardrops at her earlobes (diamonds that will later hang from the necks of her two daughters), but even these fail to compete with the elusive intimacy of her eyes. One probably heard her compared to a young Grace Kelly (did that make John Smiling a crueller and jowlier late-phase Cary Grant?) but hadn't anyone noticed that she looked about as resilient as a porcelain whip?

•

As for your story about her death, I lie awake at night thinking about it, about you and Zelda sitting in your hotel room and staring out at the mirthless heave of the sea hour after hour as it churned with the force of the spring tides under a grey blotting paper sky.

•

I also wonder what Zelda is really like. I often find myself listening to you talk about your past, an incident at school or something that happened on holiday or perhaps at a childhood birthday party, and I can never tell if any reference to your twin sister is about to elicit a dismissive shrug of resentment or a defiant crescendo of sibling pride. I wonder what it's like to grow up with your mirror image walking and talking with its own free will. I wonder what it's like to sit there and watch yourself get up off a hotel bed and knock on the door of emotional oblivion even though another part of you knew you were too paralysed by fear, confusion and anger to move.

•

One moment, you talk about Zelda as if she's the most precious person in your life, the soulmate whose bond with you no lover, spouse or parent can ever diminish. At other times, you talk about Zelda as if she were just another minor irritation of your emergent adult life, a frustration left over from adolescence that you long to be rid of. *Zelda's very different from me,* you say, *she hates anything to do with the family*. Zelda is training to become a doctor. You're training to become . . . *what?* Jean-Marc's wife?

•

Your ambivalence towards Zelda reveals itself most visibly when it comes to the subject of Jean-Marc. Zelda, it seems clear, disapproves of him. But you seem unable to decide whether you agree with her disapproval or resent it. 'She's met him once,' you tell me, 'at this wedding of a distant cousin of ours in Gstaad. She said she thought he was . . . what word did she use . . . *empty*. Came right out and said it on the first night. Can you believe that?'

Apparently, this is typical Zelda: self-righteous, opinionated, insensitive. But at other times you'll tell me that Zelda's right and suddenly it's Jean-Marc who's arrogant and self-obsessed.

•

As we spend more and more time curled up in each other's bodies, hours swindled from Jean-Marc spent in bed at the mansion, I wonder what it is you really feel about me. The telescope allows me to watch as you and Jean-Marc argue with increasing frequency. Does he suspect something? Have you found out about Alondra? Or someone else? I wonder if Jean-Marc plays around with other women besides the cleaning-girl. From the way some of the girls at Can Jazmín paw at him, I assume that he's slept with a few of them at some point in the past: perhaps there's still some unfinished business?

•

I never ask you, and you never tell me. It's simpler than that. I watch from the roof as the two of you fight by the pool or in the driveway (thankfully, I never see him move to hit you again) before you drive off. Moments later, I hear your Silentium rearing up the camino and coming to a stop outside the door to the mansion. I check that Jean-Marc hasn't followed you. We collide on the stairs.

•

But you remain engaged to him. One morning, you arrive at the mansion and we sit on my bed staring at the diamond on your finger. 'It doesn't seem right,' you say, taking it off and placing it on the floor beside your clothes. 'Can you even imagine being married? Never falling in love again . . . never sharing a first kiss. Maybe I'll meet the right man some day, but I don't think it's Jean-Marc.'

•

I don't think it's Jean-Marc either. But is it me?

26

Jay found himself alone in his bed when he surfaced. He lay there for a while, trying to remember what it was he'd been dreaming about (Ibiza? San Francisco? Or a mixture of both?). Then he got dressed and made his way downstairs to find Mrs Taft attending to the great-aunts in the room next to his own.

'Good morning, Mr Richards.'

'Good morning.'

'I found a broken lamp in one of the drawing rooms this morning,' she told him as she organized the two trays of tablets and tea. Behind her, the two old women sat impassively in their beds, Jay unable as always to determine whether their eyes were fixed on him or simply staring at nothing.

'Yes, I think that was me,' he replied. 'I was moving around in the dark last night and knocked it over. Was it very valuable? Can it be mended?'

Mrs Taft told him that it had been one of a set of lamps given to Helena and Toby as a wedding gift and was shattered beyond repair.

'I should go and apologize to Toby,' Jay replied, imagining the sharp response he would get from the man. 'Do you know where he is?'

'He's in his study but I wouldn't disturb him for a while.'

'Why?' Jay asked. 'Has Helena contacted him?'

Mrs Taft paused for a second. 'I'll let Lord Charteris be the one to tell you what's happened,' she said eventually.

In the end it was Zelda who brought him up to date with the morning's events. After his brief conversation with Mrs Taft, Jay went downstairs, collected a coffee from an empty kitchen and eventually found Zelda sitting on a bench on the loggia.

'Good morning.'

'Did you manage to sleep?' he asked. She nodded.

'Mrs Taft suggested to me that something serious has happened while I've been asleep. Has your sister been in contact?'

'In a sense.'

'What's happened? Where is she?'

'Jay, Toby and I received letters from Helena first thing this morning, couriered from a New York law firm through their North Carolinan sub-office.'

'What do they say?' Jay asked

'Helena's attorneys will be formally issuing Toby with her request for a divorce on Monday. She's written that she's begged Toby not to contest her decision and that she's made it clear that she's prepared to settle as generously as possible if it can be done quickly.'

'What does that mean?' Jay asked.

'Well, she's not contesting Jacob's custody for a start. Also, she doesn't want any money from Toby, not that he's got any to give her.'

'What about Willoughby?'

Zelda told Jay that Helena had written that ideally she wanted the house to be passed on to Jacob when he turned twenty-one, with Toby and Zelda acting as his trustees until then. But she'd also accepted that this probably couldn't happen given the reality of her and Toby's financial situation and had also written that she was prepared to sell the house if both Toby and Zelda agreed and that she was happy to divide the money raised by the sale of the house three ways: half to Jacob and the rest split between Toby and her sister.

'What about Helena?' Jay asked.

'I presume that she's planning to live on Wallace's money.'

'How do you feel about it all?'

Zelda paused.

'As far as the house is concerned, I could let it go,' she said eventually. 'Whether Toby will agree is a different matter.'

'How much do you think it's worth?'

'I don't know.'

Whatever the figure was, a quarter of it was certainly no small incentive for Toby, as Zelda had put it, to let it go.

'What about Helena and Wallace?' Jay asked. 'Surely they can't be expecting to move back to Thackeray?'

'They're not. They're planning to move to Australia. I presume Wallace will also notify Madeleine next week that he wishes to divorce her if hasn't done so already. Perhaps he's as prepared to give up Thackeray as Helena finally is to give up Willoughby. One thing I'm certain of: Wallace is in a position to be very generous to Madeleine and have more than enough to live on for the rest of his life.'

They stood there for a moment, Jay looking up at the house. Were nearly three centuries of Smiling history about to come to an end?

'So it's finally over for Toby and Helena,' he said.

'It would seem so.'

'I presume that you've met with Toby this morning?'

'Only briefly.'

'How is he?'

'I'm not sure. I think he's in shock. For a moment, I thought he'd almost be pleased by what Helena's suggesting. But he just seemed dazed.'

Perhaps Toby felt more for Helena than he realized. Certainly, it looked as if Helena and Wallace felt more for each other more than anyone had realized, Jay told himself. Even Zelda had expected their affair to fizzle out. Now it seemed as if they were prepared to give up anything in order to be together, even Jacob and their homes.

Jay also considered it all from a different angle. If Toby and Madeleine consented to the divorce (and why wouldn't they?

They were already having an affair behind Helena and Wallace's backs), they'd become impossibly wealthy whilst at the same time suddenly free of the burden of responsibility towards their respective marriages.

Something still didn't seem to add up and Jay wondered if it was simply that the fact the two couples had swapped partners was still hard to believe. And of course there was Toby and Madeleine's involvement with Dan Harrington to find out more about, and also the paranormal phenomena that he and Zelda had encountered.

It was then that Toby's voice called out across the terrace.

'Jay, I want a word.' As he approached them, it seemed to Jay as if Zelda was right – Toby looked broken, vulnerable, though Jay couldn't tell if this was as much due to the fact that he had his son cradled in his arms as anything else. Eventually Toby reached the loggia but didn't take a seat.

'What is it, Toby?' Jay asked.

'I've changed my mind,' he replied quietly, shifting Jacob's weight in his bunched forearms. Jay noticed that the child stared across the loggia at Zelda who stared back but didn't offer to hold him.

'What about?' Jay asked.

'I want you out of here by the end of today . . .'

'I thought you said . . .' Zelda interrupted but Toby merely repeated himself.

'I know what I said. But I've changed my mind. I want him out of here by the end of today. This is my house, at least for a little while longer. It's not something that's open to discussion.'

He turned and walked back into the house through the French doors that led into the dining room without saying anything else.

'I can try and go talk to him . . .' Zelda started but Jay raised his hand.

'Zelda, stop,' he said, 'don't bother trying. I think my investigation here might have come to an end . . .'

'But what about the figure we saw last night? What about the paintings?'

Jay shrugged.

'I'll try and talk to him later on,' Zelda insisted. 'What are you going to do?'

'I'm going to head over to Parton.'

'What happened last night at the ranch? I never asked. Did you see anything?'

'Nothing,' he replied briskly. 'I just need to go over there and talk to Buck. I'll come find you when I get back. I should only be a couple of hours.'

Before he left for Buck's ranch, Jay went inside and settled himself down in front of his powerpad in the hallway. There were only two entries in the log he was interested in.

02:43:21   Unit 03
03:13:13   Camera 01

The first of these was a motion detector file. The second had been triggered by the phenomenon that both he and Zelda had witnessed in the hallway and he opened it up – had the camera captured an image of the figure there under the chandelier? No, the file presented him with little more to look at than clattering static. He couldn't even make out Zelda and him creeping down the stairs amongst the buzzing murk of the pixels.

Jay sat back, scratched his head and slurped the rest of his coffee even though it had gone cold. Whatever the camera had or hadn't recorded, the apparition had also triggered the other equipment and blitzed the Geiger. And both he and Zelda had witnessed it together. While it was certainly too wild a claim to suggest that the apparition had *interacted* with the two of them, he couldn't deny that there was something in the house and that they'd kept it in more or less clear sight as they trailed it through the rooms of the ground floor . . . Jay locked and archived the file, then shut down his machine and took his mug back to the kitchen before driving to Parton in Lara's Gazelle. In the kitchen there, he and Buck sat at the table while Jay filled him in on the contents of the letters Zelda and Toby had received.

'And these letters are genuine?' Buck asked once Jay had finshed his report.

'Yes. Zelda told me they were couriered in from the New York law firm Helena's hired to handle her side of the divorce.'

Buck looked shocked at the news, surprised at the very least.

'What about you?' Jay asked. 'Any news from Freddy? What about the newspaper clipping?'

Buck said that there's been no news from Thackeray.

'But I have managed to get the newspaper article translated. It's about a teenage girl who killed herself after she got pregnant.'

'*Chica Valdez*?'

Buck nodded. 'The article says that she lived in Badalona. I looked it up – it's ten or so miles north-east of Barcelona. It seems reasonable to guess that Chica Valdez is one of the two girls in the photograph you came across. You got it on you?'

Jay searched his pockets but couldn't find it. He'd left it by his bed.

'I haven't got it with me,' he said. 'I must have left it at Willoughby.'

'Doesn't matter,' Buck replied. 'We know what was on it.'

'What's Chica Valdez got to do with anyone here in Brunswick County?'

'I don't know. Maybe nothing? Maybe Madeleine Kelly is Chica Valdez's sister and they're the two girls in the picture and that's all it means.'

'When was the article written?'

'It doesn't say.'

Jay asked about the passports — had Buck's contacts come up with any leads? The man shook as his head.

'What if Madeleine realizes someone broke into her house last night?' he asked.

'Then Freddy sees what she does and reports back to me.'

'He can hardly stop her calling the police can he, standing in the bushes outside?'

'Yeah,' Buck replied. 'But I don't think the Kelly woman is going to report four fake passports as stolen to the police. So we wait and we watch.'

Jay also told him that Toby had given him until the end of that day to leave Willoughby. Buck replied that Jay could bring his things over to the ranch.

'There's still the matter we discussed the other day to resolve,' Buck said firmly.

'And you still haven't told me what Madeleine and Toby discussed at the fishing shack last night,' Jay added. 'Or what you know about "Santina".'

Buck stared back at Jay.

'You go get your things from Willoughby and bring them back here — then we'll talk. And remember: not a word about any of this to Zelda, you understand?'

Jay nodded and said that he would be back soon before he walked out of the ranch and climbed into the Gazelle. Back at Willoughby he walked into the house to find it empty. He called out along the main corridor downstairs but no one appeared, not Sara nor anyone else, and it was the same on the floors above. It didn't matter. Jay started to dismantle his equipment, starting with the motion detector on the top floor, then the camera and its corollary units on the first floor corridor, then the camera and computer and the rest of the gear in the hallway. After about an hour, he had it all locked away in its flight cases and ready to take to Parton. After that, he went upstairs and started packing up the rest of his possessions. There wasn't that much of it, a few t-shirts, spare jeans, his Lester Young discs. Half and hour later he was done and was lining it all up in the hallway when he heard a car come up the drive. He stepped out under the portico and looked out, raising a hand to shield his eyes from the sun as a navy Meteor sedan slowly rolled to a stop on the gravel in front of him. The doors opened and from behind them stepped a man and a woman, both somewhere in their mid-forties, the man in a suit, tie and sunglasses, the woman in a pair of tailored slacks, a needlecord jacket and flat pumps. Cops. He watched as they came towards him, wallets extracted from inside pockets, a flash of black steel and cross-hatchings, heavy eye contact from the woman who led the way, her partner scanning the windows of the house, the hallway through the open front door and the passage by the coach house as he made his own slower approach.

'Detective Wells,' announced the woman, 'this is Detective Lowenstein. Is Lord Charteris on the premises?'

'I don't think he is,' Jay replied cautiously.

'Perhaps you can help us. We're looking for a Jay Richards. We believe that he's currently staying at this address.'

'That's me,' Jay replied calmly.

'Mr Richards, sir, could you come with us, please?' This from Lowenstein. 'We'd like to ask you a few questions down at the station.'

'What about?' he asked.

'It's better that we talk down at the station, sir,' Lowenstein said, hands on hips, Aviators trained on Jay's face. One hand left his belt and gestured towards the waiting sedan as if he were a waiter at an exclusive restaurant. 'If you'd care to step this way?'

'Am I under arrest?' Jay asked.

'No, sir,' Wells replied as if the idea had never crossed her mind. 'Were you expecting to be?'

Jay didn't bother to answer.

'We just need to talk to you,' she continued in a flat monotone that perfectly complemented her partner's, 'ask you a few simple questions. It shouldn't take long.'

'I should get my jacket,' he tried but Lowenstein told him he wouldn't be needing it. 'It's a warm day,' he said, the stiff rod of his arm still pointing towards the glinting Meteor. 'And we'll bring you right back once we're through.'

There was nothing else for Jay to do but climb into the car. As it pulled away he saw a pale blur at one of the upper windows. It was Zelda, watching them drive him away.

27

At the station in Southport, the two detectives pulled up in a lot full of squad cars and unmarked sedans and ushered Jay through the crowd of uniformed personnel moving efficiently back and forth across the concrete to a compact single-storey building constructed from standard-issue municipal brick and glass.

'You a visitor to this country, Mr Richards?' Lowenstein asked in a voice that could have made the words 'Happy Birthday' sound like the passing of a death sentence.

'No, I was born here,' Jay replied.

Wells held a door for him and he entered the subdued bustle of the station's lobby, thanking her as politely as he could and letting her lead him down a side corridor to a door marked 'Interview Room'. If he wasn't under arrest, it didn't feel like it. In the room on the other side, Wells pointed towards the seat he should take. Then she took the seat next to him, Lowenstein the one opposite him, and the two of them stared at him for a moment in silence, their faces all Us: unasked questions and unrevealed agendas and ultimatums with which they hoped to trap him unawares. And still Jay had no distinct idea why they wanted to talk to him. Uppermost in his mind was the possibility that Madeleine Kelly had discovered that she'd been burgled and figured Jay as a likely culprit. But as Buck had pointed out, she had as much (if not more) to hide as Jay – would she really have gone to the police?

'So,' he started, looking at each detective in turn and doing his best to smile. 'This is where I ask you "What's it all about?" and you say "We ask the questions".'

'The first thing I'm going to do,' Lowenstein said, 'is thank you for coming here to talk to us. The next thing I'm going to do is read you your rights . . .'

'Hold on a second . . .'

'What's the matter?' asked Wells.

'I thought you said that I wasn't under arrest?' Jay protested.

'You aren't,' she told him. 'Your Miranda rights are there to protect you in a number of situations and to make sure we do our jobs properly.'

What was the phrase Jay had once read in a novel? '*They had eyes like they always have, cloudy and grey like freezing water . . .*' Wells' eyes were the colour of uranium and she certainly had the voice and manner they always had, somewhere between a doctor pronouncing death and a soldier trying to organize it.

'Do you have any more questions before we start?' she asked him. Jay shook his head and Lowenstein read him his rights. After that there was another pause, the two of them content to sit there watching him for a moment longer.

'Let's start by confirming who you are,' Lowenstein said eventually, pulling out a notebook and placing it on the table in front of him. He didn't open it and kept his eyes on Jay the whole time. 'Mr Jay Richards. You're currently a guest of Lord Charteris at Willoughby, am I correct?'

'That's right.'

'Where do you live?'

Jay gave him the address of the house on Quintara Avenue back in San Francisco, all the time imagining Christoph sitting there with his sacks of weed and a clew of slumped stoners talking vaguely about Hitchcock or reincarnation or deep house.

'And you came to this area when exactly?'

'I arrived five days ago.'

'And the purpose of your visit?'

'I'm carrying out some work for Zelda Smiling.'

'I see,' Wells said. 'What kind of work?'

'I'm not sure I'm at liberty to say. My clients expect complete discretion from me.'

'Whose clients don't?' she asked without smiling.

'Ours certainly do,' Lowenstein added joylessly from across the table. Jay didn't respond to either comment.

'Well I'm sure that your professional reputation is as important to Detective Lowenstein and myself right now as it is to you,' Wells continued, 'so we'll try this a different way. What is it that you do for a living Mr Richards? Don't be too specific. We wouldn't want you betraying any important confidences. Not at this stage anyway.'

Jay cleared his throat and tried not to let himself get too phased by that last 'anyway'.

'I'm a paranormal investigator.'

'Which means *what* exactly?'

'It means that people call me up when they've think they've seen or heard what we might crudely call a ghost. I investigate their property and try to find out what's behind their experience.'

'A ghost?' Wells asked. Jay knew he might as well have said 'extra-terrestrial' or 'bigfoot'.

'That's what *they* believe they've seen. I tend to try and take a more rational line . . .'

'And what "rational line" would that be?' Lowenstein leaned across the table and stared into Jay's eyes.

'That usually there's a rational explanation behind the events that have caused my clients to come to me,' Jay replied.

'And people pay you for your services?' Lowenstein asked.

'Some of the time.'

'How much?'

'It varies.'

Lowenstein sat back in his chair and shared a glance with his partner who got off her seat and took up a position directly behind Jay's head. It was now *her* voice that he heard but Lowenstein's face that scrutinized his, watching every movement it made.

'You're a guest staying at Willoughby. Is that correct?'

Jay said it was.

'It was Lord Charteries that employed you to look for . . . *ghosts*. Is that right?'

'No. It was his sister-in-law, Zelda Smiling. She came to San Francisco last weekend to hire me. I flew to Wilmington the following day and have been staying there ever since.'

'She flew all the way to San Francisco?' Wells' tone of voice made it sound as if San Francisco was further away than the moon. 'Is Miss Smiling a good friend of yours, Jay?' she asked.

Jay wondered how to answer this. Should he tell them about him and Helena?

'I met Miss Smiling once before, several years ago, in Europe. We haven't been in contact since then.'

'So why did she hire you? Aren't there other investigators like you? Or are you unique?'

'There are others like me,' Jay replied. 'In fact, I asked her the same question when she contacted me in San Francisco. She says she read a newspaper report of a high-profile case I was involved with a few years back and that's why she chose me.'

'Which case were you involved with?'

'The murder of a young Bay Area woman called Dana Lockwood.' Jay gave them the name of Captain Hansen, the SFPD officer that had dealt with him, as well as the approximate date of the case and watched Lowenstein make a note of it all before he resumed his vigil of Jay's face.

'So, you've been at Willoughby for five days,' Wells continued from behind him. 'Zelda Smiling is paying you to hunt a ghost there. I guess what Miss Smiling does with her money is up to her and nothing to do with us and that's the end of that.'

Jay didn't believe her. Wells didn't sound as if she was at the end of anything.

'You've been here five days. Have you come into contact with a Mrs Madeline Kelly in this time?'

So it *was* about Madeleine. 'Yes,' he replied. 'She lives over at Thackeray. It's near Willoughby . . .'

'We know where it is,' Wells cut in. 'When was the last time you saw Madeleine Kelly?'

He took a second. Before breaking into her house the night before, he'd last seen her in Southport, amongst the crowds of people waiting to see the police pull the dead body out of the water the previous morning.

'I last saw her here in Southport yesterday morning, down by the cannery where you guys pulled a dead body out the sea. Zelda Smiling and I drove down from Willoughby to take a look. We ran into Madeleine and stopped to talk for a while.'

'You were at Southport yesterday?'

Jay nodded.

'Have you been in contact with Madeleine Kelly at any other time during the last few days?'

'Yes. She took me back to her house two nights ago.'

'And why did she do that?' Wells asked, her voice not quite devoid of implication.

'I had a car accident near her house. Another vehicle knocked me off the road as it overtook me. Hers happened to be the first car that came along, she saw what had happened and stopped to help out.'

'Did you get a look at the car that collided with you?' Lowenstein asked. Wells wanted to know why Jay hadn't called the police.

'No, I didn't get a look at it,' Jay replied. 'It was dark and I was too busy trying to keep control of my own vehicle. And I didn't call the police because . . . because I didn't think it was intentional and I didn't have any details to report.'

'Sir, it doesn't matter if the other driver's actions were intentional or not,' Lowenstein told him. 'He or she still committed a crime when they failed to stop at the scene of an accident.'

Jay didn't have an answer to that.

'You also met with Mrs Kelly earlier that day didn't you?' Wells asked.

'Err, yes,' Jay replied, telling himself that they must have talked to Madeleine's maid (*that's* how they'd known his name and where to find him). 'I must have called on Madeleine in the middle of that afternoon.'

'And the purpose of your visit on that occasion was?'

'I wanted to check if Mrs Kelly had experienced anything strange at Thackeray.'

'A ghost?'

'I prefer the terms *anomalous* or *paranormal phenomenon*.'

Lowenstein couldn't suppress a mean chuckle at that one. But Wells remained deadpan. 'And had she?' the detective asked from behind him. 'Had she experienced any anomalous or paranormal phenomena?'

'No.'

There was a pause and Jay felt himself starting to sweat. 'Can you tell me what this is all about?' he asked.

'It's about exactly what we've been discussing,' Wells replied cleanly. 'We need to ask you some questions about your relationship with Madeleine Kelly. So far, you've been kind enough to answer those questions.'

Jay heard her pacing around behind him.

'Could you tell us what your movements have been since yesterday evening?'

'Starting when?'

Wells said that he could start from whenever he liked and Jay realized that he would have to tell them something about

Buck Harrington or otherwise come up with an alternative that was untrue, some kind of lie that he could sustain. He couldn't think of one.

'I spent the night at Buck Harrington's ranch in Parton . . .'

That seemed to surprise even Lowenstein whose thick slate-coloured eyebrows twitched for all of a nanosecond.

'*Buck* Harrington?' Wells asked. Jay nodded.

'Do you have any previous connection with Mr Harrington?'

'No. Not before I got here.'

'So you just became friendly with him in the last few days?'

'He and Zelda Smiling are acquainted,' he replied. 'Miss Smiling's brother-in-law has asked me to leave and Mr Harrington has kindly agreed with Miss Smiling for me to be *his* guest while I arrange a flight back to San Francisco.' It was a lie, but not an important one and it meant Jay didn't have to discuss the fact that Buck too thought he'd encountered something paranormal, something Jay was sure the man would want to keep to himself.

'Why does Lord Charteris want you off his premises?'

'Because like you,' Jay replied simply, 'he's sceptical about the existence of something paranormal at Willoughby.'

'And when are you planning to fly home exactly?'

'I'm not sure yet.'

'And what did you do last night at Buck Harrington's ranch?'

'Not a lot.' Jay knew he was sounding dangerously vague.

'And did you spend all night there?' Wells asked.

That was a harder one to answer. If he said that he didn't return to the house until earlier that day, the detectives might speak to Zelda and find out that he'd been lying to them. But the last idea he wanted to place in their minds was that he was careering all over the county in the middle of the night. And telling them that he'd spent the night at Willoughby would mean talking about paranormal investigation again, a subject that Jay was sure didn't sit well with either detective, however much they dismissed it as harmless quackery.

'Yes,' he lied. 'I got back to the house early this morning and started packing my things. I've been ferrying them between Willoughby and Mr Harrington's ranch most of the day and was back at the house packing up the last load when you arrived.'

'Can anyone verify your movements?'

'Up to a point,' he replied. 'I spoke with Toby Charteris and Zelda Smiling at Willoughby this morning, and also Sara Taft who's the housekeeper there. I spent some time at the ranch today talking to Mr Harrington. A few other people at the ranch saw me as well.'

'And you went nowhere else today?'

Jay shook his head.

'You didn't call on Madeleine Kelly today, not for any reason?'

Jay shook his head again.

'No, I didn't.'

Neither of the detectives spoke for a moment. They seemed to be gauging him and didn't mind if he knew it.

'Is there anything else?' he asked tentatively.

'Yes, one more thing,' Wells replied. Jay felt Lowenstein's pupils zone in on him. 'Does the name "Bruno Santina" mean anything to you?'

'I've never heard of him.'

Jay knew he'd replied too quickly before he was halfway through the sentence. He didn't need any change in Lowenstein's expression to tell him that (and Lowenstein's expression hadn't changed of course; he just stared at Jay with his numb, shock-proof eyes).

'I'll ask the question again, just in case you misheard me the first time,' Wells said. 'Does the name "Bruno Santina" mean anything to you?'

'I heard you correctly the first time,' Jay replied as slowly as he could. 'I've never heard of him. Who is he?'

'You said you were at Southport yesterday morning,' Lowenstein told him, the words almost forming without him having to move his mouth. 'Santina's the dead guy you saw them pull out of the water.'

28

For a moment Jay felt as if he was nothing more than bones and neurones.

'How are Madeleine Kelly and this Santina guy connected?' he asked after counting to seven.

'We didn't say they were. Are they?' Wells replied.

'I don't know. I just assumed that they were connected because you were questioning me about both of them simultaneously . . .'

'We received a call from Mrs Kelly's maid,' the detective continued as if she hadn't heard him. 'When she returned to Thackeray this afternoon, Mrs Kelly was missing from the house.'

'Where's she gone?'

'We don't know. Again, we thought you might be able to tell us something about it?'

'I don't know *anything* about it,' Jay answered, realizing that he was starting to sound as if he was pleading.

'Her car is still in the drive.'

'Perhaps she went for a walk?'

'The maid looked around the house for Mrs Kelly and found blood in a reception room at Thackeray. That was when she called us.'

And Wells and Lowenstein had taken the call, Jay told himself, and they'd talked to the maid and she'd told them he'd called at the house a few days before and they'd brought him in as a matter of routine. That he'd since revealed he was a stranger in the area made him look suspicious. That he was a paranormal investigator made him look suspicious. That he'd claimed he'd had a car accident that in some way had involved Madeleine made him look suspicious. That he was staying at the ranch of a notorious (if retired) gangster made him look suspicious. And there had been the brief but undeniable combustion of recognition in his face at the mention of 'Santina' (they knew it; he knew it). When he looked up, Jay saw Lowenstein staring at him, letting him know without saying a word that he'd been watching Jay add it all up in his head.

'You sure the name "Santina" doesn't mean anything to you?' he asked.

Jay shook his head.

'Then we've got a problem.'

The words that Jay had been dreading. He heard Wells moving around behind him and she eventually came into view, circling the room until she came to a stop behind Lowenstein.

'I need you to think about something for me,' she said (she wore a wedding ring, Jay noticed for the first time. Did she have children? Was this how she spoke to them when they swore, lied or stole?). 'I need you to think about the situation from my perspective. I've got a missing woman and indications of a serious assault of some kind. And I've got *you*, showing up in the area out of the blue with some wild story about ghosts to explain your presence here. In five days, you've come into contact with the missing woman on at least three occasions that you've told us about so far.'

Wells spelt the rest out for Jay pretty much the same way he had to himself moments earlier. But what could he say? He didn't know anything about Bruno Santina. He didn't know anything about Madeleine Kelly's disappearance or about the blood in the reception room though he knew that Freddy and another of Buck's guys had staked out the place – had they entered the house and taken her? If so, why? He imagined the pool of blood on the cream upholstery of Thackeray's reception room, the Voodoo Queen and her consorts looking down from the walls.

Had they hurt her?

There in the interview room, Wells went on to tell Jay that she believed he was already familiar with the name Santina. 'Forensics are processing Thackeray right this moment,' she continued. 'If we find out that you've been lying to us about this or about your relationship with Mrs Kelly, the consequences could be very serious for you. And we haven't even started on the subject of the recent disappearance of Mr Kelly and Lady Charteris.'

Wells delivered her last point meticulously and let Jay absorb it all.

'You think something's happened to Helena and Wallace?' he asked. 'Two sheriffs came to Willoughby yesterday morning to say that Helena and Wallace are planning to fly to Buenos Aires from Mexico City in a few days time. Helena and Wallace's lawyers have also initiated divorce proceedings with their respective spouses.'

'Right now we don't know what to think.' Wells replied dryly. 'And right now we're going to leave you to think about whether you've failed to mention some connection between you and either Madeleine Kelly or Bruno Santina or both of them. You've got five minutes.'

'Can I make a phone call?' Jay asked. The detectives looked back at him blankly. 'I presume that I don't need to be under arrest in order to be able to exercise my right to a phone call.'

'You go ahead,' Wells told him, 'you've got five.'

When the door shut behind them, Jay pulled out his cell and called the office back in San Francisco, glancing across the room at the mirror on the far wall and the camera in the corner of the ceiling while he waited to be connected. Wells and Lowenstein were probably staring at him on some flickering screen in the room next door and about to listen to every word he said.

'*Penny 'n' Richards Paranormal Investigations, Mike Penny speakin'. How can I be of service?*'

'It's Jay.'

'How ya doin', buddy?'

'I've got to be quick. I'm in a police station in a place called Southport. I've been asked to come in to answer a few questions by two detectives, Wells and Lowenstein. I'm not formally under arrest yet but . . .'

'Don't say another word, buddy,' Mike interrupted. 'I'm guessin' that the situation's gone astray and a few things might've happened that you best don't talk about right there in the tank. Just tell me what you want me to do.'

'I need you to contact two people. The first is Zelda Smiling: she's the client in the case I'm working on. The second person I need you to call is Buck Harrington.' Jay gave Mike their numbers, at Willoughby and at the ranch. 'Can you let them know where I am? I think I'm going to need a lawyer.'

'This Harrington's the guy we talked about the other night?'

'Yes.'

'Sounds like you grabbed on to a pretty wild steer there, partner?'

'I'm pretty sure that *he's* not the problem.'

'Whatever you say. I'll call 'em both, let 'em know where you are. You sit tight in the meantime and call me if you need any more assistance.'

After Jay hung up, he stared round the room trying to work out his options. He was pretty sure that Buck knew something about Bruno Santina but he couldn't mention this to Wells and Lowenstein for obvious reasons. And what about Toby? Were two other detectives questioning him right that moment? Had *he* attacked Madeleine Kelly? Should Jay mention that Madeleine and Toby were having an affair? The detectives would ask how Jay had come to know about it and an honest answer would do nothing to make him look less suspicious than he did already.

Jay also faced up to the possibility that he soon might not

have any options, or less of them anyway, if the detectives officially arrested him. And what would happen if the forensics at Thackeray turned up evidence of Jay's presence inside the house? Jay felt himself panic and of course it was then the two detectives opened the door and re-entered the interview room.

'You made your call?' Wells asked.

'Yes.'

They both sat down on the other side of the table from him, Lowenstein bent forwards and resting his weight on his elbows, Wells sitting back in her chair and staring at Jay across a greater distance.

'You thought it all through some more?' Lowenstein asked.

'Yes, but there's nothing I haven't told you.'

'You sure about that?'

Jay nodded.

'You're going to have to do better than that, Jay,' Wells told him.

'I can't.'

'Really?' She looked at him with all the warmth of a striplight before taking him through it one more time and repeating her catalogue of reasons for being suspicious of him.

'I'll ask you one more time: tell us what you know about Santina?'

'Nothing.'

'What about Madeleine Kelly?'

Jay repeated that he'd told them everything he knew. 'If I'm not under arrest, I think I'd like to leave now.'

Wells and Lowenstein stared back at him.

'Am I under arrest?' he asked.

'Not right this second,' Lowenstein replied. 'But we're going to have to go talk to our superiors. You've got one last chance to go about this a different way.'

Jay repeated that he had nothing more to say and Wells told him that she'd have an officer bring him something to drink while he waited for them to talk to their captain. Ten minutes later, a female officer deposited a plastic cup of black coffee on the table in front of him without saying a word and returned half an hour later with another.

'Do you know how much longer detectives Wells and Lowenstein are going to be?' Jay asked her, placing it next to its untouched predecessor. She told him that she'd 'go check' and closed the door behind her.

The Sunday of the second weekend of September. You arrange to get away from Jean-Marc by saying that you're going to the spa in San Još and appear at the mansion a little before midday. We smoke a joint while we hunt for a pair of swimming masks and two pairs of flippers I've seen somewhere in the oily shadows of the garage. When we've found them we drive to Cala Carbo in the Scout where we rent a motor-boat and forage our way through the waves towards the horizon. I drop the small anchor fifty metres out and we strip off our clothes (I watch you take off the necklace your mother gave you and fold it into the pocket of your jeans) and throw ourselves over the side.

•

Under the surface, I watch your skin change colour in the capricious marine-green light, the fluid chaos of your hair gleaming behind you, the perfect economy of your limbs, the diamond on your finger catching a sunbeam in the flush and flux of the fluorescing murk.

•

Later we lie on the boat while the sun bakes us dry and the ghost of a moon fades into view, the sweet taste of cherries in your mouth along with the sand and surf and sea-spray, my hand gliding along your arm and coming to rest on the delicate flesh of your inner wrist. Your pulse beats away under my fingertips which then move off the wrist and along the undersides of your fingers.

'Take it off,' I tell you.

'I'm going to tell him tonight,' you tell me.

'What?'

'That I want to break off the engagement.'

•

We spend some of the afternoon drinking beer and playing pool in a bar in Cala Vadella where the men are muted by you, their faces only ever one of three things, hopeful, resentful or defensive. Eventually we get bored of everyone staring and take a walk along the headlands nearby, the sun dropping towards a bank of gauzy clouds bursting out of the sea. We pause for a moment, sit down on a rock and watch the changing light substitute one smouldering shade for another above our heads until there's a strip of raw pink across the purple horizon. After that we drive to Beniras and stroll hand-in-hand through the crowds, the sound of the drummers' bongos, congas, tablas and tambourines phasing in and out of time in the darkness.

'Where shall we go?' you ask me.

'Mongolia or Hawaii,' I reply. 'Or one of the two poles. You've been everywhere else.'

'Anywhere's okay with me,' you say. 'I don't mind.'

•

We drive slowly back to the mansion. When I bring the Scout to a stop, you turn in your seat and rest your chin on my shoulder.

'I should have been back hours ago.' Your nose brushes against my skin, your hair against my cheek and neck. 'I think Jean-Marc's known about you for a while,' you say.

'Is that why you want to end the engagement?' I ask

'No.'

I can't work out if this is the answer I want to hear.

'Has he said anything to you about me?'

'No, he hasn't said anything,' you reply. 'It's just a hunch.'

I climb out of my jeep and start walking towards the garage where your Silentium sits hidden from view.

'Leave it, Jay,' you say quietly. 'Just leave it.'

You step down on to the ground and walk up to the front door of the mansion. 'I don't want to go back.'

•

We make love upstairs in my bedroom in the fading light and then both fall asleep. You curl up into ball and I wrap myself round you, my mouth pressed against the ridge of your spine.

•

I wake up to find it's gone eleven and you're still beside me. You're still there. I watch you sleep, knowing that I should wake you, reluctant to do it because you'll pull your clothes on and leave.

•

Suddenly you sit up in bed and grab me.

'What's the matter?' I ask. You say you were having a bad dream. 'It wasn't anything important,' you tell me, moving across the sheets towards me and sliding up over my body. We make love again and then you go back to sleep. I listen to you breathe for a while, the rolling bass of the ocean in the distance, a slice of the moon visible through the open widow, and it's then that I hear a banging noise downstairs. I sit up in bed and listen. There it is again . . . you stir beside me, but don't wake up.

•

I pull on some jeans and a t-shirt and walk down to the ground floor where I place my eye to the peephole in the front door as a fist pounds against the wood. It's Jean-Marc in the fish-eye of the lens.

I open the door.

'Jean-Marc.'

'Jay.'

He doesn't say anything else for a second, just stares back at me as if he's sizing me up, a cigarette burning away in his left hand. For a moment, I think he's going to try to hit me.

'Something serious has happened,' he says finally, 'very

serious.' He pauses again. 'If you see Helena, tell her that her sister's just arrived at the villa and that she should return as quickly as she can.'

He doesn't wait for me to say anything and walks back to his Kodiak and drives off. I shut the door. *Something serious has happened.* I go up to my bedroom and sit on the edge of the bed and stare down at you for a little while. Then I shake you awake.

'What's happened?' you ask immediately.

'Jean-Marc was downstairs just a second ago . . .'

'. . . did he know I was here? Did you tell him?'

'. . . it's okay. He's gone now. But he seemed pretty sure that you were here. I didn't say anything. But look, that's not the point, he came here to say that . . .'

'Zelda . . . ?'

'. . . she's at the villa. Apparently something serious has happened. You should go back.'

'One of my great-aunts has probably died,' you mumble as you get out of bed. 'Two of my grandfather's sisters live at Willoughby. They're both very old and very senile and we've been waiting for them to die for years now.' As I watch you pull your shirt over your head and shoulders, I think of Jean-Marc's face moments earlier. Whatever's happened, it seems to be more serious than the death of some distant and very elderly relative.

•

I follow you outside into the night.

'I'll drive you.'

'I'm fine. I can drive.'

We open up the garage and you steer the Silentium out on to the dirt.

'I'll see you tomorrow,' you tell me, painting a kiss on to my lips.

•

After you drive away, I run up to the roof of the mansion and train the telescope on the driveway of Can Jazmín. A few minutes later, you appear in the beam of the security light by the front door to the villa. You stop for a moment, turn to gaze across the bay at the mansion and raise your hand for a moment. Then you walk inside. After that, I can't see you. A couple of the guests sit out on the veranda smoking cigarettes but also go inside after twenty minutes. I continue to scan the villa, looking for a glimpse of you at a window or doorway, wanting any kind of clue as to what's happening.

•

I sit there all night.

•

Or, at least, I'm up on the roof all night. The next morning I find myself face-down on the tiles, one arm nestled around the tripod's legs. It's gone ten o'clock and I scramble to my feet and stare out across the bay at Can Jazmín.

•

It looks as lifeless as my mansion.

•

The swimming pool is empty except for a lone inflatable mattress that circles lazily through the aquamarine water. The pool area itself is devoid of any belongings. I can't see any towels or magazines or coffee cups or cartons of juice. And I can't see any people. The same goes for the veranda and the windows on the upper floors. No flashes of movement. No signs of life. The only object that suggests that someone is still there is the solitary car in the driveway, your black Silentium standing there in the dust. A few minutes later, I'm pulling up alongside it and stumbling towards the front door which is shut but unlocked.

•

I go inside.
 Hello?
 Can Jazmín is silent. The hallway is as deserted the pool area. The same goes for the living room and the kitchen. I call out again.

Helena?

There's a noise on one of the upper corridors. Footsteps echo down the main staircase towards me. And then you turn the corner and appear at the top of the stairs, your hair tied back behind your head.

•

You're still here, I think to myself, *thank Christ you're still here.* I expect you to come down the stairs but you just stare down at me with an unreadable expression.

'Helena?'

'No.'

•

And then: 'I'm afraid not. I'm the other one.'

Zelda comes down the stairs and walks past me into the centre of the room where she turns to face me again. 'I'm guessing that you must be Jay.'

'That's right.'

•

I don't know what to say. Zelda's voice is a little deeper than yours, her hair a little shorter. Besides that, there was little to distinguish the two of you from each other. Zelda seemed to have beamed down from a parallel world, one which had played out your life with infinitesimal variations.

'I'm Zelda,' she says. 'You probably want to know what's happened.'

•

For a moment, it feels as if I'm looking down on myself from some external perspective, somewhere high-up, somewhere far away.

•

'Our father died early yesterday morning . . . he was involved in a car crash near where he lived and passed away in the ambulance on the way to the hospital. I came straight here to break the news to Helena.' She pauses. 'Helena was much closer to him than I was. I didn't want her to hear the news by telephone.'

'How is she?' I ask.

'She's okay. We sat her down for an hour or so while she absorbed the initial shock of it all. And she had Jean-Marc here to look after her. He's never seemed like the most thoughtful man in the world to me, but . . . anyway, they packed all through the night and flew back to America first thing this morning. Jean-Marc said the others could stay here till the end of the rental period if they wanted to but no one felt like it and they've flown home too on whatever flights they could find.'

•

I picture you flying home, your face creased with tears, Jean-Marc next to you in the closeted air of first class. For a moment, I wonder if you've left me a note but know that you haven't. As if reading my mind, Zelda speaks again.

'I'm flying back to America later today. Helena asked me to call on you and tell you what's happened. But you've saved me the trouble.'

And that's it. For a second, I wonder what you've told Zelda about me, if anything at all, but realize that it isn't worth thinking about.

•

'I should go,' I say. Out on the driveway, I tell Zelda that I'm sorry about the death of her father. She nods and says that it's very sad. In the rearview, I watch her turn and enter the villa as I round the bend.

•

Back at the mansion, I go up to the roof terrace, placing one foot in front of the other because it has nothing better to do. Up at the top of the house, I stare at the piles of litter that have built up over the last couple of months, the sandwich wrappers, juice cartons, beer cans and coffee cups overflowing with ash and oily roaches, the telescope standing there amongst it all like some kind of spacecraft that has just touched down amongst the trash. Somewhere along the hill, there's the sound of a car but it seems as remote as Jupiter. In the meantime the Earth turns and birds chirp and planes cut out fat lines of cocaine across the mirror of the meaningless sky.

29

Jay sat there for another thirty minutes. When the door opened, Wells and Lowenstein re-entered the room but didn't bother to sit down.

'Can I go?' he asked

'Yes,' said Lowenstein. 'You can go.'

Jay stood up.

'Don't make any plans to fly back to San Francisco just yet,' Wells added. 'We'll be needing to talk to you again.' She presented him with her card. *Det. Julienne Wells.* 'If you remember anything, don't hesitate to give me a call.'

'We'll contact you at Buck Harrington's ranch or on your cell phone if we need to speak to you,' Lowenstein added, taking down Jay's details.

Amongst the puppet shrubbery outside the entrance to the station, Jay found a man in a grey suit waiting for him, his briefcase on the ground by his feet.

'Jay Richards?' he asked.

'Yes.'

'Max Seeker.' He too handed Jay his business card. 'If you're contacted by the police again in any way,' he told the Jay, 'please call me without hesitation.'

'Thank you,' Jay replied. 'Did you stop them from arresting me just now?'

'No,' Seeker replied. 'They almost certainly weren't going to arrest you today. At this moment in time you're what they call a "Person Of Interest".'

'So I'm not under suspicion?'

'No, you're under a tremendous amount of suspicion.'

'So why didn't they arrest me?'

'They might do tomorrow when Thackeray's been processed.'
'Why not today?'

Seeker told Jay that the detectives would be hesitant to arrest him before they had enough evidence. 'Defence lawyers often use the fact of a quick arrest to point to a desire on the police's part to fit someone up for a crime. Also, once a person has been formally arrested, several other temporal factors come into play. By simply bringing you in for questioning like they did today, they can keep it nice and informal and retain the option to arrest you at a later time.'

'So they'll come and get me tomorrow?'

'We'll see. As I've said, if they do, don't answer any questions until I've arrived.'

'Okay,' Jay nodded. 'Who sent you? Was it Zelda?'

Seeker pointed towards the black Orca parked across the street in the shade of some trees.

'Goodbye,' the lawyer said, shaking Jay's hand before walking over to a titanium Graystar Coupé and driving away. Jay himself walked through the parking lot and across the street to the Orca and climbed into the passenger seat.

'How are you?' Buck asked. There was no one else in the car with him.

'I'm okay. Madeleine Kelly's disappeared and they figure I'm something to do with it. Forensic investigators are combing through Thackeray right this moment . . .'

'I know,' Buck interrupted. 'You tell them anything about last night?'

'I told them I'm staying at yours now that Toby's kicked me out. I said I stayed in all night and didn't leave until this morning.'

'Good,' Buck grunted.

'They also asked me about Santina. They told me he's the dead man they pulled out of the sea at Southport yesterday morning. I didn't tell them that I'd overheard Madeleine and

Toby talking about him. I didn't tell them anything in fact but they do know the name is familiar to me because they saw it in my face when they questioned me about him. That's the thing that's made them the most suspicious.'

'And you didn't tell them anything else?' Buck asked.

Jay shook his head. 'I told them why Zelda originally hired me to come to North Carolina – naturally they didn't believe me – and I had no choice but to admit that I've met Madeleine Kelly on three occasions. But I've said nothing more than that.'

'What else did they ask you? Is that everything?'

'They pushed me to make a connection between the body they pulled out of the sea in Southport and Madeleine's disappearance but I couldn't make one because I don't know anything about it. They suggested that they found my association with you somewhat suspicious. Also, I'm not allowed to leave the area.'

They pulled out into the traffic. Jay turned to Buck who kept his eyes on the road. He looked troubled, Jay thought, and he still hadn't told him what *he* knew about Santina or what had happened at the cabin the previous night or whether Freddy was connected with Madeleine's disappearance.

'What about you?' Jay asked. 'You turn up anything?'

'Kind of,' Buck replied, eyes on the road ahead. 'Something happened . . . last night'

'What?'

Buck looked across and glanced at Jay quickly. 'After I'd dropped you back at Willoughby, I went and sat in my study trying to piece this whole thing together. I don't know how long I sat there but I remember looking at the clock not long before and seeing that it was almost five thirty so that gives you an idea of the time. Anyway, I was sitting at my desk when I heard footsteps behind me. Then the desk lamp suddenly cut out and when I looked up, I saw her reflection in the window in front of me. She was standing right behind my shoulder.'

'Who? Esmerelda Smiling?'

'No, it wasn't Esmerelda.'

'Who was it? Someone you recognize?'

'It was Helena.'

Jay asked Buck if he was certain. The man nodded. 'It was her,' he said. 'There was no mistaking it.'

Had she said anything? What had she done? Buck told Jay that she'd stood there, gazing at him, a pillar of light. He'd called out her name but the figure hadn't moved or replied.

'When I turned around, she'd disappeared.'

Jay swallowed a mouthful of acidic saliva (if Helena's ghost had appeared to Buck, that would mean that she was . . .). 'Buck, what's your connection with the Smiling family?' he asked. 'There's something you're not telling me. There's a whole load of things you're not telling me, in fact.'

Buck didn't answer for a while but Jay didn't break the silence and eventually the man pulled the Orca over to the side of the road somewhere on the outskirts of the town.

'You're right,' he said, turning to face Jay. His face was all Ds, disorientation dancing in his pale eyes that were both as shiny and as dull as polished dimes. He looked as dazed as Toby had that morning and Jay noticed the big man's hands dithered as he brought his zippo up to light the end of his cigar.

'When I was nineteen, I got back from Asia and got a job at Willoughby as John Smiling's driver. He had this impressive collection of classic cars, a Consul, a Majestic, a Hyperion and even this old pearl-white Lancaster that had once belonged to the King of Sweden and been given to Smiling's father as a gift. It was my job to keep them all in good condition and also to drive John Smiling wherever he wanted to go.'

Jay remembered the photo he'd seen hanging on the walls of the library – he'd assumed the chauffeur in the picture had been a young Alfred Taft. He'd been wrong.

'I'll never forget the first time I saw her,' Buck continued.

'It was the day of her father's funeral and I'd driven Smiling to Troy for the service. It took all day, of course, and I waited with the other cars and other drivers until the evening when one of the butlers came to say that Smiling was ready to leave. I brought the car round to the front of the house and it was *then* that I saw her for the first time. She came out with him, dressed in black. The only parts of her that were visible were her mouth beneath the hem of her veil and her pale wrists between the edges of her gloves and the black cuffs of her sleeves. I didn't think about anything else the whole way back to Willoughby.'

'When did you see her again?'

Buck told him it had been the following weekend. John Smiling had invited Esmerelda Candor to stay at Willoughby and sent him back to Troy to collect her. The journey had taken three hours as it had before and he'd spent every second of it wondering what the rest of her face looked like.

'When I arrived,' he told Jay, 'I went inside and notified the housekeeper. She came down the main stairs, nineteen years old and the most beautiful woman I'd ever seen. For a moment I couldn't move. Luckily I remembered myself in time and went to take her case. But being near to her was almost more than I could bear. How the hell was I going to survive the three hour journey back to Willoughby?'

'Did the two of you talk?' Jay asked. 'What happened?'

'Once we'd been in the car for ten minutes, she leaned forward and asked me to pull over. I asked her if she'd forgotten something and did she want me to turn round — but she simply asked if she could ride up in the front with me as if the choice was mine and not hers. I told her as politely as I could that she could do whatever she wanted and she said that she felt stupid sat in the back on her own and climbed in beside me.'

Buck told Jay how they'd talked the whole way to Willoughby, jazz on the radio, Esmerelda telling him about her father and her childhood, Buck telling her about Vietnam. Only when they'd got as far as Sixty Bridge did she return to the back seat.

'What happened next?' Jay asked.

'They were married six months later. I spent half that time driving her back and forth from Montgomery County to Willoughby. It became our little ritual, me bringing the car to a halt on the bridge and her getting out and getting into the back before we continued on to the house where John Smiling would be waiting for her. And of course it was me who drove them from the church to the house for the reception when the day came. I remember looking at her in the rearview mirror, eyes like pieces of sky and this mass of golden hair pushed back from her neck, her delicate fingers arranging her skirt and train around her knees and Smiling sitting next to her the whole time with a huge shit-eating grin plastered all over his face. I almost died.'

Jay asked Buck when his affair with Esmerelda Smiling had started: before or after she'd married John Smiling. He told Jay it had started a few months afterwards.

'John Smiling kept women all round the area and he refused to give them up, right from the start.'

'Did you ever drive John Smiling to meet any of these other women?'

'Sometimes,' Buck replied. 'They weren't anything special. And that was the part I couldn't understand: he had the most beautiful woman in North Carolina and yet he continued to screw around with waitresses and dancers and teachers and bored widows. There were all so *ordinary*. And he hardly even tried to hide it half the time. Esmerelda told me that some nights he wouldn't bother to come home and that he'd arrive back the next morning and sleep half the day. He'd surface some time in the afternoon and start drinking.'

Buck stopped talking for a moment and dropped a large lump of ash into the ashtray.

'And so it started. One week John Smiling flew to New York on business. I drove him to the airport and was coming back down the drive when I saw her waiting for me on the front porch. I asked her if anything was wrong but she didn't say anything, just took my hand and led me through the garden. I asked her where we were going but she didn't reply and by the time we got to the forest, it didn't feel so strange. In fact, it felt totally ordinary, the two of us walking along hand-in-hand in the sunshine. Perhaps that's what she wanted. And then we got to the lake.'

The two of them had made love on the floor of the cupola. And so their affair had started. John Smiling was too busy and too arrogant to notice and it had been easy enough for them continue meeting in secret.

'One afternoon I was driving her to Wilmington for a lunch appointment,' Buck told him, 'it was then she told me she was pregnant and that she was expecting twins. I asked if they were mine and she said that she didn't know. I asked her if she was going to leave Smiling but she told me that it was *our* relationship that she wanted to come to an end.'

Buck told Jay that he'd continued to work at Willoughby, watching Esmerelda grow larger as every month passed.

'Eventually she stopped leaving the house so I never got to see her or talk to her. And then the girls were born.'

Buck asked Jay if he'd ever seen a picture of John Smiling and Jay replied that he had. 'So you know that he was a dark guy. People sometimes used to say that he looked Italian but I know a lot of Italian guys and I wouldn't have said *that* about Smiling. Black Irish, maybe, but not Italian.'

Buck stubbed out his cigar in the ashtray and lowered his window to let out the smoke.

'Well, you can imagine what happened when these two

beautiful blonde twins appeared, he said. 'I remember driving John Smiling to the hospital in the city and waiting in the lobby while he went to check on Esme the afternoon they were born. He was upstairs in her room for two hours and I just sat there trying to read some stupid magazine when all I really wanted to was go up and take a look at the girls. Waiting was the worst part. I didn't know if they were mine — but I *felt* they were and yet I also knew this was ridiculous, that a man can convince himself of anything when it comes to love and that I had no way of telling.

'And then John came down and I knew at once that they were mine and that he knew.'

'What did he say?' Jay asked.

'Nothing to start with. Out in the car, I asked him if he wanted to go back to Willoughby. He told me to drive to the bank where he went inside for ten minutes and then asked me to drive to the train station. When we got there he told me that "we" were going to get a cup of coffee. I followed him into the terminal building and into a café where we sat down. The waitress came and went and I'll never forget what he said next: "*Do you know how unlikely it is that someone like me could father two blonde girls with blue eyes?*" Smiling was shaking, I noticed. Then he said it again: "*Do you know how unlikely it is that someone like me could father two blonde girls with blue eyes?*" I still didn't answer him. He went on to tell me that Esme had admitted everything to him and that he knew I was the twins' father. He told me that I was fired. Then he pulled out an envelope and placed it on the table in front of me. "This is ten thousand dollars in cash," he said. "All you have to do for it is get on a train and never come back."'

'What did you say?' Jay asked.

'I told him that if the girls were mine, I was going to be the one to raise them. I told him that Esmerelda didn't love him. I told him that he should let her go so that we could be together. No amount of money could change my feelings. When I was done, John Smiling simply laughed at me. So I told him again, that I had a right to raise my girls, that Esmerelda had a right to make her own decisions, and it was then he told me that she already had. She wanted to stay with him and bring the girls up at Willoughby. I said I didn't believe him but he pulled out another envelope from inside his coat and handed it to me. It was a letter from Esmerelda.'

'What did it say?'

'You can read it for yourself.'

He handed Jay a cream envelope. On the front, a single word was written in lilac ink: 'Buck'.

'Read it,' Buck said.

Jay opened it and pulled out the single folded sheet inside.

Wilmington General Hospital,
Wilmington.

1ˢᵗ April, 1973

Dear Buck,
By now you will know what my husband and I have decided. All I can ask you to do is not fight against this and to see it as the best thing for all concerned, the girls included. You and I have shared something special but it is over now. I am certain of it.

I expect that you will wonder as you read this if it is possible for you to change my mind. Any thoughts of this kind are a waste of time. This decision cannot be changed.

Please take our help and go find your own future. I wish you luck.

Esmerelda

'John Smiling could have made her write it,' Jay said when he'd finished reading.

'Yes. But I don't think he did and I didn't then. And by that point such details didn't seem to matter any more.'

'What about going to court and proving that you were Helena and Zelda's father?'

'Again, it wouldn't have mattered to me. I knew in an instant that nothing mattered if Esme wasn't prepared to make a choice, a choice to be with me.'

'What happened next?'

'John Smiling repeated his offer: ten thousand dollars in cash to disappear and never contact Esmerelda or the girls. He would raise the girls as if they were his. He and Esme would continue with their marriage as if nothing had happened between me and her.'

'So you left.'

'Yes.'

Jay asked Buck if he'd taken the money.

'It was the most shameful thing,' he muttered. 'I wanted to tear the money up in front of his face. I sat there picturing myself doing it and scattering it over the table in front of him. But then I tried to picture what I would do afterwards. Where would I go? I didn't have a cent to my name. I didn't have a place to live. And I didn't have Esmerelda or my daughters. So I took it and left. As I reached for the money, I told myself to look John Smiling in the eye at the very least. But I was too ashamed even to do that.'

'And then you left?'

Buck nodded. 'Took the first train out of the station. A week later I was in Chicago. It wasn't a choice. I ended up there. I didn't leave for twenty-five years.'

'And you never saw Esmerelda again?'

'Not once. I tried to do everything I could to put it all behind me.'

Buck started up the engine and pulled back out on to the road while Jay pictured him and Freddy back in the old days, late night rendezvous in the streets of Chicago's boiling gangland, the trunk full of guns and drugs, Buck's past buried inside of him.

'Years passed,' Buck told him, as if reading his mind. 'It was like a bad dream. Perhaps you already know what kind of life I used to lead?'

Jay nodded. 'I know a little.'

'Well, it was violent and dangerous, enough problems for any man to carry around in his head. But there wasn't a day when I didn't think about my girls. When I married Nicole, Dan's mother, I thought it would make things easier. But it all just got harder. Every time I looked at Dan, I didn't think that he reminded me of Nicole, I just wondered how much he looked like my daughters. I'd never seen them and Dan was all I had to go on.'

'And you never tried to contact the girls?'

'No. But it was a matter of *my* pride rather than what I thought was best for *them*. Of course, when I got news that Esmerelda had killed herself, I was devastated. And I hated the thought of Helena and Zelda living with that man. But by then it seemed as if we'd all travelled too far for me suddenly to reappear in their lives.'

Jay wondered whether he should admit to Buck that he already knew the story of Esmerelda Smiling's suicide. That would probably mean discussing his relationship with Helena years before, something he didn't want to trawl through, and in the end he let Buck carry on with the rest of his story. Another eighteen years had passed by, the man told him, and then his wife had died.

'I just went on living my life and raising Dan. And then I got the news that John Smiling had died. For two days I didn't leave my study, didn't think about anything else except whether I should move back home. I probably made my decision the second I heard the news but it took that long to work out why.'

'And then you came back to North Carolina.'
Buck nodded.
'But you didn't tell Helena the truth.'
'I meant to but I couldn't do it. I just couldn't do it.'

30

'Does Freddy know any of this?' Jay asked.

'Yes.'

'Dan?'

'Not a thing.'

Buck didn't mention that he'd beaten Dan when he'd found out that his son had made a move on Helena. And Jay certainly had no intention of revealing that he knew that Helena had slept with her half-brother which meant that neither of them spoke for the rest of the journey to Parton, Jay unable to stop himself imagining Dan and her together in the echo-chamber of his head.

'Are you going to tell Zelda?' he asked Buck when they were finally sitting in his study.

'Yes. Eventually. But right now we've got more important things to deal with. Like you say, things can only get a whole load more serious now the police are searching through the Kelly house. And the whole issue of Santina isn't going to go away either.'

'What did you find out at the cabin last night? I presume Madeleine and Toby met up as planned?'

Buck nodded.

'I couldn't hear what they were saying clearly beyond the fact that Toby borrowed a whole load of money off my son and that Dan's been putting pressure on Toby to pay him back. I got my son over here this morning and questioned him about what's been going on between him and Toby.'

Buck had 'got' Dan over to the ranch? Jay wondered how this meeting had gone. Had Dan met with his father willingly?

'What did he tell you?' he asked.

'He told me that Toby loaned a quarter of a million dollars from him last year.'

No mention of whether Buck had needed to force his son to tell him what the truth was of his dealings with Toby. Perhaps it was better if Jay didn't know.

'Toby didn't say what the money was for at the time but Dan says he knew that it was to cover Toby's investment in the new complex on Windy Point. I also got an admission out of him that he's behind a lot of the problems the redevelopment has suffered over the last two years. He told me that he's been trying to sabotage the project from the beginning. He knew that Toby had put himself into as much debt as he could handle right at the start – if things went wrong, then Toby would quickly become desperate for cash.'

'I saw Dan with Frank McKelvy at Windy Point the other day. Do you think McKelvy's been in on Dan's plan from the start?'

'Yes. Dan says that when he loaned Toby the money, McKelvy had already told him that it was unlikely Charteris would be able to pay him back. Dan guessed he'd eventually be able to force Toby to sell him his stake in the complex in order to clear the debt. And that's what he really wanted, right from the start. A stake in the marina is worth more than the initial loan over the years to come. So far Toby has refused but Dan's pretty sure it's just a matter of time before Toby has no other choice.'

'What would Dan do if Toby refused to pay up?' Jay asked.

'Things you don't want to know about,' Buck replied.

'Are you going to get involved? Do you care what happens to Toby?'

'No, but I care about my daughters . . . and my grandson.'

'So you *are* going to get involved?'

'Right now? No. Like I said, we've got too much else to think about.'

They sat in silence.

'So what are we going to do?' Jay asked.

'You say the cops asked you if you know who "Santina" is and though you'd heard Madeleine and Toby mention his name, you didn't admit it?'

'I said I'd never heard of him but they didn't believe me.' Buck paused.

'I know who Bruno Santina is.'

He paused again and Jay sat there waiting patiently.

'Have you ever heard of a man called Carlo Dotto?' Buck asked.

Jay said that he didn't.

'He's the head of the Dotto family, one of the seven families that run things up in Chicago. I worked for him for over two decades. He's like a father to me and he was the first person I told what had happened between me and Esmerelda, the only person for ten years until I told it all to Freddy. Anyway, a couple of weeks ago, Carlo called me up. It was only the second time since I came home.'

Dotto had rung to let Buck know that he'd heard through the mafia grapevine that a contract had been taken out on a rich woman living nearby.

'Some guys have got what it takes to make it in the kind of business I used to be involved in. Stick to the rules, do as you're told, keep your end tidy and you should get a chance to make something for yourself. And that's where this Santina character enters the story. Apparently he's always been something of a flaky character, always talking too much, always drinking too much and getting himself noticed. As a result he's been getting passed over when it comes to getting promoted and he's never had as much action as he'd like. Anyway, Carlo calls me up and tells me that he's heard that Santina's been doing some moonlighting, says his source was out with a group of guys and that Santina was amongst them, drunk and boasting about how he was going to make fifty thousand the following week for killing a rich woman and her lover near to the ranch.'

'The targets, they could have been anyone?'

'Apparently he was stupid enough to talk about the hit, saying where it was going to take place and so on, at a party in a big house and so on. Carlo eventually heard about it and rang me, though not before Santina had left Chicago.'

'What happened next?'

'Well, I knew all about the party at Willoughby so it didn't take me long to work out that Santina's victims were Helena and Wallace.'

What had Buck done next? He didn't have an invitation for Toby and Helena's anniversary celebrations and had gatecrashed the event as Jay had already been told. As they sat there, Buck described how Carlo Dotto had got hold of a photograph of Santina and faxed it to Buck who took Freddy along with him to Willoughby and roamed the party looking for the killer.

'We knew he was posing as a chauffeur and we kept checking the front of the house where all the guests' cars were parked. Eventually Freddy spotted him sitting in his car.'

'What did you do?'

'We killed him.'

'How?'

'It was dark and he wasn't expecting anyone to be coming after him. We just walked up beside the passenger window and Freddy shot him. After that, we drove him away in his own car, stripped and dumped the body in the sea and then had the car crushed.'

Jay asked if anyone had heard the shot. Buck said that Freddy had used a .22 pistol. 'They're almost silent. What do you think Santina was carrying?'

Jay didn't answer, also glad that he hadn't known any of this when he'd been questioned earlier.

'After that,' Buck continued, 'we reckoned we'd prevented Helena's murder . . .'

'But she still disappeared, as did Wallace.'

'Yes.' Buck looked at Jay. Jay looked back at him. They were both thinking the same thing: if it *was* Helena's ghost that had appeared in Buck's study then it meant that she was dead. Possibly.

'Do you know who hired Santina?' Jay asked.

'No,' Buck replied. 'But my guess is it's Madeleine or Toby or both of them.'

'And now Madeleine's missing and her blood's all over the reception room according to the cops. Did Freddy have anything to do with that? Did he see anything?'

Buck shook his head.

'So who was it?

Buck shrugged. 'There's a back door to the house so someone else could have sneaked in the other way without him seeing.'

'Toby?'

Buck nodded. 'That's my guess. Freddy's still watching Thackeray waiting to see if Madeleine or anyone else comes back.'

They sat in silence for a few moments.

'Where did she appear?' Jay asked after a while.

'Helena? Right *there*.'

Buck pointed to a spot on the floorboards in front of him as he sat in his leather desk chair and Jay imagined him looking up into the glass and seeing her reflection standing over his shoulder. His daughter. 'What are we going to do about . . . *that*?' Jay asked.

'Again, nothing. For now.'

'I think Toby killed Helena,' Jay said, 'and Wallace Kelly.'

'Me too,' Buck replied

For a moment Jay considered suggesting that they go to the police but realized there was no way Buck would agree, and certainly no way he could agree if he and Freddy had killed Santina.

'So what are you going to do?' he asked. 'Confront Toby?'

'Eventually. I think we need to break into the cabin where Toby and Madeleine have been meeting. Let's see what we can find there. After that, we plan our next move.'

Buck got out of his seat. 'Let's call Freddy.'

Jay remains on the island for another two weeks.

•

When he isn't running errands for Pepé, he cleans up the villa that formerly belonged to the French former ambassador to Cuba. Within four days, the place is as scrubbed and as spartan as when he'd moved in, the roof terrace as clear of signs of inhabitation as Can Jazmín across the bay, the rooms inside empty except for the backpack that contains his clothes and his father's notes, the flight-case that contains his records and his toothbrush and toothpaste by the sink in one of the bathrooms. He eats one meal a day, making a solitary trip in the Scout to Portinax for a sandwich, usually after nightfall so that there is less information for his eyes to process, less sky, less grass, less water (during daylight, Jay tries to view the world in extreme close-up with minimum depth-of-field, each day a blinkered montage of single images, the dirty plastic of a beer crate he's carrying, the spout of a generator he's refuelling, a spot of tarmac on the road ahead, the glowing end of the joint inches from his nose).

•

Then Jay's stipend from Cambridge arrives, on the first day of October as it always does, and he drives the Scout to Portinax where he finds Pepé in the backroom of the Restaurante S'Illot. He hands back the keys for the villa and the jeep and tells Pepé he's leaving the island (the old man absorbs the news with a shrug and wishes him luck) before catching a cab to the airport where he buys a seat on the next available flight to Barcelona. From there Jay flies south to Marrakesh where he gets a job driving an overland truck full of backpackers across the continent to Cape Town. The trip is scheduled to last eleven months and Jay remains behind the wheel for all of them, joints the size of beer bottles hanging from his mouth as he pushes the rumbling Behemoth on through one pink horizon after another, through the Spanish Sahara and the blasted salt-flats of Mauritania beyond. At night, the sky above him more silver than black, Jay listens to the backpackers as they swim and laugh in waterfalls and oases and tries to keep them as distant as possible, happier when the Behemoth is on the move and he has an excuse not to say anything. Luckily it doesn't take long for the passengers to learn to leave him alone. And as the personnel that make up the group shift and change like the planet around them (towns carved out of mud in Mali, volcanic rock in Cameroon, the shimmering surface of Lake Tana in Ethiopia, the mountainous rainforests of Uganda), so this knowledge is passed on to newcomers. By the time they arrive in Zanzibar, Jay can see that a shroud of mystery surrounds him just as his dirty hair now straggles around his shoulders and his beard seems to swarm around his face like a cluster of black insects. As far as the passengers are concerned (all of them young, white and eager to believe in anything), they're happy enough to write him off as the group's lunatic, an 'experience' they will refer back to at some point in their increasingly surrendered futures, the 'freak that drove us around Africa in our gap year', 'the guy who didn't speak for days at a time', 'the guy who didn't wash for weeks at a time', 'the guy who only ate sandwiches' (this isn't strictly true – when bread supplies are exhausted, Jay can usually force down a small meal if it consists of only one substance). At the side of Lake Malawi, while the passengers soak the sand from their skin, Jay sits on the shore on his own, a fistful of weed ripped from his own personal cob smoking away in his mouth like a road-flare at the scene of an accident. For the first time in a while, the others beckon him to join them. 'It's beautiful.' 'You can see fish.' But Jay waves them on and swallows down another bitter image of him and Helena. How stupid of him to have squandered those final moments together (if he'd known they were to be their last, he would have done more to absorb the feel of her hair, her skin, the sound of her voice, the blue cyclones of her eyes). How stupid of him to have thought that anything could have come of it, of him and Helena. They could have travelled anywhere in the world – but where would they have gone back to?

•

Jay considers his time on Ibiza and realizes how much he'd managed to convince himself that what was happening between him and Helena at the mansion had some kind of potential. And he knows that he still feels these throbs of delusion, knows that he still wallows in the sweet logic of his own intoxication, but also realizes that he is sampling its last precious drops and that soon only the preying ache of missing her will persist.

•

Weeks later the Behemoth rumbles across the border into South Africa. By now the world seems to Jay as if it's made out of plastic. Nothing seems real. In the Matapos National Park a week or so before, they'd seen elephants off the truck's starboard bow as the sun set over distant hills, a pair of giraffes on the portside: to Jay they were just *elephants*, they were just *giraffes*, it was just a *sunset*, they were just *hills*, it was just a *horizon*. The Victoria Falls were nothing more than falling water, as mystical as a running tap.

•

The truck reaches Cape Town. Jay doesn't so much register the change as a reformulation of landscape or context, more feels it in the rhythm of his hands as they grapple with the Behemoth's hula-hoop of a steering wheel, feels it in the rhythm of his feet on the spade-like pedals. Objects like traffic lights, other vehicles, pedestrians and road-markings now present themselves to him and he deciphers their messages like a child fingering his way though his first book.

•

And then the journey ends. Jay takes a room in a hostel and sleeps for two days. On his third day he wakes up and cleans up. First the beard and hair, a barber in Foreshore demanding triple money *up front* (as well as the cost of a new set of razors for his trimmer) before he agrees to tangle with Jay's tangles. After that, Jay stands under a shower in a public gym for an hour before sitting in the steam room for the rest of the day, breathing the moist heat in through his mouth and sucking it down into his lungs until his windpipe sounds like a blocked nostril. When he finally emerges, the passing cars glinting in the streetlights, Jay coughs up yellow glops of phlegm the size of oysters into a flowerbed that will be lucky to contain anything living by the time the week is over.

•

Then back into the world of the living. Or almost. He turns down a job as a gravedigger but accepts one cold-calling for a company that sells graveyard plots. He lasts two days, his phone manner probably better suited to being an undertaker than a salesman trying to sell healthy and happy South Africans costly and tangible reminders of their own mortality. After that, he washes cars in a garage on Heerengracht, blasting water at small patches of primary colour, but only lasts two weeks. The problem now is a strange one, a problem that feels impossible to escape from by conventional means. Jay keeps thinking he sees Helena in the world around him, in the 4x4s and saloons that pull up on the forecourt, in the windows of cars that drive past or else strolling along the pavements and sitting outside cafés and on benches in the Botanical Gardens and De Waal Park. He'll be walking to the bus stop on his way to work and he'll see a tall blonde girl (inevitably Cape Town is full of them) standing there with her back to him, her face buried in a magazine and he'll tell himself it's Helena, their paths again intersecting, fate bringing her to him, bringing him to her.

•

It's never her, of course, but it becomes alarming what he manages to let his mind do to him, let it tell him that the girl's hair is slightly darker because Helena has dyed it, that the girl's hair is lighter because Helena has bleached it, that the girl has lost weight because Helena has lost weight (she hasn't been eating for thinking about him), that the girl has put on weight because Helena had put on weight (for the same reasons), that she's shorter only because she's leaning against a lamppost . . . and of course, it's never her but some frizzy-haired blonde pretender with a face like bruised fruit, cheeks and mouth exploding in all directions, or some washed-out waif with sunken green eyes and hair like dirty soap. What makes it all the more alarming is that Jay is only too aware of the deceptions he's heaping on himself. He is being tormented but knows that he is tormenting himself.

•

Another few weeks pass before Jay sees an advertisement in a paper offering work as a film projectionist and he promptly answers it. He knows he's given the job only because he's first through the door to the manager's office at the cinema and not because of the crazed look in his eyes ('I have to get off the streets,' he repeats to himself as he barges his way into the foyer, 'I *have* to get off the streets'). But he's given it nonetheless and it produces some of the desired effect. Jay now spends most of his day locked into a room on his own for hours at a time with no visual contact with anybody except the vague glimpses of the backlit heads in the audience sitting in front of him. But even though Jay rarely watches the films, he's forced to listen to the actors' dialogue, voices amplified by design but now also impossibly loud in his mind as they come booming out of the darkness with no other reference point attached except their presence inside his head. It's like being a small child in a world of invisible adults and Jay lasts only a month. He can't endure it longer than that and leaves. Raking maize stores a week later offers him no contact with blonde women of any description for ten hours each day but does require him to churn dead rats and snakes up out of the slithering yellow grain instead. Cleaning bricks in a factory in Salt River also means little contact with anyone who can be mistaken for Helena but it also means working with rednecks who seem to count down the hours until the next beer-drenched punch-up with rampant glee.

●

Jay buys a ticket that deposits him under Singapore's sheet-metal sky. There's no avoiding it — he doesn't just have to get off the street, he has to get out of South Africa and get to Asia where the streets are filled with crowds of dark-haired heads moving back and forth like the backs of glistening ants. He gets a job on a work gang painting a skyscraper overlooking the airport. For the first time in as long as he can remember (twelve years? thirteen years?), Jay isn't putting a new joint between his lips every half an hour. But he still feels as if he's floating through an unreal world and can't decide whether sobriety is now as disorientating as being high or whether it's all simply a case of vertigo, of being suspended hundreds of feet up in the air for hours at a time on the small and precarious platform. Eventually Jay can't take it any more and leaves for Thailand, flying to Bangkok and from there taking a train to Surat Thani, from there a boat to Ko Samui. He's been to the island before, before Amsterdam, before Ibiza (and before Helena) and hopes that returning might achieve the system-reset he now realizes he's been looking for these past eighteen months.

●

It doesn't materialize. Instead, he sits on the beach, at a bar, in the doorway of his beach hut, Thai-stick burning away in between his fingers, and he'll see a yellow flash in the blue sea, brown skin, a slender arm breaking the waves ... suddenly he's craning his neck to see if it's *her*. A pair of blue eyes glimpsed for a second in a nightclub, a swatch of pale locks at the store in Ban Lamai – Jay always finds himself wondering if it's *her*. Sometimes he even thinks he hears her voice (again his mind is able to rationalize any initial discrepancy between what he's heard and what he *thinks* he'd heard and simultaneously relay to himself harsh verdicts on his serial self-deceptions) only to turn round and see some dark-haired American girl ordering cokes.

•

Eventually he has no choice but to delve inland, to remove himself from the beaches and the water the colour of Helena's eyes and the sunbathing blondes on the blonde sand. He takes a series of trains that ultimately deposits him in Vientiane where he doesn't hallucinate Helena for four days until he sees her face staring up at him from the society pages of an English newspaper he finds in a pile of magazines at a bar on the Quai de Mekong. There she is, in a white wedding dress, the veil lifted from her face. Jay looks across and expects to see Jean-Marc standing next to her. But it isn't him. Jay reads the small caption and feels his Adam's apple swell in his throat.

> The Hon. Toby Charteris (30) yesterday married Miss Helena Smiling (25) at a lavish ceremony at the bride's home in Brunswick County, North Carolina ...

The rest of the short column essentially talks about how rich the Charteris family is, but also how rich the Smilings are too. All Jay can think is that Helena has married an Englishman.

He scrambles to unfold the paper and looks at the date in the top corner of the crumpled page: August the sixteenth . . . *the previous year*. Jay takes a swig of beer, anything to give his mouth, throat, tongue and hands something to do all at once and also wondering, without total certainly, whether the fifteenth day of August the previous year had been the day he'd brought the Behemoth to a halt by Lake Malawi (he can't be sure . . . he's certain . . . he can't be sure). Jay takes one last look at her picture and then closes the newspaper, raises his bottle of beer and drains it. *Congratulations*, he mutters. Helena was probably already pregnant if indeed she hadn't given birth already. As he troops off, in search of more beer, in search of opium (there was the place a Danish guy had mentioned), his eyes suddenly find themselves tracking a blonde spot on the street corner ahead of him. It isn't her . . . *no it isn't* . . . yes it is (it isn't; the girl Jay has seen has hair the colour of old cheese and is a foot shorter than Helena).

•

Four days later, Jay emerges, dark rings under his eyes, the taste of burnt plastic in his shrivelled mouth. He tells himself that he needs to move — but in which direction? He realizes he is desperate now, or whatever comes after *desperate* if desperate is what he's been for almost two years. Out on the road, he catches a lift with Boony, Lols and Quickie, a trio of Australians who are driving a Ridgeway north towards Luang Prabang and have room for one more.

•

'Mate,' says Boony, offering Jay a beer and a handshake as he climbs into the back, 'y'look like you've been gizzing it flat out.'

Jay decides to sketch out the route he's taken from Marrakesh to Laos in brief detail rather than offer any information about himself and that seems to be enough for the three lads. As Lols heaves the Ridgeway out of the city and into the jungle, it turns out that the guys have been to many of the same places and are happy to talk nostalgically about all the *wallop* they've *necked* in each and reminisce about girls they'd *rooted* and *pumped* or got *gobbies* from.

●

It takes six hours to get to Vang Vieng, an accumulation of shacks and muddy streets where they all get out and stretch their legs. Jay buys himself a plate of spring rolls (his staple Asian diet) and buys the Aussies noodles and fresh supplies of beer and *lao-lao* in return for the ride before they all continue north through the green-grey landscape, the Mekong drifting along beside them, Jay slurping from his own bottle of whisky and sucking down more weed in the passenger seat while Lols and Quickie sleep in the back.

'So . . . are you Italian, mate?' This from Boony. 'I'm Italian . . . Boony *Baggetta*.'

Jay has been mistaken in the past for a Greek, an Italian, a Spaniard, a Turk, an Indian and a Native American.

'I'm half English, half Chinese . . . kind of.'

'Oh, right.'

●

That's it in terms of conversation. After another couple of hours, Boony eventually pulls the Ridgeway over at a fork in the road.

'Why are we stopping?' Jay asks. It's the first conversation he's started since approaching Boony and the others for a lift earlier that morning.

'I think I'm lost,' the Australian says simply and neutrally.

They clamber out, Boony flattening a map out in the steam rising off the jeep's bonnet and opening another beer while Jay stares at the northern sky, the treeline stopping short of the ridge of a mountain range that stretches away to a point north-east of where they stand.

●

It starts to rain. Boony can't work out where they are and walks off towards some trees. 'I'm gonna take a piss,' he calls out, 'to clear my head.'

Jay simply starts walking in the other direction as soon as Boony turns his back, checking that he has his wallet and his passport secure in his pocket and only taking a short look back at his backpack and his flight case (his father's notes? His records? It's too late to get them, he tells himself).

•

By the time he's two hours up the slope, the rain has started to fall harder, Jay's face not so much registering the drops of water as the rare spaces in between them. His trainers slip in the mud, the sound of the cascade like a forest fire in his ears. At least there's no chance of running into Helena or anyone that looks like her.

•

Time passes. Jay tosses his watch into the jungle so that he can't keep track of how long he's been walking. Just one step and then the next, that's all he wants his universe to contain. Eventually the track he's following levels out, a deep valley plunging back to earth on his right, the mountain slope on his left ascending towards the storm clouds. Momentarily without a gradient to fight against, Jay's will to continue suddenly vanishes and he collapses against a rock.

•

He doesn't know long he sits there. The reverberations of the sky are endless and unrelenting and getting nearer all the time. The mist moves, the sky cracks its knuckles and lightning flashes in the distance, darkness approaching from the same direction. And the rain continues to fall. At some point, he loses the sensation of his fingernails at the ends of his fingers and his teeth start to oscillate in his mouth however hard he tries clamp his jaw shut. At some point everything goes blank and he feels nothing, not even his own breathing, and guesses that he is horizontal only because he trusts in his internal memory of gravity's pull.

•

When Jay finally comes round the next morning, he sits up to find a man sitting on a stool at the end of his bed.

'I . . .'

'Don't talk,' the man tells him in an Irish accent. 'And lie back down under the blankets.'

Jay does as he's told and at that moment there's a knock on the door, a small Laotian girl appearing with a plate of bread and a bowl of broth.

'My name is Father Tim,' the priest continues, ruffling his hand through his salt-and-pepper hair. 'This is Lhong. She's the one who spotted you. Ironically enough, we're only a hundred yards further up the track from where you came to a standstill but you'd have been a gonner if she hadn't looked out of her window and seen you lying there.'

•

Jay lives at the orphanage for a couple of months. During the first week, he does little more than sleep and eat in his room. After that, Father Tim puts him to work, assigning him the task of cutting the grass and tending to the trees, plants and shrubs in the old building's gardens in return for his food and shelter. Jay is grateful: the work is simple but absorbing, requires both delicacy and physical exertion, and soon he feels as if his mind is made of something more substantial than crumpled paper.

•

During the evenings at the monastery, he eats his meals (usually dry dumplings or primitive sandwiches made from cornbread which he is obliged to bake himself) in the main dining room with the priest and the children and takes his turn to clean up as required. The children seem neither interested nor uninterested in him, as if they sense more quickly and more fully than he does the inevitable frustrations presented by the language barrier between them. And Father Tim remains similarly distant. The priest never asks him what he was doing on the mountainside the night he was found, never asks him why he was there. And Jay never gets to find out too much about the Irishman. There are a few occasions when he manages to draw Father Tim into conversation as they sit together in the dining room, Jay discovering that he left County Cork to take charge of the orphanage sometime in the seventies, 'switching one set of wet rocks for another'. But mainly the priest is too busy herding the kids into their dormitories each evening or praying in the small chapel and so Jay learns as little about him as he gets to divulge about himself and is left to cloister himself away in his room where he reads gardening books and botanical encyclopedias scrounged from the orphanage's rotting library until he falls asleep.

•

Then Jay leaves. He says goodbye to Father Tim and the children and hitches a ride on the next supply truck that struggles its way up and down the mountain and soon finds himself back in Vientiane. At the airport, he buys himself a plane ticket to Hong Kong where he gets a job delivering furniture, joining a gang of six Chinese youths who haul sofas and dining tables up the towering blocks of apartments or else ride around Kowloon Tong in the back of the van, reading comic books and eating noodles while they wait for the next order to come through. None of them speak English and Jay speaks no Cantonese. It doesn't matter. He spends his time in the back of the van eating spring rolls and listening to the Prez and Lady Day. 'Ghost of Yesterday'. 'I'll Never Be The Same.' All the Cantonese he needs to know is '*Yat, ye, sam . . .*' and then to *lift*.

•

Hong Kong. It strikes Jay, who has felt throughout the majority of his life so far that he's only ever half belonged in England, that he only half belongs there too. As for hallucinating Helena in the streets, Jay does his best to exert some kind of control over the delusional reflex that tortured him in South Africa and later on. Sometimes he's in Tsim Sha Tsui catching a movie or on the Star Ferry crossing the harbour and he spots a blonde head in front of him (across the street, on an escalator), a flash of light amongst the dark heads of Chinese hair ... he immediately chokes the thought that it's *Helena*, puts his hands round the idea's throat and throttles the air out of it, and it's the same when he catches himself remembering her. Her face appears in his mind, always in context (the blue Mediterranean sky; the borrowed pillows of his borrowed bed in his borrowed villa; the Scout as it flies through the perfect landscape), sometimes her features moving, sometimes just her clear and piercing gaze ... Jay voids it, obliterates its detail from the picture, and then the context too (the hallucinations: are they only sleeping in his body?).

•

As for his real life, Jay switches jobs, becomes a valet at the Peninsula for a while and then a barman at a place in LKF where he serves beers and cocktails to ex-pats. Suddenly Jay is speaking English again for hours at a time, to colleagues and to customers, and looking at European faces again and listening to the sound of European chatter rather than its unintelligible Chinese counterpart. And for the first time in years (for the first time since leaving years before), Jay thinks about returning to London. He hears people talk about the place and it almost sounds like a foreign city to him, a *new* city. But what would he do there? Jay, as usual, can't answer this question. Thinking about it, however, reminds him of his days on the stall in Kensington Market and he e-mails Christoph, expecting to find him either back in London or else still in Prague.

•

Jay: am in San Francisco. Got a good set-up . . . if you're not plugged into anything (women, work etc.), you should get over here.

•

Jay buys a ticket and leaves for America. It's humid in Hong Kong and he's sick of the crowded streets, the dirt in the air and the unreadable Chinese faces whose continual stares always seem to be trying to *place* him. And San Francisco is where his mother had grown up and where he'd been born, even if he's never been back since. Jay packs up his things, filtering through the few extra possessions he's accumulated since his arrival and throwing away whatever he can't carry in a single bag.

•

In San Francisco, he learns that the company Christoph went to work for in Prague was bought up by MuzakCorps in Palo Alto the previous year and that Christoph had been offered a transfer soon afterwards. And his 'set-up' is definitely 'good'. His salary gives him more than enough to rent a house on Quintara out on the city's western edge while a 'random connection' he's made at work has led him to a cheap source of some of Mendocino's finest marijuana which he sells in bulk.

•

'It's like I put a whole load of ideas *down*,' he tells Jay as they drive from the airport to the city, 'and then strip most of them away until I've released the jingle *within*.' Christoph spends most days sleeping or playing computer games or watching films and most nights sitting in front of his computer writing sound bites that are eventually used for software start-up screens, automated telephone systems, radio station continuity and internet pop-ups. Sometimes he gets to write longer pieces, for elevators and computer games and the occasional commercial.

•

Jay moves into the spare room and gets a job serving coffee at Café Judah down by the beach, working with Old Don

'Giovanni' Buzcek who's been running the place since the sixties and a couple of Jewish sisters called Dinah and Elanit who both moonlight as healers, and it isn't long before he settles into a daily rhythm he can tolerate.

•

The secret, he tells himself, is to live in *shifts*. Thinking beyond the next sandwich (or beyond the last one) only gets him into trouble.

•

It was like those movies about submarines. At some point, the heroic captain was always forced to dive deeper than he'd planned in order to outsmart some ruthless but more cautious pursuer, to dodge a cowardly salvo of depth charges, to find the secret passage through the reef. The submarine's hull was never designed for such desperate tactics and always started to creak and crumple ominously. And this was what thinking too far ahead felt like to Jay. Luckily, his new life rarely asked him to plan anything more than a few hours in advance. He would simply wake up each day and cycle the three blocks down to the sea before pushing his bike along the sand to the café and attending to whatever awaited him there until it was time to leave for home. The establishment was too far away from the centre of the city ever to get busy during the week and serving coffee seemed to supply everything he needed, a feasible equilibrium between activity and idleness, a sizeable collection of increasingly familiar regulars with whom Jay could form limited and predictable patterns of familiarity and an amount of money that allowed him to eat, sleep and work. No more and no less.

•

One morning, he was out on the beach smoking his pre-shift joint and washing down his breakfast with a coffee when he spotted an old Chinese man coming towards him, a red kite high up in the gentle crosswind above him and a small dog trotting quietly beside his feet.

'Good morning,' Jay called out when the man paused nearby. 'Who's this little fella?'

He reached down to ruffle the dog's head but the mutt gently pawed his hand away before looking up at the kite hanging in the sky.

'Name's Marlowe,' the man told him, 'Scots Terrier.'

'Looks like a nice day for kite flying.'

'Perhaps.'

•

The dog seemed to grow bored of standing there listening to them talk and wandered over to the water's edge leaving a meandering set of dance steps in the wet sand behind him. In the meantime, Jay took a closer look at the man and saw that his eyes were inflamed with tears, the breeze blowing them back across the sides of his face like parachutists exiting a plane. Also, he seemed more concerned with staring up at the kite and consulting the pocket watch in his hand than in making small talk and Jay thought about walking away and giving him some privacy. But it was then that he saw the stranger's knees buckle and the watch suddenly fall from his hand. Jay quickly bent down and retrieved it, then placed a hand round the man's arm and helped him back on to his feet.

'Are you okay?' he asked.

'I think I just need some water.'

•

Five minutes later, they'd reeled in the kite and retreated inside the café where Jay sat the guy down at the table in the corner and poured him a coffee.

'You dropped your watch,' he said, putting it on the table.

'Thank you,' the old man replied, 'but *this* is my watch.'

The old man showed Jay the cheap black digital attached to

his wrist, the kind one saw homeless people trying to sell on the corner of Van Ness and Market.

'Shitronic SA-80,' the old man said with pride, 'looks ugly but has special properties.'

'What's *this* then?'

The old man flipped the lid of the device open and slid it towards him.

'It's a compass. I use it to track the direction of the wind when I'm flying my kite.'

Jay saw that there was a Chinese symbol engraved on to the inside of the lid.

龙

On the face of the compass itself were four more symbols around the perimeter:

北
西　东
南

'My name is Jay.'

'Tommy Cheung.'

The man kept his eyes lowered, took a sip of coffee.

'I've not seen you here before.'

'You don't let customers smoke inside so I don't come in.'

'Are you okay?'

The man nodded though it was a more a movement in his eyes than of his head.

'It was just a dizzy moment . . . it's passed.'

•

Tommy couldn't have been more than a couple of inches over five feet, Jay guessed. He wore grey slacks that were the same colour as most of the hair on his head, a tweed sports jacket (also grey) over a striped polo-shirt, four-hundred dollar Italian slip-ons and had a face like a Sharpei, eyelids just another set of wrinkles in the loose skin of his brown face. As for the man's tears out on the sand, Jay soon learned that he'd just returned from Europe where he'd scattered the ashes of his wife who'd recently died of cancer. She'd grown up in Scotland and Tommy had travelled to Inverness and from there to Rhidorroch Sound, a body of water near the land her family had once owned.

•

Tommy nodded towards Marlowe who sat up on the ledge and stared out to sea. 'He used to belong to her.'

'How long were the two of you together?' Jay asked.

'We were married four years ago. Sixty-five years old and the last four have been the happiest of my life. Maturity is a wonderful thing.'

'How did you meet her? What was her name?'

'Her name was Catherine and she was originally a client of mine. One day she just appear at my office. She was wearing a green dress, matching shoes and handbag. She even wore *gloves*. Real classy dame, I thought, too good for the likes of me. And then she opened her mouth and started to speak ... who would have thought an old Chinese guy from a small village near Shanghang would fall head-over-heels for *that* accent.'

Jay asked what line of business Tommy was in. The man told him.

'You're a *what*?'

'A paranormal investigator.'

Jay poured them more coffee and toasted some sandwiches and Tommy told him all about it while the ocean swelled and the gulls cried and the sea-grass whipped against the dunes beyond the glass.

'So . . . do you actually believe in ghosts?' Jay asked eventually, trying to make sense of what the old man had been saying.

'It's a little more complicated than that,' Tommy had replied patiently. 'As my wife used to say: "Best not put the cart before the horse."'

31

Jay and Freddy assembled in Buck's kitchen just after nine o'clock, Buck walking into the room a moment later with a bottle of Blue Johnny Walker. He poured out three measures and both he and Freddy swallowed theirs down in a single ceremonial gulp. 'We ready?' he asked quietly.

Freddy nodded and Jay gulped down his own shot (Tommy's hip-flasks of hundred-dollar Glen Achall tasted like cold tea in comparison) before nodding as well and following the two of them out to the waiting black Orca. Freddy took the wheel while Buck climbed in beside him and Jay got into the back. Above them the moon was full and bright but eclipsed by impatient clouds that streaked in from the direction of the Cape Fear River and still seemed to carry traces of the day's purple and orange. As for River Road, it was deserted. They didn't pass any other cars as they coasted along it and after a few minutes they took a right turn, Freddy cutting the headlamps and then the engine moments later.

'We go the rest of the way on foot,' Buck said. 'No flash-lights. No talking.'

Freddy led the three of them through the trees, the rustling sound of their feet mixing with the fervent drone of the undergrowth, and soon they reached Willoughby Pond. Somewhere an owl hooted in the darkness. Buck pointed along the bank.

'The cabins are half a mile away that way,' he whispered. Again, Freddy went first, following the narrow track than ran parallel to the water, Buck next with Jay following behind, the world around them all Es, the forest with its hidden energies and damp echoes, the ethereal night-mist that swirled around their feet, the earthshine visible at the moon's edge in the giant eight-ball of the sky. Jay was almost empty with expectation by the time they came to another halt twenty minutes later, Buck putting a hand on Freddy's shoulder and whispering into his ear.

'It's just up there . . . second shack on the left . . . let's come in from the rear . . . there's no hurry so move *slow*.'

Freddy nodded and then led them across the track to the undergrowth on the other side. Soon the first cabin came into view, as abandoned as the three on the other side of the dwelling that Madeleine and Toby used for their meetings. Freddy skirted along its back wall, Buck and Jay following, all of them moving through the waist-high grass until they came to the far corner of the structure. Freddy peered round at the next building.

'Don't see no lights on this side of it. You want me to go and take a look from the other side?'

Buck nodded and Freddy walked slowly across to the cabin, Jay watching him fade into the shadows before he disappeared from sight completely. What was it Buck had told him that afternoon? That he and Freddy had shot Santina dead in the front drive at Willoughby . . . there must have been other people nearby that night, Jay reasoned, other guests and other drivers. Yet Buck and Freddy had managed to kill Santina without anyone noticing. He pictured the two men closing in on their intended victim with the same single-minded determination with which they now approached the cabin and wondered what they'd do if they discovered that Toby had harmed Helena.

'Can you see anything?' he whispered to Buck.

'Not yet.'

Freddy reappeared, silent across the ground until he was only a few metres away.

'You find anything?' Buck asked him. Freddy shook his head.

'Okay, let's do this.'

They ran across to the cabin's front door where Freddy

jemmied the lock and pushed it open. Once the three of them were inside Buck switched on his flashlight and scanned the room. The downstairs floor of the cabin was a single open plan room with a stove, a dining table in one corner and a couple of sofas with rugs thrown over them. Freddy went over to a dresser against the far wall and started rifling through the drawers, Buck opening a set of cupboards under the small counter next to the stove.

'What are we looking for?' Jay whispered.

'Anything,' Buck whispered back. 'Freddy?'

'Nothing,' Freddy replied, moving from the dresser to the toilet under the stairs, 'and nothing in here.'

They went upstairs. There were two rooms on the floor above and Freddy took the far one while Jay and Buck took the door directly at the top of the steps.

'You look through those drawers and under the bed,' Buck told him, 'I'll check the closet.'

Jay did as he was asked but turned up nothing.

'I don't think they use this room.'

'I guess not.'

It was then they heard Freddy calling them from down the corridor.

'Boss, you should come take a look at this.'

The next room was better furnished than the first. There was a lamp on the bedside table along with some candles and an ashtray. There was an armchair by the window, a robe thrown across it. Madeleine's body lay sprawled across the bed and the statuette of Kali that Jay had seen the first time he'd called on her lay near to her waist. It was spattered with the same blood that coated the left side of her face.

'Take a look in here,' Freddy said, bending down and angling the beam of his flashlight at a section of wall that he'd already pulled away. 'I saw these scrapes on the floorboards. Found a concealed closet.'

Buck bent down and shone his flashlight into the space beyond.

'What's in there?' Jay asked, standing behind them and unable to see anything.

'I'm going to pull them out,' Buck whispered. He put the flashlight down on the floor, reached out in front of him and slid something out of the cupboard. It was a suitcase.

'There's another one'

He reached inside again and pulled it out. Both were made of leather, one in brown, one in black, and the handle of the brown case was smeared with dried blood. Buck took out a knife from his pocket, cut a hole in the top flap and pulled out some of the things inside: a bikini-top, a woman's blouse and other female items. In the meantime, Freddy had broken into the black suitcase and was pulling out shirts and handkerchiefs.

'Got anything?' Buck whispered.

Freddy grabbed one of the handkerchiefs and flapped it open. On the corner were embroidered three letters: 'W.F.K.'

Buck was still busy emptying the brown suitcase. Eventually he had a random pile of clothes on the floor and started burrowing through it, pulling out a leather wallet that was perhaps twelve inches long and eight wide. He unzipped it and opened it up: inside the pool of light they saw a set of plane tickets, a photo of Helena and Jacob, a photo of Helena and Zelda in the garden when they were little girls, sheets of unmarked cream writing paper and a sheaf of blank cream envelopes.

'It's Helena's. That's Kelly's,' Buck said. 'Charteris killed them.'

'They're . . .' Jay started to whisper until a gurgling behind him had them all spinning frantically.

'Christ . . .'

'She's alive . . .'

Jay rushed over to the bed.

'Only just.'

Buck came over and examined Madeleine in the light of his flash. 'We can't carry her all the way back to the car,' he said eventually.

'Why don't I run and get it?' Jay offered.

'Because you don't know the way,' Buck replied quickly. 'I'll have to go while you two wait . . .'

He stopped suddenly.

'I smell gas.'

Freddy said he smelled it too and by the time the three of them had got to the top of the stairs, they could see flames at the walls of the cabin on the floor below.

'We've got to get Madeleine,' Jay whispered. Buck nodded and they went back and lifted her from the bed as gently as they could, Jay wrapping her in a blanket before Buck carried her along the corridor in his massive arms.

'Okay, let's go,' he shouted at the top of the stairs and Freddy led the way down. Buck followed with Madeleine slumped against him, Jay next. When they reached the ground floor, Jay could see that each of the cabin's four walls had been set alight.

'It hasn't taken hold yet,' Freddy called across the room as he peered out through one of the windows. Jay agreed, but also thought that it might only be moments before the flames ripped upwards through the whole structure. It hadn't rained once since he'd arrived and probably not for months before then.

'Let's get out of here,' Buck shouted and Freddy went to the front door, pulling a gun from inside his jacket. Then Jay heard the sound of a gunshot and couldn't tell if it had come from Freddy or from somewhere else until he saw Freddy slumped on the ground a couple of feet beyond the cabin's front porch. Buck shouted out to him but Freddy didn't move.

'What about the side door?' he asked Jay.

'It's locked,' Jay called back and Buck lowered Madeleine

down on to a sofa before coming across the room to help Jay kick it off its hinges. Another gunshot shattered the window by Jay's left ear.

'He's got both doors covered,' Buck grunted as they both crouched back down by the sofa, 'which means he's probably positioned somewhere between *there* and *there*.' He described a set of angles with a flat hand. 'We might have to run for it. You take the side door and break left . . . I'll take the front door and break right. If we go at the same time, he'll be confused for a moment and that should give us more than an even chance.'

Jay didn't know what to say.

'If it's Charteris, it's likely that he's not that good a shot and it's likely that he'll panic which will make him even worse,' Buck told him. 'If we run, don't think about it, just keep going and get into cover. Remember it's dark out there and he's as nervous about missing as you are about getting hit.'

Jay doubted that but let it pass and peered up at the walls through the smoke. How much longer could they wait in the cabin? A couple of minutes? Would they suffocate before then?

'Have you got a gun?' he asked. Buck shook his head.

'I don't carry one. I leave that to Freddy.'

'We can't have more than a couple of minutes left in here . . .'

'I know.'

'What about Madeleine?' Jay asked.

'I'll take her. You're not big enough to carry her.'

They stayed there in a crouch for a few more seconds, flames flaring in bursts at different points all over the walls and the smoke getting thicker all the time.

'Okay, let's go. Like I said, we take a door each, try and confuse him. I'll take the front, maybe try and grab Freddy's gun as I'm going through. You bolt out the side-door and make for the bushes. Don't look back.'

Before Jay could stop him, Buck had gathered up Madeleine in his arms and was moving towards the front door and there was nothing else for him to do but crunch his way across the shattered glass towards the side door. Beyond it was a plot of high grass, beyond that some bushes . . . *it would take him only a couple of seconds to span the gap . . . Toby would panic and miss* . . . Jay looked across the cabin at Buck who nodded and then moved out into the darkness. Jay moved too, hearing the gunshot almost immediately and somehow having the time to wonder if his universe was about implode into a single point of pain but also hear Buck's desperate exclamation simultaneously . . . and then he found himself suddenly catapulting forward into the grass. He'd tripped up over a rubber tyre lying prone in the vegetation and insects swarmed at his face as he heard another gunshot and registered something flicking through the grass to his left. He slithered to his right, perhaps a yard back towards the burning shack, and considered clambering backwards into the taller undergrowth not more than ten feet behind him. What about the others? Something collapsed inside the cabin and he realized that the whole thing could come crashing down on Freddy, Madeleine and Buck whom he could hear groaning above the sound of the fire. Slowly, Jay pushed his head up though the grass. The air above was thick with black smoke and orange light, but he could see Buck's fallen body from where he was, a pool of blood soaked through the back of the man's denim shirt low down on the left side. Turning his head, Jay could also see Toby peering out from the bushes at the water's edge. He seemed to be squinting at a spot perhaps ten feet to Jay's left. Could Jay slither back towards the cabin and try and pull at least one of the others away from under the collapsing building? He ducked down again and slid a couple of feet sideways only to hear another gunshot and sense another whistling impact through the grass beside him. Then another gunshot. Then silence. Jay counted to seven and slowly raised his head again . . . had Toby spotted him? No, Toby still seemed to be staring at a space to Jay's left but it wouldn't help him ultimately: the others lay in open sight of where Toby was lurking across the track. It would be too easy for him to pick Jay off as he . . . *Jay froze*, and then watched as the undergrowth behind Toby seemed to uncoil itself and lunge forward, the dark silhouette of a human figure rearing up out of the shadows and knocking him to the ground.

32

After the ambulances had taken Freddy, Buck and Madeleine to Wilmington, Jay was driven back to Willoughby and huddled from the squad car into the library where he was left with a uniformed officer to watch over him. Were Mike and Toby being questioned in other rooms of the house, Toby furiously denying everything? *And what was Mike Penny doing in North Carolina in the first place?* Jay and Mike had only managed to exchange a few words before the police had come charging down the track and separated them and Jay hadn't been able to find out anything from his partner.

At some point a pair of cars started up outside the library window and an hour later there was the sound of cars returning, though Jay realized that they may have been different vehicles. More time passed, perhaps another thirty minutes, the cop and Jay not exchanging a single word. Then the door to the library opened and a man Jay hadn't seen before entered the room.

'My name is Detective Sergeant Chris Andrichak,' he said as he took the seat opposite Jay, the same seat Toby had occupied when Jay had first arrived at the house. 'How are you?'

'What's happening?' Jay asked, ignoring Andrichak's question.

'We're talking to everyone,' the detective replied quietly. He was a tall guy in his late forties and seemed more like a college professor than a detective, with his knitted tie, lightweight blazer and tidily parted hair.

'I need to ask you a few questions,' he said.

Jay nodded and Andrichak read him his rights before reaching into his pocket.

'Okay,' he said. 'I need you to tell me who these people are.'

He pulled out an evidence bag and flattened it out in front of Jay on the small table between them. Inside was the photograph of the two girls Jay had found with Madeleine's cache of passports.

'I'll ask you again: who are the two people in this photograph?'

Why were they asking him? *And where had they found the photograph*? Jay thought through his options as quickly as he could: the police had searched his things, either at Buck's ranch in Parton or in the hallway outside . . . what had Toby told the police so far, if anything at all? One thing was certain, Jay couldn't admit to breaking into Madeleine's house the night before. Perhaps denying everything was the best decision for now.

'I've never seen it before,' he replied and then waited for Andrichak to tell him that he'd just pulled it out of Jay's bag. The detective didn't reply however and just stared back at him doubtfully.

'You were questioned today in relation to Madeleine Kelly's disappearance,' he said eventually. 'You told my colleagues that you had no previous connection with Mrs Kelly prior to the twenty-sixth of August. At this point in time, I have some reasons to doubt the truth of that statement.'

'Why?'

'I have reason to believe that one of the girls in this picture is Madeleine Kelly and that this picture belongs to you.'

'Why?' Jay asked again, still determined to bluff his way through. Andrichak told him he wasn't at liberty to say which had Jay thinking that he or one of his colleagues *hadn't* found it amongst Jay's things. If that was the case, then where had it been? Jay also wondered what would happen if Madeleine Kelly regained consciousness. Would she tell them that the picture belonged to her, that she was one of the girls sitting on the bench, and that someone had broken into Thackeray the night before and stolen it? Perhaps not, given that the photograph had been hidden away with the fake passports which she might guess the police knew nothing about and whose existence she might still want to keep from them. Whatever Madeleine might say, Jay decided he'd deal with it as it transpired.

'Could you give me a complete account of your relationship with Madeleine Kelly?' the detective asked. Jay repeated what he'd told Wells and Lowenstein earlier in the day.

'I'd never met Madeleine Kelly before coming to North Carolina five days ago. Since then, I've had only the briefest contact with her on only a few occasions.'

Andrichak stared at Jay.

'That's all you've got to say?'

Jay nodded.

'Well, I've got some more questions. What were you doing down at Willoughby Pond tonight? What was Buck Harrington's involvement with all of this and how do the two of you know each other?'

Had they already questioned Buck at the hospital? There was no way Jay could tell. 'I've only known Mr Harrington a few days,' he replied. 'He was considering employing me. That's my only connection with him.'

'He's an interesting choice for an employer.'

Jay shrugged. 'I didn't force Mr Harrington into thinking about hiring me.'

'As a . . . what do you call it . . . *paranormal investigator*?'

'That's right.'

Jay knew that Andrichak would have already read through Wells and Lowenstein's notes on him and he could see that whatever he'd said to them or whatever he said to Andrichak now, nothing would stop the man being suspicious. That was okay. At least being a paranormal investigator wasn't against the law, even if withholding evidence from the police almost certainly was.

'And what about tonight?' Andrichak asked.

Jay looked at him. 'It was Buck's idea. He said he had a hunch that Toby was up to something but didn't say more than that to me.'

'And you just happened to tag along with Harrington and his sidekick for the hell of it?'

'Buck asked me to go along with him,' Jay replied simply.

'You always on first name terms with known mobsters?' the detective asked. Jay didn't answer, suddenly tired of being questioned and tired of Andrichak.

'Wait here,' the detective snapped eventually, scooping the evidence bag from the surface of the table and putting it back into his pocket before leaving the room. Another thirty minutes passed, just Jay and the uniformed cop sitting there in the library, before the door opened again. This time it was Wells and Lowenstein who appeared and told the cop he could leave.

'Hi,' Jay said.

'Good evening,' Lowenstein replied with all the finesse of a dump truck.

'Seems like things have progressed since we last spoke,' Wells said. 'You think any of this mess tonight could have been avoided if you'd been straight with us today?'

Jay didn't answer.

'Goodnight, Mr Richards,' Lowenstein said. 'Don't go making any plans to leave the area. I'm pretty sure that we'll still be needing to talk to you in the very near future.'

They left, shuffling out into the hallway. Mike Penny walked in a few moments later.

'As far as I can make out, they're still talkin' to Toby and his housekeeper. Apparently we're no longer under suspicion though we ain't allowed to leave the house just yet.'

Mike walked up to the pool table and picked up a cue.

'You fancy a game? I need to slow down and get my head round a few things.'

'Mike,' Jay started, almost laughing at the ridiculousness of the question, 'what are you doing here? What were you doing by the cabin?'

'Well, buddy, it's kind of a strange story and I'm still piecin' bits of it together myself.' Mike pulled out a cheroot, lit it and then poured them a pair of brandies while Jay went over to the table and racked up the balls. 'When you rang me from the jailhouse and asked me to call Zelda and the Harrington fella, I did as you told me. But I also decided to get on a plane and fly down here myself and see if I could help out *personally*, what with me now bein' your wingman an' all.'

Mike bent down and took a shot, the triangle of balls scattering towards the four corners of the table. Outside, green reality pawed at the glass as a breeze picked up over the drive.

'So I call here again and leave a message for Zelda with the housekeeper. After that, I pack my things, say goodbye to Mei Han and hop on a plane at good ol' SFO. Seven hours later, I find Zelda waitin' for me at the Arrivals gate. I asked her where you were and she told me that you were at the house. After that, we catch a cab and as we're drivin' along, I'm askin' her what's been goin' on and she spends most of the journey tellin' me about your investigation and how the police took you away for questionin'. Then she tells the driver to take this side turnin' which brings us out by the side of the lake and she tells me that it's only gonna be another coupla minutes . . . and then the car goes dead. The engine, the lights, the whole darn caboodle. The driver tries the engine but can't get it started again and me and him get outta the car at that point and take a look under the hood. Didn't seem be nothin' wrong with the car but it was hard to see with it bein' so dark an' all. So I walk round to the trunk to get a flashlight from outta my bags and *that's* when I see that Zelda's gone.'

'Gone?'

'Disappeared. I hollered out her name but she didn't call back. I asked the driver if he'd seen where she'd gone but he says he ain't seen nothin'. Then I scan the side of the track with the flashlight to see if she's taken a walk or somethin' but she ain't there.'

Mike stood up from the table, puffed away on his cigar and let some ash fall into one of Toby's marble ashtrays.

'Then I see this light suddenly flare up down the track and it looks like somethin's burnin'. I tell the driver to stay with the car and take a closer look and that's when I hear the gunshots. I tell the driver to call the police and then start movin' faster towards the noise, hearin' more shots and wonderin' what the heck's goin' on. And it's then I see that Chateris fella shootin' at you guys in the house. Before I can do anythin', you're all comin' outta the house and he's takin' more potshots. All I had to do was creep up behind him and smack him over the head with a log. It was pretty easy. I'm just sorry I didn't get there in time to save your buddies.'

The Nebraskan sipped his drink while Jay considered what he'd been telling him. *Where had Zelda gone*? At that moment there was movement out on the drive and Jay and Mike moved to the window to see Toby being led to a car in handcuffs, a detective's firm hand on the back of his head guiding him *down* and *in* through the door frame.

Then there was knock behind them and Jay and Mike spun round to see Zelda in the doorway.

'Zelda? Where have you been?' Jay asked.

'We've been talking to Detective Andrichak,' she replied.

'What about before?' Jay asked. 'Mike says you disappeared.'

'I'm sure Miss Smiling can explain all that,' Mike interrupted before she could reply. 'You walk right in, ma'am, and take a seat.'

He put down his cue and moved towards the doorway. 'You wouldn't happen to know where a man might get some chow around here?'

'If you follow the corridor on the other side of the hallway, it'll take you round to the kitchen. You'll find Sara in there.'

'Much obliged. I think I'll leave you two songbirds to talk amongst yourselves while I go find somethin' to eat.'

He walked out through the wide doorway and Zelda entered the room.

'I saw them take Toby away just now,' Jay said.

'He confessed.'

She came over to the pool table and the two of them sat down on the window seat.

'He killed her?'

'He killed her *and* Wallace. They've been under Sixty Bridge ever since the night of the party.'

So they were dead. Helena was gone forever, Jay told himself. He reached out a hand and took hold of Zelda's arm. Her skin felt cold, brittle.

'I'm sorry.'

She looked back at him.

'Detective Andrichak talked us through the whole story.'

'Do you want to tell me?'

She nodded.

The story as Toby had told it to the police started three years before when Toby and his partners had bid for the contract to redevelop the marina at Windy Point. When the project had failed to achieve completion on time by the following summer, it had been impossible for Toby to make the interest repayments on the loan he'd borrowed.

'Toby says he managed to get another loan off one of his brothers in England. But this only went so far and it wasn't long before he was facing bankruptcy again and also about to forfeit his place as one of the principal investors.'

Toby had become desperate and borrowed a quarter of a million dollars from Dan Harrington. He hadn't been able to get that much money from a more reputable source and obviously intended to pay back at least some of it by the end of the following summer once the marina started generating revenue.

'That never happened. The marina continued to incur unforeseen expenses. And though business improved, Dan Harrington started becoming increasingly impatient for his money. Apparently it was then that Dan first offered Toby the chance to sell his share in the marina to him and clear the debt. Toby refused.'

And of course, Jay told himself, it was Dan Harrington who was behind the problems the marina redevelopment had suffered in the first place, with Frank McKelvy working as his inside man.

'Toby soon worked out that Dan was behind the marina's problems, and he knew that Dan was trying to squeeze him from two directions at the same time. But it meant very little in real terms. And Dan ultimately presented Toby with a choice: either he could pay what he owed along with the accumulated interest, or he could give up his stake in the marina at a fraction of what it was worth, let alone what it might make in the future.' *Or have his legs broken*, Jay thought to himself. Of course, Toby had nothing. And he couldn't ask Helena for any money. She didn't have any. All she had was the house.

Jay said that he thought that Toby had no claim to the property. 'And you'd given your half to Helena which means that it's hers and that Jacob gets the whole place when she . . .'

He didn't bother to finish his sentence.

'That's true,' Zelda nodded. But when Jacob was born it was agreed that should one of them die or become incapacitated through injury or mental illness, the other would act as a trustee for Jacob until he turned twenty-one and assumed full control of the Smiling estate.

'And Toby thought that by killing Helena, he might be able to use his position as Jacob's trustee to sell off at least some of the estate?'

She nodded again.

'Zelda, how does Madeleine Kelly fit into all this? You know she was having an affair with Toby?'

'Yes,' Zelda replied, 'I do now. When did you find out?'

'Two nights ago. I thought I saw an apparition in the garden, trailed it to the lake and came across Toby creeping his way through the forest to Willoughby Pond. I followed him and watched him meet with Madeleine.'

Zelda stared at him. 'Why did you keep it from me?'

Jay didn't answer her, aware of all the other secrets he was withholding, the truth of Buck and her mother, of Dan and Helena (and Dan was *her* half-brother too).

'I . . . I was planning to.'

'I suppose it doesn't matter,' she replied neutrally. 'Apparently it started last Fall.'

According to Toby's confession, he and Madeleine had started meeting in secret a few months after Helena became pregnant. Madeleine had made it clear that she wanted sex and Toby had obliged her. It had been as simple as that. They'd started meeting at motels, later at the cabin which Madeleine had bought and patched up in secret. Toby claimed that when Madeleine found out about his financial problems, it was *she* who came up with the plan to kill Helena and Wallace in order to get him some money.

'Do you think that's true?' Jay asked.

'The answer to that question might matter to a judge, but not to me.'

Jay paused for a moment. He took a sip of brandy before asking Zelda what happened next. She told him that Toby and Madeleine had decided that all they needed to do was to get rid of Helena and make it look as if she'd disappeared. They'd guessed that Helena had run off so many times before that the police wouldn't consider it suspicious, especially if a man she was known to be having an affair with went missing at the same time. Madeleine had told Toby that she suspected that Wallace harboured a secret attraction for Helena and also knew that he was a hopeless romantic and steadily she and Toby had started pushing their spouses together.

'Madeleine told me,' Jay interrupted, 'that she and Wallace found Helena and Toby arguing upstairs in his study on Helena's last birthday because Toby had allegedly flirted with Lara and that Wallace had walked in and stopped Toby from hitting her. Madeleine said she believed that *that* was the moment Wallace fell for her. I guess the whole thing was staged by Madeleine and Toby.'

'I guess so,' Zelda replied.

Whatever they had or hadn't staged, she told him, by the end of April they knew their plan had worked. Helena and Wallace had started seeing each other and the gossip it generated spread around the local area as Madeleine and Toby had hoped it would. Then they set about the next part of their plan. Toby had already started to organize the anniversary party for the first night of August.

'Are you okay?' Jay asked when she faltered.

Zelda didn't answer. It didn't matter. Jay could easily piece the next part of the story together himself. Who would suspect Toby of getting rid of his wife while two hundred guests were in the house? Helena's history of running away with other men would have everyone assuming that she'd taken off with Wallace, especially if they both went missing at the same time, their passports, clothes and car gone. Jay also reminded himself that the fact that Helena would have appeared to have absconded so publicly (and so *maliciously*) would have been put down to her proven waywardness. He asked Zelda about the flight booked from Mexico City to Buenos Aires: had Madeleine and Toby booked it in their spouses' names? Zelda said that they had, a last detail designed to keep everyone thinking that Helena and Wallace had run off together and were doing their best to make it look as if they were trying to avoid being located. After that there had been one last major obstacle for Toby to surmount. Toby had admitted during his confession that he knew he wouldn't be able to kill Helena and Wallace himself. He wasn't naïve. He knew how hard he'd find it to murder Helena in cold blood and didn't want to take the risk that his nerves might get the better of him at the crucial moment. Apparently he'd claimed that Madeleine had advised him against hiring a contract killer, saying that involving a third party was too risky, but that he'd remained adamant. Whatever the case, he started on a chain of enquiries that eventually led him to Chicago.

'You remember we saw the police pull a man out of the water down in Southport the other day?'

Jay nodded, trying not to give anything away.

'The police say that he was the hitman, a guy called Bruno Santina who used to be some kind of mobster.'

'Really?'

'Toby and Madeleine's plan was for this Santina guy to come to the party posing as a chauffeur. He'd been paid half the money up front and was due to collect the second payment from Madeleine and make a positive identification of Helena and Wallace on the night of the party itself.'

After that, Toby and Madeleine planned to lure Helena and Wallace there at pre-designated times where they would be shot. Santina would then take away the bodies . . .'

'So what went wrong?' Jay asked, picturing Freddy and Buck in the emergency room right that moment. 'You said that Toby killed Wallace and your sister.'

She told him that Santina's body had been found with five

small caliber rounds in it. Obviously he'd been killed before he could carry out his job but the police still didn't know who'd killed him.

'Toby says he doesn't know either although he's denied that it was him. An explanation may lie with Madeleine, of course, but she isn't in a state to talk to anyone yet.'

'So, Santina's dead,' Jay continued. 'How did Toby kill Helena?'

Toby had gone on to confess that he'd left it until the last moment to remove Helena's passport from the safe in his study in case she went to fetch some jewellery she also kept there and noticed it missing.

'At around six-thirty, Toby finally went upstairs to get it but found Helena taking it out of the safe herself.'

Toby had told the police that she hadn't spotted him and he'd just watched her. Helena was on her cell at the same time and he'd listened as she told whoever it was she was speaking to that she was going to say goodbye to Jacob and would be at Sixty Bridge in twenty minutes. Toby then called Madeleine and found out that Santina still hadn't shown up to collect his second payment. Worse than that, she'd lost sight of Wallace ten minutes earlier and had just been told by Sara Taft that he'd been seen heading down Willoughby's drive in his car.

'It was then that Toby says he realized . . .'

'That Helena and Wallace had planned to run away together . . .'

'. . . on the night that he and Madeleine had planned to kill them and make it *look* as if they'd run away together.'

Zelda and Jay stared at each other.

'In different circumstances,' she said bleakly, 'I'd be struck by the ironic symmetry of it all. As it is . . .'

Jay sat there on the window-seat, imagining Toby's face as the realization materialized in his mind. Jay could see him, suddenly lost in a vertigo of desperation, his ego punch-drunk. 'What did Toby say happened next?' he asked.

Toby panicked but managed to retain enough presence of mind to guess that Helena was planning to walk through the party and then on through the woods, past the lake and out to Sixty Bridge. He'd decided at that point that Santina had decided not to show and that he had to take matters into his own hands. Suddenly he found himself chasing after her.

'This is a strange part of the story.'

'What is?' Jay asked.

'Toby claims that there's a secret passage behind one of the bookshelves in his study. He even took the police upstairs and showed them. It runs all the way . . .'

'. . . under the garden and the woods to the cupola by Willoughby Lake.'

'You knew about that too?'

Jay admitted that he'd heard Toby talking about it with Madeleine at the cabin.

'What else do you know that you're not telling me?' she asked him.

'I think that's about everything,' he replied, wondering if she could tell that it wasn't.

'Toby says he ran down the passage, using it to get ahead of Helena, and waited for her at the side of the track that leads up to Sixty Bridge.'

Jay felt his stomach trying to climb up his throat as he imagined Helena picking her way through the darkness, her shoes dangling from her fingers, a slip of silver amongst the shadows. *He smashed her over the head with a rock . . .* he heard Zelda tell him but her voice was little more than a set of subtitles reluctantly attached to the grisly film of events that played out inside his mind . . . *then he waited for Wallace.* And Wallace had appeared minutes later. And Toby had waited for him to get out of the car and come looking for Helena before he killed him too.

After that, Toby dragged their bodies into an engineering lock-up under the bridge and hid their car deep inside the nearby woods before running back to the party. For a moment, Jay pictured Zelda standing with Sara Taft amongst the crowd of cops, the forensics unzipping the body bags and Zelda suddenly confronting her own mutilated double. Helena's body: it had been rotting down there the whole time, he told himself, also remembering all the occasions he'd passed by a only few metres above.

'Presumably, Toby used the tunnel to get back inside the house without being seen and cleaned himself up.'

Zelda nodded. On re-entering the house, Toby had hidden his blood-spattered tuxedo and dress shirt, put on clean replacements and then rejoined the celebrations.

'Another sick irony about this whole thing is that Toby had an identical tuxedo and dress shirt in his closet but he was forced to re-enter the party wearing white studs rather than the black ones he'd originally been wearing because they were covered in blood. He says he was sure that someone would notice, but no one did.'

Jay gulped back another surge of nausea and considered that it was the kind of detail that a wife would have noticed, the kind of detail that Helena would have noticed.

'And since then, he's been trying to hide the fact from everyone,' he said. 'Did the cops say if Toby told Madeleine what he'd done?'

Zelda shook her head.

'I guess he couldn't trust her,' Jay continued, knowing they were both thinking the same thing. 'He was a murderer, twice over. He couldn't trust anyone.'

'The detectives have said that he broke down in the interview and claims that he keeps seeing Helena's ghost in the house. They don't believe him, of course. But he keeps swearing it's true.'

'Perhaps it *is* true,' Jay replied. Zelda had seen something in Jacob's room two nights before. Later, they *both* thought they'd seen something here in the library. And there were the paintings that had moved and the apparition Jay had seen at Thackeray. And of course there was Buck's certainty that Helena's ghost had appeared to him at the ranch.

Zelda didn't answer and they sat there in silence for a few moments until Jay asked her if there was anything else Toby had told the police. She nodded.

'From this point on, Toby's confession is fairly messed up. According to Detective Andrichak, Toby seems to have admitted to trying to stay calm and reminding himself that he'd got what he wanted, a chance to sell off all or some of Willoughby to get himself out of debt with Dan. But as the days went by he felt himself going crazier and crazier.'

Jay pictured the last few days from Toby's point of view. Toby probably saw Helena's last horrified look in his mind over and over again (Jay imagined it, her brilliant blue eyes swashed through with shock, pain and betrayal). Perhaps Toby had seen a ghost too. *Was Helena really haunting the house*? That strange events had started occurring all over Willoughby in the wake of Helena's death would have unsettled him and Zelda's arrival at the house could have only made things worse for him, worse because she would have reminded him of Helena every time he saw her but also because she took the others' claims that they'd experienced something paranormal seriously. And then Jay himself had arrived after that, again claiming that ghosts existed. If things had started moving with their own horrendous momentum the second Toby found himself watching Helena finalize her own plans to leave him, then things must have quickly become terrifying for him. Jay could only imagine what Toby, in such a state, might have imagined each time he saw Zelda, his wife's double. And he would have thought of Helena constantly and all the things they'd done together, perhaps even dreamt about her at night, alive and beautiful, before waking up to his terrible and unforgiving reality.

'Toby keeps saying that he's been having nightmares, hallucinations of Helena around the house. He's also been too scared to move Helena and Wallace's bodies and has been living with the fear that someone might discover them at any moment.'

'What about Madeleine Kelly?' Jay asked.

Apparently Toby had confessed to attacking Madeleine at Thackeray that afternoon and taking her body to the fishing cabin, believing that she was dead or about to die. The police were still unsure why he'd attacked her but it seemed that the photograph Jay had found at Thackeray was part of the reason. It didn't make sense . . . *yet*. Again, he wondered what would happen if Madeleine regained consciousness.

'Toby was about to go on the run and wanted to burn down the cabin with Madeleine inside before he went. He went off to get some fuel when it got dark but found you, Buck and Freddy Graham inside when he got back. You know the rest.'

Yes, Jay knew the rest.

They sat there in silence, the library around them all Os: the globe in the corner with its swirling ochre oceans, the pool balls on the table in an approximation of Orion, the handful of chess pieces locked in their obdurate endgame on the board on one of the shelves and the opaque woods flickering away on the other side of the glass.

'I've got one more question,' Jay said eventually.

'What is it?' she asked.

'The letters from New York? Were they real or did Toby and Madeleine forge them?'

She told him that the police had contacted the law firm

in New York who attested that she'd met with them a few months before and organized it all personally.

'If Toby hadn't killed me, I'd have run off with Wallace anyway.'

33

She stared through the window at the garden, fingertips moving to push a strand of hair away from her face, the muscles in her neck trembling under the white skin.

'Jay . . .' she started, turning so that her blue eyes found his.

He saw that she was beginning to fade away just as he realized that he already knew what it was she was about to tell him.

'You're . . .'

He couldn't continue. His vocabulary seemed to have been instantaneously reduced to a single word.

'You're . . .'

Helena looked back at him.

'How . . . ? When . . . ? I . . .'

Words crowded out of Jay's throat and dropped off the end of his tongue. She reached out a translucent hand and took hold of one of his.

'Slow down,' she said quietly, her fingers squeezing his.

'Was it you in San Francisco . . . and here at the house?'

She nodded.

'What about that afternoon at the marina hotel?'

She shook her head.

'But it was you who disturbed Clemmy and Lobelia and scared Mrs Taft out on the drive and moved the paintings . . .'

'Jay . . .'

'Is it all like you just told me – Toby killed the two of you?'

'Yes,' she said quietly.

Again, Jay couldn't speak again for a moment.

'I guess there's a lot you want to say and a lot you want to ask.'

'What happened . . . after he . . .'

Helena stared across at him.

'It's confusing . . .'

'How come I can feel you right now?'

'Are you sure that you can?' she asked, squeezing his hand again.

'What are you saying,' Jay stammered, '*that everything's taken place inside my head*? You spoke to Mike on the phone . . . and you spoke to *me* on the phone, as soon as I'd got back to Buck's ranch after searching through Thackeray . . .'

'Jay, I don't know how it works. I wish I did, probably more than you, I'd say. But I don't.'

That silenced him for a little while. 'What's it been like since . . . ?' he asked eventually. It was all he could think to say. The million other questions he had seemed to cancel each other out. And still she was fading steadily away.

'I'm not sure,' Helena replied. 'You know how people who have near-death experiences often seem to relearn the value of their lives? Well, it seems the same for . . . for *us*. So far it's been like a mysterious dream where I feel the essence of everything I've done right in my life but also feel the shame of every mistake I've ever made at the same time. Sometimes I even think I know what people are thinking or feeling too but this may just be a result of getting to look at them for hours when they think they're on their own.'

'What happens next?' Jay asked. He felt her other hand close around his.

'I don't know. I guess we'll just face it and see.'

'*We?*'

'Wallace . . . he's out there.'

Jay peered out into the garden where he saw the shape of a man waiting in the moonlight beyond the glass. Then he turned back towards Helena's face, scared to look into her eyes but knowing also that it would be the last time.

'Why didn't you simply tell me what happened in San Francisco or when I first got to Willoughby?' he asked. 'You could have taken me to Sixty Bridge. I could have gone straight to the police and . . .'

'Jay . . .'

Helena placed a cold fingertip on his lips (there were supernovas in there, in the deep space of her eyes), then her mouth.

'I never said goodbye before. Now I get my chance. So long, Jay. I'm sorry. I hope I've made amends . . .'

'What do you mean? Wait a . . .'

But she was gone.

Jay sat there for a second. Then everything imploded into a knocking sound, Sara Taft suddenly opening the door.

'Mrs Taft?'

'I thought Zelda was in here?'

Jay stood there. 'She was a second ago . . .'

'Well, I guess you deserve to know too. I've just found out from the hospital: Freddy Graham's condition has stabilized. But Buck died twenty minutes ago. Madeleine Kelly passed away on arrival.'

Jay could see that there were tears in Mrs Taft's eyes.

'I know about Buck and Esmerelda Smiling,' he said. 'I presume you do too?'

She nodded, walking from the doorway to the pool table.

'So, he told you. Have you told anyone else? Zelda?'

'Not yet,' he replied.

The light in Sara's eyes seemed to collapse. 'You seem to know a lot, Jay, for someone who's been here less than a week.'

'You're not the only person to say that to me tonight,' he replied, also realizing that it was the first time she'd called him 'Jay'.

'Did Buck tell you that he was my brother?'

Jay shook his head.

'I'm guessing you know that Buck came to work here at the house when he got back from Vietnam and that John Smiling forced him to leave for Chicago when the girls were born. And you probably know that Alfred went to Vietnam too.'

'Yes.'

'He came back with shell shock and he hasn't spoken since,' she said, sounding more than a little shell shocked herself. 'When he first got back from Asia, he could barely move and had to stay in an institution in Fayetteville. I lived nearby until he'd recovered. After that, we came back home to live in Parton, only a little while after Buck left for Chicago. I looked for work but couldn't find any. And then I heard that John and Esmerelda were looking for a nanny and I applied. I didn't tell them who I was, of course.'

Jay looked at her and realized that she'd been Buck's source of information inside the house (and had mothered his daughters in his absence).

'So now you know everything,' she said, watching him join the last of the dots. There was no blame in her voice, just exhaustion. 'There'll be some food ready in an hour. Come to the kitchen then if you're hungry. If you see Zelda, will you pass on the news about Buck and Mrs Kelly?'

She turned, walked out of the library, and left Jay alone on the window seat. He didn't get up for a moment and sat there listening to the sound of her footsteps recede. Then he took one last look at the spot where Helena had vanished before walking out into the hallway. The paintings were still up on the walls in the positions she'd left them, Katherine Smiling's pale eyes staring down at him as he opened the front door and stepped through it. Looking across to the empty space by the old coach house, Jay saw that the cars of the detectives and other police officers had dispersed and that the only people left at Willoughby besides the great-aunts and Jacob upstairs were Mike, Sara Taft and himself. Alfred and Lara would be at home.

He took a sniff of the night air and then put his hands in his pockets where he found a half-smoked joint which he pulled out and lit. For a few moments the front of the house was simply J. Then he heard the sound of a car engine and saw the glimmer of headlamps down the drive. It was probably Bessie Flowers, he told himself. She would have just heard the news and was coming back from Southport to check on Zelda and the baby.

And Zelda wasn't there.

What would Jay tell them all? Perhaps he should keep the fact that he'd encountered Helena's ghost to himself and play dumb when 'Zelda's' disappearance was discovered? The sound of the car got nearer and then a cab appeared, clearing the trees and pulling up a couple of yards from where Jay was standing. The door swung open and Zelda Smiling stepped out on to the drive.

'Zelda?'

She stared at him. 'I *know* you don't I?' (Like Helena, Zelda's hair was the same searing chrome yellow as sun-bright dahlias, her eyes the same pure delphinium blue.) She squinted at him. 'Wait a minute, you're . . . ?'

'We met once before, on Ibiza, just after your . . . after your *father* died.'

'That's what I thought. What are you doing here?'

'That might take some time to explain,' he replied.

The driver hauled Zelda's suitcase out of the trunk and placed it by the front door before getting back in his car and pulling away.

'Well I'd like to know what's going on. Is Helena here? Is she back? How's the baby? I got this letter from Toby a couple of days ago saying that she's run off with Wallace Kelly. I would have got it sooner but Toby sent it to the wrong place . . .'

'Zelda, come inside,' Jay told her, picking up her suitcase. 'There's a lot I have to tell you.'

For some time afterwards, Madeleine Kelly's exact role in The Smiling Affair continued to reveal itself in fragments.

•

The day after Zelda returned from Kosovo, Andrichak arrived at Willoughby with another detective around noon and we had another stilted conversation in the library. Andrichak asked me repeatedly if I had any prior connection with Madeleine and how I'd come to be in possession of the photograph of the two dark-haired girls while Max Seeker looked on from the window seat. I simply repeated that I'd never seen the picture before until he gave up and dismissed me.

•

Zelda was next, entering the library to talk to the detectives while I waited nervously with Mike on the loggia (I'd told her the whole story the night before, going through it several times and leaving nothing out, but it was a lot to take in all at once). Eventually she reappeared, saying that Andrichak and his accomplice had just left.

•

'Apparently Toby's claiming that he searched through your room yesterday morning while you were down here talking to me . . . he thought you were on to him and was looking through your room for clues and says it was then that he found the photograph of Chica Valdez by your bed. At that point he says he wondered if you and Madeleine were working together in some way and drove to Thackeray looking to confront her only to find her in the process of packing up to leave . . .'

'. . . because she'd discovered that Freddy and I had found her passports.'

'I guess so. Of course, the fact that she was about to leave without telling him only increased his paranoia. He says they started arguing and she tried to push past him and he panicked and hit her over the head with the statue.'

Kali. Goddess of Death. That still didn't explain Toby's connection with Chica Valdez. 'So who does Andrichak believe when it comes to the photo?' I asked. 'Me or Toby?'

'He certainly doesn't believe you,' Zelda replied. 'But I don't think it really matters. Madeleine's dead and Toby's confessed to everything.'

'I guess so.'

•

As it turned out, it wasn't Chris Andrichak who filled out the rest of Madeleine Kelly's story but Freddy Graham. Two weeks later, Buck Harrington was buried at the ranch in Parton and Zelda and I sat in the front row with the Tafts and Freddy while Mike sat at the end of the row behind us with a line of tan gentlemen in dark suits. Carlo Dotto and his crew, I presumed, trying not to get caught staring at them too closely but eventually getting a good look at Dotto himself when the man embraced Zelda after the service as if she were his own granddaughter.

•

At some point at the wake, I found myself standing next to Freddy who said that he'd finally got some information back from Buck's contacts in the FBI about the fake passports I'd found in Madeleine's bedroom.

'You want to know what Toby's connection with Madeleine Kelly is?'

I nodded.

'He was one of eight guys who raped her sister at a beach party in Spain nine years ago.'

'And that's why she committed suicide?'

Freddy nodded and I asked if he knew why Toby and the other men involved hadn't been arrested.

'According to our contacts, the case file in Spain says that her parents were too ashamed to allow her to press charges. Anyway, the cops now reckon that Madeleine Kelly is the girl's sister and that she's been tracking down the men responsible.'

'How did they link this with Toby? How do they know Madeleine was out looking for revenge?'

Apparently Toby had given detectives the names of his seven accomplices on the night that Buck and Madeleine had died. When they checked out the first name, they found that the man had been killed in a hit and run accident a couple of years before in Marseilles. The second, a Londoner, had been electrocuted in his bath-tub. The third, another Londoner, had gassed himself in his own garage, the death originally registered as suicide.

'Madeleine?' I asked.

'Probably. Who cares?' Freddy replied.

•

'Perhaps she wanted Toby to murder my sister so that she could inform the police and then flee and change her identity,' Zelda suggested as we drove back to Willoughby later, saying out loud what we were both thinking but could never prove. 'After all, Toby said that it was her idea in the first place to kill Helena and Wallace and that she was against the idea of hiring a contract killer.'

'Perhaps,' I replied.

•

And that's it. Andrichak never bothered to talk to me again and I got a call from Max Seeker the day after the funeral to tell me that I was free to go back to San Francisco.

•

Or, rather, that was *almost* it. The afternoon after Max Seeker called me, Zelda and I were in our room in the old coach house, Zelda's sleeping body curled against mine while I lay there trying to piece together what Helena had told me before she'd disappeared.

●

As usual, I wasn't getting anywhere in terms of working it all out. *It had been her and not Zelda*, she'd told me in the library, *right from the beginning*, and I thought back yet again to that evening in San Francisco, the bar on the roof of the Buchanan, Helena sitting across the table from me . . . she'd asked for the drinks to be charged to her room and I'd spent money that she'd given me on sandwiches and cabs and weed and renting a car . . . I got out of bed and pulled on a pair of jeans and a t-shirt before walking across to the house where I dialled the operator from the phone in the ground-floor office and asked him to connect me to the airline. A moment later an airline sales agent listened to my question, said he'd transfer me to the appropriate department and then put me on hold again. There it was, 'This Year's Kisses', the Prez strolling through the introduction, then Lady Day like a ghost whispering into my ear . . . *This year's crop of kisses don't seem as sweet to me* . . . finally a bored voice came on to the line and identified herself to me as Janice.

'How can I help you today?' she asked wearily.

'Janice, I'd like to know who paid for my flight from San Francisco to Wilmington on the twenty-fourth of August of this year?'

'I'm sorry sir, I don't understand. You want to know who paid for a flight you've already taken?' she asked.

'That's right.'

'You don't know already?'

I said that I didn't.

'Your name?'

'Richards,' I replied, 'Jay Richards.' I stared out into the garden and listened to the distant sounds of Lara and Marlowe playing somewhere outside (she was trying to teach him to chase sticks but would never succeed) while Janice clicked and tapped away on the other end of the line.

'Sir, I have it on record that you paid for your ticket in cash at our sales desk at San Francisco International.'

'Your computer says that *I* paid for my ticket?'

'That's correct, sir.'

'In cash?'

'That's correct, sir. I have a code C-47 here on my screen: the customer paid in cash. Is there anything else I can help you with?'

Janice's voice grew clipped with growing suspicion and I quickly said that I had all I needed before hanging up. After that, I dialled the operator a second time.

'Could you please put me through to the Buchanan Hotel?' I asked. 'The address is Union Square in San Francisco.'

While I waited for the click of connection and the long electronic drawl of pips, I considered what Janice had just told me and wondered how I could have paid for my ticket in cash when I'd had little more than a few dollars to my name in those final days in San Francisco. Then a desk clerk at the Buchanan came on the line.

'My name is Raymond. How can I help you?'

'I'm sorry to disturb you, Raymond' I answered, 'but I'm in the process of querying my wife's credit card statement and I need to confirm how many nights she stayed at your hotel. She says that she was only there for two nights but her credit card company *swear blind* that she charged three nights to her card. Can you help me?'

Would a whiff of betrayal pique the clerk's curiosity enough to override any sense of duty or confidentiality? It seemed that it would.

'Certainly, sir,' Raymond replied, sniffing for more, 'what name was your wife registered under and on which nights?'

What name was your wife registered under? Not: *What is your wife's name?*

'Her name is Zelda Smiling,' I continued. 'She was booked into one of your rooms on the twenty-second and twenty-third of August.'

'Twenty-second and twenty-third? I'll check the register. Please bear with me.'

I waited for a few moments.

'I'm sorry, sir, but I have no guest registered at the hotel under that name on either of the dates you specified.'

'Raymond, can you check again for me?'

Raymond said that he'd already checked twice but put me on hold again. Then he came back on the line and told me that there was no one with the name *Smiling* listed in the register on either the twenty-second or the twenty-third, nor on the twenty-first nor the twenty-fourth.

'Perhaps you've got the wrong hotel?' he said helpfully, and then more salaciously, his voice inevitably lowering itself: '*Perhaps she was registered under a different name?*'

'Perhaps,' I said before thanking Raymond for his time and hanging up.

•

I sat down on the swivel chair by the desk for a moment and tried to picture my passage through the airport three weeks earlier. I'd checked in my bags at the desk and then surrendered myself to the inertial ritual of the airport with its metal detectors and scanners and serged security guards. And then I'd climbed aboard my plane . . . I stood up and walked back to the coach house where I rooted through my bag of clothes. Of the money that Helena had supposedly given me, there was a little over a hundred and forty dollars left, a single hundred dollar bill, a couple of twenties and some change. I picked up one of the twenties and tore it in half. It was real: hard, tangible cash.

•

After that, I rummaged around in my bag some more but

couldn't find the letter that had come to my office nor the box containing the necklace.

'What are you looking for?' Zelda asked sleepily from the bed.

'Nothing important,' I said, looking across at her and her bare unadorned throat (she'd told me that she'd never worn *her* necklace, not once). 'I'm just trying to work something out, that's all.'

●

Where was it? When had I last seen it? Had I lost it or dropped it somewhere? Had I ever really had it in the first place? I went and checked the flight cases containing my equipment which were stacked up in the corner of the library by the old globe. I couldn't see the letter anywhere amongst it all but eventually found the small cardboard box in one of the side pockets of the bag for my powerpad. I pulled it out and opened the lid.

There it was: Helena's necklace.

●

I picked it up and let the cool metal slip around my fingers. I'd received it in the mail back in April, I reminded myself, around the time she'd started her affair with Wallace and months *before* she'd been killed.

●

Why had she sent it? Why had Helena – the real, living, breathing Helena – sent it to me at the same time she'd started her affair with Wallace Kelly? What message had she been trying to send? Was she trying to say goodbye? Or was she trying to tell me that she couldn't?

●

I put the necklace back in its box and locked it away with the rest of the equipment, telling myself that I'd never know the answer as I walked over to the tray of drinks, poured myself a scotch and drank it down in a single meditative swallow. After that, I walked through the house and out on to the terrace where Willoughby's grounds stretched away from me towards the river, the world all As for a moment, the tingle of Glen Achall on my lips, the arcing flight of the departing seabirds over the estuary in the distance, the abruptions of the ambivalent clouds in the sky above. Around the garden, the insects chittered and a breeze stirred while blood-red leaves waited to fall from the branches of the antique trees and the whispering grass shone amber and orange in the sanguine brilliance of an autumn afternoon.

Acknowledgements

Thanks are due to the following for their friendship, inspiration and support: Ellah Allfrey, Julia Bell, Lula Bennett, Stephanie Cabot, the Chus, the Corbetts, the Everetts, Dan Franklin, the Fungs, the Hillson-Dugmores, Paddy Grey, Hannah Griffiths, Charles Lambert, Joanna and Sue Johnston, the Knoxs, the Peels, the Pennes, the Moody-Stuarts, the Morrisons, the Schoepf-Jordans, the Scotts, the Sheldons and the Turners. Special thanks are also due to Damian Peel, Julian Sheldon and Deepak Sikka.